D1137174

The Summer Holiday

Jo Clegg's brief stint as a stand-up comic ended when a promoter told her she was really funny until she got on stage. After ten years as a producer in TV and radio comedy, Jo became a scriptwriter. She writes for children's TV shows including BAFTA and Emmy-award winning *Hey Duggee*. She lives in London with her family. *The Summer Holiday* is her first novel.

The Summer Holiday

Jo Clegg

ORION

An Orion paperback

First published in Great Britain in 2021
by Orion Fiction
an imprint of The Orion Publishing Group Ltd
Carmelite House, 50 Victoria Embankment
London EC4Y 0DZ

An Hachette UK Company

1 3 5 7 9 10 8 6 4 2

available from the British Library.

ISBN (Mass Market Paperback) 978 1 4091 9813 0
ISBN (eBook) 978 1 4091 9814 7

Typeset at The Spartan Press Ltd,
Lymington, Hants

Printed and bound in Great Britain by Clays Ltd,
Elcograf S.p.A.

www.orionbooks.co.uk

For Mum

Chapter 1

How could it have gone wrong already?

It had been her New Year's resolution to know where her keys were, but a week into January here she was needing to borrow the spares. It was, *she* was, disappointing. Ben had given her one of those key rings for Christmas that peeped when you clapped, but it had piped up at anything over the level of everyday conversation, raising her family's stress levels, until Pearl had pleaded with her to go back to her old one.

Claire clutched each side of her straggly blue coat across her chest. Her knuckles were stinging. Her feet, in worn baseball boots, banged numbly off the pavement.

She'd had her keys this morning, in her hand. Then the strap of Pearl's book bag needed sorting, and Charlie fussed that his hat was too small (which it was, you jammed it down, it rose back up and perched on top of his head); and she'd put the keys down.

Somewhere.

Ben hadn't yet gone into work, he'd been on the laptop in the kitchen, so she'd slipped from room to room looking for them, hoping not to alert him to the familiar rigmarole of helping her. Lovely Ben. It must be crap living with someone who never knew where their keys were.

Claire had reached the parade. Nearly home and she'd forgotten to notice the ice on the trees, or check how the sun was casting shade on the blue iron frame that once housed Headleigh's giant circular gas holders. Pope's Hill had presumably been clogged with traffic snaking from Headleigh towards Luton. Oh well. There'd be more frosty school runs.

She turned into the alley. Birdsong. Complex and beautiful. A robin was perched on the frosted edge of a mattress at the end of the alley singing its tiny heart out. Claire gasped and exhaled, her breath pluming into the air. She crept towards the bird. It warbled, pinprick eyes looking her up and down. Claire held back laughter. It was as though it was chastising her for her outfit choice.

'You're right,' she whispered. 'Totally inappropriate, I'm freezing.'

She gently slotted her chilled hands in her pockets. The warble switched to important-sounding trilling, then back to warbling. It had a lot to say.

'Thanks, robin. That was magic.'

She was going to have to go and raise Edna for the spare keys. She took a right onto her street at the end of the alley, passing boxy semis like her own. The bird had fallen silent. Maybe talking to it had disturbed the natural order and she'd broken it. Phew, there it was, singing again.

Claire reached the twiggy calf-height hedge that separated her house from next door and walked up Edna's path, psyching herself to knock. She would have to bash like a bailiff; Edna was in denial about her hearing. The shaky note on the door said that if there was no answer, *try Mr and Mrs Swift next door*, which, as Claire was Mrs Swift, wasn't much use. She pulled her cuff over the heel of her hand, banged three times and stood back to wait.

A neighbour passed, holding hands with his young daughter. She was in a parka, pyjama bottoms and football boots, her hair a bushy tangle.

'Happy nearly new year,' Claire called.

'And you. Yours gone back today?'

'Yeah,' said Claire. 'Monday for St Joseph's?'

The man nodded and Claire smiled. It was kind of mad that Pope's Hill Infants and Juniors went back on a Friday, but it was a nice soft start for Pearl and Charlie, in for a day then off again. She'd be back to her part-time work there herself on Monday and they'd have a nice chilled weekend in between. *Wait. No.* Claire's heart sank a little. On Sunday they were going to see their friends Honor and Chris and their kids. It would be exciting to see their new house, and good to see them, and lunch would be delicious, but Honor always secretly put her on edge.

Ben had written 'Lunch at the Wellbeloveds' in their Luton Town FC calendar he'd got from his work Secret Santa, and she'd thought that it was odd; he must have meant to put it in April to fit with the pattern they'd fallen into in the last few years, of get togethers near Halloween and then near Easter. Ben saw Chris in between: they were best mates, but that was the routine. So lunch this Sunday did seem kind of... soon.

She raised her hand to thump again, then the door to her own house opened. Ben came out in a slightly creased scarf, buttoning his coat. 'Thought you'd left for work,' she said, knowing he would know why she was at Edna's.

He smiled and pulled the door shut behind him. 'Oh no,' he said, mock-horrified, hands to his face. 'I've shut the door. Hope you've got keys.' He raised an eyebrow, reached into his pocket and slowly pulled out her grubby bubble-writing CLAIRE key ring.

'Amazing. Where where they?'

'In the fruitbowl,' he said, as though the idea of anywhere else was ridiculous.

Claire laughed. 'Cheers, Ben.' She opened Edna's letterbox

and peered through. 'Think she's still in bed.' She stepped over the hedge and reached up to kiss him.

'You wouldn't have got much joy there anyway.' He pulled out more keys.

'The spares?' said Claire. 'No way.'

'Way. That's why I waited for you. It's fine, though. I got more work done at home than I thought I would.'

Claire shook her head in disbelief. 'I thought I'd dropped them back to her after last time.' She put both sets in her pocket and held it shut. 'You're brill, Ben.' She rubbed his bristled jaw. 'You're the Key Finder General, I don't deserve you.'

'You do, and you're welcome. How was drop-off?'

'Fairly fun in the end.'

'Cool. Right, just one quick thing before I go, and there's no need to freak out.'

'What is it?' She laughed. 'Ben! When did dramatic pauses help with not freaking out?'

'OK. So Chris and Honor on Sunday. Change of plan.'

'Oh. Is that all?' Claire exhaled. 'I mean, it would have been nice to see them, but I'm not going to freak out that they've cancelled lunch.'

'That's the thing. They haven't cancelled. They're coming here.'

Claire's left ear whooshed like a boiler lighting. 'Honor and Chris, coming to *us*? But they never come to us!' She was pretty sure this was what Ben had meant by not freaking out but it was happening anyway. 'I mean they came that once, years ago, but ... Are you sure, Ben?'

He shrugged. 'Well, yeah. Chris texted *Looking forward to lunch at yours on Sunday*.'

Claire pushed hair from her forehead. 'We always used to say it was our turn to host, d'you remember? And they'd say *no no no come to ours*, so we stopped. I thought that's how they liked it.' Claire cringed. 'Oh God, Ben. Are we *those* people, who don't return invitations? Did they get fed up waiting?'

Ben smiled. 'I think Honor would have said something sooner if that was the case.'

He had a point. Honor did let her views be known.

'The main thing,' he said, 'is not to overthink it. We're cooking lunch for our friends. I know we eat the food of our lives when we go to theirs, but it'll be nice. We'll keep it simple.' He laughed. 'It'll be an adventure for them.' He mimed holding something in the air and scrutinising it. "Pot-ay-to waff-ull. Interesting." They'll love it. It will be like a visit to a primitive tribe.'

'You're ridiculous.' She looked at him sternly. 'I'll cook.'

'You sure? I was kidding about the waffles.'

'I know.' Claire glanced around. There were weeds coming through their crazy paving. 'But it's a bit true and I'm stressed.'

'Don't stress. They're our mates. Look, we'll clean to-morrow, then on Sunday we'll jiggle the sticks in the per-fume thing and bung something in the oven. There's no need for it to take over the weekend.'

Ben's hazel eyes regarded her warmly. 'OK.'

He held out his arms and enveloped her in a hug. 'Just, you know, keep it in perspective.' Claire looked round his shoulder, imagining Honor and Chris Wellbeloved's enormous shiny spaceship of a car pulling up. Wondering how the Miseries, the cheerless couple opposite, would react when the most beautiful woman they'd ever seen outside *Hello!* magazine emerged and graced them with a smile.

'Sure. I'll keep it in perspective,' she said.

'Good,' said Ben, letting go. 'Have a nice day. Doing anything fun?'

'Er, yeah,' said Claire. 'Illustrating a leaflet for a nail salon.'

Ben's head tilted. The side of his face squeezed up. 'Those photos you took before Christmas?'

'That's right.'

'New client?'

'Yeah, new client.'

He beamed, eyes crinkling. 'Great. Hope it goes really well.'

'Thanks. See you later.'

Claire watched Ben walk down the thawing pavement towards the station. His thick hair neat above his scarf. He crouched to say hello to a neighbour's Jack Russell and toddler. Kind, upbeat Ben. She'd got so lucky.

She stepped to the edge of the pavement to see what Honor would see when she arrived at the home Claire loved.

A hip-height brick wall. A curly metal gate. A weird stain on the roof tiles at the base of the chimney. The chimneys on all the houses had one. The houses were the same, all made out of ticky-tacky or whatever that old song was. She and Ben had planned to paint the pebble-dash when they'd moved in six years ago but something always came up. Talking of which, those weeds were thriving. Claire tutted. *Give me a break, it's January, why are you here?*

Also, the cheery shade of coral she'd painted the front door had faded. A fresh coat would brighten things up. Would it be feasible to do that by Sunday, or was she losing perspective already? *Must. Not. Lose. Perspective.* She'd just quickly go round and note things they did need to fix, then get to work on the leaflet, and only start the fixing when it was done.

Despite freaking out that Honor Wellbeloved was stepping into her house, her life, appraising every aspect of her existence, perspective would be maintained throughout.

Chapter 2

Claire pulled out a set of keys and hurried into the house. She grabbed a red pencil that was lying on the stairs. Back outside she picked a scrap of paper out of the recycling box by the gate and wrote:

OUTSIDE AT THE FRONT
Weeding
Repaint door
Plant winter flowering stuff???

She went back in the house, shut the door and breathed in. Hints of coffee, Nutella toast, a bit of dust. A good hoovering would sort that out. She smiled, looking round the little hallway because there were also hints of calling up the stairs and of small people bumping down them on their backsides. Of laughter and games set up on the hall floor, bath taps running and films on the sofa. Love swelled in Claire's chest. As she knew, not all houses were this happy.

The front room was a jumble of toys, scrunched throws and cushions. Along with photos of her and Ben and the kids, the mantelpiece held a shrivelled apple core, a half-chewed sweet and a doll's brush full of real hair.

'Ugh, how long has this been here?' She picked up the mess and pulled the hair from the brush as she walked to the kitchen. She dropped the hair and the sweet into the bin, whose lid hadn't clicked shut in months, and put the brush on the cluttered kitchen worktop before rinsing her hands and running them up and down her jeans.

It's just Honor coming. It's not that big a deal. Shit, Honor's coming.

Claire opened the cupboard next to the cooker to check supplies. The shelves were oily and sticky and sprinkled with pepper. The Wellbeloveds moved to a more gobsmacking house so frequently their cupboards hardly had the chance to get sticky. She'd add it to her list to clean it out *if there was time*. Nice perspective!

She took a couple of steps away. The cupboard seemed to pull her back. What if Honor saw inside? She sighed and dropped to her knees and whipped out the tubs of gravy granules, salt and pepper and bottles of oil and vinegar and stood them on the floor. She sat back on her haunches, queasy with the familiar feeling that she hadn't worked out where she was trying to get to and was already striding off in the wrong direction.

Don't clean the cupboard now. Step away from the cupboard.

She glanced at the cooker. Not a lot of magic happened there. Honor had always been an effortless, brilliant cook. Right from when Claire first met Ben and he'd taken her to meet Chris and Honor, and Claire had sat in their house feeling every inch the flakey ex-art student who worked in a shop, impressed to the point of intimidation by Honor who juggled a tray of potatoes in hot fat, a glass of wine – always a glass of wine – in the other hand while giving forth on current affairs. Her roast potatoes had been exquisite. Everything Honor cooked was always exquisite. Listening to the satisfied sounds of people eating a meal she'd made, you'd think it was the soundtrack to a porno.

Cooking overwhelmed Claire. All the things you had to

remember, the decisions and the timings. Scrambled egg with beans and toast taxed her to her limit. It just wasn't how her head worked. How was she going to cook Sunday lunch for Honor Wellbeloved? She'd be hot of cheek and cack of hand and trying to hide her burns, spills and curses with no hope of keeping up with the conversation. And what she produced would be ordinary. Possibly not very hot. Honor might pick at it and shake her dark, glossy hair at the offer of seconds.

She sighed and stretched back her shoulders. It wasn't *all* about the meal. And their house was a nice place to spend the afternoon. When Fran had dropped her phone back here that time, when they'd just started their teaching assistant job-share a couple of years ago, she'd said the house was welcoming and friendly like Claire was. So what if Honor did think their pub banquette that Claire had re-covered in seventies fabric was gaudy, and the boot-sale dining table wasn't elegant, and the painted wooden sideboard and lamp-stand were fey. Claire liked them.

She went round to the table and picked up the junk model horse she and the kids had made from a cardboard box. She opened the back door. Three steps across the frosty paving took her to the shed at the back of the garden, which the property details had fancifully called a summer house. It had a glazed door and windows and stored bikes and trampolines and DIY stuff. She pulled the door open and squeezed the cardboard horse inside. Its back leg ripped a little and Claire bit her lip. *I'll fix you after Sunday, sorry.*

She shut the shed, and went back in. Not having a junk model horse inside did a lot to increase the floor space. Although they'd have to bring in garden chairs. Not that there was really room for them.

The wall Ben had started putting her artwork on – Pearl and Charlie's pictures dotting other walls in the kitchen-diner

– bothered her. He'd been framing copies of the illustrations she'd done since he'd persuaded her to make more time for her art. She worried that people would think the wall was her idea. She'd have to tell Honor and Chris it was Ben's … although that might sound like a humble brag.

The fact was, the idea of Honor seeing her work made her shudder way more than a smeary cupboard. Her work was *her*. She scanned the frames and stopped at her favourite. A poster for a jumble sale. Alongside the hand-drawn lettering, she'd illustrated a table of clothes and two women who'd just grabbed the same cardigan. Their expressions said 'Ha ha, look at us, how funny!' But you could tell who'd go on to claim it. She'd drawn a short, thickset man too, holding up a slim tuxedo with a look of infatuation that suggested he thought it was a perfect fit for him. It was Claire's take on the world and Honor's judgement could be brutal.

Claire unhooked the jumble sale poster and the one for the allotment sale, and the Christmas street party, and laid them on the floor.

Picture hooks studded the wall. She could harvest other pictures from around the house and hang them instead. Or take out the hooks, fill the holes and repaint the wall.

Claire gazed out into the garden. Damn it. She really was letting this visit hijack her Friday. And it wasn't just the leaflet she had to do. There was something else, something lovely. She'd thought of it earlier and squeezed her thumb as a prompt. She squeezed her thumb now. It didn't give up its secret. Honor didn't squeeze her thumb to remember things and then not remember them. If Honor was doing anything with her thumb right now, she'd be pressing a switch to tell someone to get her a protein shake, or China on the line, while she signed off a confidential bank-related contract with a Mont Blanc pen.

Claire. Stop thinking about Honor. There's not another soul in the house. Use this lovely silence to do the illustration for that leaflet.

Claire pulled her drawing board from behind the banquette and two trays crammed with brushes, paints and pencils from the sideboard. She set them on the table with her laptop, a pad of paper and water in an old yoghurt pot. She'd pop to the loo, grab some tea and then focus.

Her hand juddered on the banister. Jam maybe. She must clean the bannister. Where was that list?

Claire sat on the loo and the seat did its alarming slide-clunk. It needed tightening, maybe replacing. The bathroom would have to be blitzed and Ben's on-loo reading matter curated. Claire flushed, washed her hands. Honor might look in the bathroom cabinet; *she* definitely looked in Honor's bathroom cabinet. She chucked the gungey Calpol and cough medicine bottles and the fake tan she hadn't got on with and the part-used sachets of shampoo into a carrier bag and dumped it in the bath to sort out later.

How much time did she actually have? There would be some today after she'd done Karmel's leaflet, and the thing… the thumb thing, if it came to her. Then she had all of Saturday, so there was no need to freak out now. Honor coming for lunch was a spur to do a good clean, maybe weed the front, that was all. Everything else she'd ignore. Honor and Chris and their kids were their *friends*. That was the important thing, seeing their friends.

'Hey, hello perspective. I lost you for a while there.'

She went back downstairs, found the list, added the things she'd thought of, then put it in the living room under a sofa cushion.

'Be gone, list. I'm busy.' She closed the living room door. She made tea and sat at the table. She opened the laptop and looked through the photos of Karmel she'd taken in Karmel's tiny nail salon a couple of weeks ago. Karmel had closed that minute for Christmas and Claire had drunk Prosecco with her and her friends and taken close-ups of Karmel's gorgeous face with her friends' hands round it like petals round a flower to showcase her nail art.

Ben had looked so happy when she'd said 'new client'. Karmel had already given her an eye-watering – *way* too enthusiastic with the filing – pedicure as payment, so it wasn't quite the business transaction he would hope.

Claire switched paints and brushes around so everything she needed was in reach. She had five hours of quiet to do this. It had been boisterous and joyful at Karmel's and Claire had felt that come the new year, illustrating the leaflet would be easy. But since then, old well-known insecurities had woken up and crawled out of a deep place inside her.

It was always the same. The worry that the marks and shapes she made weren't worth making. That what she hoped was funny and real was just... silly. She knew what a proper, serious artist looked like. Not like her.

Maybe this was the year things would change. Something would click and she'd have the nerve to say, 'I'm an illustrator', and charge for her services.

Claire searched out her favourite pencil. 2B but not too smudgy. Karmel's vitality shone from her. She was fresh, warm and great company. Claire would really need to catch all that in her work and HONOR WAS COMING TO HER HOUSE. Her ear did its boiler whoosh again. *OK. Honor coming wins. Jeez.*

Claire pushed back her chair, threw on a jacket and grabbed the gardening box from the shed. No. Not this. Better to do inside stuff while no one else was here. She put the box back and ran round the house, tidying and putting away. She put the shower curtain in the machine and scrubbed the bathroom with the ferocity of someone hiding a murder. She pulled the hoover out of the understairs cupboard. No. Not this now either. Shopping. She threw together a cheese sandwich and grabbed an apple to eat in the car.

The Silver Bullet, named for its laughably slow acceleration, was parked by the end of the alley. The frost on the mattress had melted. No sign of the robin.

At B&Q, she unchained a trolley and tucked her phone between her ear and her shoulder.

'Hi Claire.'

'Hey Katie.' Claire walked through a veil of heat into the store. 'How was the dentist?'

'Really good! Apparently, if Luke stops wobbling it, it might firm up and be fine.'

'That's great.'

'Although he sort of wants it to fall out.'

Claire laughed. 'Anything to be different from Jake.'

'Exactly. Another medal in the twin war.'

'Katie, have you got a minute?'

'Sure, but only just.'

'Thanks. I'm freaking out. Honor and Chris are coming on Sunday and I'm in B&Q and I need a loo seat and loo brush and paint and plates and glasses and I'm thinking of looking at doorknobs.'

'Right.'

'There are three different kinds of doorknobs in my house. How have I never noticed this?'

'Claire, you're lovely and so are all your doorknobs. Your home is a real achievement.'

'Thank you, that's a lovely thing to say. And I need silicone to reseal the bath.'

'Are you like this before I come round?'

'No, course not. Apart from anything else, you're round all the time.'

'OK, well, I *think* I'm flattered. Why do you care so much what Honor thinks?'

'I know. It's nuts. I don't want to. Its just she's so confident and precise. Wait. I need a new bath mat. We got bleach on the nice one when you were doing my highlights, remember?'

'Claire, could you maybe *lie down* on the bath mats, do some deep breathing?'

'No room. There's a shelf above them, nice idea though. Listen, rather than fill and paint the wall by the dining table, maybe I could stick a big plant in front of it.'

'I don't think you need a big plant. I think you need some perspective.'

'Oh, perspective schmerspective, you sound like Ben. That ship sailed hours ago. "Jiggle the perfume sticks and bung something in the oven." Try telling that to the voice in my head yelling *Get a new bin! Paint stuff! Weed the garden! Hire a chef!* Why are they coming to us, Katie? They've got a massive new house that was on *Grand Designs*. I want to see it.'

'I want you to see it.'

'Anyway. I rang because what should I cook? What's hardest to mess up but not too basic? Honor never just boils peas; she'll do peas in, I don't know, kumquat and anchovy foam.'

'Sounds horrible.'

'If she makes it, it's delicious, crispy, melt-in-the-mouth, whatever it's supposed to be. This is too stressful, you know what I'm like with cooking.'

'Let Ben do it.'

Claire leaned on her trolley. 'He *could* do it. But weirdly, it doesn't feel like an option, sort of like asking him to give birth wouldn't be an option. Does that make sense?'

Katie sighed. 'I have a meeting. Do chicken. I'll see you in the morning, we'll talk then. You know I'd help but the weekend is—'

'I know. It's your busiest time. Chicken, OK. Thanks for the chat, lovely friend. Maybe I could lie down on some towels.'

She hung up and saw a message had arrived from Fran.

How's it going with the birthday card? X

Shit, *that* was the thumb thing! She scrolled back to Fran's text from Wednesday.

Yo, happy new one! Hope Xmas was good. Just remembered that first day back is Grant's birthday. Shall I get bubbly from you and me? And would you have time to make a card from us both? He'd really like that. Fran x

She had replied:

Yes and yes! X

Twenty minutes later Claire pulled up in front of the house and hurried inside, leaving her B&Q stash in the car.

Oil and vinegar bottles scattered as she rushed to the sink to fill the yoghurt pot with paint water. She put it on the table with her painting things and pulled out a sideboard drawer to riffle through a box of stationery. She found a good-quality envelope, laid it on the table and measured watercolour paper to fit. She sat down and scrolled through photos of Grant and the class on her phone. She settled on one of him telling a story. Burly and bearded with playful blue eyes, his entire demeanour infused with 'you'll never guess what happened next'. Mr Reader, a teacher kids would remember.

She set the display to 'always on' and propped the phone against a pot of paintbrushes. No time for blank page panic or unhelpful thoughts about her abilities. She dipped her pencil to the page, her consciousness hovering somewhere hopeful, and tried to catch the joy of him.

★

Pearl and Charlie were chatting happily with Grant and Fran in the emptying playground as Claire rushed in.

The sun caught the ends of Fran's halo of dark hair and turned it orange. A tweedy tie showed at Grant's neck. He turned twenty-eight today but he loved that old-style teacher look. There was probably a cord jacket under his coat.

Pearl frowned at Claire. She had a whole head over Charlie now. Standing next to her brother was the only time she looked tall.

'Mummy, I'm going to be late for Edna,' she said. 'It's piano day.'

'I know, love. Sorry I'm late.'

Charlie barrelled over for a hug. Claire handed Grant the card, still warm from the hairdryer. 'Happy birthday, Mr Reader.'

'Did you put it from me as well?' whispered Fran.

'Yes, Ms Achibe, I did.'

Grant pulled out the card and laughed. 'Oh, wow. My own Claire Swift original.' Claire's cheeks heated. 'Thank you, that's fantastic.' He opened the card and read it, Fran peering over his arm. 'Thanks, Claire and Fran.'

Claire grinned. Fran curtseyed, her calf-length pleated skirt pooling round her elegant legs. Grant bent down to show the picture on the front to Pearl and Charlie.

'That's you,' said Charlie, pointing to the card and looking earnestly at Grant.

'He knows that already,' said Pearl, rolling her eyes.

'It *is* me,' said Grant. He studied the card and laughed. 'And there's Ryan, *listening*,' he looked up at Claire and Fran who smiled at each other because they knew that wasn't a given. 'And, that's … Tegan?' Claire nodded. Grant laughed. 'You've made them *enthralled*.'

'Well they would have been,' said Fran.

Claire was touched by Grant's response. Fran handed him the gift bag with the champagne inside and he gave them a kiss each on the cheek and said, 'Best teaching assistants ever,' which made the kids laugh.

They said their goodbyes and Claire rushed Pearl and Charlie out of the gate.

'Too fast, Mum.'

'Hold my hand then, Charlie. Guess what? The Well-beloveds are coming to our house on Sunday.'

'Why would they come to our house?' said Pearl.

'I know, right? That's what I said to Dad.'

'Does that mean Honor isn't making the food?'

'Sorry Charlie. Next time.'

'You'll have to tidy up,' said Pearl.

'Yeah, there's masses to do. Come on, let's get you to Edna. Wait till you see how I've parked the Silver Bullet.'

The car was half on, half off the pavement. It was filthy. If there wasn't time to clean it by Sunday, she'd have to park it round the corner.

'How are we going to fit in too, Mum? It's like a jungle in there.'

The pot plant was squeezed between the front seats into the back. 'Yes, it is a bit.'

'Mummy, why have you got a new bin?' Charlie squashed a finger on the window. A silver bin filled the passenger seat. 'We don't need a new bin. Dad sent off for a new closey thing.'

'Did he?'

'Yes. The packet's in the bits-and-pieces drawer.'

Claire's phone buzzed in her pocket.

'Your phone's ringing, Mummy.'

She pulled the phone out. 'That's great about the closey thing. This is Dad now. Ben, hi, I was going to call you.'

'Yeah, I—'

'Listen, Katie thinks chicken is hardest to mess up and I bet Edna's got a meat thermometer we could borrow and maybe she'll have a food timer.'

'But there's no—'

'A few timers would be useful. Not that we should try and make it fancy. We should keep it simple, but not boring simple. We haven't got anything planned, have we?'

'When, because Sunday—'

'If you could take the kids out tomorrow, then I can fill and paint the wall in the dining room and do the door. Oh, and I got a new loo seat. We can't have Honor doing one of those horrible clunky side slides, plus there's a gazillion other things, I made a list. Not sure where I put it.' She took a massive breath.

'Hmm,' said Ben, mildly. 'Doesn't sound like you kept it in perspective.' He sounded loving, but … long-suffering. Like he'd suffered for a long time. And he was right. From *his* perspective anyway.

Charlie tugged her arm down to speak into the phone. 'Mum's bought plants and a bin, Dad. We can't hardly fit in the car.'

Claire held out a hand to fend Charlie off and angled herself away from the kids. 'Fine. I haven't kept it entirely in perspective.'

'OK. Well. Anyway. Chris has been in touch. He had the wrong end of the stick, we're going to them.'

'Seriously?'

'Seriously.'

Claire leaned against the car. She threw back her head and fully inhaled for what felt like the first time since that morning.

'Better go. See you later.'

'Yes. Love you.' Claire put her phone in her pocket. 'Right.' She smiled at the kids. 'After Pearl's had her piano lesson and we've done Edna's shopping, who'd like to take some things back to B&Q?'

Chapter 3

Charlie squirmed and giggled as she walked her fingers up his spine. 'Spider spider on my back, which finger did that?' Her thumb pushed gently between his shoulders.

'Er... was it your fum?

'It was!'

'Again.'

Claire complied, yawning. She'd been up late. Only starting Karmel's leaflet after she and Ben had cleared away dinner. She'd scanned over a draft for Karmel's approval at quarter to midnight and Karmel had emailed back, potentially drunk, at 2.20 a.m.

Approval? Are you kidding?? Queen I bow to thee. Like, approved!!

The doorbell rang. Charlie grumbled and Claire kissed the whirl of hair on the back of his head and clambered off the sofa. 'We can play again later, love, I'm having a walk with Katie.'

Claire opened the door. Katie was posing like she was at the end of a catwalk. Claire recognised her leggings but the trainers and camo running jacket were new.

'Woah, Katie. Outfit.'

'Christmas presents from Ed.'

Claire beckoned her into the hall. Cartoon voices jabbered from the front room.

'How's the getting ready going?' asked Katie. 'I thought you'd be re-sanding the floors or something.'

Claire laughed. 'Turns out we're going to theirs.'

Katie visibly relaxed. 'Thank God for that, and you *do* get to see the new house.'

'Yes we do.'

'Right.' Katie pushed back the lengths at the front of her short dark hair and looked at her watch. 'You'd better get changed. I've got forty minutes until I have to open up the Halls. I'm not leaving Karate Club waiting outside again. Someone practice-kicked the bin over last week.'

'I'm ready,' said Claire.

Katie frowned. 'Aren't they your pregnancy yoga pants?'

Claire tugged the stretchy cotton. 'Yep. Couldn't find my leggings. Don't worry. They won't fall down.' She lifted Ben's fleece and the baggy T-shirt under it to show Katie her belt. 'Anyway, I won't be running.'

'Says who?'

Claire sat on the stairs and pulled on her floppy greying trainers, stifling another yawn. 'Are you really making me do this? It's cold, and I'm me and—'

'Couch to 5K will get your energy up. You are taking those multivitamins?'

'Y— no. I will.' Claire pushed open the living room door. 'Charlie, one more cartoon after this, then go and see if Daddy's up.'

''Kay mum.'

It was cold but not frosty. The street lights splashed yellow pools along the dark pavement as they walked down Bevan Way.

'I've worked out our route,' said Katie. 'We'll go past the Halls, through the play park, along the parade, up Pope's Hill past school, down the dual carriageway past the gas holders and home.'

'That's miles,' said Claire, instantly exhausted.

'About a mile and a half.'

Claire faffed with the hat she'd put on and and folded her arms. 'All right, but I'm not running. I don't want my body to go into shock. Why aren't we starting on the couch? Doesn't Couch to 5K have a couch phase?'

'We've been in the couch phase for years, Claire.' Katie swerved her pristine trainers round a lump that probably wasn't mud. 'I'm getting fit. I want to keep up with the kids in Norfolk this summer.'

'You're going camping again?'

'Hell yeah. Outside in the evening with a beer, knowing Luke and Jake are safe and off having fun, it's the best. Shall we try a little trot?' She swung her arms athletically.

'No thanks.' Claire walked a bit faster. 'Will that do?'

They reached the end of Bevan Road and turned onto Attlee Way where three pairs of semis butted on to the grounds of the Halls, an early Victorian beauty of a building philanthropically gifted to the people of Headleigh.

Katie waved to a groundsman. She and her team ran the Halls as a community hub. 'So let's talk about your freaked-out phone call yesterday.'

Every inch of Claire did not want to do that. She stopped and crossed the pavement to the the Halls' noticeboard. 'Daffodil Club Quiz Night, Katie, d'you fancy it? We could make a team with Ben and Ed.'

'You're changing the subject.'

Claire smiled, she hoped winningly.

Katie looked at the noticeboard. She *hmph*ed a laugh. 'Great poster. Really funny.'

Self-consciousness curled through Claire. She hadn't been fishing for compliments. She glanced at the poster. Four people sitting at a table, their expressions exaggerated and silly. Three of them were racking their brains about a quiz question, and one of them obviously had the answer.

'Thanks.'

'Did the Daffodil Club pay you?' asked Katie.

Claire sighed. 'With raffle tickets. But it's a fundraiser so don't go on at me about it.' She made a shooing motion at Katie and headed to the edge of the pavement. There was a break in the traffic and she scurried across.

Katie caught up with her. 'Oh go on, Claire. I haven't been on at you for weeks.'

'Yeah, I know,' Claire smiled as they headed down the tree-lined path to the play park. 'It's been great.'

'January though, innit? Month of new beginnings.'

They joined the path that circled the oval of grass next to the playground. A woman with a bouncy dog rolled her mobility scooter into the middle.

Claire sighed. 'Fine. You can go on at me for thirty seconds.'

'Right,' said Katie, tapping her index finger. 'First off, send your work out to some illustration agencies because why not. Next, put an advert on the Headleigh Forum: "prices from x pounds" kind of thing so it's out there and people stop expecting freebies. Three. Send samples to companies who'd like your Italiany fiftiesy vibe for their packaging. You know, artisan muesli and beer people.'

'Hmm,' said Claire, counting the seconds in her head. They were at seventeen.

''Cause you have way enough talent to do it for a living, Claire. And isn't it what you want?'

Agreeing to that question would be like stepping off a cliff. Claire rummaged for safety and found it. 'People round here do nice community things in their spare time, and my hobby is to help publicise them. Like Karmel, that nail technician.' She was warming to her theme. 'I've just done her a leaflet. She's offering low-cost nails to people with income and health difficulties.'

Katie nodded slowly. The woman in the scooter slotted a ball into a gizmo and tossed it for the happy dog.

'That's decent of Karmel, Claire. But she'll still be paid. Plus, I've seen her normal prices and she charges like a wounded buffalo.'

Claire snorted with laughter. 'I'm fine, Katie. I've got my school job. We're careful, we keep our costs down. I don't buy new clothes. It's enough just to be doing the odd poster. In fact, it's kind of too much. Seeing my work around here the last few months, it can be ... uncomfortable.'

'There's *such* an easy answer to that. If you don't want to see your posters in shop windows and on the Halls' noticeboard, then spread your net wider than Headleigh.' Katie hurled her arms in front of her.

Claire remembered the clock she'd put her on. 'You've got five more seconds.'

'You should dream bigger, Claire.'

'You're not the boss of my dream size.'

'You sell yourself short. You're a fucking artist too.'

'Cheers. Time's up.'

'Claim the space Claire. It's not just ring-fenced for your mum. There's no sign saying Margo Macklin only.'

'That's all, folks.' Claire circled a hand in the air.

'No one's comparing your mum's huge, scary paintings with your work except you. It's not a hobby. You're an artist.'

'Ding a ling a ling a ling,' Claire trilled. They must be walking faster; her breathing was quite shallow.

'We both know that's what holds you back, Claire.'

Claire put her hands over her ears.

'Fine. If you won't talk about that, we'll talk about yesterday. Why were you wigging out so hard about Honor?'

'Okaaaay.' Claire opened the gate to the empty playground and squeezed herself through the chains onto the seat of a swing. 'Sheesh, did someone make these smaller? Give us a push.'

Katie pulled back and let the swing go. The ground swooshed past and Claire gathered her thoughts. 'I think I wigged out because tomorrow would have been my first chance to show Honor I've got my shit together, which is debatable but, you know, that I'm a grown up.'

'Uh-huh.' Katie moved towards the front leg of the frame and leaned against it.

'Because when I met Ben, and then obviously her, I was kind of a scrapey pisshead, and then the party years rolled into the pregnancy years, and they rolled into the baby-and-toddler years, and all through it she was this sleek, high-functioning individual and I thought maybe since she was coming to our house for the first time in ages, I'd like to come across a bit like that too.'

'Because wigging out about bathmats and doorknobs is really sleek and high-functioning.' Katie walked back to the gate. 'It's so wrong.'

'Which bit?'

'The fact you're obliged to have a relationship with Honor Wellbeloved, that she's a de facto' – Katie jabbed savage air quotes with her fingers – '"*friend*" because the men you went out with and married and had kids with are best friends.' She picked up a drink can and popped it in a bin. 'We've never expected it from Ben and Ed, have we?'

'They get on.' Claire rose from the swing unsteadily.

'Yeah but they don't have a relationship, do they?' Katie opened the gate. 'And they spend zero time giving shits what the other might think of them. It's like, because you and Honor are women and mothers, there's an expectation that you're important to each other. God, the patriarchy makes itself so hard to like.'

They set off towards the exit on the other side of the park, Claire laughing. 'But it's different,' she said. 'They've got kids the same age as ours. Charlie and Pearl get on great with Ottie and Ollie; well, the boys have their moments but it's mostly great. Also,' Claire laid a hand on Katie's camo arm. 'You're saying her surname wrong. I watched her correct a maitre d' about how it was pronounced once. He was tiny and she leaned right over him and said, "It's not Wellbelove-id. It's Wellbe*loved*, as in I loved you once".'

Katie's mouth fell open.

Claire laughed. 'Her maiden name was Hoarecock, by the way.'

'Hoarecock? Ouch.' Katie laughed. 'Don't get me started on *maiden* names.'

A ball landed near their feet and the bouncy dog panted up and grabbed it.

'What it is with Honor,' said Claire, hoping her analogy would land, 'it's like if conversation was dancing, I never quite know where she's going to put her feet. And she always leads, but if it goes wrong it feels like *my* fault. Does that make sense?'

Katie gave a sturdy nod and Claire smiled at the relief of being understood. She leaned on Katie and tugged her sock, which had folded over under her heel.

'The night I met her she said I wasn't what she was expecting, and that Ben obviously didn't have a type because I wasn't at all like his ex.'

Katie scowled. 'Why did she say *anything* about his ex?'

'I know. And she was all smiley like it was a nice thing to say; meanwhile I was almost puking. Then she said she wouldn't tell me anything about her, because that wasn't fair. But I wouldn't have asked. It made me feel like I'd rushed up and gone, "Tell me *everything* about Ben's ex".'

Claire wriggled her foot on the ground. Better.

'So why do you want to impress her?'

'Who said I want to impress her?'

Katie had one excellent eyebrow raised.

Claire sighed. 'Because she's kick-ass and stunning and she knows how to do stuff and does it at a million miles an hour. And when I'm with her I sometimes think well if *she* likes me, maybe I'm a bit kick-ass too, and then I come back here to Headleigh and our idyllic gas holders and our little houses, and realise I'm me.'

'You are kick-ass. And you love Headleigh, that's why you got me and Ed to move here.'

'I know. I do. Of all the Luton suburbs Headleigh is the concretey best.'

They turned down the passage that led to the parade.

'So the Wellbeloveds' new house, is it the one from the *Grand Designs* episode where the woman's pregnant with twins, and she's handling it like a megastar and then she finds out they won't be able to move in till after the babies are born and they'll be dealing with two newborns *in a caravan*?'

Claire smiled. That was such a Katie angle. 'Yeah, that's the one. Honor and Chris bought it from the couple. Those twins are about nine now. I'm sure Honor will have loads of plans to improve it.' She laughed. 'I love how your review of a *Grand Designs* didn't refer to the house that was being built *at all*.'

'It's the twin thing. Unless you've had two living beings leave your body and then exist on different time clocks...' Katie shuddered and clutched her chest and Claire laughed again.

They turned onto the parade of shops. The grille at the front of the bakery cranked into life and rose up. The woman in the baker's with a face like a cottage loaf nodded at them and they waved back.

'The one time Honor and Chris came to visit us here,' said Claire. 'Honor had had her son Ollie like ten days before and she was glowing, her hair shone, she'd put on make-up and earrings—'

'She'd managed to leave the house.'

'She'd managed to leave the house, exactly. Anyway, I knocked a jug of water over the bread, and Honor says, "I'll come out with you for another loaf after I've fed the baby," and I'm thinking *oh well, that's lunch delayed for an hour or two*, not that it mattered, it was shop-bought quiches or something, but about ten minutes later she's at the door in this amazing cream wrap coat, having done a complete breast feed.'

'A ten-minute feed?'

'I know. Everything about her is ultimately efficient. Her breasts, her babies. Basically, she makes it sound like her two slept through and got up to make her coffee and put their sleepsuits in the wash from about eight weeks.'

Katie laughed. 'She was sugar-coating it. No one has it that easy.'

Claire shrugged and blew out. She did a quick scan of the charity shop window, crammed with New Year declutterings. 'Anyway, she and I walked into the baker's and when the woman we just went past saw Honor she stopped wiping the counter and went all flustered like it was a royal visit, I'm not even kidding. She was genuflecting as she handed her the bloomer, I felt like a serf.'

'I thought you felt kick-ass when you were with her?'

Claire cocked her head. 'I suppose it's more basking in reflected kick-assery. That's when it's just us and them. When we used to eat out with them before kids, waiting staff would look at me and I'd feel them think, *She's a normal dobbin kind of person we can largely ignore, but the other one is a thoroughbred we want to impress.*'

Katie fixed Claire with a look that was somewhere between pity and puzzled. 'I think most of this is in your head, Claire. She's gorgeous, but so are you.'

'I'm glad you've met her, I virtually only persuaded Ben to have a proper wedding so you could see her in the flesh.'

'She wasn't massively high on my list of priorities to be honest. Me, the size of a *Grand Designs* house, giving you away at the register office. Trying to search out your mum from wherever she'd slid off to puff a Sobranie. But look, we're going off topic. If Honor makes you wig out at B&Q, maybe it's time to …' Katie ran a finger across her throat with the noise of a blade.

'Katie!' Claire's voice came out louder than she expected. 'Oh, I shouldn't have said all this. I'm going to run as penance.' Claire lumbered off. She was running. Get a load of this. It was kind of all right. *Oh God*, no it wasn't. Splitting headache, no air, *whoops, nearly tripped on the hem of the yoga pants.*

Katie caught up with her. 'Sorry about the throat-slicing.'

'Doesn't matter.' Claire swatted behind her. 'Look. We ran miles. All the way along the parade to the corner.'

'It's about forty metres but *go team.*' Katie held up her

29

palm. Claire went to slap it and missed. 'Every time, Claire, every time. Aim for my hand.'

Claire brought her hand to Katie's in slow motion and Katie's fingers interlaced with hers.

'Claire, you're tremendous. I wish you knew your worth. I don't like how people get your work for free and I don't like how Honor gets to you. If she doesn't make you feel tremendous about yourself tomorrow, that's on her.'

Claire unlaced her fingers 'OK.'

'Right.' Katie checked her watch. 'There isn't time to go up Pope's Hill now. Let's bomb round the park again faster.'

Claire sucked in air. 'I don't think we should chance it. I bet Karate Club are eyeing up that bin already.'

Katie narrowed her eyes. 'Fine. Next time. Take it easy tomorrow. And get some photos of the house.'

Claire laughed. 'I will. And I'm going to have a great time and feel great about myself, OK?'

'Deal.'

Chapter 4

They were late leaving. It was Claire's fault, agonising over clothes and make-up, fiddling her hair into a bad mood.

She and Ben had hunted for her bag, then Claire remembered it was with Charlie, who was in the back of the car with his love-grubbied cuddly dog, Dog, under his chin and the bag on his lap.

Claire willed them along the B489. *She'll know it's your fault you're late.*

'Mummy, you didn't take the label off the flowers.'

'You take it off then, Pearl.' *Without mentioning how much they were.*

'It's a lot of money for flowers, isn't it?'

'They're nice though, don't you think?' She glanced at Ben.

'Eight pounds,' said Pearl. 'That's loads, isn't it?'

Even if Ben thought it was loads, he ignored the bait. She patted his leg. 'Lovely driving, Ben. Can we please not mention we watched their *Grand Designs* twice?'

'Why?'

'Because I feel like a tourist when we look round their houses anyway and it just seems extra-stalky.'

'It's not stalky,' said Ben. 'Our rich mates bought a big house that was on a TV show and we watched it. What's wrong with that?'

'Can we just not say we watched it twice?'

'Mummy, let it go.'

'Yeah Mum, leave it.'

Charlie's hoodie had been navy and belonged to Katie's twins, then Pearl. Claire noticed its worn cuffs in the side mirror. She'd never seen Ottie and Ollie in the same clothes twice.

She caught her reflection. She looked even more knackered than she felt. *Come on Claire. You're going to have a great time and feel great about yourself, remember?* She pushed her shoulders back, lifted her head, saw a fleck of mascara on her cheek and wiped it. The car banged through a pothole and her finger jabbed her eye. The sting took her breath away.

'Oops,' said Pearl. 'I banged the flowers.'

'Let me take them.'

Claire wiped and blinked and put the lilies on her lap and looked in the mirror. Her eye was pink and all the make-up had gone. She took out her ponytail and bundled her hair into a bun, thinking it might take the focus off looking so *Clockwork Orange*. The elastic snapped, she felt the ridge across her hair. She moved the flowers and the lilies left powder down her cream jumper. Fantastic. Pink eye, shit hair, stained brown. She had truly aced not looking like she'd tried hard.

Just after eleven they passed some streets of prefabs that had seen better days. Then there was a hedge, and then a huge cedar, glass and steel house, solar panels on its roof, glinted into view.

'Looks bigger than on the telly,' said Ben, turning onto the sweep of drive. 'Their window cleaner can't need many other clients.'

'Look, Daddy, they've got three cars now.'

The family spaceship and sleek runaround had been joined by a tiny city car.

'I wish we had three cars,' said Pearl, as though three was a sensible bare minimum. Ben and Claire smiled at each other.

'How about four, one each,' said Ben.

'Really, Dad?'

'I don't want four cars, Daddy,' said Charlie, like it was an awful possibility. 'Too many keys, isn't it Mum? And we'd forget which one to look for in the car park.'

'What would the neighbours say about us parking four cars on Bevvy Way?' said Ben.

'The Miseries would hate it,' said Pearl. 'It would be brilliant.'

They laughed. Pebbles crunched slowly under the wheels. The front door flew open and Chris and Honor's kids hurtled out, faces gold from skiing. Ben pulled between the spaceship and the runaround.

'You and Chris are such a laugh, Ben, don't disappear with him, will you?' said Claire quietly.

Ollie banged his hands on their still-moving bonnet. Ben braked hard.

'Ollie!' called his sister.

'Careful there, bud,' said Ben in his measured way.

Claire smoothed through the massive *ker-lunk* the door always made as it opened because it was dented.

Ollie had grown again. His skinny arm flew out and ruffled Charlie's head and Charlie unstuck himself from Claire's side. Ottie, more solid and knowable than her brother, swept a curtain of dark hair behind her ear, and with a smile that reached warmer, soulful versions of her mother's chocolate eyes, held out a hand to Pearl.

Claire glanced back at their car, dwarfed between the shiny black motors. 'The Silver Bullet is filthy.'

'It looks cool,' said Ben. 'Like a low-rent cop car on a stakeout.'

Chris and Honor were at the door, shoulder to shoulder. Honor wore a dark, slouchy jumper. A slash of caramel collarbone showed at one side. Her slim legs were in black jeans, hair in waves reflecting window shine. Her tanned and polished feet were bare.

Nerves shimmered from Claire's stomach and she pulled the edges of her straggly coat across the pollen stain. It was a little warmer than yesterday but bare feet was brave. *Wait, heated floor.*

As usual, Chris's jumper and jeans looked new and pulled a little tight like there hadn't been the chance to ask for a size up before Honor, wanting his waistline kept in check, had waved their credit card. He had the air of a man kept in check, somehow. Wistful, a bit surrendered.

'Hey you Swifts, it's been too long,' said Honor.

Claire braced herself for a brisk grab and the knock of Honor's cheekbone against hers. But Honor threw out her arms and Claire crossed the threshold into an unexpected hug that smelled of jasmine.

What have I done to deserve this?

Chris and Ben's bear-hugging paws slapped each other's backs.

'Good to see you mate.'

'And you, fella.'

Claire was released.

'Hey.' Ben held locked arms towards Honor.

'Ah Benj.' Honor draped herself around him.

Claire and Chris half-hugged and kissed on the cheek. 'That eye looks sore,' he said, kindly.

'Oh, it's fine. Looks worse than it feels, I expect.' They smiled at each other awkwardly. Claire loved Chris and Ben's easy affection for one another. But left alone, she and Chris were a little like becalmed boats waiting for the wind of their partners to set them on their way.

Honor was still hugging Ben. He was valiantly holding back. Close contact with his leggy, beautiful friend must be a thrill but he made it look like it wasn't.

Honor thanked them for the lilies, which she transferred at arm's length to a shelf.

'We saw your house on *Grand Designs*,' said Pearl, copper curls bouncing as she and the others ran back into the hall from wherever they'd already been.

Charlie gasped, squeezing Dog into his chest. 'Pearl!' he stage whispered. 'Mum said don't say we watched it twice.'

'I didn't say we watched it twice.' Pearl was fuming. 'You just did.'

Claire pulled a bunch of faces and sweated. 'Yep, well, we did, we watched it twice.'

'We've watched it loads more than that,' said Chris.

Charlie grinned at Chris and pointed over the door. 'All that bit there was wonky wasn't it? And they bashed it down and made it again and the people were really *"Grrrrr".*' He made his Incredible Hulk face. 'And the lady who had two babies in her tummy, when she was talking to the man, she went …' Charlie mimed someone overcome with emotion, '"*This has been the hardest thing I've ever done. I'm sorry I just can't …*"' He waved to stop imaginary cameras and walked away.

Honor applauded first, fast ringing claps. Everyone joined in. Claire's chest squeezed. Ollie looked like he was considering Charlie in a new light.

'Oh Charlie,' said Honor, 'what a great little actor you are.'

Charlie looked stunned, turned red and walked into Claire to hide. 'Mum, is that what acting is?'

'Yes,' said Claire. 'Pretending to be someone else, you know that, Charlie.'

'You should sign him up for classes,' said Honor.

Charlie's hand shot up. 'Yes please.'

'We'll have to look into it, Charlie,' said Ben.

Chris took their coats. 'Oh Lord,' said Honor. 'Look at your jumper, Claire. That lily pollen gets everywhere, doesn't it?'

'I'll give it a wipe,' said Claire. 'Can I borrow a cloth?'

'Don't wipe it,' Honor said urgently. 'You'll push the pollen into the fibres. It needs soaking in cold then washing in biological gel.' Pearl cocked her head, full of interest. Honor smiled at her. 'If you're travelling with lilies, Pearl, it's best to pull off the anthers, those brown bits in the middle, with a tissue. But then throw away the tissue, because, fact fans, lily pollen is poisonous to cats.'

'Wow,' said Pearl, her face lit up. 'You know a lot about lilies.'

Honor smiled and shrugged agreement and Claire's pink eye twitched.

They had to put their shoes in the boot room. Claire held Pearl's hand as she hopped, undoing her laces. Their coats were hung with Wellbeloved coats in a wall unit. There were sports kits too and ski and judo suits. A long bench seat ran opposite with a door that led outside at the end. Under the seat were cubbyholes, half of them home to riding boots, walking boots, wellies and sailing shoes. Even if it smelled of used footwear, it was testament to the wealth and the wealth of experience Honor and Chris were giving their kids.

Ben and the kids found cubbyholes, deposited their shoes and left. Claire took off her baseball boots. It had been a bad morning for socks. Her better sock was patterned with bananas, the other was orange and grey stripes with a hole. In fact, it was a bad day for feet too because the hole revealed a toenail painted with Santa's face. She'd thought her feet would be hidden under jeans and boots. How could she have forgotten this would be a shoes-off house? She sighed. Her choice was mismatched socks with a trashy glimpse of Santa, or go all out and parade Karmel's pedicure in full: two big toe Santas and eight red and green beribboned presents.

'Hey.'

Claire scrunched her feet, hiding Christmas.

'Would these help?' Honor held out soft camel socks. 'They're cashmere. Not to be showy, I just know you feel the cold.'

'Thanks. That would be great.'

Claire returned what was definitely a warm smile.

'I'll put those lovely lilies in water.'

Wow. Honor was being so nice. Claire stuffed her socks in her boots and pulled on Honor's socks. She took a breath. How was she feeling? She pictured a little Alpine weather house with a tiny Claire fixed to each end of a stick. An emotional barometer. Feeling Good Claire was right out there and Feeling Bad Claire was nicely tucked inside the cabin. Excellent.

Honor sighed onto an upstairs window, her breath misting the glass.

'Upsetting yourself again, my love?' said Chris.

'It's this horrible view,' she told Ben and Claire.

They'd reached the guest bedrooms upstairs on the house tour. They'd had tea before they'd started and, as lunch wouldn't be till much later, peanut butter flapjack.

'I got the nanny to make it for you, Claire,' Honor had said. 'I remembered how much you liked it last time.'

The kids had apple juice and the adults had all chosen

37

different teas. Honor had removed the bags with a spoon and casually tossed them one after the other into a wooden caddy she'd flipped open, an arc of ten feet, as though it were nothing. If Claire had done that, everyone would have known about it.

Honor had delighted in everything she'd shown them when they'd toured downstairs. The kitchen that opened into an area Ben and Claire's entire house would fit inside with room left over for a stable of junk model horses. The geometic-patterned rugs on the polished concrete floor. The glass dining table big enough for a cabinet meeting, two streamlined sofas and a shiny black grand piano in the corner. The smaller room with carpet, a snugglier sofa and big TV, blankets neatly slotted in a basket. The study, adorned with one of Claire's mum's canvases, taking her by surprise like it always did that Chris and Honor had it. The games room with table football, utility room with laundry area and fridge-freezer as broad as an American footballer. The shower and loo off the boot room. The garage full of bikes, and sports accessories.

Honor had delighted in every aspect of it.

But upstairs in the guest rooms things weren't to her liking. Claire stepped closer to the window. Beyond the Wellbeloved's lawn and fence was the back of a row of the prefab houses she'd seen as they drove in. Some had nets, ramps and grab handles, others blinds and swing sets.

'They're so close,' said Honor. 'It was almost a deal-breaker for me.'

'They're a bit like our house,' said Ben.

'Oh,' said Honor. 'What? No. Your house is sweet.' She peered out gloomily. 'Those are grim. I don't want to see them. And I don't want them looking at us.'

'To be fair, sweetheart, this is a guest room. You don't

spend much time here. Also you can do this.' Chris flicked a button and the glass turned opaque, then he flicked it clear again.

'I actually have a cunning plan for those houses,' said Honor.

'Oh, cool. So do I,' Chris looked suddenly brighter.

Honor smiled. 'We'll plant mature trees along the boundary so we can't see them. Loads of twelve-metre-high jobs. Then it will be all private and we can have that lovely pool, Chris, the lagoon.'

Chris laughed. 'Oh, OK, well your plan's not the same as mine.'

Honor pecked him on the lips, slowly, with eye contact. 'I'm sure it is.' She moved to the doorway and smiled at Claire and Ben. 'Come and see the real view.'

Claire glanced at the garden. Honor had shown no interest in Chris's plan. She took it as read that her big trees and pool would prevail.

Ottie's bedroom looked out the front over fields. A leather-edged school backpack with a slip attached filled out in Honor's beguiling hand sat near the door, as it had in Ollie's room.

'Ben,' Claire whispered, 'Monday tomorrow. Have we washed the uniforms?'

'No. But the kids only went back for a day.'

'Pearl dropped a yoghurt on her trousers, and Charlie's sweatshirt's painty.' She sighed.

'We'll sort it when we get home.' Ben rubbed the small of her back.

Honor and Chris's bedroom at the end of the wide landing had gorgeous leather chairs and carefully chosen furnishings but the vast picture window beyond the end of the bed took Claire's attention. There were fields and hedges. A hill swept behind, a clump of trees tufting its crest.

'Oh,' said Claire. 'That is stunning.'

'It's what I like best about the whole house,' said Chris. He pointed through the window. 'There's a telegraph pole there. And that bit of road sign. And that's it. Not a building in sight.'

They could keep their giant sofas and boot cubbyholes and the space and the bathrooms. This, she envied. 'It's perfect,' she said. 'To enjoy the changing beauty of the countryside, but *from bed*.'

Everyone laughed.

'We'll have a walk up that hill in a bit,' said Chris.

'You've spoiled it now,' said Claire and they laughed again. Chris and Ben went off to assemble a cross trainer. Claire tried to join them but was called back by Honor.

'Claire.' Honor pulled a grey jumper from a stack of knitwear. 'Do you want to wear this?'

Claire looked down at her pollen stain. 'Yes please.'

Her jumper crackled with static as she removed it. She peeled her T-shirt away from it.

'Lovely T-shirt. Where's it from?'

Claire laughed. 'Headleigh Beavers' jumble sale, the label's been cut out. I made them posters and they paid me with a ten-minute rummage before they opened.'

'God, how exciting.' Honor looked sincere. Maybe she was bored of proper shopping. Claire pulled on the light-as-air jumper and felt immediately cosseted.

'That reminds me,' said Honor. 'I have some clothes for Pearl and Charlie downstairs, I'll see you down there. Enjoy the view.'

'That's brilliant, thank you.'

Claire was alone. She peered around the room and into

the bathroom from where she stood, as though invisible sensors might be set off by moving. She'd been greeted with a hug, lent socks and a jumper and given kids' clothes. Had any of that felt like a judgement? Did she feel she had blundered in some way? She checked in with her barometer. She was surprisingly OK. Feeling Good Claire was still outside the Alpine weather house.

She stepped back towards the linen headboard and took a photo of the hill and fields and messaged Katie.

Honor and Chris's view… from their BED!! All good! xx

★

'Looks delicious. Did you make it?'

Claire had taken a bottle of wine and a jar of chutney with a printed cotton hat to Honor in the kitchen.

'No I didn't. Sorry it's not more meaningful. It's from the Christmas fair at the local allotments. I did a poster for that too.' *Jeez*, she was the poster girl of posters.

'Wish I had a talent I could swap for home-made chutney.' Honor smiled with an admiring intensity, as though she'd swap *her* talent, for being paid enormous sums of money by a multinational bank, for receiving chutney for her efforts in a heartbeat.

'Is it delicious?'

'Um,' it suddenly seemed like a careless present. 'I haven't actually tried it.'

'Russian Roulette chutney, how exciting.'

Honor glanced at a recipe on her phone then without rechecking it, produced ingredients from a cupboard, pull-out larder and fridge, nothing falling out or being knocked over.

Claire wished she had it on film. 'This,' she'd say to Katie. '*This* is what the fuss is about.'

Honor was the opposite of the pinnied cook with flour in hair. She'd remain pristine as she stirred and oversaw the gadgets that flashed and beeped her culinary bidding. She would never spatter her phone screen with tomato and send it into a blinking fit.

'I've put the bag of clothes outside the boot room but don't feel you have to take them.'

'We'd love them, thank you. Shall I put it in the car now, so it's not in the way?'

Honor thought that was a good idea, so Claire put on her baseball boots and wrestled the huge laundry bag outside to the car. She spluttered an embarrassed laugh as she wondered if Charlie's wrecked hoodie had prompted Honor's offer.

She put the bag by the boot and unzipped it. The quality clothes were barely worn. Keeping them in their folds, she laid some in the boot, checked no one was looking and, thumbs-upping in the corner, snapped a photo. Dithering over whether to send it to Katie, she glanced at the house.

Honor was behind the glass in the hall, shaking her head and smiling. Claire flamed red and busied herself in the boot. And just like that, in a one hundred and eighty degree stick swivel, Feeling Good Claire flipped into the weather house, and Feeling Bad Claire – really bad, idiotically bad – swung out.

Chapter 5

Curls of mud squelched under the borrowed wellies. They were too big and Claire gripped hard to keep them on. They'd gone down a track across the road from the house and Chris was pointing out a route to Ben and the kids, arcing his arm across the horizon.

They were definitely going up that hill. Honor had said they needed to set a fair pace to be back for when the slow-cooker finished the beef, so it would be a lot faster than the rate Claire tackled Pope's Hill with the kids.

When she'd come in from putting the clothes in the car, Honor had said, 'You do make me laugh, Claire.' She'd clasped Claire's fingers and fixed her with those huge dark eyes. 'Don't ever change.'

In reply, Claire had simpered. She had *simpered*.

'Don't ever change,' she muttered to herself now in an uncharitable impression of Honor.

If I want to change, I will. I do not exist for your entertainment, Honor Wellbeloved. Her foot almost came out of a welly. She tugged the zip of Honor's spare cagoule down her chest. Her coat had been deemed 'fun, but not remotely breathable', but it would have been fine and she wished she was wearing it. She clomped a little faster to catch up with the others. No one else was having this problem with their borrowed wellies.

Honor was waiting for her with an expression of fervent sympathy. 'How's your mother, Claire?'

'Oh. Um...' It was a wholly unexpected question. Honor usually asked if Claire and Ben had eaten at Nobu yet or ever been to Val d'Isère or were planning to see anything at the ENO this season, and then insist that they *should*, like you could on a part-time teaching assistant and voluntary-sector worker's salary.

'Margo's fine, thanks. We spent Christmas in Scotland with her. It was nice. Low key.' Honor still looked fervent. Despite her better judgement Claire continued. 'Her phone's broken. So we were on the train to Glasgow with me not entirely sure she'd remember we were coming, but she did.'

She had said more than she wanted to. 'How are Andrew and Katrina? Did you all have a nice ski trip at Christmas?' Claire hadn't met Honor's friends but they were always off on family jaunts with the Wellbeloveds.

Honor sniffed sharply. 'I have no idea how they are, we went on our own. I'd rather not talk about Katrina.'

'Sure. No worries.' That told her.

Up ahead Chris was gesticulating as he explained something to Ben, pushing his hands together to make a sphere.

'...Burns up all the waste underground and returns it as power to each household.'

'Sounds amazing,' said Ben. 'Email me the link, I'd like to read about that.'

It sounded more fun than the conversation Claire was having. She chewed her cheek, wondering how to end the lengthening silence.

'So, Honor. This will make you laugh. I started changing all my passwords the way you told me, and you won't believe it but—'

Honor goggled at her. 'You *can't* have got my password hack wrong. It's foolproof.'

'Well this fool messed it up.'

'Let's go through it again.' She put her arm through Claire's. 'It's the first four letters of the opening of a song, then an exclamation mark, then two digits, then the start of the website name.'

'Yeah, that's what I was aiming for, and I was fine with the words from 'Funky Town', but I got about halfway through and then realised that sometimes I was putting the digits *before* the exclamation mark, so I tried to check and redo it but I ran out of time and just left it in a mess.'

Honor threw her head back to laugh. 'That's hilarious. So my life hack has made your life more complicated.'

'Yup. Can't get in anywhere without going round the houses.'

'And "Funky Town"? Classic, Ding. You're a one-off.'

Claire flinched at hearing the nickname.

'So if your mum's phone's broken,' said Honor, 'how do you get hold of her, email?'

Oh. Margo again. 'God no, Margo is the sixty-something tech forgot. I have to phone her neighbour.'

'Is she painting?'

'She must be. If she video calls me from the neighbour's she always has flecks in her hair.'

'Tell her to get a phone.'

'You can't tell Margo anything. She's only a slave to her muse.'

Honor pushed an overhanging branch away. 'I do admire how you're parenting so differently to her. Being there for your kids, working at their school. Mine would hate it, but then they've always been so independent.'

'Help me, Mum.' Charlie sidestepped towards them with thick snot snailing from his nose.

'You need a tissue, Charlie,' said Honor, not hiding her distaste.

Claire ferreted though receipts and crumbs and bits of pen and action figures in her bag.

'Eugh. Disgusting,' yelled Ollie. Charlie whimpered. Honor whisked her arm from Claire's.

'Ollie,' she barked. He dropped his head.

Claire offered Charlie a rumpled paper napkin from a café.

'It's got coffee on, Mum.'

Honor tugged forward a tissue from a pack. Charlie reached out, Dog swinging from his hand, the snot having reached his lip. Honor flinched. 'Better take them all, Charlie.'

'Thanks.' He squidged the rest of the pack into his pocket and patted it. 'Dad!' he yelled. 'I've got my own tissues!'

Easy, Charlie Bucket, it's tissues, not a golden ticket. 'Thanks, Honor.'

'No problem. How's Katie?'

'Good. We've started running.'

'I can't imagine you running.'

'Me neither,' said Claire. 'It's her idea.'

'I'm like you, Claire. If Linton didn't turn up at my front door at the crack of dawn three mornings a week I'd do very little, but I have to be fit for my job. And seeing him in Lycra is very motivating.'

'Cool,' said Claire, at a loss for how else to respond.

'Is Katie still pressuring you to charge for your illustrating?'

'Did I mention that?' Claire felt a pang of guilt. 'A bit. It's just a hobby really. I don't feel it's right to ask for money.'

'Who says you have to be wealthy to be an artistic philanthropist, eh?'

They crossed a field, the hill rising up before them. It was
a whole palette of greens and browns, beautiful. Claire hung
back and watched everyone climb a stile and jump clear of
the mud in front of it. They made it look so easy. She fiddled
with the gate beside it. Padlocked. The others had gone out
of sight but Honor was waiting. Claire hoisted herself up
then faltered as she turned, her handbag swinging.

'Why did I bring my handbag? I'm such a townie.'

Honor reached across the mud and took the bag. 'You
can do it my lovely, over you come.'

Claire climbed one foot over, then the other. Wobbling
on the top step, she adjusted her feet, caught the toe of one
wellie with the heel of the other and splatted into the mud
on her knees. Her heel throbbed from kicking the stile as
she fell and the humiliation throbbed as hard. Her jeans and
the cagoule were slathered in mud. Honor helped her up.

'Sorry about your cagoule, Honor.'

'You're creating quite a lot of laundry today, Claire.'
Honor laughed. Like she'd said something funny.

'Yes.'

'Anything hurt?'

'Nope, nothing hurt.'

'I'd give you a tissue, but Charlie—'

'It's fine.' Her eyes brimmed with tears. 'I'll catch you up.'

'Here.' Honor turned back and handed her a bottle of
water.

Claire poured the water on her hands and wiped them
with the coffee-infused napkin that Charlie had rejected.
She should have started with the mud that was drying on
her face. She rubbed that with the top of the kagoule sleeve.

47

This is shit, and I do not feel good about myself, and home, I want to be home, I want to be home.

When she caught up, the others were making their way up the slope like mountain goats. Ben turned around.

'You OK?' he called down to her.

'Fine. See you at the top.' Her voice was shrill.

A scar of stones cut its way up the hill. From Honor and Chris's window this hill had looked grassy and undulating, not steep and stony. There must be easier routes to the top. It was going to be a hands and feet job. She reached forward and made her way up the slope, picking a toe position, rejecting it, finding another one. Picking a hand position, retracting, pricked by something.

She turned to see if she could see the house, lost her footing and scraped a hand down rock. She held her wrist. Tears in her eyes.

Keep going. Keep going.

When she emerged at the top, palm stinging, heel pulsing, everyone was gathered waiting. 'Here she is,' said Honor, 'huddle up.'

Claire lumbered into the space Ben made between himself and Chris as the kids bunched in front of them.

'Smile, everyone.' Honor, at the front, raised her phone and took pictures. Before Claire could organise her features into a a version of her photo face, the phone was put away.

*

'Arms up.'

Honor tugged the strings of the apron and tied them at Claire's back.

Laughter drifted from the TV room. She wished she was in there with the kids. Never once in close to fourteen years had Claire been asked to help Honor with cooking. Was it a promotion? She wondered if Katrina had helped before Honor started having no idea how she was.

'Could you do me a white sauce please, Claire?'

Bail, Claire, bail now. Say that following a series of traumatic white sauce incidents you only deal in packet mixes.

A jug of milk, a butter dish and a pot marked 'flour' appeared in front of her with a pan and wooden spoon. Maybe the universe would smile on her, or perhaps, since she'd borrowed jersey lounge pants now too, so was mostly in Honor's clothes, the universe might mistake her for Honor and bless her efforts accordingly. She set a low flame under the pan and picked up the butter dish, clattering the lid on the worktop. The butter melted. She poured in some flour. Too much or not enough? She never knew. She stirred it to paste. Maybe it was OK. She picked up the jug and poured very, very slowly then milk whooshed out half into the pan and half onto the hob with a hiss.

'Whoops.' *Concentrate.*

Claire paddled milk around lumpy islands with the spoon. She turned up the heat a little. The sauce chunked up like burnt Playdoh. 'Honor, what's the definition of sauce?'

'God, that's a mess.'

'Ha ha ha,' Claire flashed, sweat on her upper lip. 'Isn't it?'

'Bless you, Ding. Don't feel bad about it, we can't all be good at everything.' Honor flipped up the lid of the food waste caddy. She upended the pan and the sauce fell in with a thud. She snorted with laughter again and Claire joined in. It was shocking to hear her old nickname. It had been so long since anyone called her Ding, herself included. Short for dingbat: like binge drinking, she'd left it behind years ago.

'Let's start again,' said Honor.

It was an intense, hands-on experience, Honor at her shoulder, but the new sauce turned out well. When it was done, Claire said she was going to wash her face. Once she had, grazed hand stinging, she slipped though the door in the boot room and leaned against the weathered cedar outside wall to phone Katie.

'So then she said, "we can't all be good at everything," like she's saying, "*I'm* good at everything but we can't *all* be like me," then she threw away the sauce I'd made. That's probably enough motive to get you off homicide in France.'

'Where was her stick blender?' asked Katie.

'That's what *I* thought. I suppose she's never made a white sauce that needed saving.'

'That's not normal.'

'Anyway, then she stood behind me and put her hands over mine and we made another batch.'

'Oh God. She's the puppet master.'

'Yeah. It felt like an unerotic power-play version of *Ghost*. And another thing that annoyed me, when we got here, Charlie acted a bit from their *Grand Designs* and she said, "He's good, you should sign him up for classes." I mean Ben and I know he's a good performer. And I felt proud but I felt bad too. Like we haven't been doing enough for him.'

Katie tutted reassuringly. 'You know what, Claire. Just dig deep for another couple of hours and you can leave her wizarding Oz and come home to Kansas.'

'You're right. Just a couple of hours, and lots of that will be eating, then I won't have to see her for months. I'm so having thirds.'

'That's the spirit.'

★

Lunch. Was. Delicious.

The tenderest, richest beef. A rainbow of tasty vegetable dishes. Insanely good roast potatoes. Once they'd cleared up, and Chris had filled both dishwashers to his satisfaction, and his wife's glass with the rest of the red wine, Claire wiggled her eyebrows and Ben picked up the message.

'We should hit the road,' said Ben. 'Uniform wash and all that.'

Ottie and Pearl insisted on doing a recital. One of the long sofas was turned to face the shiny piano. The girls sat on the velvet stool and played a short duet that Ottie had taught Pearl on her bedroom keyboard. They stood for a bow. After setting her shoulders back having seen Honor point at her own, Ottie played a solo piece. It was lovely. Claire glanced at Honor. Imperious, implacable. Proud or bored, it was hard to tell. At the end, everyone clapped and Claire whistled, fingers in her mouth.

'My turn.' Pearl plonked 'Chopsticks' out of the piano. Claire whistled again, just as heartily, not wanting Pearl to hear a difference, then the kids disappeared again and Chris went with Ben to find a book.

'She's just had a few lessons next door,' said Claire. 'I mean she and Edna have fun really, I leave Pearl there and me and Charlie do Edna's shopping.'

'Is she hard of hearing, Edna?'

'She is, actually, yes.'

'Just a hunch.'

Claire found herself pretend-laughing again. It was exhausting.

Honor was checking through photo frames propped on the piano. Claire's gaze landed on a photo. One of a dozen of Honor and Chris with Katrina and Andrew and all their kids around a restaurant table, pink-cheeked, raising colourful fruit-adorned drinks.

Honor passed Claire a silver frame. 'Remember this, Claire? Our holiday together.'

The photo was herself, Honor, and Ben in Cornish drizzle with Pearl in a buggy with a rain cover on. Honor's shoulder-length hair tucked behind her ears, her own in wild strands over her face.

'Oh gosh, yes, Bodlowe. That really brings it back.'

Claire had been pregnant with Charlie. She'd felt like drizzle the whole week, even when the sun came out. A sleepy, ravenous, despairing, ill-equipped mess, trying to keep Pearl quiet in her travel cot in that tiny thin-walled cottage. Unable to say or make heard what she wanted to do, or eat, and if she did, torn up with the sense it was wrong. No wonder Honor and Chris had upgraded to Katrina and Andrew for their next holiday, and the accommodation they could all afford. 'So how are Katrina and, oh…' She remembered too late she'd been warned off.

Honor smiled and surveyed the piano top. Then she stacked each photo of Katrina and Andrew into her arms, and put the whole pile on the floor, the noise ringing off the polished concrete. She swept specks of dust from the piano's shiny black surface with the sleeve of her jumper. Then taking the drizzly buggy photo from Claire, she placed it with a ceremonious flourish in the centre of the piano on its own.

'Does that answer your question?'

'N— yeah, kind of.'

Inside Claire, something shifted. A change in the tiny alpine weather house. Feeling Bad Claire had been replaced with another Claire. One who felt a bit scared.

'All set?' said Ben.

'Yep. Just get my stuff.' Claire went to the kitchen for her jumper and jeans. Honor was dropping Charlie's Dog into a ziplock bag with a pair of tongs at arm's length. Claire started to take off Honor's jumper.

'Oh, keep it all for now, Claire.' Honor carefully zipped the bag shut. Claire had the ridiculous thought that Dog wouldn't be able to breathe.

'Throw this in with your next hot wash.' Honor handed Claire the bag with a wrinkled nose.

'Good idea,' said Claire, following Honor into the hall, opening the bag an inch behind her back.

Claire put on her baseball boots, stuffing her odd socks in her jacket pocket. In the hall, Honor pressed a box of cake and flapjack onto Ben.

'Saturdays are jam-packed for us,' said Honor. 'But let's do another Sunday really soon. Let's do lots of Sundays. We don't see you nearly enough and we want to see you loads this year.'

The kids cheered. Claire could just see the edge of the Bodlowe photo through the living room door.

She crunched the Silver Bullet into gear and the moment Ben ker-lunked shut the passenger door, she reversed from between the Wellbeloved's cars quite fast.

On the way home Ben and the kids were chatty, then they sang like hooligans to a bunch of fun, punky songs Ben had found on Bandcamp.

Claire unclenched her hands on the wheel and took a long breath. It would be all right. What Honor had said about seeing them loads this year was just what people say when they've had some wine and their guests are leaving.

Claire glanced in the rear-view mirror. Pearl was leaning over a notebook. The gonk on a spring at the end of her pen waved wildly back and forth.

'What are you up to there, Pearl?'

'A letter to Ottie.'

'That's nice. What are you saying?'

'I'm saying today was the best day ever and she's my best friend.'

'She's a honey, but what about Connie and Seraka, aren't they your best friends?' *Please say yes, their mums don't scare me.*

Pearl tapped her pen on her chin, thinking.

'Ottie is *one of* my best friends.'

'Ollie is one of my best friends!' said Charlie, like it was a great coincidence.

'He's not too rough for you?' asked Ben.

'Sometimes, but it doesn't matter. Chris is your best friend, isn't he Daddy?'

'Yes. He's my bestie.'

Claire flashed Ben a smile.

'Is Honor your best friend, Mum?' said Charlie

Claire locked her eyes on the road. 'Katie's my best friend.'

'But Honor's one of your best friends, isn't she?'

Pick carefully up this stony slope, Claire. 'Honor's incredible,' she said. 'She's an amazing cook, and she knows tons, and she's always got what people need, and she's really generous with advice.'

Charlie seemed satisfied. Claire was pleased. Her cautious phrasing felt like the only thing she'd done with any style all day, saying things that sounded like compliments when they were sugar-coating for the reasons she didn't like Honor at all.

Chapter 6

Monday morning. Grey and bitter. Huffing up Pope's Hill to school with the kids, the top of the gas holders hidden in cloud. It was great to be back in Kansas.

'Why are you smiling, Mummy?'

'Katie said something funny about the Wizard of Oz.'

'Okaaaay,' said Pearl.

Claire's phone vibrated. She let go of Charlie's hand. It was Honor. Her coat felt suddenly non-breathable.

'Hey, Honor.'

'Morning.'

'Thanks so much for yesterday.'

'Our pleasure.'

'Did I leave something behind again?'

'Nope, nothing. I had a gap between meetings so I thought I'd try and catch you. I meant what I said about seeing more of you. How's Sunday the twenty-third?'

'Of, er, when? Which month?' The kids were fighting over who got her non-phone hand. She removed it from service into her pocket.

'This month. January. In two weeks.'

Absoruddylutelynofreaking way. 'Um, the twenty-third rings a bell. I'm not with the calendar at the moment.'

'Is that your nickname for Ben, "The calendar"?' Honor chuckled.

'Ha, yeah, very good. Can I let you know?'

'Of course. Call me back later.'

Claire launched into her morning with the invitation heavy on her mind and Honor's jumper light on her shoulders. She collected the register, wrestled shut the classroom coat cupboard, and took the kids down to assembly.

'Gorgeous jumper.'

'Thank you.'

'Is that cashmere, Claire? Very smart.'

'Yes, it belongs to a fr— I'm just borrowing it.'

At break, washing her hands, she remembered Honor's on top of hers, pouring milk for the second batch of sauce.

Ring her back, say you checked and the reason you can't go on the twenty-third is because you don't like her.

'I can't say that. Oh, morning, Mrs Benjamin.'

The school secretary nodded, somewhere between quizzical and disapproving, and shut herself in a cubicle.

The staffroom was scattered with teachers and support staff. A few sat gulping a moment's respite, the rest were busy with exercise books, the laminator, the inputting of caffeine.

Claire stood at the counter spooning at unmelted coffee granules. The twenty-third didn't ring a bell. But she couldn't bear to go. She should share her Honor issues with Ben.

She should.

But then he would know how flimsy her resilience was.

And he had enough on his plate with work, dealing with funding cuts and a boss on the brink of long-term sick leave.

Perhaps she could make them busy on the twenty-third, fill the empty space. In fact, with Honor determined to see more of them, she'd need to fill more spaces. The Wellbeloveds had jam-packed Saturdays. She had to jam-pack their Sundays. She took her coffee to her pigeonhole and riffled through the letters and leaflets that had built up inside. French lessons, judo, football, it didn't really matter what it was, even if one of the kids just went for a few sessions, it would be job done.

'Anyone know any kids' activities or clubs that run on Sundays?'

Heads shook.

'No. Sorry, Claire.'

'Nothing springs to mind.'

'Can't think of anything.'

'There's football at the rec.'

'Oh yeah,' said Claire. 'I'll put a pin in that, cheers.'

'Maybe check online. Fantastic jumper by the way.'

'Thanks.'

'Mum.'

Charlie was at the staffroom door. Claire shoved the papers back in her pigeonhole.

'What's up, Charlie?' He was leaning on his friend Serenity, his trouser leg pushed up.

'He hurt his knee,' said Serenity, excitedly.

Claire took his hand. 'You're supposed to go to Miss Keen, remember?'

'But I always want you.'

'Just quickly then.' She returned from the sink with a damp paper towel. As she applied it to the penny-sized graze, she heard the unmistable thud of Gunnar's patent Footgloves. Busted.

'Is that better, Charlie?' asked the Head.

'Yes thank you, Mrs Gunnarson.'

'Next time, find Miss Keen. Miss Keen *loves* making knees better.'

'OK. Take me to the playground, Mum?'

'Go with Serenity,' said Claire. 'Good boy.'

He threw an arm round the girl's shoulder and limped off as though back to the trenches.

Mrs Gunnarson leaned towards her. She smelled tired.

'You need to believe he should go to Miss Keen too, Claire.'

'I know, you're right, yes.'

Claire went in and drank her coffee. What if she couldn't make the kids go to Miss Keen? What if she could never let them go? What if she had to get a job at Charlie's workplace so he could bring her to difficult meetings? She smiled at the thought of him performing in a meeting room. Performing... Drama class! She'd look for a Sunday drama class and hoist Honor by her own petard for her talent-spotting.

The bell rang for the end of break.

Claire set off to the playground to bring the kids in. Grant was coming the other way. He touched his head, trying to remember something.

'Ooh, yes, Claire. Could you try reading practice with Strawberry table before lunch rather than after? It might solve the attention problems.'

'Great idea, Grant.'

Ryan struggled with his book about King Canute, whose name kept going *seriously* wrong. Claire held her phone under the reading table. Was this OK? Ryan was benefiting and even if she wasn't giving him full attention it was a nice break for the kids on his table to have him out in the corridor.

'That's it Ryan, cover up the rest of the word.'

Claire searched for drama classes. This one had potential, the kids in the photo looked natural and free. *Rats, Saturday only*. She clicked on another site, Luton Luvvies, her hopes low. Top hats and tails, cheesy grins and a Sunday class with *Last places for the new term!* at the top. Exciting. She should wait till lunchtime to contact them, pay some attention to Ryan. But it seemed suddenly plausible that she wasn't the only person online looking to avoid Sunday lunch invitations. She'd buzz them a quick email.

'Mrs Swift?' said Ryan.

'Just turn the page, love. You're doing really well.'

'But Mrs Swift.'

Claire looked at Ryan. And then at Mrs Gunnarson, standing behind him.

She jolted and slid her phone into her back pocket. Where was the unmistakable thud of Footgloves when you needed it?

'Will you pop by my office at lunchtime, Mrs Swift?'

Claire hurried upstairs to the classroom.

'Where were you Mummy? We're fed up of waiting, aren't we?'

Connie and Seraka, like the other kids who dropped in to Claire's Monday lunchtime art club once they'd eaten, didn't look especially bothered.

'Sorry guys. I had a meeting with Mrs Gunnarson.' *Where I was told off for having my phone out at school, like I was twelve.* She unlocked her art cupboard and set out the box of fabric scraps and pile of glue-wrinkled works in progress.

The children settled to work. She left them to chirp bursts of commentary on what they were doing and shrank into the sink bay to send the email.

Shelby Herrington, Creative Director, Producer and Founder of Luton Luvvies, replied while Claire and the kids were walking home from school. She was excited to meet Claire's 'tiny trouper' on Sunday.

A glow spread across Claire's body. *I heart you Shelby. Jam-packed Sundays here we come.*

'A drama club?' said Honor, when Claire phoned her back late that evening. 'Great stuff.'

'Yeah, thanks for the idea.'

'So important to encourage them, Claire. Even if it turns out there's only a particle of talent, you *have* to push it.'

Particle? *Particle* of talent? 'The thing is, it's twelve till three on Sundays.'

'Then come for brunch before the club.'

'Brunch. Um, that would mean *leaving* yours at half ten to get back, so—'

'Does sound a bit punishing. Come after. You'll be here at four thirty, we'll have early supper. Perfect.'

Not perfect. Kill it. Kill it, Claire, or like Ben said, 'it's two hundred quid we don't really have to be knee-deep in eyes and teeth'... and still seeing Honor.

Claire rubbed her forehead, catching sight of her rounded shoulders in the mirror by the wardrobe. So tired. *Try tiredness.* 'I think' – *be firm* – 'Charlie would be too tired?' *You asked! You made it a question. She'll railroad you.*

'Will he have acted his little socks off?'

'Yeah. Plus he's in bed by seven so ...'

'Well that's it. No more Sundays.'

Ha ha, she'd done it! She'd killed it with tiredness.

'It's not that we don't want to see you,' said Claire. 'We love seeing you.' *Easy now.*

'Aww, likewise my lovely. Well, who knows when the next time will be.'

'Who knows.'

Who knows was perfect. Lovely and wafty and open ended.

'Ooh, wait a minute,' said Honor.

Claire sat down on the bed.

'Here's an idea. I'm flying to Geneva in a couple of weeks and some derbrain booked me out of Luton. I was going to get them to rebook but I'll pop in and grab dinner with you on the way.'

'OK. Excellent idea!'

Honor ended the call. Claire fell backwards on the bed.

Chapter 7

Claire bought olives and carrots, houmous, posh tomatoes, pitta and haloumi. Then she worried the olives might be the kind that tasted soapy, so she bought two more kinds. And then because it was only February she thought she should have more hot things than grilled haloumi, so she bought some falafel, and then because Honor wasn't a vegetarian, in the early evening before the pop-in dinner grab, she went to Luton Waitrose for chicken and lamb skewers and a bottle of wine from their fancy section.

And taramasalata.

And vine leaves even though she suspected no one really liked them.

Charlie wanted beans on toast for tea but Pearl wanted to try the 'Honor food', and even though she hadn't liked a lot of it, she said, 'Mummy, can we have this kind of tea every night?'

Claire put them to bed.

'Love you too, Mum.' Charlie turned on his side and slotted Dog under his chin. He sniffed the clean toy and shook his head.

'Dog is still wrong. No more washing machine.'

'OK honey, I agree.' When she'd pulled Dog out of the hot wash, he'd looked sort of stunned and a lairy bright cream, not himself at all. 'We'll give him a bath in the sink again next time. But not for ages, promise.'

Charlie happily jammed his eyes shut.

'Even if I'm asleep, Mummy,' said Pearl, who'd spent ages tidying her tiny room, stowing all the cuddly toys that were usually out on her bed into her laundry basket, 'get Honor to come in and have a look at me.'

'I will.'

Claire went downstairs. Katie was nibbling an olive.

'Did I get enough, Katie?'

Katie looked in the fridge, pushing her fingers through the front of her dark hair so it sat near where it was short at back of her head.

'Looks like a Greek restaurant in there.'

'Wait,' said Claire. 'Halloumi's not Greek. Isn't it from Cyprus? I should have got feta.'

'Relaaaax,' said Katie, swinging the fridge shut.

'I'll try. It's just all that money on drama classes to avoid her and yet here she comes, like the Terminator, ruining my evening.'

'Popping in on the way to the airport, yep that's typical Terminator behaviour. Look, Claire, she doesn't *have* to ruin your evening. You do have some control.'

'OK, I see your point.' Claire set back her shoulders. 'I will rise to the challenge. Honor Wellbeloved will not ruin my evening.'

'Word. I like your top by the way.'

'Oh, thanks.' Claire felt the ruched fabric at her neck, then pulled a bit more hair out of her loose bun. 'Fifty pee clearance rail for some reason.'

'Right,' said Katie. 'I'd better go, she'll be here in a bit.' She moved towards the front door, her long denim pinafore rippling around her hardy brown boots. 'Just stand your ground, keep things light and don't let her in.'

'You mean *emotionally*?'

'Yeah, you kind of have to let her in the house. And yes,' Katie squeezed Claire's shoulders. 'The house looks lovely.'

'It's the candlelight. Hides all its wrinkles. Did you see the new bathmat?'

'Great bathmat. And the loo seat is *solid*.'

Katie took her scarf from the stair post and looped it twice round her neck. 'I meant to say, thanks so much for remembering my mum and dad's anniversary. They went nuts about the card.'

'Aw.'

'Dad said the allotment detail was amazing and it must have taken ages, and Mum said you caught the absolute best of them and it made her think she could handle staying with him another forty years.'

Claire laughed, suddenly emotional. 'I love your mum and dad.'

'Well, good luck.' Katie reached for the door. Claire tried to smile goodbye, but her face wasn't working. 'You want me to stay, don't you?'

Claire's hands flew together like her prayers had been answered.

'Fine. I've got till Ed needs to leave for tai chi.' She unlooped the scarf and hung it up and followed Claire back to the kitchen. 'So can I do anything?'

'Er, oh, yeah. Look for a little corner of newspaper. I wrote something on it that I need to do.'

'Is this it?' Katie picked up a scrap of paper.

'Ooh you're good. Have you seen my phone?'

It was under the jar of olives like a coaster.

'I'm Googling which UK mature trees are the most expensive.'

'Que?' Katie posted another olive into her mouth.

'Honor wants to—'

The doorbell rang.

'Oh God, she's early.'

Three was a crowd. Honor was kind of a crowd on her own, but straight away she was ... a lot.

'Hey, you,' she said to Katie. 'Were you scared to leave her alone with me? Ha ha, I'm joking. *Mwah*,' she knocked Katie's cheekbone in greeting. '*Lovely* to see you.'

She'd brought wine and Prestat chocolates and a big square thing in bubble wrap and a combination laptop-and-cabin case. She took over, changing the lighting, serving drinks, setting out the food, and deciding where they all sat.

'See you've left the food prep to the experts,' she joshed, nudging Claire, who now wished she hadn't persuaded Katie to stay.

Honor's trip was to her bank First United's European headquarters in Geneva to meet a colleague she might work with.

'It would be a fabulous promotion.' Her eyes glinted as she assured Katie and Claire that her experience in various global banking capacities made her eminently qualified.

Claire nodded, and wolfed down food, and wet her lips with the wine from the fancy section, which was too acidic for her unrefined tastes. Honor seemed to like it though.

'I'd be working alongside this incredible guy, Asif. We'd head up the initiative jointly. It's such a great opportunity to stretch my legs, and for Asif too. It would really allow me to input at a global level, alongside Asif, obviously. I'll be on top of the world.' She threw out her arms.

'Next to Asif,' Katie muttered through a mouthful of taramasalata.

'It's Asif's department, and I'm always very sensitive

around people who are obliged to share their world with a newcomer.' Honor sucked houmous from a carrot stick. 'Claire knows why that is.'

Claire didn't know.

'Abbie,' Honor whispered.

Now she sort of knew. 'Abbie's Honor's sister,' Claire told Katie, as Honor wasn't explaining.

'Adopted sister.' Honor wiped her mouth with kitchen roll. Apples of pink flashed on her cheeks. She sank what was left in her glass and refilled it. 'Her dad and mine were army surgeons together. He and his wife died in a sailing accident on my eighth birthday, and then Abbie turned eight the day she came to live with us.'

Katie glanced at Claire in alarm.

'Her welcome-slash-birthday gift from my parents was a pony.' Honor's eyes glazed. 'They'd given me a new bow for archery. I'd wanted a pony for ages but Abbie was their new priority. Part shares in someone else's pony is no compensation when you've been replaced. It's why I feel such an affinity with Claire. Growing up second place to her mother's painting.'

Claire startled. 'I don't think I've ever said—'

Honor put a hand on top of Claire's. 'You didn't need to.'

'I'm proud of my mum, though, Honor. She's a huge talent.'

'I'll take your word for it. I can't be doing with abstract stuff. I like my art to look like life. Maybe she'd be less temperamental if she did nice landscapes.'

'Well that's not her at all, she—'

'You mentioned once that you took her some tea when she was engrossed and she roared and chucked it at the wall.'

'Did I tell you that?' said Claire, embarrassed. 'She was

very apologetic. She had money worries and the work was going badly.'

'It reminded me of Daddy laying into me about Maitland. Yelling about Abbie having "lost too much already".'

'Who's Maitland?'

'The pony.' Honor's shoulders raised and her palms turned out. 'I just thought he looked like he needed a run in the field. I didn't know the gate was open.'

'Was he hurt?' Katie asked urgently.

'Oh, he was all right. Anyway, these experiences bond people.' She gazed meaningfully at Claire. 'Didn't Margo move to Glasgow while you were pregnant with Pearl, Claire?'

'Well yes, but she'd studied there and she'd been planning to go back for ages.'

'She chose her painting, and put all those miles between you.'

Katie crossed her arms.

'She helped us a lot when she sold up,' said Claire. 'We'd never have been able to buy, even somewere like Headleigh.' Claire pulled up her sleeves, suddenly hot, aware of how rude that was to Headleigh and to Katie.

Honor drew back her lips in a half smile and lowered her chin, confidentially. 'You should see where Abbie lives. I mean, the woman's a surgeon but it's just a terrace. In Westminster, but you know, a *terrace*.'

'Do your mum and dad still put Abbie first, Honor?' asked Katie.

'It's a rule of mine that I don't discuss her with them.' Honor glittered as though this was a zinger of a move and proved that she'd won. 'I think your childhood was quite normal, Katie, am I right?'

'Yeah. Really, really normal.' There was tension in Katie's

face. 'I'm lucky. I had a good start, but my parents both had rotten ones. It just shows, you don't have to pass on the hurt.'

Oh that was good. And strong, and also wise.

'Absolutely,' said Honor. 'Amen to that. And go us, because we're not, are we Claire?'

Claire raised her shoulders and blew out. Katie and Honor laughed and Honor stood up.

'I'll pop upstairs. Then I've got something for you to open before my taxi gets here.'

'Great. Will you look in on Pearl? She asked if you would.'

Honor looked touched. 'I will.' Her heels clicked towards the stairs.

'Sorry, Katie,' said Claire once the bathroom door had closed. 'I don't know why I said "even in Headleigh".'

'*You've* got nothing to apologise for. That was classic frenemy behaviour. Looking for the pain. Humiliating you about your mum.'

Claire cleared things off the table.

The bathroom had opened. Honor was coming downstairs. She hadn't looked in on Pearl. The floorboard would have creaked outside her room. She clicked back in and passed Claire the package.

'Thank you.' Claire took off the bubble wrap. 'Wow.' She turned it to show Katie. 'What a photo.' It was a canvas enlargement of the photo Honor had taken at the top of the hill when the Swifts went for lunch, everyone huddled up. Honor front and centre, knockout gorgeous. Herself at the back grimacing, red-faced. A muddy latecomer.

Honor looked around the kitchen diner. 'You could hang it over there.'

She would hang her posters back up there when Honor's visit was over. 'We'll find somewhere,' said Claire, wondering if she could hide it in the shed before Ben got back.

His key turned in the door.

'Benjy,' bellowed Honor, leaping up to hug him. He kissed them all. He smelled of cold evening and post-meeting beer. He looked at the photo as he undid the poppers of the black motorbike coat Claire had found on eBay for his birthday, having waited years for one to show up.

'What a great photo. Thanks Honor.'

'Grab a plate, Ben. Loads left.'

Ben smiled at the table. 'So I see.'

'The photo says it all, doesn't it?' said Honor. 'Everyone's friends and we've each got our best friend.' Her eyes darted to Katie. 'Within the group, I mean. Not trying to compete with you, Katie.'

'Oh crap.' Olives rolled across the floor. Ben dropped to his haunches to round them up.

'I'd better get home,' said Katie. 'Ed's off out in a minute. Have a good meeting, Honor.'

Honor's phone had beeped. She was looking at the screen.

'Thanks. Great to see you,' she said without raising her head.

Claire followed Katie to the hall. She looped her scarf back on.

'Evening ruined?'

'Pfft. Nah,' said Claire.

Katie mock-punched her in the chest. 'Atta girl.'

Claire waved Katie off and shut the door as Honor's boots clicked towards her from the kitchen. 'Bloody taxi's broken down. They can't get another one here for forty minutes.'

'Oh no. Er…' Claire rummaged in the everything bowl on the hall table, picking out a handful of cards. 'There are lots of local taxis. Not sure which ones are good.'

Honor studied her phone. 'Closest Uber is quarter of an

hour.' She looked at her watch, and made a calculation. She strode back into the kitchen.

'Ben. I'm stealing Claire.'

'Er, OK, what for?'

'Airport. Come on Claire. You hardly touched the wine, you're driving me.'

Claire ker-lunked opened the Silver Bullet. It was this bashed-up passenger door that had made it such a bargain a few years ago. She tried not to see the crumpled school letter and cheese string wrappers. But the smell ... Eau de Dropped Salami?

'Sorry about the car.'

'Any port in a storm, Claire.' Honor pinched her nose, ker-lunked the door shut, swapped the hand on her nose and pushed home her seatbelt. 'Ah, there's something squidgy in the footwell. I'll hop in the back.' She ker-lunked the door open, pushed the seat forward, shoved Pearl's crumb-filled car seat onto Charlie's, fully opened the window, climbed in the back and ker-lunked again. Claire set off, gasping under the weight of her succession of car fails, chauffeuring Honor with the self-consciousness of her driving test.

Worried she'd be thought a pushover, she sped up and rushed through amber lights onto the parade. Concerned she'd overdone it, she grew cautious, letting through too much traffic before taking a right up Pope's Hill. Honor looked out of the window as they passed the gas holders.

'So, um, I went back and did all the passwords,' said Claire perkily. '"Funky Town" lyrics, exclamation mark, door number, first three letters, boom.'

'Oh well done. That should make your life simpler. By the way, so glad you like the photo. We have one on our piano.'

'Cool.'

'Now look Claire, I know you were desperate to know what happened with Katrina.'

'No no, it's fine if you don't want—'

'I don't want to keep anything from you. I trust you. True friendship equals full disclosure. Basically, I was a rock for Katrina for years. No one was happier than me when her hair grew back, alopecia is devastating. Exit coming up.'

'Oh yeah, thanks.'

'And when everything fell into place in her life, I more than anyone was delighted. To say otherwise is ridiculous. But she became rather full of herself, Claire. Then she said some horrible things to me. "Home truths" she called them. All absolute lies. She is now in my past.'

Claire swallowed noisily, her hands tightening on the wheel.

Honor's head jerked.

'Claire. You've missed the turn.'

'Oh, *fucknuts*.'

'Need to catch this flight.'

'Sorry. So sorry.'

Claire came off at the next junction, found her way back to the dual carriageway and floored it.

'Here, Claire, now. Left lane, left. This exit.'

Shiiiiiit. Claire streaked across and took the exit.

'Take a right.'

'It's taxis only!'

'Take it anyway.'

Claire pulled up in a taxi bay and braked hard, flinging them forward.

'Gosh. What a ride.' Honor pushed the seat forward, ker-lunked the door open and slid her legs out.

'Sorry about that. Good luck, Honor.'

'Thanks.'

Honor ker-lunked the door shut and banged the roof a couple of times. Claire pushed a happy foot on the clutch and slotted into reverse.

Ker-lunk. The door heaved back open. Honor really was the freaking Terminator. She leaned her arms on top of the car and lunged like she was stretching for a run, which she well might have been.

'I've just thought how we could see more of you. It's genius.'

'Honor, look, I think that bloke is about to start a ticket. And shouldn't you ... your flight?'

'Never missed one yet. Claire, the cottage we rent in Cornwall is huge. Come with us in the summer. We'd have an amazing fortnight. The kids would *love* it.'

'Oh gosh, wow,' said Claire. 'I don't know what to say.'

'How about yes?'

No. Not yes, because no no no no no. 'I'll um, I'll ... I'll need to check with Ben.'

Honor looked at Claire as though that was adorably unnecessary. And the look went on and on.

Claire was going to have to say something to make Honor *go*.

'So er, yeah. I mean thanks ... for the invite.'

'That sounds like a yes to me.'

Ker-lunk. Evening ruined.

Chapter 8

Sunday morning a couple of weeks later, Claire was inching herself into a hot bubble bath while Ben rounded up the kids for Luton Luvvies. Enamoured by the cheesy glamour when they'd taken Charlie, Pearl had gone off piano. Ben had brought his bass guitar from the loft to try and inspire her. It made him wistful, and Pearl more determined to be a tiny trouper.

'Just had a text from Chris,' Ben called through the bathroom door, his tone causing Claire instant discomfort.

'I can hear you, Ben. No need to shout.'

'He's asked if we want to go to Bodlowe with them.'

'Really?' Her voice sounded strangled. Since no parking ticket had materialised, she had convinced herself that Honor at the airport had been a bad dream.

'Yeah. Last week in July, first in August.'

She landed her back against the freezing metal of the bath. 'Can we mull it over? Not say anything to the kids for now?'

'Sure. See you later. I'm going to pop into work while they're at drama.' Ben couldn't bring himself to say Luton Luvvies.

Claire mulled until it was warmer outside the bath than in, and all her mulling led to the same conclusion. She was not spending a fortnight with Honor Wellbeloved.

She stood, water sloshing onto the floor and threw on her

robe. She found a used envelope in the bedroom bin and a pen in her make-up bag and flopped onto the bed to write down her thoughts.

OPERATION GET OUT OF BODLOWE (G.O.O.B.)
1.

She hovered pen over paper. What or who could save her? Her first thought was audacious, but these were crazy times.

1. Margo

Her mother returned the call unusually fast while Claire was staring into the fridge wondering if the kids would mind penne and cheese for lunch again and how many slices she could squeeze from a watery cucumber stump.

She ran to the table and the wall of pixels on the laptop shimmied and corrected into Margo against the tall sash windows of her upstair's neighbour's Glasgow flat. Her hair was piled on top of her head, a smear of oil paint on her sharp cheek.

'Hi Mum.'

Claire sat on the banquette. There was a breeze from under the back door. She was glad she'd put on sheepskin slippers.

'Is everything OK?' said Margo. 'What's wrong?'

'Nothing's wrong.'

'Oh.'

'You sound disappointed, Mum.'

'I'm not disappointed. It just sounded urgent and I was working.'

'Sorry.' Of course she'd interrupted Margo's work. It was a bloody given.

'We mustn't be long,' Margo said under her breath. 'David is extra grumpy today.'

Claire rolled her lips over her teeth. It wasn't the time to say find a better way to keep in touch than via your grumpy neighbour.

Margo scrutinised her in a flustered way. 'You look rather nice.'

'Thanks.' Claire put a hand to her damp hair. 'I've just got out of the bath.'

'How long ago was Christmas?' asked Margo. 'I've missed you.'

'You only miss me when you see me,' Claire said amiably.

'That's not true.'

'How are you?'

'Fine I think. My head's still downstairs in the studio, I haven't been talking much.'

'Well we don't have to chit-chat. I've got an idea to put to you.' Claire rubbed her palms on her robe. 'I've been thinking about the summer and I'd love it if we could come up for a longer stay with you. It wouldn't be oppressive, you'd barely see us some days. The kids are much better sleepers now, and we'd taser them if they disturbed you.'

'Gosh. Taser?'

'Figure of speech, we don't have a Taser. We could do odd jobs, bring a toolkit, and obviously we wouldn't expect meals. Does that sound good? We're kind of boxed in date wise so it would be the last week in July and first week in August. What do you think?'

Margo sighed. 'That's a super and very detailed plan, Claire.'

'Really?' Claire's feet tapped a slippered dance under the table.

'But perhaps next year.'

'Oh.'

Margo melted into a smile. 'I'm having a big solo show up here in the middle of October. I had confirmation from the gallery a couple of weeks ago.'

'Oh Mum.' Claire clapped her hands. 'That's absolutely brilliant, why didn't you tell me?'

'I'm just so engrossed. I've never known flow like it, Claire. It's like being in love, but tons better because it comes from within.' Margo flung out her fists and knocked the laptop, giving Claire a view of her throat wattle, and Grumpy David's silver orb light fitting.

'That's great. I can't wait to see the paintings.'

'What about you darling?' Margo pulled the screen forward. 'School and the little ones running you ragged?' She scratched at the paint on her cheek.

'Oh yeah, lots going on, but look, we can come for our usual visit in August, can't we? Maybe a long weekend in the first week?'

Margo blew out and shook her head. 'I'll need to clear the decks through to the show. It's going to be work, work, work. Best you make your own plans for summer. Go ahead without me.'

Claire pressed hard on the paper.

1. ~~Margo~~

In the kitchen, she tore off a sheet of kitchen roll and wiped her eyes. 'Go ahead without me', that's how things always were with Margo. *Did you really think she'd put you first, Claire? Did you really think she'd save you?*

OPERATION GET OUT OF BODLOWE (G.O.O.B)
2. In-laws

'Luton Luvvies? How comical. Angela loves musical theatre.'

'How is she?'

'Much better than when you were here for New Year. Just up once or twice in the night. All quite manageable.'

'You must be shattered, Graham.'

'Oh, I'm right as rain, thinking about the Lakes. The gang want to go earlier this year.'

'Any idea when?'

'Last week in July, first week in August.'

'That's absolutely perfect for us.'

'Ah, now hold on young Claire. You and Ben are not helping out with Angela's care this year. We're booking respite. I've heard good things about the home.'

'We could look after your house and visit Angela.'

'All bases are covered. You and Ben must take the kids on a proper holiday this summer.'

'If you're sure. We'll come up and see you soon anyway.'

2. ~~In-laws~~

Claire met Katie in the pub. She'd nabbed their favourite sofa near the fire.

'So Ben's parents and your mum aren't options.' Katie applied some lip balm. 'What's next?'

'You are,' said Claire. 'Option three, go camping with Katie.' She grinned, showing all her teeth.

Katie laughed. 'You look like Pearl when she's after something.'

'I could play with the twins, fetch and carry.'

'It's camping, Claire. You know, in a tent.'

'Would I hate it more than going away with Honor?'

'I'll test you. Head torch, sleeping on the ground, noise keeping you awake, She-wee, thought so.'

'OK, you lost me at head torch, but can I tell Ben it's on offer?'

Katie frowned. 'You'd be dreading it nearly as much as you'd dread Bodlowe. Don't you think that might take the shine off for me?'

'Ugh, sorry Katie. You're right, I'm a terrible person.'

Katie squeezed Claire's knee. Claire yelped and her leg shot up. They laughed and then Katie winced at the heat from the fire and shifted them both down the sofa.

'I've got it, Claire. You could *kill* her. Honor killings are already a thing.'

Claire laughed.

Katie plucked a beer mat from the table and tapped it on her chin. 'Or here's a radical idea, tell Ben you don't want to go. He knows what Honor's like. He must know what effect she has on you.'

'He doesn't know. He really doesn't know how deep it goes.'

'So tell him.'

'Katie, I can't. He's invested so much time helping build my self-esteem over the years. I don't want him to know I'm not stronger.'

Katie sighed and shook Claire's empty glass. Claire nodded. She checked her phone. There was an email from Honor. She clicked on the attachment.

When Katie put down the beer, Claire thrust her phone out. 'Look. Blue Gables. This is the cottage.'

Katie waved Claire up the hot end of the sofa and plonked down. She tapped and pinched the screen. Her mouth dropped open.

'Woah. Well, Blue Gables looks terrible, Claire. I mean the helicopter access is weather dependent for goodness' sake. Also, uninterrupted sea views are unsettling for us townies plus the beds are way too big, freestanding baths are annoying and how would you ever find a dropped earring in a carpet that thick?

'Have you found anything you like about it?'

'Nothing. It can be slippery around outdoor pools and hot tubs are about seven per cent semen so that whole area of the huge garden would be a no-go.' Katie frowned. 'Why do you look happy?'

'Because I think Bodlowe might be its own get-out-of-Bodlowe. Blue Gables is three thousand two hundred pounds a week, Katie. With all the days out and meals out, we genuinely won't be able to afford it.'

'Nice one, Blue Gables. Here's a plan. Bodlowe comes in at ...' Katie worked things out on her fingers, 'meals a hundred times fourteen, maybe seven doing-y things at fifty quid ... that's just shy of five grand, probably more. So we find you a nice all-inclusive fortnight, then you show Ben and say the Wellbeloveds' offer is awesome, but you need time together as a family and this is way cheaper.'

'I love it. Let's find me that summer holiday.'

They grabbed their phones off the table, slumped back on the sofa and got stuck in.

A tut. A chuckle. 'Look at you two. Friendship rut? Lost the spark?'

Claire and Katie glanced at each other and laughed.

'Hey Fran. You look lovely.' She wore a long-sleeved print dress and long lashes. 'Katie's helping me find a holiday.'

'Cool. I'm on a date.' Fran said flatly, pointing over her shoulder.

Katie and Claire meerkatted to look at Fran's burly, bearded companion.

'Looks a bit like Grant,' said Katie.

'Doesn't have the Mr Reader twinkle,' said Claire.

Fran sighed. 'Tell me about it.'

'Looking for someone like Grant then?'

Flustered, Fran picked up the pub menu and swatted Claire's arm. 'No. Just someone nice. Anyway, you two have fun not talking to each other.'

They waited until the loo door had shut behind her.

'Ms Achibe, fancies Mr Reader,' said Katie.

'Knew it,' Claire replied.

They walked home huddled together against the cold, Katie filling Claire in on the new rota for which of her twins had top bunk, the box room being their home office.

A bus went past with a holiday advert on the side, a family of four holding hands and laughing as they ran through waves. Claire buried her nose in her scarf. 'I want to be like that family.'

'Photoshopped?'

'I know it's an advert and they're probably not even related, but they look happy and free.'

Back on Bevan Road, Claire hugged Katie and went inside. She hung up her coat. The kids were watching TV in the front room. She went into the kitchen and picked up a tea towel.

'Nice time?' Ben was washing up.

'Good thanks. Saw Fran. She definitely fancies Grant. She was with a disappointing lookalike and got a bit flustered about it.'

Ben laughed.

Claire twisted the tea towel. Off we go.

'Ben,' she took a plate from the drainer. 'I got an email from Honor. The Bodlowe house, Blue Gables, it's so expensive, and it made me think. Apart from Disney Paris, we've never properly gone away just us and the kids.'

Ben shook his hands over the sink and turned round.

'And if you add on what we'd spend in Cornwall, I mean we wouldn't be eating at Greggs with the Wellbeloveds, would we?'

She tapped in her phone PIN. 'I've found some great holidays. All inclusive, well over a grand cheaper. I think it would be great.'

'What holidays?' said Pearl, hurrying in.

Ach, those bat ears. Not much point trying to shove the genie back in. 'Two weeks in Spain, or Ibiza.'

Charlie padded in holding Dog under his chin. He screwed up his face. 'Ebeefer, what's that?'

Claire showed them a hotel on her phone. 'Do you know what all-inclusive is?'

'It's free ice creams all the time,' said Pearl, jumping up and down as Charlie gasped.

'Well, you have to ask your mum and dad,' said Claire, 'but that kind of thing, and every meal you choose anything you want and just put it on your plate.'

Charlie jumped up and down too.

Ben folded his arms. Things seemed to be going a bit fast for him.

'I think Connie goes to that hotel, Mummy, she told me about her wristband.'

'It's probably not the same hotel, lots of places do it.'

'It is. It looks the same as that one.'

'It could be the same, let's ask her.'

'You don't believe me.'

'I do.'

'Ebeefer,' said Charlie, sticking his face under Pearl's. They leapt around the kitchen.

'And the sea is lovely and warm. What do you think?' Claire looked hopefully at Ben.

He rubbed his chin. She was rushing him, but it could go so beautifully, like surfing a wave to the beach. 'I'll show you properly on the laptop,' she said.

Claire went to the table. The kids jostled as she clicked on the hotel.

'Come and see, Dad,' said Charlie. 'Let's go to Ebeefer. How do you get there, Mum, in the Silver Bullet, or on the big train like to Gogo's?'

Claire stroked his head. 'We'd go to Luton airport and catch a plane over the sea.'

Charlie clutched Dog. 'What's a different way to get there?'

'That's the only way, but it's exciting.'

'I don't want Ebeefer.'

'Charlie!' said Pearl, like no one on earth was more irritating.

'I've got some news about holidays,' said Ben. 'You know how Chris invents clever ways to make plastic from vegetables?' Charlie shook, Pearl nodded. 'Well, he's just invented a cheaper way of doing it and sold his company. He wants us to go on holiday to Cornwall with them, and he wants to pay for us.'

'With Ottie and Ollie?' said Pearl. 'We're going on holiday for free, with the Wellbeloveds?'

Ben glanced at Claire.

Pearl ran manic laps into the hall and back.

Charlie narrowed his eyes at his father. 'In the Silver Bullet, Dad?'

'Yes. In the Silver Bullet.'

Charlie joined in with the manic laps, crashing into Pearl.

'I wish you hadn't said that in front of the kids, Ben. We were going to talk about it.'

'Oh right.' He was angry. 'Different rule for me, is it?'

Charlie grabbed Claire's hand. 'We can have free ice creams and no aeroplane and Honor can make our food and tell Ollie to be nice. This is the best day ever, isn't it Mum?'

OPERATION GET OUT OF BODLOWE (G.O.O.B)
Final option. Tell Ben how you feel around Honor

The kids were asleep.

Claire had apologised to Ben. It had been a mistake to talk about holidays while Pearl was awake, and she should not have pursued it like that.

She lay on her side now in bed. Ben ran his hand along her hip. Bed was a good place for confessions. If they were warming up for sex, Ben would listen to anything. She once talked about what she thought might be blocking the bathroom drain then showed him a mole on her arm that had sprouted a hair and he had looked at her throughout like she was utterly captivating.

Tell him why you don't want to go.

'Ben, you know I love you.'

'You do sometimes mention it.'

She put her hand through his dark blond hair then along his jaw. *Say it. Tell him the truth about how Honor makes you feel.* He kissed her slowly.

Last chance. Say it or say something. She pulled back gently. 'Remember when we went to Crete for two weeks before the kids? And how we said a fortnight's long enough to feel like you live somewhere.'

'Sort of.'

'Well a fortnight of feeling like we live with a whole other family would seem really long, don't you think?'

'We could do our own thing sometimes. And it's a big house.' He looked at her compassionately. 'I know you had a shit time in Bodlowe before. Being pregnant was tough.'

Tell him your shit time wasn't just being pregnant. Ignore how he's running his hands over your bum.

'I don't feel comfortable about someone else paying for our holiday.'

'Chris is so chuffed he can offer. Look, it'll be fun, Claire. You, me, the kids. When don't we have fun?'

'We do have a lot of fun.'

We do. Us.

Ben smiled at her, and touched her. And the more he touched her, the more free, strong and beautiful she began to feel, like life was a gentle jog through warm, shallow waves. And although she knew she felt this way because oestrogen was flooding her body, and her hormones were strong-arming her instead of helping her put a case to him, it seemed to her that she and Ben could handle anything.

'All right,' she said. 'We'll go.'

Operation Get Out Of Bodlowe = Failed.

Chapter 9

Over the weeks that followed Ryan crawled to the end of *King Canute* and Claire chivvied him through more Green Level reading books. Something fell into place during *Anansi the Spider* but had evaporated again by *Ra the Sun God*. She took supplements and was less knackered and tried to blank out Bodlowe, but so many things, a bird sounding like a seagull, Honor popping up on social media, even hearing the word 'holiday', triggered the sensation that a shotputter was using her stomach for target practice.

When she woke early she'd wonder whether Honor was at a meeting with Asif – of *course* she'd got her promotion – or at home, making a flask for her commute, tossing a teabag across the kitchen into her pristine caddy, or engaged in sweaty combat with Linton, and Claire would pull the duvet over her head.

One afternoon Honor tagged her in a photo.

Can't wait to return to Bodlowe with this Goddess Claire Swift, wife of my gorgeous uni friend Ben Swift who took the pic, and their adorable kids.

Claire bristled. When Ben shared the photo with Honor five years ago, it would probably just have been a nice sunny beach picture to him. He wouldn't have noticed Claire's puckered second-time-around maternity swimsuit. He probably hadn't clocked that his whey-faced fifteen-weeks-gone wife was slumped and squinting, crossed legs exposing stuff they shouldn't.

And maybe he wouldn't notice now, or be too polite to say. But what Claire knew for sure was that gimlet-eyed Honor, all shoulders and long tanned limbs in a halter top and board shorts in the photo, *she'd* noticed Claire's broken fibres, rolls and stray pubes. She'd noticed Claire was sat on her and Chris's towel holding cool sparkling water from their supply. Honor was saying, 'This is how it's going to be Claire. This is who we are to each other.'

It couldn't be like that. It had to be better.

So Claire had to be better.

★

Monday early evening, Couch to 5K, halfway up Pope's Hill. Milder than it had been, but damp on the pavement, weaving round dog walkers not going much faster than they were. Lumbering they called it. It had to be slow enough for conversation. If they couldn't chat, what was the point?

Luke's aggressive outbursts, mostly aimed at Jake, were worrying Katie, as was how much shouting she was doing. Claire said it sounded tough, and Katie was a great mum. Katie slowed from a lumber to a panting walk. 'You're going too fast. I preferred you in the yoga pants.'

Claire laughed. 'I hadn't realised how much energy was going into not catching my foot in the bottoms. Proper leggings are way better. Come on, you're supposed to be the fit one.'

They crossed a side road, then Katie broke into a near jog alongside her. 'Do you think we'll ever run the whole five K circuit, Katie?'

Katie laughed. 'You do know five K is *twice* our circuit?'

'What? Well, that's not going to happen then, is it?'

'Not with that attitude.' Katie pulled down the zip of her running jacket to let in some air.

Claire remembered her pledge to be better and clicked her fingers. 'Attitude changed. Now then, it's the middle of March which means it's time to stop wanting to puke about Bodlowe and start planning Bodlowe.'

'Bodlowe is ages away.'

'But there's all the research, and all the kit to get hold of. Then there's me.' She jumped over a slippery looking man-hole cover. 'I'm going for a full transformation. Like Sandra Bullock in *Miss Congeniality* only less beauty pageant and more family holiday. You'll help, won't you: be my Michael Caine?'

Katie scoffed. 'Why would I do that? I'd be up for helping you not give a shit about Honor, but the only change you should make is to accept yourself as you are and stop giving your art away.'

Claire agreed to work on accepting herself and nodded when Katie mentioned perspective again.

They passed school and intermittently jogged and walked back down the dual carriageway, talking about Grant and how one of the mums from Luke's class had leaned on him at pick-up time, supposedly to get a stone from her shoe but really to present him with an advantageous view down her top.

They stopped on the parade so Katie could buy orange juice and Claire went back to hers to pick the kids up from Ed. Luke was coming down the stairs, a dark-mopped doppelganger for Jake except where it mattered to him the most. He was noticeably shorter than his brother.

Claire hugged Katie and took the kids home.

Ben came in from work with pizzas and Claire unwrapped

them and put them in the oven. It was actually him she needed to get on side about changing.

'I've been thinking, we should do Bodlowe differently this time,' she said.

'How do you mean?'

'Well, let's not show up for a day at the beach with some digestives and a beachball. Not this time. Let's have all the right stuff and be really organised.'

'Yay.' Ben looked at his phone. 'Sounds fun.'

'Come on Ben, work with me.'

He put down his phone. 'I don't want it to be work. It's a holiday, I want to look forward to it.' He flattened a pizza box. 'Honor and Chris must have it down to a fine art, we'll just ask them what to bring nearer the time.'

Claire squeezed a cloth and wiped the worktop. 'But remember that beach barbecue we did? We set up in the wrong place and the waves came in and we had to use bits of wood to pick up the tray of sausages and leg it up the beach.' *And Honor almost laughed out her kidneys.*

'Yeah. I remember. Burnt sausages and warm beer. It can be our signature dish.'

Claire rubbed dried ketchup and chucked down the cloth. 'I don't feel jokey about it. Do you remember Honor and Chris's barbecue later in the week? Chilled wine, chicken and chorizo kebabs, couple of salads?'

'Vaguely.'

'I just *can't* spend a fortnight saying "Mmm, delicious!" one minute and "Sorry, here's our shabby offering" the next.'

'Are you overthinking this?'

Claire sighed. She wished Ben could experience how it felt in her body when Honor produced spray for cuts and home-made energy bars for hunger. When she came up with solutions and decisions. How whatever Honor provided, it doubled down in Claire as a lack. What would that look like as an existential equation?

(+) Honor = (- -) Claire, maybe. OK, she might be over-thinking this.

'I don't want to scrape through relying on them, Ben. I want to hold my head up.'

She flashed with panic as she remembered the pizzas and peered into the oven. The cheese hadn't even bubbled. *Of course it hasn't you muppet, you've only just put them in.*

Ben gave her a hug. His body said he understood. That they were a team.

'I want it to be different. I want me to be different.'

He frowned at her. 'You don't need to change, Claire.'

Ben went to tell the kids it was five minutes to pizza, which turned into an improvised song, Ben drumming on the door as the kids jumped around.

'Fiiiive minutes to pizza! Ooh, five minutes! Five minutes!'

Claire peeled a carrot. There were people who'd understand her need to remake herself. Not only understand but encourage and hold her to it. It was time to share her woes in the proper arena. With strangers on the internet.

Chapter 10

Claire filled a glass with water and drank it, poking at the jar of liquid on the kitchen windowsill. The floating fungus looked like a jellyfish, why would she want to drink it? Still, she'd agreed to illustrate a pregnancy yoga flyer in return for this kombucha baby, or mother, or whatever the jarred freak was called, so that's what she'd been doing.

She glanced at the clock. Just over an hour till pick-up. She'd tidy her art stuff away and then jump online to seek out those kind strangers.

She rinsed the glass and her paint water pot then at the table, tidied her sketches and drawings inside an A3 pad. She folded her drawing board flat and slotted that and the pads behind the banquette. Her pencils were returned to their pot, the tubes of gouache and watercolour into boxes, and the trays went back to their place at the bottom of the sideboard. It was like she'd never been there.

Table clear. Restored to family settings.

When Claire was a kid, clearing tables hadn't been high on Margo's agenda. The table in the Brixton flat they'd shared had been strewn with paint tubes and turps and painty cloths and sketches and ashtrays and mugs *all the time*. The table was part of Margo's studio space. Claire hadn't minded. She would perch on a chair by the table with a cheese and tomato sandwich and gnaw the bread Margo bought from

Brixton Wholefoods that had the texture of rubble. Her mum would perch and eat too. They'd chat about Claire's day or Margo would talk about what she was trying to express in her work if it was going well, or be out in the garden wreathed in smoke and lost in thought if transporting onto canvas the injustice and sorrow and beautiful pain in the world was going badly.

From when Claire was tiny she'd had her own studio space in a sunny corner of the living room with a desk and books and all her art things. She'd sit for hours filling sketch pads. Making comics and books. She liked being near her mum and was *excellent* at not interrupting her. She'd only had to experience Margo's furious bewilderment at being dredged back from her work a handful of times to prefer to sort out her own problems, answer her own questions or just go and have a bath or watch the telly in Margo's bedroom and forget about them.

Sometimes Margo would ask Claire about *her* work and with trepidation Claire would show a drawing she'd done, and wait for things to get complicated.

'What's the drawing of a princess *about*, darling?' Margo would ask. 'What are you saying about the princess and the world she lives in? What's her struggle?'

'OK.' Claire clapped her hands, returning from childhood memories to find herself gazing at the cardboard horse that she'd shoved in the shed when she'd thought Honor was coming.

She plonked herself down and opened the laptop. She typed **Not looking forward to family holiday Mumsnet** into the search engine. And clicked on the first result.

Really not looking forward to my holiday

Maybe this was a kindred spirit.

Onebubandoneontheway
My sis in law is a bossy cow. We're off to her Florida timeshare this summer. There's plastic covers on the sofa and she's all about how bigger and better her life is. It starts when they collect us from the airport in a hired Hummer. How will I cope?

Onebubandoneontheway felt a bit like she did. Claire smoothed out the envelope from the water bill ready to copy down the wise advice.

CharlieAndZola
You sound really ungrateful. I'm glad I'm not your sister-in-law.

BigBoo(ze)
Free holiday in Florida? Get your big girl pants on and enjoy it.

User146988
I wish my bitch sis in law had a nice holiday house and invited me to stay.

The strangers on the internet weren't as wise or kind as she'd hoped. Maybe she'd have to do this on her own.

She rubbed a hangnail on her thumb. She'd told Katie and Ben she wanted to change, so change what exactly? At the top of the envelope, she wrote

BE BETTER BEFORE BODLOWE

She shook the intermittent biro and cracked on with a list.

Be more organised around the house – watch tidying videos.
Keep taking vitamins.
Learn to be less splashy at swimming and put head in water.
When I notice I'm thinking about or comparing myself to Honor repeat distracting phrase (in my head) like 'Taj Mahal!'
Get better at remembering where I've put things.
Get fitter – 2 whole circuits?
Make list of holiday kit needed and get it.
Look up tips for acing holidays.
Don't let Mum/Honor make you feel bad.
Change all your passwords cos you've told H what they are!
Learn how to fake laugh convincingly.
Make feet nice. (Start soon)
Wear keys round neck?
Start things and see them through without starting another.
Roof box for car!!
Carry tissues and wipes at all times.
Weekly coconut oil on hair.
Get business tips for charging actual money.
Stop being a dingbat.
Buy a beach tent.
Be more of a leader. (Look up what Leading From The Front and Leading From Behind mean)
Be more adventurous and less clumsy at cooking.

Her ear made its whooshing noise. She ought to deal with the cooking stuff first. Or maybe as it was so stressy, build up to it and do it last?

Look up tips on decision-making.

She read over her list. If she wanted to be more organised, she should start right here. She grabbed scissors and snipped the list into individual items and grouped them ready to glue to a piece of paper.

Stuff to get for the holiday in this pile.

Skills to acquire in this one.

That one for fitness, health and beauty.

Other people would type this into a computer, Claire.

Well, screw them.

She picked up cooking. Was that general or holiday? She propped her elbow on the table and parked her chin on her hand. Cooking on holiday would be un-fun. What if Honor bulldozed her into making another white sauce? It would be so sweet to knock up a silky smooth one and be *Kerchow! Eat that!*

Sod it. She'd make one now.

She scanned Youtube videos.

Basic white sauce

Simple white sauce

My perfect béchamel

No one wanted to be 'basic'. 'Perfect' was asking for trouble.

'Simple' was good.

Claire set the laptop by the hob, and pulled out butter, milk and flour and the scales. Honor would doubtless know how much to use by sight. Maybe. One day. If Claire became a real boy, she'd be able to do that too.

The video chirped 'everything's fine' music and Claire did what SueChef247 said, melting eighty grams of butter, adding eighty grams of flour and stirring for two minutes. She took the pan off the heat and swapped to a whisk, and added a little, then the rest of the milk.

At the end, she had made simple white sauce, which just happened to also be perfect. Simple was the way.

It was time to collect the kids. She scooped up her strips of list, so they didn't fly everywhere when Pearl and Charlie bowled in and dumped their stuff. She picked up a sock she found on the floor and popped the strips inside to keep them safe.

They had her white sauce that evening, warmed up with cheese and pasta, wolfed down with appreciative noises.

Ben put on a load of washing and took the kids up for baths. Claire cleared up. She wiped bits of grated cheese from the curve of the washing machine door and noticed flecks of paper among the dark clothes – someone had left a tissue in their pocket. On closer inspection it was her Be Better Before Bodlowe list disintegrating in the water. She must have left the sock somewhere random.

It was hard to be simple when you were so good at making things complicated.

Chapter 11

Losing her list was a sign. A sign that important notes should not be stored somewhere that could be misconstrued as laundry.

Claire bought a lined notebook and rewrote her list, bringing all her shortcomings to mind and thinking of new ones. She kept her notebook, keys, purse and phone in her bag on a peg in the hall at all times. When she took her phone or the notebook upstairs, she only ever put them down on the chest of drawers. It changed her life and filled her with optimism about what she could achieve before Bodlowe.

Claire and Katie found they could move faster while still managing to chat. They'd settled on calling their evening sessions 'jog'n'jaw' but were working on a better name.

On her non-school days, Claire popped to the Headleigh leisure centre climbing wall, hoping to awaken her inner mountain goat for scrambles up Cornish hillsides.

She redid her passwords. 'Eye Of The Tiger' didn't sit right, so despite it being 'classic Ding,' she reinstated 'Funky Town'. She decided to change just her digits, bouncing herself out of the *Sophie's Choice* conundrum of which kid's birthday to use by going for Katie's instead.

She booked Charlie and Pearl swimming lessons and began them herself. Watching the winning-at-life people zipping up and down the fast lane across the pool, she learned how to streamline her half hour of wet putzing in the changing room and be out in less time in drier clothes, valuable transferable skills for the beach. One day, when she found she was still wearing her blue plastic shoe covers out on the pavement, she resisted the urge to post a picture. If she didn't want Honor to think she was a dingbat, she had to stop inviting the conclusion.

She signed up for free combat classes at the Halls. Afterwards, in the damp basement reading room, she used the whirring computer in the reference section to familiarise herself with the Bodlowe area, and search message boards for holiday tips. *Talc,* she wrote in her notebook, *makes sand come off skin.* She looked up what doctors packed in their holiday first aid kits and booked herself on a first aid course.

In a Luton charity shop she unearthed a faded but sturdy canvas windbreak. In a supermarket clearance bin, a boules set and kids' goggles. She lurked on giveaway and auction sites and hustled up a beach umbrella here, a coolbag there.

Ben had said that Honor and Chris would provide what they needed. But Claire remembered how it felt to muddy that borrowed cagoule. She knew that to share or borrow would open her to Honor's condescension and ridicule. And because persuading Ben they needed all this stuff would be another thing on the to-do list, she hid the stuff away instead. In the loft or the shed, or the cupboard under the stairs.

One evening Edna brought round a parcel she had taken in. It was wrapped in brown paper and packing tape. That it was a bodyboard was immediately apparent.

'It's very big, dear, isn't it?'

'Thanks so much for signing for it, Edna.'

Edna jiggled the brown paper parcel up and down. 'Light though. What on earth is it?'

'It's a bodyboard,' said Claire, big on mouth movement.

'A what?'

Claire took the parcel and mimed jumping on. 'Body-board.'

'Who?'

'Bodyboard.'

'Buddyboard?'

'It's for in the sea. BODYBOARD.'

So Ben, on the living room sofa, did know about that particular purchase.

Claire began to give the school address for deliveries, passing parcels off as resources.

One Wednesday lunchtime at handover, Fran was distracted by something out of the window. 'Look at that.'

Claire joined her. There was a woman at the gates delivering a box emblazoned with a photo of a portable barbecue. 'Shit,' she muttered.

'What a great-looking pair of humans.'

Fran wasn't looking at the barbecue. Isobel Keen and Grant were chatting as they strolled to the gate to help a theatre company bring their props in.

'Oh, yeah. Gorgeous.' Claire's eyes flicked back to the box she would not be able to pass off as school related.

'Isobel looks like she's just got off a horse and who wouldn't want to ride Grant?' said Fran. 'Just a question of when they get together, I reckon.'

Claire watched as Isobel took the barbecue and then Grant took it from her, saying something that made her laugh. Grant would bring the box to the classroom, bypassing Mrs Benjamin; panic over.

'Would that would be all right, Fran? Grant and Isobel?'

Fran gestured *what's it to do with me?* Then sighed. 'I had a crush but I'm almost over it. Surprised, aren't you? I've played my cards pretty close to my chest.'

'Fran, you've been flashing your cards since September.'

'No way.' They laughed.

'Not that you weren't enthusiastic with Mrs Gilbert, but your clothes, your posture, your *laminating*, everything's upped its game.' Fran facepalmed. 'Mind you, maybe mine has too,' said Claire. 'I mean even Mrs Benjamin cracks a smile for Mr Reader. And anyway, why not you and him? You've got great rapport.'

'Grant has rapport with everyone. He has rapport with the freaking coat cupboard, I mean can *you* get that door to stay closed?'

'No, never.'

'I hate that cupboard. I wish it would Mary Poppins itself sorted; I reckon there's clothes in there from kids who've started sixth form.'

'Seriously, what makes you so sure you and he aren't a possibility?'

'Oh he's all fresh and tufty, he wouldn't want an old been-through-it bird like me.'

'Fran, you're my age. Thirty-six is hardly old. Yeah there's an age gap but—'

'Don't drag me back. I'm working on getting over this. And for the record, if, *when* Grant and Isobel get all two-become-one, I'll be the first to congratulate them.'

Grant came into the classroom without the barbecue.

Fran zipped her coat. A lovely olive-green wool that warmed her skin. 'Enjoy the rest of your week, guys.'

'Cheers Fran, and you.'

Grant went to his desk, then paused and pointed at Claire, grinning. 'Forgotten something, haven't I.'

She grinned back. 'Cheers Grant.'

The bell rang before he was back. Claire brought the kids in, and they started paintings about Tudor life. She forgot to ask Grant where he'd put the barbecue.

Later, when she was helping find slots in the drying rack, Grant called across the classroom.

'Ms Swift, Mrs Benjamin for you.'

Mrs Benjamin clung to the stair rail like she expected to fall.

'Sorry about the delivery, it—'

'Your son. Medical room.'

'Oh gosh. Again?' Claire trotted down the stairs and across the foyer. Charlie was splayed on the bed, a wad of damp paper towels across his neck. 'Hey, what's wrong?'

Isobel pulled her curly ponytail over her shoulder. 'He seemed floppy and said his neck felt strange so I'm observing him.'

Charlie sat up. 'Hello Mum,' he said, like it was a lovely surprise she'd dropped by. 'I was dizzy in my neck but I think I'll be OK, especially now I've seen you.' He climbed from the bed and held out his arms. 'Hug please.'

Claire hugged him.

'I have to record this Claire, sorry.'

'It's fine,' said Claire. 'He's doing it less this term though, right?'

Isobel scrunched up her nose and shook her head.

Claire leaned down so she was face to face with him. 'Charlie, unless something is really wrong, you have to be in your classroom.'

'But I like seeing you,' he whispered.

Isobel held out a hand to him. 'Come on, back to class.'

Claire watched them go. Mrs Benjamin cleared her throat and muttered. Claire sighed, suddenly defensive, and went to her hatch.

'Sorry, Mrs Benjamin. But you see, this one time, when I was little, I was in the medical room with a fever. The school phoned home but there was no answer, which meant Mum had taken it off the hook because she was working. The clock clanged every second, and I thought I'd be there forever. I don't want my kids to feel like I won't show up.'

Mrs Benjamin pointed her pen at the floor. 'You've received another parcel.'

Claire glanced at the portable barbecue. 'It won't happen again.' Wait, she'd given the school address for a Thermos flask. 'Actually it will happen again, but then it will stop.'

Chapter 12

Claire approached the entrance to Lidl.

Carrier bags, check.

Debit card, check.

Shopping list but sense of foreboding anyway, check.

She grabbed a basket and stopped immediately by the magazines.

Claire, you absolute twonk, just get the shopping done.

How kind is the voice in YOUR head?

She reached for the magazine that was asking the question. Interesting. She wasn't sure she had a voice in her head.

Er yup ya ninny, hello, ya do.

She flipped to the article.

The way we talk to ourselves is an ingrained setting. Great if it's positive, but if our self-talk is locked on negative, it can cause us damage.

That's you. That's your setting.

Because if we don't approve of ourselves, how can we expect anyone else to approve of us?

Claire, this should be on your list of things to change. It's kind of mortifying you weren't aware of it; what else might you have missed?

Good news? Once you're aware your self-talk isn't as kind as how you talk to others, you can flip a switch. When you catch yourself being negative, flip it. Rather than 'I'm always late, I'm such an idiot,' flip it to 'I can work at being on time and improve.'

Claire set off along the fruit and veg aisle and put a pack of easy peelers in the basket.

Hi Claire, I'm your new self-talk voice. We're going to catch ourselves being negative and flip it.

Well, good luck with that. She added a lemon to the oranges.

Thank you, I appreciate it.

I was being sarcastic. She picked up a punnet of red grapes.

Positive self-talk could be helpful when it comes to Honor.

If you think it will help you hold your own next to a global alpha high-achieving precision-engineered Michelin-starred swimwear model, then go ahead, positive self-talk your heart out.

Honor's not all that.

Ooh, listen to you.

Claire shook her head. Inner voices falling in and out with each other. Ridiculous. She grabbed peppers, and spinach because they hadn't had any mouldering in the salad drawer for a while, turned out of the aisle then reversed back in to hide and watch.

Grant and Isobel were by the upmarket ready meals. Isobel had wine in a basket and was playing with her hair. They were deciding. Grant picked up a big foil tray. The picture on the front was maybe lamb shanks. His face was flushed.

Claire messaged Katie.

Guess who's in Lidl? She added a few shocked emojis.

Katie: Orlando Bloom. No, Venus Williams?

Claire: Grant and Isobel. Looks like they're going to be *Eating In*.

Katie: Oh no. I mean, yay. Love heart emoji but sad face emoji for Fran.

Claire: Should I maybe tell her so she's got a few days to get her head round it?

Katie: Yes. Would be worse for her to see them all cosy at school if she didn't know.

Claire: Cheers x

Claire: Hi Fran. Hey ... feel horrible telling you this, but I've just seen Grant and Isobel and it massively looks like they're spending the evening together. Sorry but hope it's right to mention it. C xoxoxo

The message had arrived. Fran had read it. No sign of her typing a reply. Claire was struck by how shit it would feel to read that text and be sick at every aspect of it yet want to ask a billion questions.

Claire: To clarify, it was in Lidl. Maybe it's nothing, but I think it's something and I'm really sorry.

Claire: You continue to be beautiful, exciting, smart, funny and special.

Claire: OK I think I'm being annoying so I'll stop. And I hope I'm wrong. And I'm here for you xxx

★

'What's up?' The way Ben had bunged the peppers and spinach in the fridge … *something* was up.

'I went in the shed.'

Ah, that would do it. Claire folded a carrier bag.

'How long have we had a roof box, Claire?'

'You're making it sound like a *horse* box. It's not an especially mental thing to have. I got it a while back, second hand.'

'We didn't talk about getting a roof box.'

Plonk. *There you go fruit bowl, have some apples.* 'Gently, Ben, they'll bruise. I know. But the kids need more room now they're bigger and we'll be taking loads of stuff to Cornwall.'

'So I saw. Quite a collection in there.'

Wait till you see the rest. 'Just making sure we're ready.'

'It's still months away.'

'A roof box won't go off though. Unlike apples.'

Ben undid the apple pack and placed them with exaggerated care back into the fruit bowl.

'Sorry,' he said. 'It annoyed me. It feels like this holiday has all your attention. You're swimming, you're running, you're "popping out" somewhere. And when you're here you're on the laptop. When did we last watch TV together?'

'Sorry you feel like that. Swimming and running are good, though. It's not *all* about the holiday.'

'Feels like it. Climbing wall?'

The climbing wall was all about the holiday. 'It's good to be challenging myself, don't you think?'

'I thought your project this year was building up your illustration.'

Her knees bucked like a lift had landed her on an unexpected floor. 'Well. Yes—'

'Oh, yeah.' Ben clicked his fingers, smiling. 'Healthy Start, one of the charities I work with, have got funding for a new brochure. They'll need illustrations.'

'Their last brochure was fantastic. I'm sure they'll want to use the same person.'

'They'd love what you do, at least send some samples, Claire. Your work is absolutely professional standard.'

He'd seen into her fear. Claire grabbed a pen and stepped over to the Luton FC wall calendar.

'We should go out, Ben, let's go out. It's been *ages* and Ed and Katie owe us a babysit.'

'Now you're talking. How about tomorrow?'

'Tomorrow's Combat.'

'Friday?'

'Ah, no, sorry. I'm on a first aid course. It covers drowning and they don't all do that.'

He screwed his eyes up trying to read her writing, 'What does it say on Saturday?'

'It's a Summmer Swish. You know, you swap clothes.'

Ben deadpanned her. 'Right. It was five degrees when I last checked, so you wouldn't want to miss that. Claire, our end of April is full of your August.'

'Shit. I am a bit obsessed, aren't I?'

'Yes. You are. You need to be in the moment.'

He looked at the calendar again. 'Sunday I've got five-a-side beers. Monday's my team meeting.'

'Tuesday,' said Claire, a plan forming. Ben had been saying it had been too long since he'd seen live music. 'How about Tuesday? I have an idea. I'll see if Katie's free.'

'OK. Where d'you want to go?'

'Can it be a surprise? For you. It can't be a surprise for both of us.'

'Fine, next Tuesday, surprise.'

Katie was happy to have a night away from her battling boys. 'What are you doing, meal and a movie?'

Claire jumped over a crack in the paving. 'Spring show at my old college. I haven't been back in ages. Wine, art, live music, great weirdo watching. The email came last week.'

'Will Ivan the terrible will be there?'

'Oh God, The Letchurer. No. He left the year after me. Pretty sure it was in disgrace. It could be great, Katie. I looked up the band that's playing, really punk and fun, Ben will love them. It will be one of those nights that reset everything. The ones where you go sheesh, yesterday things were rubbish but today we're super close again. It will be the best date ever.'

Claire attempted a heel click, whacking herself in the ankle.

Chapter 13

Early Tuesday evening, Claire and Ben stepped onto the bus to Luton. He was wearing her favourite shirt and he smelled fantastic.

'Your hair looks nice,' he said.

'Oh, thanks.' She'd wanted to put waves in it but ran out of time so left it where it fell.

His gaze rested on her in a way that made her more excited. Under the blue straggly jacket she had on a dress he liked. She'd done a double take when she'd seen it in the window of the charity shop. It made her feel neat around the waist, and finished below her knees right where she started to like her legs, which were in black tights and cherry DMs.

The bus braked sharply at traffic lights. Claire fell against Ben, her breast pressed against his arm.

'So what's the surprise?' he asked, looking at her like he wanted to take her home to bed. 'San Lorenza, Thai Orchard or that pop-up place?'

'None of the above. We're getting outta Luton.'

His face fell. 'Where? Not *London*.'

'Yes, London.'

He shook his head. 'Claire, I'm tired, I've had a hard day. You can't just spring London on someone.'

'Come on Ben, trust me. It'll be great.'

They shuffled over to accommodate people who were getting on. One was a man who leered immediately at a seated girl in school uniform. The girl, make-up free, high ponytail, glanced up and raised an effective middle finger from behind her study guide.

Claire and the girl exchanged a smile. She wondered if Ivan the letchurer ever did turn up to these college shows, despite his disgraced send-off. And on a happier note, what about Andrea Byers? Would Claire's tutor be there? What would it be like to see her again?

It struck Claire that Ben wanted her to be in the moment. But she was taking him into her past.

She handed him a Coke and a warm cheese slice from the concession on the station platform.

'Want anything else?'

'This is fine,' he said.

It IS fine, Claire. A delicious cheese slice in a nice bit of sun while you wait for the London train.

Woah, where had that voice come from? That was quite the flipped switch.

On the train she looked up the band who were playing and passed Ben her headphones. He listened to one of their songs, and nodded along, smiling.

He likes Ear Snail! He listened to the whole song. You knew he'd like them! Stay positive. It'll be a great evening.

Out of the Tube into drizzle, they zigzagged the streets to the familiar Georgian terrace. She folded her hand into his.

'Looking forward to that band,' he said.

Claire smiled. They reached the building. There was a tall thin man at the door trying to find his mouth with a cigarette. He turned round and Claire's smile disappeared.

'Claire … Macklin?'

'Hello, Ivan.'

'Well, this evening's taken an upward turn.' He circled the

end of the already-lit cigarette with a flame. His eyes were pink and puffy.

'This is my husband, B—'

'I thought it might be.'

Ignoring Ben's outstretched hand, Ivan dropped his cigarette and put his hand in the middle of Claire's back to usher her in.

A student hung their coats on a rail. Ivan passed Claire a flimsy cup of wine. She handed it to Ben and took one for herself. Ivan shepherded her off like they'd arranged it, touching her back to orient her from one artwork to another, asking her what she thought of the piece and when she started to answer, cutting across to say what the student had been attempting, and how they'd fallen short.

'I'm getting another drink,' said Ben. 'Want one, Claire?'

Ivan said, 'Yeah, I'll have one.'

'Thanks, Ben.' Claire poured *sorry*, and *this is not what I want to be happening* and *bear with me*, from her eyes towards his.

'Age has definitely not withered you,' said Ivan with a confident smirk as though all the ladies loved it when he told them they hadn't withered.

Claire turned towards a piece on the wall and screwed her eyes shut. Ben returned. Claire linked his arm and took the wine. 'Thanks for showing us around, Ivan,' she said. 'We'll be fine from here.'

'But I like showing you around.' He swayed after them.

'So sorry about this, Ben.'

'Hold up,' called Ivan.

Ben let go of Claire and turned round. Too slow to get the message to his reedy booze-fuelled limbs, Ivan and his cup of red crumpled into Ben, soaking his lovely shirt.

'Oh fuck,' Ivan said, as though Ben was an inanimate object. 'I'll have to get another drink now.'

'Anything to say about this?' Ben held his shirt out. Ivan focused on the wet stain, looked into Ben's face and shrugged provocatively.

Oh God, they weren't going to have a fight, were they? Claire tugged Ben's arm. 'Come on, Ben. Let's disappear.'

Ben stepped back and she took his hand and pulled. Techno pulsed from the basement as they strode through connected rooms, towards the far exit, the students' work waving and smiling as they passed.

You messed up. Resetting to super-close best date evers doesn't include almost-fights between husbands and drunk ex-lecturers.

But wait, it's not over. The band. You brought Ben here for the band.

'Ben, let's not leave. You could rinse your shirt in the gents, then we could go down to the basement and wait for the band.'

Ben sighed and pushed his hair back. He was flustered and smelled of oaky wine.

'All right.'

The crypt-like basement was empty apart from a tech taping a cable to the stage and another behind the sound desk. Claire found a student with a tray of wine. She and Ben clinked flimsy cups.

'About getting home on time,' she said. 'We'll need to leave at nine for the fast train then hope to get lucky with a bus.'

He smiled warmly. 'Nice planning. The tech says the band are on at eight, so they should start by half past and if the rest of the songs are as fast as the one you played me earlier, they'll burn through their set in about twenty minutes.'

'You're looking forward to them aren't you?'

He smiled and brushed at his shirt. 'I am.'

A hand touched her shoulder. 'Hello Claire.'

The same kind of Saxon-looking silver earrings she'd always worn, hair twisted into the same kind of leather clasp.

'Andrea.'

They hugged. Andrea gave it her all, so Claire relaxed into it.

'It's amazing to see you.' Andrea said it like it was unequivocal. That was so Andrea. Encouraging, celebrating. A memory rushed back to Claire of a time she hadn't believed her.

'And you, Andrea.'

Claire and Ben followed her out to the stairwell to chat where it was quieter. Claire had been back twice since the end of college, her social urge stronger than her sheepishness, but Andrea had been away or on sabbatical.

They shared updates about Claire's contemporaries.

'And how did you meet this gorgeous chap?'

'It was a couple of years after college,' said Claire. She beamed. She loved telling this story. 'He came into the art supplies shop where I worked. I was building a tower of erasers and when I saw him I knocked them all on the floor.'

Andrea smiled. 'Are you an artist, Ben?'

Ben shook his head. 'I'd seen Claire through the window. I said I was looking for a pen.' He grinned at Claire. 'We tried them all out, didn't we?'

'Yep,' Claire grinned back. 'All the pens.'

Andrea smiled. 'So what are you up to these days, Claire? '

'Well, I do some illustration. Leaflets, posters.'

'That's superb. To you.' Andrea raised her cup. 'You got over your wobble. It's just fab when students make a living doing what they love, and in your case are so excellent at.'

'Oh, it's just a hobby,' Claire waved her hand. 'I don't

make any money. It's all for community groups and start-ups. Throw me a jar of chutney and we're good.'

'Literally chutney?'

Claire nodded. 'But it's OK. I work part-time in our kids' school.' She glanced at Ben. 'I'll maybe get another part-time job. I was doing two days in the art supplies shop on our local parade as well, but it closed last year.' She was wittering. And none of it was making the 'literally chutney?' look disappear from Andrea's face. Ben didn't look that thrilled either.

'I still think about your final-year project, Claire.'

Claire dropped her head. 'Oh. Don't.'

'I wish I'd known how you felt.'

'It wasn't good enough,' Claire said quietly.

'It was better than good enough. Objective fact. You were on track to do very well.'

Ben wrapped his hand round Claire's.

'Well it's all in the past now.' Claire swallowed a big mouthful of wine. 'We've seen Ivan by the way. Really drunk.'

'You shouldn't give work of your standard away, Claire. That's not good for any of us.' A thought seemed to cross Andrea's mind and she riffled through the swirl of leaflets and business cards on the table behind her.

'Here.' She passed Claire a flyer, tapping it, like it was the answer.

'My professional practitioners course for illustrators. It's next month. It empowers, enables and equips.' She pointed out the words on the flyer. 'Do you do much marketing?'

Claire pulled an embarrassed face. 'I don't do any.'

Ben's head tipped up and his shoulders straightened. Claire followed his gaze. Ivan was weaving his way down the stairs.

'Well. I've found this *wunderkind* who comes and does a marketing session, and you should definitely come.'

'She *should* come, shouldn't she Angela?' Ivan teetered on the bottom step.

'It's Andrea, Ivan. Lord, you've only known me twenty years.'

'If Claire comes I'll come. Where are we coming?'

'My professional practitioners course,' Andrea sounded it out carefully. 'You should consider it, Claire. Don't worry, Ivan won't be there.'

'Angela doesn't know that for sure.' He gave Claire a low shutter speed wink that was like groping.

'She does. *Ivor*,' said Andrea, scarily.

'Why is she calling me Ivor?' He eyed Claire conspiratorially.

'Because you're getting her name wrong.' Ben's voice was a growl.

Ivan shrank backwards up the stairs. 'Was going to the little boy's room anyway.' He pinballed off a woman in a voluminous robe, faced forward and staggered out of sight.

Andrea and Claire grimaced and sighed and then laughed and Ben joined in.

'I'm so sorry,' said Andrea. 'His wife chucked him out and he's started hanging around here, talking his way round security. Nightmare. Anyway Claire, I've run the course a few times. People find it invigorating. They support each other after. It could make the difference. Help you have the career you deserve. I'd better circulate. Great to see you both.'

Claire folded the flyer into her bag and kept her hand on it as they went back into the vaulted room to wait.

They made their way to the exit at nine. As they stepped outside, the band's opening chords thrashed into the night.

'Thanks for nothing Ear Snail. *Pff*.' Ben shrugged his

shoulders. 'With hindsight, do any of the words Art School Punk Band suggest punctuality?'

They walked to the Tube. 'I'm sorry it was such a shit night, Ben.'

'It was certainly surprising.' He rubbed his temples.

'Ivan is a twat.'

'Not your fault. His life's messed up so he might as well get himself into more trouble.'

'He's a twat, Ben. You're too nice about people.'

They arrived at St Pancras twelve minutes before the train.

'Could have heard at least five songs,' Ben muttered, then he sighed and smiled at her. 'You should do that course.'

A weight pulled in her chest. 'It's a lot of money.'

'Doesn't matter, you should do it. Are you going to do it?'

'Pressure!'

'It's encouragement.'

With trepidation, she took out the flyer. 'Ah no, look.' Relief spread through her. 'It's on during the Halls' Open Weekend.'

'You think the people of Headleigh couldn't manage without you?'

'Don't say that. You make it sound like I think I'm important.'

'You are important. You're worth investing in.'

'Platform's come up.' She put the flyer back in her bag.

They got to Luton and raced to a bus.

Ben flopped onto the seat, breathing heavily. 'Wish I hadn't drunk so much. Not that I've drunk *too* much.'

'Good.' She put a hand on his leg.

'Don't start chatting with Katie, then.'

'I won't. I'll just say thanks and good night and run upstairs peeling my dress off.'

'Yes to that. I'll be waiting for you.'

Ben was waiting for her. Claire chuckled, rushing a brush round her teeth.

Thanks sex. Thanks for existing to salvage date nights that have gone largely wrong.

She took her phone from her bag to switch it off. She'd missed six calls from an unknown number. What on *earth* could have happened to warrant six—

She startled as the phone vibrated in her hand, accidentally accepting the call.

'Claire. I'm in Hong Kong.'

'Honor, hi. Are you OK?'

'Shit news. Just put on my personal mobile to find out Blue Gables is being sold.' She tutted. 'Hold on. I've got a numpty intern outside who's forgotten his instructions. Don't go anywhere.'

Claire perched on the edge of the bath, annoyed. Like she didn't have something way better to do. Mind you, Honor's bank's hold music was nice, hopeful. A thought popped into her head. If Blue Gables was being sold, then there was no holiday cottage. Technically, they were *currently not going on holiday with the Wellbeloveds.*

She should say they needed a holiday like Honor and Chris had with their kids a couple of times a year, like the ones on the bus adverts, to Ebeefer, or somewhere you could get to by car. Maybe Charlie would be OK with a ferry? The second Honor came on the line, she'd say it.

The music soared, distorting a little. Claire could almost feel French or Spanish sun on her skin and Pearl and Charlie's hands in hers, the four of them running through warm sea, laughing.

Honor's jewellery clattered on the handset.

'So no Blue Gables. Really sad. Now look Claire, I'm

crisis managing an uber-shit show here. It will be a challenge for you, but there'll be something if you put your mind to it.'

'Put my mind to what?'

'Finding new accommodation in Bodlowe, Ding. You're going to be the hero that saves the holiday. I'll forward a guidance email setting out parameters tomorrow. Find somewhere perfect, then liaise with Chris. If he's happy it's up to spec, he'll sort the payment. Thanks a million, got to go, love you, bye.'

Claire switched off her phone.

Woah. So much to say about that phone call.

So much to unpack and discuss.

When Ben was naked and waiting.

'Your lovely man is in your bed,' she whispered to her wild-eyed reflection. 'It was supposed to be the best date ever but someone picked a fight with that man and flirted with his wife, and then he missed the band he was looking forward to. So you get out there and be in the moment. The first rule of that phone call is do not talk about that phone call.'

The duvet was at the end of the bed. Ben lay against the pillow with his arms behind his head.

'You've still got the dress on. Weren't you taking it off?'

She pulled the dress over her head and bent to untie her DMs, seeing clear evidence he was definitely in the moment.

She must not think about Honor's call. If she started telling Ben, she would not be able to stop. What was she supposed to say to herself to stop intrusive Honor thoughts? Taj Mahal! That was it, Taj Mahal.

She pushed down her tights. *Taj Mahal.* Took off her underwear and lay down beside him.

Taj Mahal Taj Mahal Taj Mahal Taj Mahal.

Ben rolled onto his side and cupped her face. He frowned. 'What's on your mind?'

Taj Mahal. 'Nothing.'

'You've usually got things to tell me.'

Taj Mahal! 'Not tonight. I'm in the moment here with you.' She took a stuttery breath. 'So what's on *your* mind, Ben?' It was meant to sound sexy, but at best it was sexy dalek.

Ben's smile faded and he flopped onto his back. 'To be honest, fucking loads actually.'

It was not the response she'd expected.

'At first,' he said, 'it was just one or two things that needed putting right, but now that Carlos has actually gone on sick leave, what I'm realising is that all the time he was struggling in on painkillers waiting for his back op, he was dropping balls all over the place.'

'Oh no. Ben, that's awful.'

'I know. Thanks boss. It's worse than if he hadn't been coming in. I'll be trying to put shit right for months. There's stuff he's agreed to deliver that we can't deliver. He's let deadlines pass on things we *could* have delivered. It's a freaking shambles.'

'Why haven't you told me?'

He glanced at her and sighed. 'S'pose I'm a bit like my dad sometimes. "Trouble shared's a trouble doubled". He laid a hand on his chest. 'I'm all stressed now. We'd be shagging if you hadn't asked me.'

'*Did* I ask you?'

'You said, "what's on your mind?"'

'I meant what's on your *sexy* mind. We can still shag, can't we?'

'D'you know what, I've got that weight in the chest feeling. Funny old night. Can we just have a cuddle?'

Ben rolled a heavy arm and leg onto her and it was official: DATE NIGHT FAIL.

'Whether or not I can get it sorted,' he said, his breath warm on her neck, 'what I'll hold onto is the thought of messing around in a dinghy with Chris and the kids in Cornwall.'

Claire would have to be the hero that saved the holiday. She would have to salvage Bodlowe, for Ben.

Chapter 14

'All right lady, keep it coming,' said Fran.

Claire read out the next line of assessment information.

'Hey,' she said gently to the top of Fran's head, 'you didn't answer my message last Friday.'

'Uh-huh.' Fran moved her ruler down the page.

'I'm sorry about Grant and Isobel.'

'It's not your fault.'

'Do you want the details?'

'Sure. Go for it.' Fran busied herself lining up the ruler exactly.

Claire swallowed. 'So yeah. I mean it's not like they were holding hands or anything, but he was lit up like a Christmas tree and she was at maximum hair toss. And she had wine. And they were choosing a fancy ready meal.'

Fran nodded. 'It's fine Claire. It happens. We move on.'

'You're being very dignified.'

'When am I not dignified?'

Claire grinned at her. Grant arrived in the doorway. He looked flustered but good, like he'd spent too long in a sauna.

'Hey Grant.'

'Hey Claire, hey Fran.'

'Hey.' Fran kept her eyes on her work. Grant pointed at his desk like he was asking permission to enter his own classroom. 'Jacket.' He flipped the jacket from the back of his chair and backed out.

They finished their cross-checking. Before she left, Fran pushed at the coat cupboard doors then held out her hands in anticipation. They wafted back open.

'Thought I'd cracked it. See you later, Claire.'

Claire watched Fran leave, pained for her, and then jumped as her phone sounded a notification.

Honor's 'Guidance email'.

She read it at afternoon break, skulking behind a tree in the playground.

Claire
Let's take a time-limited approach and get somewhere booked by end of Friday (ie day after tomorrow).

'I know when Friday is,' Claire muttered.

'And I do,' replied a little kid, crouched nearby, scraping a stick on the ground. Claire smiled and looked back at the email.

For the search, please stick within the following parameters:

'I don't even want to go,' Claire hissed, 'so how about *you* stick within *these* parameters.' She turned away from the kid and poked a finger at the email like bus girl had done to leery bloke.

– Definitely a place in Bodlowe, not Sandham (knit-your-own-yoghurt) or Chievehampton (full of knobs), go all out for Bodlowe.
– 6 beds. Or deffo 5. Let's not slum it. No one must sleep on a sitting room pull-out and Ollie needs his own space

- Close to beaches and amenities
- Parking for two cars (better make it three Ding, I've seen how much wiggle room you need!)
- Sea view. Holy grail, right? But let's try.
- Finally, not near Waverley Park, the caravan site. Huge slow-moving families with tatts and sunburn blocking the pavements.

Find whatever's most suitable, no upper budget, Send the best to Chris by six on Friday and he'll pick and pay.

Love

H

When they got back from school, Claire stuck a film on for the kids and got online. That Honor could find enough time to list all her parameters and take a swipe at a bunch of people who weren't like her was enraging and Claire felt tempted to look for two caravans at Waverley Park. She would feel comfortable there. Blue Gables hadn't been her style at all, too slick and neat with those cream carpets and sofas. Somewhere a bit more rough-and-tumble with character was what she wanted. She searched 'Hand Picked Cornwall' and 'Cornish Gems' and five or six other sites, tapping through to tiny coloured-in grids that represented August. She could see now what the challenge was. Cornwall was very popular in August.

As in full.

If she was going to be 'the holiday hero', she'd have to keep searching.

She continued after dinner, left jolly voicemails for letting agents in Bodlowe asking to be contacted with any cancellations.

Pearl spat out her toothpaste. 'Mummy,' her mouth was

ringed white. 'Try not to sound weird or they won't ring back.'

'Mum is doing her best,' Charlie told his sister, Dog tucked under his chin like a floppy violin.

Thursday morning. Claire loaded a worksheet into the school copier and pressed start. Honor would be in touch at 6 p.m. tomorrow. She mulled over whether she'd ever used the word 'parameters', or given Katie a task and a deadline. The answer was no.

She cursed under her breath. She'd forgotten to press collate and the worksheet had copied into one big bundle.

She popped into the staff room to sort out the copying. It was empty so she called a Bodlowe letting agent. The number rang.

Mrs Gunnarson marched in, heavy on her heels, to the fridge. 'The copier does collate, Claire.'

Claire stuffed her phone in her bag. 'Oh I know, I just forgot to press the button.' A voice from her bag said, 'Holiday Homes To You, good morning.' Claire invented a coughing fit. She didn't know if it had been effective cover, but Mrs Gunnarson went on her way with a carton of milk. Claire told the agent the parameters and that she was desperate.

'I might know of somewhere,' said the agent. 'I haven't seen it because it didn't meet our criteria but it's two three-bed farm cottages on the headland to the west of the harbour.'

Claire took the contact details. 'Seriously, that's the email address? Deathmetalfan at mailme dot co dot uk?'

'That's what's on file. As I say, our criteria weren't met, so it's very much your decision to make inquiries.'

★

That evening on the way back from combat class, holding her phone with difficulty in her punched-out arms, Claire listened to a voicemail.

'Evening Ms Swift. Further to your call, we might have a super property for you. The wedding party to whom it's currently booked is wrangling over cancellation terms, but do peruse our website for Perriwinton Manor.'

Claire sat next to Ben on the sofa. He was deep in season three of the show they were meant to watch together. She teased open her laptop, as though by doing it slowly he wouldn't notice she wasn't watching, again.

She looked at the website and her trembly combat arms were joined by a thumping heart. Perriwinton Manor's sandstone turreted exterior was stunning. Inside it was bonkers. There were taxidermied cows among the suits of armour, it had what appeared to be an erotic mosaic on the wall of its indoor pool and an inglenook fireplace the size of a large shed, completely lined with glued-on ring pulls. The kitchen was straight out of the seventeenth century and all the pans on the open shelves were gold. It was mini Hogwarts on an acid trip. Each family could have its own wing. The house was a perfect curve ball, such an oddity that however Honor might try to be its queen, she, like the rest of them, could only really be a tourist. She emailed to say she was definitely interested.

At break on Friday Claire was laminating flashcards, half an eye on Isobel, tending her curls and cooing at Grant, when the agent rang back.

'Lovely news about Perriwinton.'

'I can have it? That's fantastic, thank you.'

'Oh dear, I've said the wrong thing, sorry.'

'How? You said "lovely news".'

'For the groom. He's been forgiven and the wedding is back on.'

'So we can't have Perriwinton Manor.'

'No.'

'So ... not lovely news for me then?'

'Sorry. My romantic side got the better of me.'

Claire sighed. 'How likely is a five- or six-bed house to come up in the next week or so?'

'Bodlowe? Five or six beds?' He snorted and Claire rolled her eyes because she kind of had to wait for the answer in actual words and say thank you even though she already knew what it was.

Back home after school on Friday, Claire checked her spam folder for an email that hadn't arrived with copy for the Halls Open Weekend flyer. She found it, along with a reply from Deathmetalfan@mailme.co.uk. The subject line was Murdon Farm Holiday Cottages. Claire clicked on the attachment. An out-of-focus photo of two houses on a headland taken from a boat. They looked right in a no-nonsense, rustic kind of of way, but also wrong in a 'then he turned the shotgun on himself' kind of way. Maybe the email would help.

Thank you for the interest in our farmers cottage's. Their ideal for two familys who dunt want to be in each oth'ers pockits! Playbarn for the kiddies. Steps to the beach.

Not being in Honor's pocket, and having her own front door massively appealed so Claire emailed Deathmetalfan to ask for more photos. An email came back with bank account details in the name of Baxter Holdings. Underneath was written: **No other photos currently availabul.**

Six p.m. came and went. Was she supposed to contact Honor? It was one in the morning in Hong Kong. Chris rang five minutes later. 'Hey Claire. Honor said I should ring you about Bodlowe. That is one booked-up part of the world. Don't suppose you've had better luck?'

Don't mention Murdon Farm. 'Errm. Well ...'

'Tell me you've found somewhere,' he pleaded. 'I've given our nanny notice so I'm *fully* in the dog house.'

Why had he let the nanny go? Presumably they were being replaced. Poor Chris though. Being in Honor's dog house would not be fun. Claire's resolve slipped. 'I've *kind* of found somewhere.'

'Hallelujah. Whereabouts? Location's always a huge deal for Honor.'

'Just round the headland from Bodlowe to the west. Like, on the headland.'

'Sounds amazing.'

'It's maybe not though.'

'But on the headland with full-on sea view?'

'Yeah. It's two three-bed farm cottages. Parking. Steps to the beach, but we're not talking picture postcard. In fact I think we should probably leave it.'

'Steps to the beach? Claire, you're incredible.'

'We should hold on though Chris, for cancellations.'

'Why? Let's just snap these up. Text me payment details and thank you, thank you.'

Panic whirled through her. 'You should wait until you see the photo.'

'Claire, to be honest, it would be a break for me *not* to look at the photo. I sometimes look at up to five potential holiday accommodation photos a week. Text me and let's just do it.'

'But Honor hasn't seen it, Chris. And seriously, we're talking the opposite of Blue Gables here.'

'Pfft. Don't worry about that,' he said dismissively. 'I would seriously not want to interrupt her with anything at the moment. Not even holiday plans. Her work with Asif has turned super intense.'

A picture pinged into Claire's head of the sweaty hands-on intensity of an Honor v Linton personal training session, only on a massive conference table with Honor and Asif half out of their business suits. Chris didn't sound worried. Maybe Chris should be worried?

'Please just send me the details, and let's get Claire's cottages in the bag.'

Claire and Katie were on their second circuit, pausing to walk up Pope's Hill.

Katie was talking about Luke. 'I know you're supposed to speak to kids like they're the best version of themselves, but Ed's anxiety is kind of contagious.'

Ed had been catastrophising about Luke's attacks on Jake, worrying his son was a future thug. Claire reminded her of half a dozen sweet and thoughtful things Luke had said and done in his nine years on the planet.

'It's a phase, isn't it?' said Katie, looking more relaxed.

Claire nodded slowly. 'This too shall pass.'

Katie asked for an update on the holiday cottage situation and Claire tried to walk the talk as her own anxiety whipped back up.

'"Claire's cottages"?'

'That's what Chris called them. And Honor hasn't seen them, so they're my responsibility.' She showed Katie the photo that gave her the heebies.

'Rustic and authentic?' she asked hopefully.

Katie pulled a face. 'I'm going to be honest, Claire. It's like one of those pictures in the paper of somewhere something bad happened.'

'Hmm. That's what I thought.'

'Could be worse though. They'll be a lot bigger and better soundproofed than a tent.'

Claire got up early and jogged on her own. It had occurred to her at worry o'clock that Honor and Chris would assume the cottages had come through a letting agent. What if the 'criteria' that hadn't been met were things like being attached to utilities, or free from asbestos and carbon monoxide? What if Murder Farm Cottages had rotten stair rails and floors?

She'd just called it Murder Farm. Murdon. *Murdon* Farm Cottages. What would Honor think if she knew Claire's contact at Claire's cottages was Deathmetalfan?

She swigged some water and flopped on a bench in front of the shuttered shops. The skittery feeling in her chest was exactly how she'd felt in January when she'd thought Honor was coming for lunch and their loo seat was wonky. That feeling had fuelled painting plans, cupboard emptying and freaking out in superstores at exposing her home, her standards, her choices to judgment. And now it was nearly June and these feelings she had were about *August*.

In August it would be a year since the art supplies shop had closed down and Ben had encouraged her to make a go of her illustration. The beer shop that had opened in its place was flourishing and yet Claire had remained lashed down by the *same feelings* of inadequacy. She was bumping along a runway like a flimsy little biplane, never actually *taking off*. What kind of a way to live was this? Her loyal spectators Ben and Katie kept on willing her to take flight.

'I've been commissioned to do a flyer!'

'Yay Claire!'

'By Edna next door!'

'Oh.'

'And my reward – if the flyer does its job – is less dog poo on the pavement.'

'Ah ...'

Claire sighed and lay down on the bench, the soles of her trainers on its arm.

'Hello.' She gazed at her legginged thighs in surprise. They seemed to be a bit less triangle and a bit more parallel than last time she'd checked.

Things can change.

She tipped her head back and stared up. She could hear a plane but the sky was filled with cloud, white with a brush tip of black and blue mixed in.

What would it feel like to soar into the air? Get off the bumpy runway. Be a biplane *taking off and climbing*.

'Neeeeeeeeeeeeoowwwwwwwww.' Her voice vibrated through the wood of the bench.

You had to do something different to make things different. To jog up Pope's hill and down the dual carriageway and past the gas holders and along the parade and round again, you had to start going out for runs, and keep going out for runs.

Do something different, Claire. Fill your head with stuff that isn't 'Honor-will-judge-me-about-Murdon-Farm' jibber jabber.

Yes, positive self-talk voice! I will. I'll do that.

She leaped off the bench and went home. She found Andrea's course leaflet and put it carefully in her notebook with her to-do list.

Chapter 15

'Mummy, we're walking very fast.' Pearl bobbed along, frowning up at her.

Claire mimed that Pearl should rub cornflake milk from the corner of her mouth.

'I need to get to school early, love.'

It was Monday and she was on a mission, up and out even earlier than on her days in school. She'd been thinking about Fran and how it must feel to lose hope and how much hurt she must be hiding inside. Claire was going to do the one thing she could think of to help make life nicer for her.

The playground was almost empty except for Mrs Benjamin on a bench in a hi-vis tabard, knitting.

'Where is everyone?' asked Pearl dramatically.

'I don't want to play with Mrs Benjamin,' Charlie whispered.

Claire gave him a hug. 'It'll fill up in a minute, don't worry. I'm going inside.'

'Why Mum? Monday's not your day.'

'I know but I'm going to do something nice for Fran and clear out the coat cupboard.'

'That's nice.' Pearl skipped off to chat to Mrs Benjamin. 'Is Fran sad?'

Claire stroked Charlie's hair. 'Yes. She can't have something she wants.'

He nodded then broke into a grin. 'She can have it for her birthday.'

'She'd love that. See you later.'

Claire was buzzed into the building by the caretaker. She went upstairs to the classroom and put her things out of the way and flung open the double doors of the walk-in coat cupboard, stepping into the mayhem of coats, jumpers, P.E. kit and water bottles.

You can do this. Put everything from the pegs on the floor. If it belongs to someone in class, hang it back, if not, put it in this box for lost property.

Or maybe empty one peg at a time?

No, stick to plan A. It's Honor-y and will work. You planned the work, now work the plan.

After a good fifteen minutes she sat among the almost-sorted clothes, hands smelling of floor, for a breather. Everything was always harder than it looked.

The classroom door opened and closed. Claire was about to announce herself when there was a short gulp of laughter. A rustling noise was followed by an appreciative sound like a good banoffee pie had arrived in front of someone. Definitely female laughter came next then something like kissing. Intermittently pecky then snoggy kissing.

When it didn't stop, Claire peered round one of the cupboard doors. It *was* kissing. Fran and Grant were kissing.

She crept back into the cupboard. There was a more pressing sound now. Feet had tapped up the stairs, and heavy-heeled court shoes were approaching along the corridor, and two of the three people in the classroom seemed too preoccupied to notice.

Claire rushed from the cupboard and yanked the classroom door far enough to stick her head out.

'Morning Mrs Gunnarson,' she trilled. The head reared sideways, a neat stack of paperwork held up to defend herself. She continued down the corridor.

'Good morning,' she said, like she was really saying 'For fuck's sake, woman.'

Claire went back into the classroom and leaned against the door, shutting it with her bum, exhilarated.

'Thanks Claire,' said Grant. Like Fran, he was smiley and making only brief flicks of eye contact with her. 'Didn't think it was your day.'

'Oh but it *is* my day. My day is made.'

Fran laughed in a weird gulping way. 'Awesome idea to sort the cupboard.'

Grant rubbed the back of his head and gestured a thumb towards the door. 'I should probably collect a register or something.' He fumbled with the handle. Once his steps had faded, Claire and Fran snorted with laughter.

'Oh my God, Fran. But, what about Isobel?'

'There's no Isobel.'

'But I saw them.'

Fran shook her head. 'Last week, after I told you how I felt and you said that thing about our rapport, he came down to the lobby as I was leaving.' Her cheeks filled with smile. 'I said, "Do you want to go for a drink and if you don't it's cool." And he said "I do, how about Friday?"'

'No way.' No wonder Grant had forgotten to bring her barbecue upstairs.

'Way. Best three-second conversation of my life. Anyway, it was that night you saw him in Lidl. Isobel just happened to be there. I had to stay in for my landlord, so he brought dinner round and here we are.'

'This is amazing. You were all dignified. I thought you were broken-hearted.'

Fran shrugged. 'Just keeping it under wraps.'

'You've got game, Ms Achibe.'

'I've got Grant. Sometimes you make a leap that scares you and it turns out to be the right thing to do.'

The news about Fran and Grant put Claire in great mood. As soon as Ben got back from work, they had fantastic sex. Claire had been coming down the stairs with the laundry basket, grinning. He'd come in and their eyes had met and it was 'I see you' and 'I see you too,' and he'd smiled and taken the washing from her and put it at the bottom of the stairs and set the kids up with a TV show and followed her up.

Later, drying plates that Ben had washed, making contact with her body against his as she picked another from the rack, Claire thought about Fran's scared leap that had got her what she wanted.

'Ben, I've been thinking about Andrea's course.'

He turned round and smiled. 'I saw the flyer in your notebook. That's really great. Just a shame it clashes with the Halls thing.'

'I know. I don't *have* to go.' She put a plate onto the stack in the drawer.

Ben held her shoulders. 'No, it's great. You should do it.'

Claire's chest swelled with possibility. What she'd wear, what art materials she'd take. 'I'd leave early on the Saturday and be back Sunday night.'

'Right. Didcot isn't it? You'd have to get the train into London and out again. It'll take half the time in the car.'

This was sounding very real. 'Sure you won't need it?'

'You have it. We can get the train to Drama.'

She reached for another plate. 'OK, I'll take the car.' Yep. She was doing it. She was going.

'Might be worth seeing Steve to have the clutch checked.'

'I will.'

'Great. I'm proud of you.'

Claire swallowed. 'Thank you.'

Chapter 16

She dropped the Silver Bullet with Steve on the Wednesday morning before the course. When she went back, his straggly pate was glistening under the bonnet. She leaned against the garage wall to wait.

It was Ben who'd told Katie she was going on the course. He'd been at a meeting at the Halls, and Katie was there because she basically *was* the Halls and Katie had run round to Claire and hugged her so tightly that Claire's ear studs pushed into her neck drawing tiny spots of blood.

She was going on Andrea's course.

The course was for professional practitioners.

Therefore, she was a professional practitioner.

Eurghhh. She leaned forward and crossed her arms protectively.

That feeling's excitement *Claire. It's not* fear. *You're not shitting yourself, you're just really* REALLY *excited.*

A really excited imposter.

What? No! Stop that, we've been through *this. It'll be awesome. You'll be golden. You'll come back having met a bunch of super nice illustrators who are new or need a boost and you'll all climb your ladders together.*

Bet none of them messed up their degrees at the last minute.

That makes you the plucky underdog. Everyone loves an underdog. Am I right? Hmmm?

Positive self-talk voice, sorry, but you're sounding kind of desperate, and I feel like kind of puking.

Steve shut the bonnet and wiped it affectionately with his overall cuff. 'Take it slow and Didcot and back should be OK.'

Claire smiled. Her little biplane with its dents and wonky wiper, gaffer-taped wing mirror and ker-lunky door was taking off. Leighton Buzzard, Aylesbury, Abingdon then the A34 down to Didcot. Pearl had made her look up the route.

But what about that longer drive...

Taj Mahal!

When Honor's Space Ship would rip down to Bodlowe at warp speed.

Taj Mahaaaaaal!

You have to be practical, Claire. You've blanked it out with the course but Bodlowe hasn't gone away.

'Steve. Do you think we'll be OK driving to Cornwall and back in the holidays?'

Steve rubbed his jaw, turning a speck of oil into a streak. 'I'll check the exhaust.'

He slid under the car and Claire eyed the line of chunky, shiny second-hand cars beside them on Steve's forecourt, plastic signs offering great discounts on the windscreens next to all the numbers.

Steve rolled out and clambered to his feet, shaking his head. 'I wouldn't fancy it, personally.'

The Silver Bullet was old. Anything could go wrong with it. What if they rammed it full of stuff and it conked out before they even got to Bodlowe? She had to be practical. Wasn't it better to start with a car that would get there?

Claire looked at the cars on the forecourt. And the prices. A big silver one was the cheapest.

'Out of interest, Steve. How easy are the easy terms?'

Steve took Claire for a test drive. She couldn't believe how high up she felt, and it might have been her imagination but other drivers seemed to be giving way to her a lot more.

Do it Claire. Buy the car. You want to fly? This is a solid plane. This is a jet. This is making changes.

But it's ridiculous. Second gear slid into third. *I can't just buy a car.*

Says who? People buy cars all the time. Feel how light that steering is. Check out all the leg room.

'D'you like it?' Steve asked absent-mindedly. 'The boot is massive.' He was staring out of the window at a strolling woman's rounded rear.

She did like it.

She went back to the garage and completed the part-exchange paperwork in the office, unable to look the Silver Bullet in the eye.

She drove off the forecourt in what to some would be a banger but to her was an extremely fancy new car. She caught the Silver Bullet's reflection in the rear-view and burst into tears. It was like leaving an old pet at the vet's, but waltzing out with an immediate replacement. One with an incredibly flattering light-up mirror. She turned into a back street and pulled up to take a moment. She was breathing very fast. She clapped her hands to her cheeks and burst out laughing.

'I sound mad,' she said, still laughing. She hadn't parked properly. She'd just stopped near the pavement. A couple of cars held up behind her sped on, beeping.

There was a nice big space opposite the house and Claire

reversed into it, stopping as Steve had shown her just as the parking sensor peeps flatlined. The Miseries parted their nets to gawk. Claire waved and pressed the key fob which locked the car with a cheerful tock-tock, and went inside. She made some tea then was magnetised to the window to gaze at the car, surprised it hadn't drawn a crowd of admirers. When they'd last been in Bodlowe, the Swifts' car had looked like a grovelling flunky behind the Wellbeloveds' Space Ship *du jour*. This August, Silver Bullet Two – no longer an ironic name – would hold its own. It wouldn't look like it was *following*, just like it was *driving behind*, a deputy not a flunky.

This was a good idea. There are worse things you could do than surprise your family with a new car. Honor would do it. Ben might think it was brilliant.

She took a photo through the window and sent it to Katie.

> Claire: Bought a car.
> Katie: Whaaaaat?! Someone is thinking way beyond their course. Where'd the £££ come from?
> Claire: Just call me the loan (ar)ranger. If you see Ben don't tell him. It's a surprise.
> Katie: Okaaaaaay ...... scream emoji

Claire's adrenal glands needed a break so she went on foot for her afternoon in school. She walked to the alley backwards, drinking in the gleaming hulk of kerb appeal she'd manifested.

Pearl cantered home under the impression Claire had deliberately bought a new car on a day Charlie had a play-date so that she could see it first. They went for a drive.

Pearl was beside herself. 'It's so blingy and big.'

'Is that good?'

'Definitely. I feel like a rich gangster.'

Claire laughed and glanced in the rear-view at her daughter in her Pope's Hill sweatshirt. 'Cool. I mean, is that cool?'

''Course it's cool. Mummy, my booster seat is minging, so's Charlie's, can we get new ones?'

'I'll wash the covers.'

'We should keep it just like this. No one is ever allowed to bring *anything* inside it. It'll look like one of Ottie's cars.'

Claire stopped for petrol. The numbers flickered up and up. OK, so Pearl wasn't even eight until the end of August, but she liked the car and her opinion counted a lot.

Stunned you could pay so much to fill a car, Claire's resistance was low. She let Pearl come with her to pay and agreed to a bag of foam sweets and a tin of travel barley sugars 'for Bodlowe', like they'd last.

'Let's get one of these.' Pearl plucked a car air freshener from a stand.

'All right, but not vanilla,' said Claire, hooking it back. 'We'll get a really gangster one. Which is the most gangster air freshener?'

'Mummy, stop saying gangster.'

'OK.'

Pearl thought long and hard. 'Strawberry.' She placed the cardboard packet into Claire's palm.

They went out later to collect Charlie. He gave her his school bag and ritzed down the road practising a Luton Luvvies routine.

'We've got a really big surprise for you Charlie,' said Pearl, trotting along beside him, exaggerating how far she needed to bend to be on his level.

'What is it?' he asked, unhappily.

'There.' Pearl tock-tocked the fob she'd been hiding. 'That's our new car. Silver Bullet Two.'

Claire patted the air near the car so as not to dirty the shiny metal. Charlie frowned.

Pearl bent towards him. 'Don't you like it, Charlie?'

'I don't like it.' He burst into tears and Claire felt her eyes fill.

'But it's bling,' said Pearl. 'And look,' she scrambled into the car and patted her brother's seat. 'It's our old car seats, Charlie, all mingy like usual.'

'I want the Silver Bullet.' His face crumpled and he squidged it into Claire's stomach. She held his head.

'Oh Charlie, sorry. The Silver Bullet was very old. It was time to say goodbye.'

Charlie howled. 'But I *didn't* say goodbye.'

'Would you like to?'

He nodded.

'Charlie, wait.' Claire jumped out of the car as her boy pelted across Steve's forecourt, leapt up and straddled the bonnet like a starfish.

'It's alright, Mummy. Let him,' said Pearl.

From his office, Steve smiled then pulled a sad face.

'All right, Charlie. That's enough.'

Fair play to Pearl, she'd given him a full three seconds. Charlie slid off the bonnet, newly grimy. 'I feel a bit better now, Mum.'

Two Swifts happy, one to go.

'How has this even happened?'

Ben didn't think it was brilliant. The skin of his neck flushed red. The Miseries' net twitched behind him.

'Steve did a trade-in. He gave us five hundred quid, which is more than we'd have got in a private sale.'

'We weren't selling it.' Ben threw out his arms and Charlie ducked out of the way.

'The clutch was a gamble, Steve said so. And the exhaust.'

'So why not come home and tell me that?'

Claire shut her eyes. He was right. Why hadn't she?

'We talk about stuff, Claire. Well, we used to. I'd say let's get a whatever, and you'd say, "Don't just go out and *buy* one, let's think about it for five years or swap one for an illustration." But you've bought this car? You own it?'

He was gesturing at her like she and the car were separate from him.

'Yes. It's our car. I got a loan from Steve and the insurance is sorted.'

He rubbed his eyes. 'I can't believe this. Do you remember the grief you gave me when I bought a new kettle without consulting you?'

Claire looked at her hands.

'I'm going for a walk,' said Ben. 'I can't talk about this right now.'

'Wait Daddy,' said Charlie. 'I'll come.'

They took off with their heads down, Charlie scuttling to keep up.

Claire gulped tears and turned to the porch to share a moment with Pearl.

Pearl's arms were folded. 'You didn't say Dad didn't know.'

'No. No, I didn't.'

'So even though the car is amazing, and when you've been on your course you'll learn how to get paid, I'm not talking to you either.'

Chapter 17

Tock-tock, the car announced into the 6 a.m. quiet.

Claire shoved the holdall packed with clothes, her laptop, notebook and art materials into the massive boot. She climbed into the car and drove out of Headleigh.

It was going to be fine. No one on Andrea's course would guess that she and her husband hadn't really spoken for three nights because there'd been no cooling-off period on the loan and Steve had sold the Silver Bullet.

Really, it would be fine.

She could busk this. In her gold trainers, vintage Levi's and abstract patterned top, she barely looked like an imposter at all.

The course would be fine! She wasn't even going to be late. She had tons of time to get to Didcot for 8.30 registration.

Somewhere around Leighton Buzzard, she punched on the radio and smacked out a heavy metal drum beat on the steering wheel. Deathmetalfan still hadn't sent more details on Murdon Farm. What were they trying to hide? What if the Wellbeloveds drove down when school broke up to find Claire's Cottages uninhabitable? That would be very shit. She had absolutely no idea what she was going to be dealing with there. The course was an unknown too. Andrea might make them go round the room. Some of them might not be recent graduates, but they'd all be graduates, they'd have degrees and contacts, and maybe confidence.

How would she introduce herself?

Hi, I'm Claire. Andrea was lovely about my final-year project, so I went home and ripped it up because that made perfect sense to me. Then I started something different, but I'd lost my way and fell into a depression. Anyway, it's great to be here!

Claire shuddered. It *had* made sense to rip up her final-year project, at the time.

She'd taken the project to Andrea and laid it out and showed her tutor how elements linked between paintings and line drawings and answered the supportively probing questions on the themes. Andrea had seemed excited and moved. She said the work was 'joyful' and 'hilarious' and 'really quite brilliant', and her chunky earrings swayed back and forth like they agreed.

Claire had floated back to her clothes-strewn room and landed on the bed in a state of amazement. Andrea had been *so* enthusiastic, *so* positive.

Bless her though, that's how Andrea was. Her comment on hearing a loo would be installed on the third floor of the art building had been, 'That's *phenomenal* news.'

She'd said Claire's work was 'really quite brilliant'. Claire had hoped the work was *good*. She'd never have dared hope it was brilliant. Brilliant was ... too much. It was nothing like the feedback Margo gave her. 'That's not quite it,' her mother would say, 'look again.' And her highest praise: 'That's pretty much there.'

Claire lay on her bed and thought about it. A new toilet on the third floor wasn't 'phenomenal' even if the current nearest *was* on the the first floor. A new toilet was 'great' or maybe 'much more convenient'. Andrea's thing was to gussy stuff up with well-meaning hyperbole. Claire's eyes suddenly widened as she stared at her poster-covered ceiling, the air gone out of her. Andrea gussied everything up, so ergo, her work was almost definitely *not* brilliant, which meant, it seemed to her in that untethering moment, that it could be *anything*.

Margo said art was pain. Claire's work made Andrea 'happy just to look at it'.

Like a kid's work.

Margo's work was serious.

Her own was ... silly.

Perhaps it was awful.

It *was* awful.

That was all it had taken. A flash of doubt which spread, collapsing each cell of self-belief to lay bare the gauche silliness of what she'd made.

It was amazing how small you could fold and tear months of work. How mundane it had looked when it was done. One swing bin liner, handles in a bow.

'Devastating. *Total* tragedy,' Andrea had said, and she had done her best to nod and smile at the work Claire began to produce in its place, but Andrea had known, they both had, that Claire was out of the game.

*

Claire pulled up behind a truck. Somewhere between Leighton Buzzard and Aylesbury she'd switched off the radio to attend to her breathing. In for four, hold for four, out for seven.

Of *course* she was going on the course. She was feeling the fear and doing it anyway and once this traffic cleared she'd swing a left onto the A34, get to Didcot, have a nice breakfast and go and register. *Hey, hi, I'm Claire, and you're …?*

She pulled a hair off her patterned sleeve. She tried to flick it away, but it stuck to her sweaty hand.

It wasn't mandatory to force yourself to go somewhere if your panic increased with every mile you drew closer. She didn't *have* to go to Didcot. She had options.

Option one. Go to Didcot, leak panic, pollute the course for everyone, feel like an arsehole.

Option two. Go home, tell her favourite people that she'd panicked, shred their last morsel of belief in her, feel like an arsehole.

Hideous rock. Vile hard place. Wait. There was a third option. Go to *Bodlowe*. Go to Bodlowe, check the cottages weren't a crack den, *tell no one* she'd gone there, feel like an arsehole but in *secret*. She could swing right, go round Oxford, pick up the road to Swindon and drive on to Cornwall. The clock on the dash said 6.45. She'd be there by lunchtime.

So, what, like, just not go on the course at all? Ha ha ha ha, that was a ridiculous idea.

She took a right.

*

The closer to Bodlowe, the greyer the sky. Then rain. So much rain. The wipers on Silver Bullet Two did their job admirably and went like the clappers and she couldn't help but love her car.

She stopped for coffee but couldn't face breakfast. She called Andrea, hands trembling. 'I'm so sorry, Andrea. I can't get there. I've got a personal situation. A family thing.'

Andrea said she'd refund the money, and that Claire should come on the course another time. Claire drove on, wretched at how little she deserved the kindness. It was only when she was sitting in traffic just outside Bodlowe that the enormity of what she'd done really hit her.

She hadn't gone on her course. She'd come to Bodlowe.

If Ben knew, the chilliness between them would freeze hard.

So what now, Claire? Are you going to spend two days wailing to yourself about how terrible you are? Or are you going to make the most of it, turn it into a fact-finding mission?

Positive self-talk voice had a point. She could get to know Bodlowe. If she could hustle up the necessary boldness, she could pop into cafés, ask customers to rate the coffee and check menus. She could suss out which deli and beachy tat shop had the edge for cheese or the best rainy-day toy fun. She needed somewhere to stay. She spotted a B&B with vacancies. A thin white townhouse, with black window frames. She parked at the rear, getting soaked as she ran back round.

A woman with a jumper full of static and dandruff at her temples said they didn't do early check-in but grudgingly took Claire's holdall, and, less grudgingly, payment for the night and lent her an enormous golf umbrella.

Claire headed to the centre of the towllage. The word had risen from her memory to annoy her. Honor called Bodlowe a towllage because it was a villagey small town. The umbrella began to close so she pushed it up harder, skinning her finger.

Dear universe, I know I shouldn't be here but I'm a long way from home, so please give me a break.

The rain stopped like a tap turning off. The sun's heat was instant. Gulls bickered overhead. Claire hurried to the seafront where light sparkled on the water and on the harbour boats and brought out the colours of the lovely cafés and ice-cream parlours and with it rolled a heinous waft of weapons-grade sewage.

People recoiled around her. Claire threw an arm across her face and tried to outrun the smell by rushing back up the slope. The village centre was being taped off. She called to an unhappy man in waders. 'Any idea when it'll be sorted?'

He shrugged. 'It's shit creak down there, burst main. We're closing off the harbour next.'

What now? It filled her with dread, but she should go and look at the cottages. The sea was high on the sand so she wouldn't be able to reach Murdon Farm from the beach. She passed a cash machine near the B&B so got her bank card out. The screen said insufficient funds, twice. She pushed her card back in and asked for a tenner. Nothing. It must be a mistake, there hadn't been any big bills lately. Wait, she'd bought a freaking *car*. The first instalment and down payment must have left her account. Just as well she'd paid for the B&B. She opened her purse. She had seventeen pence for two days in Bodlowe. Her budget for what had become her get-one-step-ahead-of-my-spendy-toxic-frenemy fact-finding mission was eight and a half pence a day.

She staggered to a bench and slumped like a town drunk. Hopefully, the B&B didn't have anyone of a nervous disposition staying, because in around twenty hours she'd be falling on that Full English like George Clooney's Fantastic Mr Fox. At least her card had worked to buy that coffee on the A30 before the money cleared. Shame she hadn't bought petrol for the journey home. She was trapped in a stinking towllage where she shouldn't even be. She clapped her hands to her thighs. *Ah well, best get on.* There were derelict holiday cottages she was responsible for to visit.

Claire asked directions, and as a carpet fitter's van was blocking her in at the B&B, she headed on foot up a lane

towards the coast road, making herself notice her surround-
ings: gulls, salty air, weeny packed together houses with
twisty bricks.

Well done Claire. You're coping really well.

'I have seventeen pence.' She opened the Bodlowe leaflet
she'd picked up from a stand.

*You can't go to the town museum or try the horse-drawn tour,
but once Bodlowe opens, you can visit the beaches and suss out the
play parks and keep an eye out for any food that—*

She let the thought trail off. Her positive self-talk had
some life-enhancing ideas but searching bins for chips was
not one of them.

She stopped for a breather. The coast road might be a
longer route from Bodlowe to the cottages but you got a
good view of the harbour and the lanes that cobwebbed back
from it. The houses had become sparse now and up ahead,
beyond some trees, a field of corn swayed in the breeze.
She'd focused so much attention on Honor, she should take
a moment to appreciate everything else about coming to
Bodlowe, starting with the fact that it was stunning.

She hadn't spent much time at the seaside as a child.
Margo had thought holidays were feeble, something that
purposeless people who didn't have art filled their empty
lives with. They'd been on the odd day trip to Brighton
and Hastings and once, an overnight visit to Whitstable but
Margo had spent the whole time painting, her equipment
strewn across the stones like she owned the place.

Claire and Ben and the kids weren't travelling to Glasgow
this summer, so they wouldn't have to fit round Margo's
crazy painting hours, and they wouldn't be at Ben's parents
either. It could feel like freedom to be at the seaside for
two weeks with Ben and the kids; maybe it could even be
wonderful.

Claire continued along the coast road. She spotted a rusty metal sign for Murdon Farm Cottages and turned onto a track with farm outbuildings either side that looked one hundred per cent messy farm and zero per cent welcoming holiday home. 'Oh shiiiit.'

She could hear nothing except birds and the sea. The only vehicle had no wheels and was under a tarpaulin. She walked further, trying to give off an aura of *I know I shouldn't be here but I'm harmless so please don't turn a gun on me.*

'Hello,' she called. 'Is anybody here?'

Nothing. The cottages had been whitewashed at some point but were now grubby and stained, with flowering weeds growing out of the gutters and cracks in the walls. Claire slapped a hand to her forehead. They were worse than the photo. They were joined in a T with the sea beyond the top. A broken window was covered with cardboard. The frames were grey, cracked and flaking. The window glass was filthy with blown sand. Junk mail stuck out of both letterboxes.

The space between the cottages and the clifftop was strewn with rusting spiky farmyard machinery, bags of rotten potatoes, bits of old greenhouse and chopped-up tree. There was definitely no room to land a helicopter. In fact the utter un-Blue Gablesness of Murdon Farm Cottages, their complete unsuitability as anyone's, let alone a Wellbeloved, holiday residence was almost laughable. They hadn't even been cheap.

Sweat coated her as indignation rose. Her face felt as brightly patterned as her top. She knocked on both doors and waited. When no one came, she circled the buildings, calling out hello, then knocked again.

She leaned her hand on the dirty glass of a window to see into the cluttered hall. The inside handle of the casement fell off and the window opened. Claire's indignation met a compulsion to see inside. She checked the track and called again through the window. Standing on a boot scraper, she reached up her other leg and poked her gold-trainered foot through. Leaning forward to grab the frame, she pulled herself to mid-thigh, then toed up the wall to inch in. Six months ago, she'd never have had the strength, flexibility or desperation for breaking and entering.

She was halfway through the window when she heard an engine. Her instinct was to shut her eyes and hope for invisibility, even though it never worked for Charlie. A car door clanged shut and slow footsteps crunched towards her.

'What on earth are you doing, young lady?'

Chapter 18

'Sorry, please don't be angry.' She was shaking.

The craggy man in checked shirt and utility trousers looked amused. His massive straggly eyebrows rose and fell above his eyes like two clumps of tumbleweed. 'You're climbing through the window.'

'I know, I'm sorry.' She shimmied out, her thigh scraping on the frame. She hid her face. 'I don't know why I did it.'

'Me neither. Why would you? Keys are in the usual place.'

This was weird. He pointed at her, smiling. 'I know who you are. Come on, let's get that hoover he promised you. Sandy, isn't it?' He ambled to the front door and took a key from under the mat. 'Dad said his cleaner was a nice young blonde.'

This was mad. But she'd get a look in a cottage if he thought she was Sandy. And if she admitted she wasn't, the mood would change, abruptly.

'Brian, by the way. Brian Baxter.'

He might be Deathmetalfan's dad. Perhaps he'd spent years yelling, 'Turn that Godawful racket down!'

Claire took his enormous hand. 'C—Sandy.'

'Short for Cassandra is it?'

'Er, just Sandy.'

She picked up the golf umbrella and rubbing sweat off her lip, followed him into a cluttered cottage living room, dark behind a tattered curtain.

'So he's settling in well at the home, me Dad.'

'Glad to hear it.' Claire rounded her voice to sound a bit like Brian's as her eyes roved the room.

'Not cheap, mind.' Brian patted the wall. 'But we don't want to sell, we was born here me and my brother, so we're renting them out, Mike's idea. Couple of families have booked for a fortnight in the holidays.'

'Right.' Worlds crashed into each other, giving Claire a sudden headache. The lies were piling up like kindling.

'The agents give some pointers to get them to spec. I'm going to clear them out, fix 'em up, put in a few bits.' He whacked his massive hands together. 'Sorted. Mike's busy but I can handle it, I know what I'm doing.'

Something about the way Brian seemed to be convincing himself emboldened her. 'So there won't be that stuff out the front?'

'Oh no, Sandy. They've got kiddies. I'm going to make a good job of this, throw a few hundred quid at it. Do you think I can't make a good job of it?'

Claire held up her hands. 'No no, I'm sure you can.'

'Mind you, I en't got the foggiest where to start. I could do with some help with the sorting.' He looked almost bashful. 'I don't suppose you've got time today, have you? If you can do a few hours I'll give you fifty quid, make it sixty as it's the weekend.'

Claire was suddenly so hungry that if he'd handed her sixty quid she'd have eaten it. *Do not rush into this.*

'Let me have a think. Can I pop to the bathroom?'

'Help yourself. Either way I'll find that hoover.'

Her whole body throbbing with wrongness, she peeked into the kitchen on the other side of the hall. Like the sitting room it was crammed full of papers and farming magazines and murky old jars. The floor had sticky-looking vinyl over the flagstones. Sandy was obviously pretty laissez-faire. Claire climbed the creaking wooden stairs. The bedroom doors were shut. The bathroom was filled with sun from a skylight. It smelled of mildew and TCP.

She didn't feel like she was really there. In the smeary mirror, the pale-faced Claire with the dark circles under her eyes looked gobsmacked. She was tired from the drive, and dehydrated, and not much more than five hours ago she'd closed the door on her family's home in Luton, and now she was a Cornish cleaner bequeathed a hoover by a fond elderly client.

Think this through, Claire. How big a hole are you digging?

If she said no to helping, and slipped away, Brian Baxter might not remember her, but if she spent a few hours with him, she'd have to look different when she came back in July. A radical hair change, big sunnies, a baseball hat, a false beard. She'd have to skulk around in the background and let the others deal with him ... but then, sixty quid.

She splashed cold water on her face with trembling fingers. Brian said he could handle sorting the cottages, that he knew what he was doing. But 'put in a few bits' was vague. Plus he'd said he didn't have the foggiest where to start. It was in her interest to influence him. Being Sandy today would mean helping the cottages be better, and eating. And maybe it was Mike, the brother, who was Deathmetalfan. Who knew, maybe Mike would be the one around in August if he was busy now, maybe Brian was doing this part and wouldn't be here. Perhaps she wouldn't need to spend her holiday in disguise.

Well done, Claire. Even when you don't know where this is going, you're travelling hopefully.

She took some long gulps from the cold tap and went downstairs.

Brian was carrying a tower of old telephone directories outside. He'd taken his checked shirt off. His T-shirt was printed with a maggot-eyed skull with the name of a band underneath.

'Does that say "Hullfire"?' she asked.

'Yeah.'

Yeah. Brian was probably Deathmetalfan. Did this mean she was digging a bigger hole? She couldn't keep up with her spadework.

'They en't from round here.'

'Are they from Hull?

'That's right.' He looked impressed. 'You know 'em?'

'Don't think so.'

He quarter-turned the Land Rover key and poked a CD into the player. An assault of the fastest, most unpleasant music she'd ever heard drilled from the speakers. He laughed and switched it off.

'New album. Bit softer than usual. European tour starts fourteenth July. I've got tickets for every gig, Sandy, I'm away six weeks straight, it'll be magnificent.'

She did a quick calculation. 'Does that mean you're away till the end of August?'

'Yep, back first week September.'

'Sounds great.' She fizzed with gratitude, certain she did not deserve this. 'Hey, so I've thought things through and I *can* help you today.'

Brian was delighted. He rang someone to bring a trailer.

'I'll be all over Germany when these families come,' he said. They were transporting a trunk full of what looked like antique milking equipment through the cottage. 'In fact I'm looking for a helper to see 'em in like, Mike'll be too busy I expect. Someone to check they're legit and be on hand to sort any problems. Don't suppose you'd be up for that would you?'

Claire could almost feel her mind bending as she dropped her end of the trunk onto the ground. 'Sorry Brian. I don't think I'm the right person for the job.'

★

Brian and Mike had already removed what they were keeping from the cottages. The other one had been empty a couple of years and the electrics and boiler had been fixed. It had the same layout and similar furniture to its neighbour but was known as 'the Fancy House'. Brian said he'd tell 'Sandy' the story about it later.

Brian's gangly employee arrived with a trailer. Claire kept back vases and various knick-knacks, some lovely woollen blankets and lamps and old tins and small bits of furniture. Brian wasn't convinced, but complied.

The bedrooms had built-in cupboards that looked like they'd been installed in the nineteen thirties. She persuaded him he shouldn't tear them out. The mattresses, pillows and carpets however, had to go. The floorboards were in great shape underneath. He wanted to get rid of the cottages' worn brown wooden-legged sofas and easy chairs, but Claire thought they had potential. Out in the barn he showed her replacements he'd bought from a friend, massive boxy things that would suck all the space out of the small rooms. She suggested keeping them in the barn for the kids and getting a table-tennis table and some other games, maybe putting in a sand pit.

Brian thought this was a 'smashing idea', it reminded him he'd mentioned a play barn to 'the woman', after something Mike had said.

Claire wrote 'table tennis' on Brian's list of things to source, then shuddered a yawn and rubbed her gritty eyes.

'I told the woman there were no more photos 'cause I didn't want her put off,' Brian admitted sheepishly.

'Maybe you should send her some when it's finished.'

He agreed he would.

Once the loaded trailer had left, Brian wondered if a better use of Sandy's time would be to accompany him shopping, as he didn't have 'a ruddy clue' what he needed to get.

They went to a huge out-of-town supermarket and filled and refilled trollies with duvets and bedding and tea towels and oven gloves, then cutlery, knives, pots and pans, trays, kettles and toasters, table lamps and plates and cups and saucers, and a few small pastel artisan-style ceramic bowls.

'Them bowls is all wonky,' said Brian.

Claire smiled. 'It's on purpose, it's the style. They've all been made wonky in the same way by a machine.'

'Ruddy bonkers.'

Claire picked out a notebook for Brian. She found a list of condiments and groceries that the internet decreed holiday properties should provide and they gathered them up while adding things to Brian's list for sorting out. Brian bought them meal deals for the journey back and Claire had never been more grateful for a freezing soggy Ploughmans.

She'd eaten three bites when her phone buzzed in her pocket. She licked her fingers and pulled it out.

Ben: Hope all going well xx

Her fingers flew over the screen. If she wrote back fast it was done.

Claire: Great thanks! xx

Because that, at least, was not a lie. She couldn't face the rest of the sandwich.

When she and Brian had locked the homewares safely in an outbuilding, he showed her a path, beyond the gate at the edge of the property, that became steps down to a stretch of beach. Beyond an overhanging crag some way beneath were barnacled rocks and a crescent of dark wet sand. It was beautiful. She grabbed the rail by the steps. She was in the wings looking down to a stage where her holiday would play out. Who would she be, its hero or victim?

While Brian lopped garden overgrowth, Claire sat in the sun on the straw-like grass, leaning back against a raised bed of weeds beyond the rusty machinery. She made sketches in Brian's notebook of how the rooms might look with the little wonky bowls among the lovely old tins and other Baxter bits on the dresser. With the sofas and chairs re-covered and a mix of the new bedding and the old woollen blankets.

She and Brian sat and pored over the pictures.

'This is ruddy amazing, Sandy.'

Claire's whole body felt like a big smile. Pride. She was proud of herself. She might have rescued their summer holiday.

She left with three twenties in her purse. He walked with her up the track to the coast road.

'The hoover,' he exclaimed. 'You've gone without what you come for.' She smiled. She'd achieved so much more than what she'd come for. 'It's fine,' she said. 'You'll need it. It's on your list to get cleaners in the week before your guests come.'

'Aren't you going to do it?'

'Sorry Brian, I won't be available then.'

'You'll have to pop in at some point. See how they look all painted up.'

'I'll see them, don't worry. They're going to be great.'

'Yeah, they are. Thanks a ton for getting things started. I'm going all out on them cottages, every spare moment between now and the fourteenth of July. Mike's going to see I *have* got what it takes.'

He danced around then jabbed with both arms like a boxer. 'He'll see. And the wife might think about coming back an' all.'

'There's lots to do. I hope it all works out.'

'We can rent them through the year when they're done. I tell you Sandy, I haven't felt this pumped since the I Wish You Torment tour in twenty-sixteen. That was Hullfire at their peak. Things run their course, don't they.'

He looked down the track. 'D'you know what, I could give the tour a miss.'

The fields behind Brian seemed to rush nearer.

'What? No!' said Claire. 'Look at you. You love them. In your T-shirt and everything.'

He touched his huge palm lightly on her shoulder. 'But Sandy, I want to give them families the care and attention you've given me today.'

'But you've got all those tickets, Brian. Every Hullfire gig. They're bound to play some of your favourites.'

He nodded and smiled. 'I'm going to sell 'em on, Sandy. I'm staying put. I'm going to be here to welcome my first guests.'

Chapter 19

Claire walked back through open, but still smelly Bodlowe. Brian's Hullfire U-turn had somewhat enlived her central nervous system. On the way back to the B&B she found herself checking out a random selection of cafés and pubs, jangling like she'd caught herself on the wrong end of a cattle prod.

She entered the damp and lavender-scented B&B and went upstairs to shower. Although the loo was down the landing, the shower cubicle was in the corner of her room: *in*-suite.

She dressed in black jeans and a sweatshirt with a scribble pattern on the front, the clothes she'd picked out for day two of the course. As she appraised herself in front of a wall mirror, her stomach curdled like it was fertilizing an ulcer from her guilt and shame. Objectively she was not especially memorable. Pale, blonde, thirties. Smallish boobs, a pear if she were any fruit. She disguised her hair in a quiffy half-up, half-down arrangement, thickly lined her eyes top and bottom, and instead of her usual clear balm, painted blusher on her lips because it wasn't just Brian she didn't want to be remembered by. It was everyone.

She went out into Bodlowe with the golf umbrella, which she definitely shouldn't have assumed it was still all right to borrow. People dressed for more rain passed either side of her. The sky rumbled threateningly. She caught the toe of a trainer on a cobble and then her garish reflection in the window of a bar. She wasn't Sandy and she didn't look much like Claire.

She passed the Pheasant, a restaurant Honor raved about, went in and ordered a main course, more self-conscious about her made-up face than eating alone. She'd have thirty-eight pounds left of her ill-gotten wages.

Her review of the Pheasant was 'a bit up itself and pricey', not that she knew much about eating fish in fancy restaurants. The sorrel sauce was nice though, lemony.

Afterwards, she was drawn to the flashes and bloops of an arcade. Machines said 'Uh-oh,' and 'You're going the wrong way!' Claire dropped a pound into a machine that changed it into smelly coppers and watched a woman with glazed eyes slot coin after coin into a cakewalk full of two-pence pieces. Claire picked a machine and tried to time her drops to nudge the lake of enmeshed coins teetering over the exit to break apart and fall.

Turning up here in the summer, trying to look different, insisting this 'Sandy' she apparently looked the spit of must be a doppelganger was a horrible extra anxiety. She'd have to tell Brian who she was, email a confession in a few days when she felt calmer and hope he didn't respond badly. She won a few coins, and posted them back in, and then all fifty coins were gone. It seemed like a lot of careful input to walk away empty-handed. A bit like life.

It was much darker outside when she left the arcade. It wasn't the Vegas effect, it was only ten past seven. She legged it to the B&B and lay in the dip of her single mattress as rain thundered. This was not how she'd imagined her Saturday night away.

She remembered a rack of leaflets in the B&B's hall and brought a handful upstairs, laying them on the ridged cotton bedspread. She pored through them sussing out the attractions and how you got there, looking them up on Trip-advisor and taking notes. She opened out a Bodlowe street plan with shops, eating places and galleries marked on, and kneeled on the floor with her elbows on the bed learning the street names and routes between them, preparation for tests Honor would probably set her next time she was here.

Eventually, she cleared them off and thudded back into the dip. What might Ben and the kids be doing? What might Honor be doing while she was lying on a tatty camberwick cover in rainy Bodlowe?

It had been weeks since she'd delved into Honor's online existence. Katie had made Claire mute her, and she definitely felt better for it. But even though she knew it would hurt more than heal, she binged through Honor's social media. Unlike the random pictures Claire posted herself, of the kids being nutters, or a water spill on a table in the shape of a guitar, or a fox on a fly-tipped sofa by a dumped TV, Honor featured in every picture she posted, often in sunglasses, her mile-long legs taking centre stage, in ski wear in cable car selfies, or hot-dogging in the sun. Even her drinks photos from mini-breaks with Chris or solo retreats featured at least one posed lower limb and always a comment like 'At last', '… and breathe', or 'Can't believe I'm finally here.'

Bursts of panic and sporadically creaking bed-springs punctuated the long night. Claire would have to confess to Brian face to face. If she could sort things out with him, and pay him back all his money down the line, then Ben, Katie, and what they thought about where she was, well, that might never need dealing with.

She went in to breakfast achey and wretched and watched purposeful oldies heaping bowls with buffet prunes while the B&B owner, flushed and flakey-scalped, ferried hot plates of food to tables. It was as though pretending to be someone else had dehydrated her soul, and bacon and eggs had never seemed less appealing. So much for Fantastic Mr Fox.

She checked out, and drove round the coast road wondering if there was an angle that would make her sound less like a lunatic. As she neared the turning where she'd left Brian the day before, she remembered him dancing around at the thought he might impress his brother. Maybe she and Brian had something in common.

She could hear him before she saw him. It sounded like the Hullfire tour had begun a few weeks early, in Cornwall on a Sunday morning. He was up a ladder sanding window frames and came down delighted to see her. He switched off the music.

'Morning Sandy. Guess what? I put all my Hullfire tickets on Stub Hub and Stuttgart sold in ten minutes. You all right?'

'I've done something really bad, Brian.'

His unruly brows shot up. 'What have you done?'

'I'm not Sandy. I'm Claire Swift.'

His eyes closed to slits. 'Why do I know that name?'

She told him. And she told him about Honor and how rubbish she made her feel and what an incredible cook she was and how anxious Claire had been about the holiday and what the cottages were like. Part way through, Brian got his flask and his pack of Tunnocks Teacakes and they went down the stepped path to the beach and sat against rocks.

'So there you are Brian, that's my story.'

She held out the money. 'Here's what's left of Sandy's wages. I'll transfer the rest as soon as I can.'

'What? Don't be daft, you earned it.' He threw some pebbles into the shallows.

'There's some people what get in yer head, isn't there? It's

Mike for me. I've spent my life trying to be more like him. Even though he's a bastard.'

'You don't seem like a bastard Brian, you seem nice.'

'Well you're a nice lady Sa— I mean Claire. It's a shame this Honor makes you feel bad.'

'I wish she didn't have such a hold on me. I just want a lovely holiday with my family. And the thing is, Brian, they don't know I'm here,' she swallowed. The magnitude of what she was saying was written all over his concerned face. 'No one knows, and they can't know.'

'Is it our secret?' he whispered, anxiously.

Claire gave one small nod, as though barely moving her head made them less complicit.

Brian tapped his nose. 'Not a dicky bird.'

She looked up at the cottages. 'Did you say there was a story, about the cottages?'

Brian chuckled. 'Oh yeah. You'll love it. So, back in eighteen sixty odd, the Murdon brothers, me ma's great-grandad and his brother, had to build their farmhouse as two cottages because their wives didn't get on, just like you and whatserface.' He circled a finger at her. 'The wives wanted them separate but it was too dear, they had to be joined, so they was made with a connecting door inside for future generations what got on all right.

'The cottages was supposed to be the exact same but Great-Great-Grandad's brother's wife who was a bit above herself, she tweaked this and that on the plans to make her cottage better, but Great-Great-Grandma always got wind of it, and *she* wanted decorative wood in the porch, bigger boot scraper, whatever. Anyway, the twist was just before they start digging the foundations, her ladyship gets them to angle the plans round, so her sea view is more advantageous. Her sister-in-law never called her by her name again. She was always "her at the Fancy House".'

Claire chuckled. 'I think that's the cottage Honor should stay in.'

It was time to go. Claire thought she should have a paddle before she left. She took off her trainers at the water's edge then hopped back as liquid ice hit her toes.

She thanked Brian and left him putting his 'I'll show Mike' energy into the window frames.

She drove to the petrol station in Bodlowe then parked up, realising she must have left the golf umbrella at the arcade the night before. She rushed there but the umbrella had gone. She jogged along to the B&B and drenched the woman with apologies, promising to send a replacement.

On the way back to the car, she had a quick look at the town's crazy golf course. The obstacles were planks and treasure chests and telescopes with a big pirate ship for playing on.

An older couple in head-to-toe taupe were encouraging a teen to try a hole. Things were tense. The teen's shot went awry, and he mic-dropped the flimsy club. Once he'd stomped past, Claire gave the couple a sympathetic smile.

The woman held out the club. 'Like to join us?'

Because it was nice to be asked, Claire did. She looked down at the club and the hole she was aiming at, then twatted the ball into the litter-strewn scrub. Classic.

'Oh dear. Let's take you back through it,' said the man. 'Plant your feet square to give a nice base. Shirley will show you.'

Shirley bent and wriggled her rear.

'Have at it my love,' her husband enouraged. She had at it. 'Well played. Now young lady, try again.'

'With you in a sec.' Claire was counting how many holes

were still to play, tempted to mic-drop her own club and escape more mansplanation. Then her phone rang and she excused herself to pick up the call.

'Hey Katie.' Guilt crumbed her voice and she cleared her throat. 'How's it going at the Halls?'

'Lovely, even better than we hoped, and you've been missed. How's the course?'

'Yeah, good, just on a break.'

'Cool, this won't take long. I just wanted to say I think Ben's come round a tiny bit about the car. I reminded him about all the disagreements you had about buying the last one and he said that was the one benefit of not having been consulted this time.'

Claire laughed. 'Thanks, Katie.'

'Your turn, young lady, Long John Silver Corner awaits.'

'Who's that?'

'I don't know,' said Claire, panic making her uppity. 'Don't worry about it.'

'You playing or what?' called the man. 'We've to drop the lad back to Newquay in a bit.'

'Newquay?' said Katie. 'Claire, where are you?'

'It's … I'm …'

'Oh my God, you went to Bodlowe. You're in Bodlowe, aren't you?'

'Don't tell Ben. Please don't tell Ben.'

There was muffled conversation at Katie's end.

'Ben's right here, Claire. Just putting him on.'

'All right? How's things?'

'Great, great, really good. Just going in for another session right now.'

The man was approaching with her club. She backed towards the pirate ship feeling like a hand was round her throat.

'Come on, young lady, finish what you've started.'

'Is that ... that's not Ivan is it?' said Ben.

'No! It's not Ivan. Hold on a sec.' Claire mouthed, 'Sorry,' at the golfers and ran towards the car, gulping back tears.

'Ben, I love you, I've missed you. When it rained, the wipers on the car were brilliant. I could properly see out. It felt really safe.'

'OK. Well, I guess safe is good.'

Chapter 20

She was home in time to read to the kids.

'Did you make any friends?' asked Pearl.

'The people were very nice.' Claire turned to hang up Pearl's school sweatshirt, screwing her eyes shut as Brian's craggy face and eyebrows came to mind.

'Who was nicest?'

'Tanya,' Claire blurted, plucking the name out of nowhere. 'There was someone called Tanya. She was lovely.'

Ben stroked her back. 'I'm really pleased you went.'

They watched Ben's TV show. She told him there was no need to try and explain anything.

On Monday afternoon she went out for some air and bumped into Katie with a cardboard tray of hot drinks in each hand.

'I've been getting coffees for everyone at work,' Katie said, blowing at hair that had fallen in her eyes. 'We're knackered from the open weekend.'

Claire looked down. Her feet straddled a crack in the pavement.

'I was so happy thinking of you on that course, Claire. I thought you'd turned a corner. I thought you'd finally real-ised the value of your work, that you'd stopped comparing yourself with your mum, but it turns out that like everything these days, it was all about Honor.'

Claire glanced at Katie's face. 'Are we not all right then?'

'Not particularly.'

She felt the acid sting of a bit more ulcer construction. 'OK. I'll let you get back. I could collect the boys later.'

'In the motorised sore point?'

'Ben's coming round. You said so yourself.'

'And I'm supposed to come round about where you spent the weekend?'

'I hope so. The course fee's being refunded and I could go another time. I'm glad I went to Bodlowe, Katie. It was worth it, to me anyway.'

'You know what,' Katie lifted a tray and rubbed her chin with her forearm, 'I'm glad I was there the evening Honor came over. I'm glad I got a look at the woman my best friend's been hijacked by.'

Claire couldn't remember a time Katie had said anything so painful. She watched her walk a few steps, then stop and sigh and turn round.

'I'm not *not* talking to you, Claire. But please don't give me any more reason not to.'

★

Days went by and the secret of the weekend hung heavily. It was too horrible to think about confessing. Ben would feel so betrayed if he knew. She arranged an overdraft to cover the next car payment and was scrupulous to buy no more than usual from their joint account in case it looked like Peter being robbed to pay Paul. She found a wooden-handled golf umbrella in great condition for a quid at a boot sale and sent it to the B&B landlady. She worked through bags and boxes of brown freezer food, cooked a double quantity of macaroni cheese from a finicky recipe, labelled it BODLOWE and froze it.

At the start of the penultimate week of term, Claire and the kids were squeezing their way through the muddle of buggies and scooters at the school gates when Fran rushed up and took her hand.

'Glad I've caught you.'

'What is it? You're beaming, Fran, did no one tell you it's Monday?'

'I'm moving to St Joseph's in September. The wife of one of their teaching assistants has just got a job in York.'

'What? Why are you leaving? Wait, I know why.'

Fran nodded. 'I can't work with my boyfriend and thirty kids, it's not appropriate. Minds are definitely not on jobs.

Claire looked at Fran's bright face. 'So it's the real deal?'

'Yes, it's the real deal. We're going to see his parents next weekend, apparently they'll love me.' She pressed fingertips into her cheeks.

Claire laughed. 'That's fantastic and of course they'll love you. I'll miss you Fran, I love our job share.' She pulled Fran into a hug.

'Me too,' said Fran, squeezing tightly. 'We'll hang out though.'

'Excellent.' They let each other go. 'What did Gunnar say about you leaving?'

'I thought she'd be pissed at the lack of notice, but she was grateful for my honesty and praised our "discretion".'

'Jeez. Only because I saved her from seeing you "discretion" all over each other in the classroom that morning.'

Fran laughed and punched Claire gently on the shoulder. 'So, my hours are available. And Isobel wants a classroom role, and I want her to spend every day with Grant this much.' She held up a tightly squeezed finger and thumb, 'So why don't you go get those hours, crazy massive car-loan lady.'

Claire walked back down the hill. The air was humid,

the trees were completely still and her chest was thumping. Should she go for Fran's hours? Another car payment would go out before Bodlowe. If she had a contract for full-time hours she could extend her overdraft further over the summer. But Ben would be pissed off. He'd think the course had been a waste of time if she wasn't going to build her freelance work. But then she hadn't gone on the course, so she was damned if she did and damned if she didn't and just plain damned anyway. Not that there was anything wrong with being a teaching assistant. The work was rewarding. But the thought of telling Honor she was going full time made her queasy. It was like saying yes, I've entirely surrendered to the part of me you see as small and docile, so go ahead and sneer your high-flying smile.

Of course she should go for Fran's hours. She should go for them like gangbusters and get the car paid for and she was bloody lucky for the opportunity.

Claire emailed Mrs Gunnarson to apply to go full time. At collection a couple of days later, the Head was in the playground, her demeanour screaming *I'm here and can be approached, but, you know, don't.* Claire squirmed past her, embarrassed not to have heard back from her email, tailed by Pearl and Charlie bickering over who was bashing who with their lunch bag.

'Claire,' Gunnar's voice ripped across the playground. Claire scurried back. 'Are you free for interview next Tuesday, say ten thirty?'

'Absolutely. Yes, yes I am.'

'Good. See you then.'

She decided to wait and see how the interview panned out before telling Ben. She was boosted by going back through resources she'd used for her job-share interview.

She knew way more now about the realities of working with kids.

On Tuesday morning Claire did her make-up and put on a white shirt and wide black linen trousers that were a step up from her usual school outfits, and with shaking hands put in a pair of earrings Gunnar had complimented once.

It was already hot and set to be hotter so she twisted her hair from her face and fixed it in place. *I want this job*, she told her reflection. *I need it and I will be invincible.*

Her keys and purse were in her bag on the hook in the hall. She left the house with loads of time to spare, having factored in contingency for emergencies. Factored in! Contingency!! This is who she was now. If nothing else came out of her Be Better Before Bodlowe campaign, she'd smashed getting into and out of her house and setting off on time, and no one could take that away from her.

Rather than arrive at school too early and get more anxious, she went into the charity shop to kill some time. She was flipping through a book of ways to be calm when the shop assistant brought out a wetsuit and hung it from a hanger on a rattan room divider. Claire stared at it. It looked like the shape of her body.

'How much is the wetsuit?'

'Twenty-four ninety-nine. It's a winter one, nearly new. Woman said it cost just shy of three hundred.'

'Can I try it at home and bring it back if it's not right?'

The woman narrowed her eyes. 'You've asked me that before.'

She had asked that before. And whether they'd hold something. That had been a 'no' too. Claire looked at the time and smiled. She'd factored in a contingency and here was sort of an emergency. 'OK, I'll try it now.'

She pulled the changing room curtain. The wetsuit was

nothing like the baggy short-sleeved suits she'd got the kids from the supermarket. She had no experience of wetsuits apart from one she'd worn for an ear-aching scuba dive with Ben in Crete but it seemed to her that everything about this suit, the trim and seams, the zip which purred down smooth and even, was excellent quality. She took off her shirt and trousers. When they'd last been in Bodlowe, swimming, even just bobbing around letting the water take the weight of her bump had been out of the question because it had been so frigging cold. She'd sat and watched Honor crawling back and forth, emerging endorphined up and energised.

She clambered into the wetsuit, coaxing it up her legs, smoothing and persuading and wriggling in her arms and torso. She felt behind her for the zip cord and pulled and arched her shoulders and inched it home. She backed to the wall and strode in slo-mo towards the mirror. *Oh yeah, look at me striding into the sea.* So what if Honor was tough enough not to need a wetsuit? This was Claire's twist on the farm cottage plans, her fancy suit, a second thicker skin. Maybe she wouldn't take it off all fortnight. She chuckled to herself then checked the time. Contingency was definitely over. She reached up and pulled down the zip and yanked at the wetsuit, tussling, heating up wetly as she wrenched back and forth like an escapologist's anxiety dream, tangling herself in the curtain.

'You having trouble.'

'I'm fine,' she called, sweat beading her lip.

She checked her watch again. Her contingency was beyond over. She pulled the zip back up, buttoned her shirt and rolled the sleeves down over her wetsuited arms, put on her trousers and folded the legs of the suit until they were hidden underneath.

'I'll keep it on,' she said, swishing open the curtain,

because people did say that about normal clothes. The woman cracked a side smile. Claire chose a red and gold silky scarf that she wrapped like a cravat round her sticky neoprene neck and handed over the money.

Running. This was definitely running not jogging. It wasn't elegant, she felt like she was wrapped in layers of clingfilm with a massive sanitary towel wodged between her legs. But she was, unprecedentedly, *running* up Pope's Hill.

Break had nearly finished when she waddled into school. Pearl was doing a clapping game with her friends by the path. Claire rushed on up the steps. 'Hey Sereka and Connie. Hey Pearl.'

'Mummy, it's not your day.' Pearl looked at her suspiciously. 'Why are you here? You look all hot and that scarf is bulgy and wrong.'

'I've come to talk to Mrs Gunnarson.'

'What about? About me?' Hope and worry fought across Pearl's face.

'No, Pearl. About me working here.'

'What about you working here?'

Sweat rolled into the small of Claire's back. 'About me working Fran's half of the week as well.'

Pearl whacked her forehead. 'You'll be here *all the time*.'

Claire nodded and carried on up the steps. She pressed the door buzzer and turned to see Pearl giving her a thousand-yard stare.

Nothing like being wished good luck before an interview.

Chapter 21

Every now and then Claire caught a cool flicker of air from the desk fan aimed at Mrs Gunnarson. All through the interview, the Head had sat ruler-straight with her hands together on her desk. Claire had mirrored her except that Gunnar looked composed and cool in her cotton shift dress and Claire's hands were only together to stop herself touching her face and drawing attention to how much she was sweating.

Claire had convinced herself the protective curtain from Gunnar's fan meant the smell of the wetsuit, which since her run had released the aroma of seaweed and pee, would be contained on her own side of the desk.

The interview had been straightforward. Gunnar hadn't asked why she'd treated the school like an Amazon locker this year. Or why a while back she'd leapt out of the classroom and scared her. And when they'd discussed Ryan's reading and Mrs Gunnarson gave her credit for his progress, she hadn't mentioned catching Claire on her phone that time. So all of that was good.

'Now Claire,' said Gunnar, like their real business was beginning.

'Of course it's wonderful to have you at school. The children love you, you work well with Mr Reader and you give us so much with your art club and help with displays and backdrops for shows.'

'Thank you,' said Claire, blushing. 'I know my focus hasn't been a hundred per cent this year, but circumstances will have changed by September. I'd be totally committed.'

'Your reference to increased focus is noted. But I must say, I was surprised to get your email. I often see the fruits of your labours from the days you aren't with us. Charming flyers and posters up here and there. I assumed you might want to expand in that area.'

Claire smiled and shrugged. When you panic-bought a car it could change your priorities.

Gunnar unlaced her fingers then slotted them back together. 'Claire, I'd like to talk to you about someone. Do you remember Lynne Pike, mum to the Pikelets?'

Claire shook her head.

'Lynne had four sons come through the school. She'd been a research scientist, gluten proteins. She spoke at conferences and was part of international projects. When the first Pikelet began with us she gave it up to come and work here.'

Claire shifted in her seat. The neoprene creaked.

'Lynne Pike gave us ten indifferent years of her life, Claire. Fussing over her boys, teaching them nothing about self-reliance when she could have been stimulated and modelling all the things her career in science gave her.'

'I'm not indifferent,' said Clare. 'I like being a teaching assistant.'

'No, but perhaps the other point resonates.'

'That I fuss over my kids?'

'You are a little overly attentive.'

Claire looked at her lap and tugged where the high neck of the wetsuit was clutching round her throat. What Gunnar said hurt a bit. She always wanted to be available to the kids. She tried to do the opposite of Margo. She cleared her art materials off the dining table without fail, it was a reflex.

'My mum wouldn't even stand at the school gates,' she told Gunnar. 'If she did drag herself away from her painting she'd skulk down the road under some ostentatious hat. Although I did like the purple fedora.'

Gunnar nodded as though she'd liked that hat too. 'Just to go back to Lynne, Claire. When her boys moved on, and she tried to return to her career, to her dismay she found all things gluten had moved on too.'

'That must have made her feel really intolerant, you know like—'

Gunnar gave Claire a withering look. 'Yes. Look, I know illustration isn't a research-based field, but isn't that where your heart lies? Isn't that where you feel most alive? You know better than most that your children are very well looked after. Pearl and Charlie might actually benefit from mum being here less than she is now rather than more.'

'You mean,' Claire swallowed. 'You don't think I should work here at all?'

'That's entirely up to you. I have a strong candidate looking for Monday to Friday, so you wouldn't be leaving us in the lurch.'

Claire recrossed her legs. A rubbery air pocket guffed from the wetsuit. 'Sorry.' She flamed all over. 'That wasn't actually a f—' *Don't tell her what you're wearing.* 'I mean, pardon me.'

'Yes, er, fine.' Gunnar nodded. She wanted things to move on.

Claire ran her clammy hands over each other. Maybe Charlie wouldn't have fizzy necks and need damp paper towels if she wasn't here to check on him, maybe he'd toughen up. Maybe Pearl would be more pleased to see her if she'd seen less of her. Maybe she should be *more* rather than less like her mother. Could that really be right?

'So what do you want to do, Claire?'

This was mad. She had gone from having a half-time job to being shown a good view of the door. She had to protect Grant from Isobel. 'I know it's none of my business, but could you tell me who your candidate is?' Gunnar frowned. Sweat trickled down Claire's chest and back. 'It would really help me decide if I knew.'

'The candidate is a parent of one of our pupils.'

So not Isobel. 'Thanks.' Claire exhaled loudly. 'OK. So, I think I'm resigning.'

Chapter 22

It was Friday night and school had broken up and Claire was packing the car with Tetris-like precision using tips from the internet. She'd waited until Ben was giving the kids a bath, then she'd whipped the roof box and everything she'd stashed for the holiday from its hiding place.

Finally packing for Bodlowe was surreal. In fact the last few days had been surreal, with *what the hell have I done?* on a loop in her head.

When she got back from the interview she'd wrenched off the wetsuit and while the adrenaline was still pumping, sat in her underwear and posted on the Headleigh Forum with a link to a website of her art that Ben had put together ages ago.

CLAIRE SWIFT ILLUSTRATION
Dear Headleigh Forum folk.
Thank you so much for the kind things you've said about my work.
Just to let you know, my new business is up and running. Bring me your projects big and small. I'm happy to quote for anything. Spread the word!

Presuming the post was fuelled by Andrea's course and not shocked desperation, Ben, who was on his last legs from work exhaustion, had declared it 'amazing'.

Claire had cooked him egg and chips to soften the blow then told him she'd resigned from school, at which point her stock plummeted considerably.

'I've always encouraged you, Claire,' he'd said in despair. 'I love what you do, you're a fantastic illustrator. But you've just dammed up your only revenue stream.'

Charlie hadn't really taken in the news she'd left school as September was apparently '*years* away'. Pearl had cried and slammed her first door.

When they went running, Katie said, 'Leap and a net will appear.'

'I'll take the sentiment,' said Claire, 'although I didn't leap, Gunnar took me to the edge and I stumbled off.'

'Work will come. Just go and have a great holiday with Ben and the kids.'

'I'm worried he'll find out I went to Bodlowe instead of the course.'

Katie shook her head. 'That, I have no advice about.' She jumped a fried chicken box. 'But maybe you should take a grab bag of things to help survive an Honor apocalypse. Wine. Chocolate. Book of affirmations.' She was joking but it was a good idea. They agreed to keep up their running and Katie told Claire she and Ed would be minding a kid each, 'man to man marking', to try and keep the peace in Norfolk.

School had broken up midday Thursday.

Honor had texted: **Hey Claire. Bodlowe weather will be a bit of everything. Thunderstorms from out of the blue, so pack for all eventualities xxx**

Brian had finally been in touch with a photo. The cottages were freshly painted. The windows sparkled; he'd laid a lawn and planted roses that trailed around the door. Thanks be to Brian. Hullfire's loss had been her gain.

So here she was, jobless and off on jolly old holiday in the morning. *Whoop.* She pushed the car boot shut and placed a tote bag of croissants, bananas, water and juice boxes on the front seat, because she'd read online that breakfast at home on travel days was 'a time suck'.

The kids were finally asleep. Claire had a shower, brushed her teeth and wrote a few morning things on her list. She must remember to bring her macaroni cheese, brownie dough and salad dressing from the freezer. If she got to Bodlowe first and had the smell of freshly baked brownies to greet Honor, that was *literally* brownie points and would soften the blow, and cover the smell if Claire's Cottages needed it. She climbed into bed, setting the alarm for 5 a.m. They'd leave for Bodlowe by 5.45 latest.

At 2.37 she woke with a galloping heart from a dream where she was a Shetland pony with a racehorse pounding behind her. She looked at the back of Ben's head. He wasn't a fan of loading up the night before. It was 'putting all your eggs in one basket'. What if the car was stolen tonight? It wouldn't get them out of the holiday. They'd have to hire a car or go on the train, and they'd *have nothing to take with them*. They'd be back to carrier bags and cadging. She'd put the breakfast bag on the passenger seat. What if someone saw the bag, broke in and, disappointed by its contents, stole the car out of spite?

At 3.50 Claire dragged herself out of bed and pulled leggings under her T-shirt. She unlocked the front door, tock-tocked and got the breakfast bag. There were a couple of guys in hoodies at the end of the road. Were they harmlessly hanging around or loitering with intent to steal a car?

She unloaded the car. Reverse Tetris when you've gone nowhere was the crappest game ever. She lined the path and then, with arms stacked with a holdall and the kids' suitcases, she opened the door, tripped over the breakfast tote and slammed the luggage onto the stairs.

Ben appeared in his boxers. 'What's happening?'

Claire rubbed her elbow. 'I unpacked the car and fell over.'

'Where's all this stuff come from?' He came downstairs and unzipped a holdall. 'Oh look. New things. I can see why you wanted to load the car now. An enormous thermos flask, great. And what's in this beach bag I've never seen before?'

'Ben, it was two fifty from the charity shop. Please don't take everything out.'

'I want to know what woke me up. Let's see. Crepe bandages, support bandages; sensitive, waterproof and giant individual plasters?'

'Don't go through everything.'

It was like she'd put the idea in his head.

'Thermometer, diarrhoea tablets, ibuprofen and paracetamol and, oh look, in bottles too. Antiseptic wipes, steri stitches, constipation tablets.'

'Stop, please.'

'Bite cream, sting cream. Is this a tourniquet?'

'Yes.'

'Are you planning on opening a field hospital?'

'Why are you rowing?'

'Go back to sleep, Charlie.'

Charlie plonked down on the stairs and threw back his head.

'I've been going back to sleep ALL NIGHT.'

Pearl stomped along the landing. 'You're being really bad parents.'

'Sorry you feel like that, Pearl.'

'Guys, Mum and I are sorting out what we're taking. Pop back to bed or you'll be grumpy in the car.'

Charlie flailed upstairs. 'I'm already grumpy.'

Ben gestured at the first aid kit.

'When we get to Bodlowe we can check out where all the town defibrilators are as well if it helps.'

'Don't take the piss, Ben.'

'What time's your alarm set for?'

'Five.'

'You can wake me and the kids at seven-thirty if they're still asleep and we'll leave by eight.'

Ben went upstairs. Claire wasn't sure whether to laugh or cry that one of the things she'd noted on her secret trip to Bodlowe was the location of the defibrilators on the town beach and at the harbour.

They got away at ten to nine. They inched out of Headleigh surrounded by other grumpy people in packed cars, while flights to Kefalonia and Lanzarote and all the other places you could go with your family on a bus-advert holiday soared out of Luton Airport over their heads.

*

Claire was driving a second stint. The kids were asleep. She chanced a quick stop for petrol. She didn't want to wake them but she didn't want to get to Bodlowe on empty.

'Not a bad idea, filling up.'

It was the nicest thing Ben had said to her all day. Claire paid and came back to the car. The kids were awake.

'Hello Mum. Can I please have Darth Vader from my suitcase?'

Charlie's case had gone in first and every fibre of her being wanted to say no, but he'd asked so nicely. She re-parked by the car wash, tried to persuade a pale Pearl to eat some lunch, took everything out of the boot, found the toy and reloaded. 'Here you go.' She handed Charlie the figure. He beamed and she wondered whether what Honor called pandering was actually love.

The satnav took them round Bodlowe from the west. The rusty metal sign for Murdon Farm Cottages had been newly painted black. Claire turned onto the track. Before the cottages came into view, there was a gulping sound from the back. Claire checked the rear view. Pearl was white as a sheet and swallowing.

'Pearl, are you going to be sick?'

'No,' said Pearl and retched.

Claire braked hard, unbuckled Pearl and helped her out. Moments before she hurled, as though she'd decided being sick on the ground would count as littering, Pearl spun and puked over the pens and toys in the door side pocket and footwell.

'Oh, bad luck, love.' Claire swore silently. 'If you're going to be sick again just do it on the ground, yeah?'

Ben wiped at the door with napkins from lunchtime. Claire steered Pearl round the back of the car and held back her hair as she bent to be sick again.

'The Wellbeloveds, Mummy.' Pearl pulled her hand across her mouth and waved as the Space Ship purred in.

Claire glanced at the vom scene in the car. *Honor will make a disgusted face and probably laugh but just join in. Hahahahahahaha, yes, we're in a hilarious scrape, already.*

They chit-chatted greetings, Chris leaning towards them from the driver's seat, Honor's arm framing the passenger window.

'We've got a new car,' said Pearl.

Honor scanned their car, found it uninteresting.

'Pearl sicked in it,' chirped Charlie. Claire tensed every muscle.

'Oh dear. Chris, bring the bag.' Honor climbed out of the car. She wore old trainers, jeans and sweatshirt. 'Snap,' she said, squeezing Claire's shoulder. 'Ollie hurled all over himself and the seat.' The skin round her huge brown eyes creased as she shook her head. Her hair was in a lopsided ponytail that can't have involved a mirror. Claire didn't think she'd ever seen her with no make-up on. She looked lovely.

'Never fear, puke bag is here,' said Chris bringing a back-pack over to the Silver Bullet Two and pulling out water, wet wipes, kitchen roll and bicarbonate of soda which he shook like percussion.

'We stopped to get this on on the way down.'

'Cheers Chris,' said Ben.

'Honestly.' Honor grinned at Claire. 'Car puke. What a crock of shit.'

Claire felt a laugh bubble up her throat. It was the funniest, crappest start, and it had happened to both of them. Chris and Ben bantered about whether there were cultures in which this would signify an auspicious holiday. It was hilarious that the Wellbeloveds had a puke grab bag. The kids were chasing around on the track, Pearl fully restored. And Claire was genuinely laughing with Honor. They wiped their eyes, and laughed some more. Then they both jammed hands into their sides, and now they were pointing at each other about that, and incapable of speech, and Ben and Chris were befuddledly smiling at them and it felt *so good* to be laughing. And laughing with Honor! Maybe Claire had got it really wrong. Maybe she'd turned coming on the holiday into a whopping great stupid mountain when it was a nice molehill. What an idiot. How funny!

'Why don't you and Claire go ahead and open up the cottages,' said Chris, as laughter turned into sighs of recovery.

'Shall we, Claire?'

A fader seemed to open and fill Claire's head with noise. 'Sure,' she said. 'Why not.'

Chapter 23

'Oh wow. That view, Claire. The sea, and Bodlowe behind the trees. Amazing. Well done.'

'Um, thanks.' She couldn't take credit for the view. It had been there for millennia. But it was amazing. It really was. Claire's body tingled with post-laugh feel-good as they approached the rose-adorned, whitewashed cottages and lush lawn.

Honor stopped and grabbed Claire's wrist. She shrieked. It was laughter. Honor was laughing again. 'Claire, look. The lawn and the roses. They're *fake.*'

Claire felt her face turn red. 'Uh huh huh huh huh huh huh huh.' She was deploying her first fake laugh less than ten minutes into the holiday. The AstroTurf and fake roses had looked so convincing in the photo. What else had Brian done?

The cars trundled down. Claire found the keys under the frayed mat and handed them to Honor. Everyone piled into the side cottage to look round. Claire stayed outside, wanting distance from Honor's discovery of further howlers. Beyond the fake lawn, the scrub had been shorn and the rusty thresher and shards of old greenhouse had gone.

So that was good.

The kids piled out with the other keys. 'What's it like, Charlie?'

'Nice,' said Charlie, air-punching with Dog.

Claire stepped into the cottage and opened an eye. The sofas and chairs were recovered in green linen. The sticky vinyl had gone, leaving the original flagstones, the floor dotted with patterned runners. The Baxter family's lamps and vases and old homewares that she'd saved, and the little wonky bowls she'd chosen, were laid out on the dresser and window ledges just as she'd sketched them.

Claire went upstairs. Honor was lifting an heirloom Cornish blanket off new white bedding. She sniffed it, pulled a face and moved her head from side to side before smoothing it back out. The bathroom was scrubbed and hung with fresh shower curtains. Downstairs in the kitchen, Ben was switching on the fridge. Honor turned a circle on the flagstones.

'Where's the work surface?'

Chris tapped the worn farmhouse table. 'Somehow, for centuries, people chopped stuff on these.'

Claire bit her lip at his snark. Honor shrugged and rummaged in a cupboard.

'The pans have got stickers on. Everything's new, we're guinea pigs.' Her expression was a mix of excitement and suspicion. Honor searched for a router. It was found and the signal was good and Claire raised her eyes in thanks to Brian.

They toured the other cottage at the front and Claire stopped herself from telling the Fancy House story because how would she know it?

Outside, Chris negotiated Honor's folded arms to put his hand round her waist. 'They're great,' he said.

'Very nice,' said Ben. 'And stunning location.'

'Thanks, Claire,' said Chris. The view's better than Blue Gables, which, to be fair, was a bit pretentious.'

Honor flashed at him. 'I thought you loved Blue Gables. We can't even eat together here.'

'We could bring the tables outside,' said Ben.

'There you go. What's your verdict, my love?'

Claire's chest beat a drum roll.

'Well,' said Honor, 'they're basic, but they're trying so hard to be liked, it's kind of adorable.'

Hallelujah, Claire's cottages APPROVED.

'We can do the table thing tonight,' said Claire. 'I'll make dinner.'

'Oh God Claire, no need.' Honor looked as though she could hear Claire's white sauce thudding into the food recycling. 'Honestly, don't put yourself to the trouble.'

'It's no trouble. I've brought a huge macaroni cheese, it just needs heating up.'

'A ready meal?'

'It's home-made,' said Claire. 'It defrosted on the way here.'

'Wow, how's that for organised?' said Honor.

'So who's going in which cottage?' Ben was heading to the car.

'Claire should choose,' said Honor.

'Well I'd like the side cottage, if that's OK with you, Ben?'

'Sure, whichever.'

'Claire, come on,' Honor looked at her open-mouthed. 'Are you kidding? Chris and I have *loads* of holidays, you should take the front cottage, it's so obviously the best.'

'I prefer the other one.'

'Well as long as you're happy.'

'I am.' To be "her in the Fancy House", where Brian's one-upping ancestor had lived, that particular honour should be Honor's.

They had tea and coffee. Honor had brought a cafetiere – unlike Claire who knew they had them in the cottage – and pulled in the luggage, and Claire put the brownie dough and dressings in the freezer and macaroni in the fridge and while the others joined the kids in the barn to play table tennis, Claire wrote a text.

Everything is GREAT Brian, thank you so much! What a brilliant transformation.

Her thumbs hovered over the screen.

Hope it's OK to hold off visiting us for a few days until we're settled. Thanks again. Claire.

She sent it and shuddered. How very rude of her. Although not as rude as what she wanted to say, which was *please don't come all fortnight.*

Honor was taking on Ollie and Ben, bat aloft. Chris and the girls were on one of the sofas. Charlie was driving a toy stretch limo he'd brought from home through a big sandpit on the barn floor. Claire yawned. She was full of biscuits but hungry in that insatiable way that comes with exhaustion. She couldn't wait to eat the macaroni cheese. The sauce was textbook, velvety smooth with a little kick of mustard and lots of seasoning and all that special cheddar that came top in a taste test. Claire yawned again and her jaw cracked.

Chris laughed. 'Early start catching up?'

Honor turned round. 'We're having a tournament. You can play the winner, Claire.'

Chris chuckled. Claire had clearly not sufficiently hidden her horror. 'I think Claire might need a kip,' he said.

Claire looked at her watch. Had they really only been here an hour? It was several eons until bedtime.

'Yeah, maybe just a micro nap. Is that all right?'

'Sure.' Ben pecked her hair with a kiss.

189

Each stair made its own ancient complaint as Claire climbed up them. She entered the bedroom. It smelled of recent paint. Through the window, the Space Ship and Silver Bullet Two looked like they were making stilted conversation, their fronts angled towards each other. It was still the motorised sore point. Too much money, zero consultation. How hard was it to get licensed to Uber? Maybe she could sneak out at night and make some cash taxiing round Bodlowe.

She hung up a few things from her suitcase. A maxi, a cagoule, a button-through shirt dress, a fleece, culottes, a jumpsuit. She had definitely packed for all eventualities. If Honor dressed up she would dress up too. The more like Honor she tried to be, the safer she'd be.

She put the hessian bag she'd embroidered flowers and a sunset onto years ago in the bottom of the wardrobe. Katie had thought she should leave it at home, that it was like Claire wearing her heart on her sleeve, but Claire always took it on holiday.

She pulled the curtain and climbed into the cotton bed-linen she'd picked out six weeks ago. It would be OK with Ben. When he saw her happy and holding her own around Honor, she was sure he'd start to like her again.

There. Feeling better Claire? Now have a nap already.

She'd set a twenty-minute timer. She probably wouldn't sleep in any case. Ach, her phone was in her bag across the room. She'd count to ten and then ... she'd ... go ... and ...

'Mummy.'

'Hmm?'

'Mummy, you've been asleep ages.'

Claire felt around on the bed table. No phone. 'What time is it?'

'Twenty to seven. Dad says you've been here nearly three hours.'

'What?' Claire sat up. 'You're kidding.'

'I'm not kidding,' said Pearl, affronted. 'Everyone's starving.'

Claire shot out of bed, jammed her feet into plimsolls, pummelled the stairs and emerged through the open door like a groggy long-haul arrival.

Ben and Chris were playing boules with the kids. Honor was watching, lounging on the AstroTurf, clean and freshly made up in a chic shirt and black jeans. She looked energised and like she'd spent three hours *doing things,* not drooling on a pillow.

'Hey, sleeping beauty,' said Honor. 'You must have been shattered.'

'Sorry, that was a complete accident.'

Charlie ran over and took Claire's hand. 'I had the sea on my toes, Mum.'

Claire glanced out at the expanse of undulating ocean.

'Oh Charlie, what was it like?' And why did I have to miss it?

'Freezing,' said Charlie, as Claire thought he would.

'I'll put the oven on,' said Claire. 'It'll be on the table in twenty minutes, maybe half an hour.'

'Oh, your macaroni cheese,' said Honor as though it was problematic.

'It's nice, I promise. I've been working on my cheese sauce. Ben, can you help bring the tables out?'

Ben was rubbing his eyes. He didn't move. They all looked shifty, maybe they'd been talking about her cooking.

'Thing is, hon,' said Honor, 'we've got a first-night tradition of chips and ice cream at the harbour. You love it, don't you Ott?'

Ottie looked hunted, then nodded.

'Sorry Claire, should have mentioned it. I mean we *could* have your macaroni cheese tonight ...'

Pearl locked eyes with Claire and slowly shook her head. She was right. Let it go.

'Your plan sounds great, Honor.'

'Fabberlus.' Honor jumped to her feet. 'Ready to roll?'

Claire's skin, hair and the inside of her mouth felt like dirty carpet, but she couldn't keep them waiting any longer. 'Ready to roll.' She smiled massively to show that spurning the meal she'd worked so hard to get perfect, that she'd driven here, that just needed popping in the oven, was zero skin off her nose.

They walked through the gate at the edge of the property, and onto the cliff path. A walk along the beach. Gorgeous. When they got to the harbour, she'd feel fine. She had to feel fine.

Pearl bounced over.

'Hi, Skippy.'

'Hi Mum. Me and Ottie went to the supermarket with Dad and Honor while you were sleeping.'

'Did you? What did Dad buy?'

'Um ... Cheese, bread, milk and cornflakes. He said he wasn't sure what you'd want.'

'What about Honor?'

'She got loads.' Pearl's eyes spoke of bountiful feasts.

'Cool,' said Claire.

Chris led them down the steps. The tide was going out. There was just room to walk along the beach round the craggy headland. The kids took off their shoes and flung them at their fathers and splashed along in the froth. Claire slowed so she was bringing up the rear, and watched them all *ooh* and *ahh*. Look, seagulls! Rocks! A dog that shouldn't be on the beach because it's July! Pearl fell into step next to Honor, lengthening her stride and *wow*-ing as Honor told her things about Bodlowe that Claire could have told her.

Stupid tears pricked Claire's eyes. She mustn't let anyone see her being pathetic. She rolled back her shoulders, trying to rid herself of the push in her chest. She wished she could talk to Katie, even if Katie did bang on about perspective. Maybe calling her mum might be helpful. Ah, no. The first thing Margo would say was, 'Who's *Honor*?'

Ben was transfixed by the harbour. He got Charlie to sound out the names of little boats that were bobbing up and down. Bodlowe didn't smell of sewage. And that was the most positive thing Claire could come up with. The weight in her chest tugged further down. Ugh, here it was. Despite all she'd done since February to try and avoid it, here, on day one, was the exact feeling she'd frantically worked to avoid. All it had taken was a spurned macaroni cheese. Not even spurned! *Deferred*. A deferred macaroni cheese had pulverised her feeble wellbeing.

Ben put his hand on the railing and nudged it against hers.

'Having a good time?'

'Sure,' she said. 'Absolutely.'

Chapter 24

They had chips. Honor banged on about how delicious they were but they were no better than the ones from the chippy by Headleigh station. Afterwards, Claire helped Pearl and Charlie decide which flavour ice cream they wanted. Yes, just one scoop. Then Honor said the ice creams were on her and everyone could have two scoops. Honor inveigled Ottie into sharing with her as though it was some kind of snuggly mum-and-me treat like she'd done with the chips. And just like she'd done with the chips, when it was her go on the ice cream she popped it into a bin because they'd had enough hadn't they?

They went to a seafront hotel. Across the road in front was a beer garden. Claire went into the hotel, the Clifftop, with Honor. In the bar there were balloons that said '80', and several generations of a family squeezed across a pair of sofas noisily embellishing an anecdote about a false eye. As she and Honor gave their order, the family's vocal energy floundered and Claire knew they were clocking the stunning presence of her holiday companion.

The anecdote picked up again and the barman handed Claire and Honor a tray each. Honor put a bottle of red and two large round glasses and two pints of lager on one and Claire began to load the kids' drinks on hers. Her tray was not at all flat. In fact, if she'd hit it with beaters it might make a passable steel drum. Claire thought about asking to swap it, but Honor was waiting, so she picked up the tray. The drinks wobbled and clinked and the journey down the dark corridor to the front of the hotel where all five foot ten of Honor was framed in the doorway had the feel of a sports day ball on a tennis racquet, only with more at stake.

'You know what, Ding,' said Honor, head to one side, 'pop it on that table and I'll come back and get it from you.'

Claire put down the tray like she was told, and watched Honor check the road and stride out of sight. Lemonade bubbles burst on her arm. She threw a casually confident smile at the flicky-eyelinered receptionist to convey *There is no hierarchy here, and I am in complete agreement with this plan.* Time passed. An elderly couple with walking frames also passed, *very* slowly. Claire examined her nails to avoid making eye contact with the receptionist again.

Really, Claire? Waiting like a patsy because you've been told to. Come on. Do something. Go and get another tray and bring it here or take this tray back or fuck it, she was going over the road. Ollie's bottle of fruit juice tumbled onto the tarmac and smashed.

'Bollocks.'

'Oh no,' said Honor, appearing and taking the tray. 'Did you think I wasn't coming back for you?'

Claire went back to the bar with the broken bottle and to replace Ollie's drink. When she finally arrived in the beer garden, Pearl popped out from behind an azalea bush to bestow upon her another slow headshake. The earlier one had been don't-rock-the-boat, this one was you-tipped-the-boat-over. Claire did *not* want to see another of those headshakes.

The garden's small tiered sections were planted with overblown flowering shrubs. The children were receiving disapproving looks from the smattering of hotel guests at the white plastic tables. None of this seemed to be bothering anyone at her own table so Claire put her wine to her lips and a few large mouthfuls went down like the water she should have asked for too. It wasn't long before Honor topped up her glass.

'Cheers, Claire. So here we bloody are. And how is my favourite philanthropist? All well with the good work? Are you knee-deep in gifts of jam?'

'Oh, I've given up philanthropy,' said Claire, swinging her glass to her mouth. 'I'm sure I'll still do stuff for charity but I'm a capitalist now.'

'In what way?'

'I've left my school job. I'm going full time with my illustration.'

Honor pulled back in surprise.

'That was kind of my reaction too,' said Ben. Claire flinched.

'Mummy.' Ollie was by Honor's shoulder. 'Come and play.'

Honor froze in her retracted chin pose and shut her eyes. 'Mummy is talking.' Ollie went away. 'But what about school, Claire? I love thinking about you in your pinny, selling cakes and washing up paint things. It's like you do it for both of us. Wow, self-employed. How are you on the business side?'

'That will be a bit of a learning curve.' Claire caught Ben's eye. 'Although I've been on a course. How's your work, Honor?'

Honor inhaled and leaned towards her, leaving Chris and Ben to start their own conversation.

'It's been an utter mare. Asif and I, it's been like a cage fight. My bank win awards for their ethical practice but they chucked me in the ring with him, and no bastard is admitting I was a Trojan Horse, d'you know what I mean?'

'Oh no,' said Claire, like she understood. They both drank some wine.

'I think people thought he'd surrender, *as if* Asif would do something so decent, the cheery little public-school wind-up. So there's been this ridiculous panel process and whoever comes out on top will head up the department solo. I've put a shit-ton of work in. It was delivered yesterday, and I'm not going to lie, Claire, Honor Wellbeloved will ace it. I'm better than Asif. I'm faster, more proactive. I am un-a-fucking-ssailable.'

'I'm sure you are,' said Claire. 'I'm sure you'll get it.'

Honor nodded. 'They'd be loons not to pick me.'

'When will you hear?'

'I think it's safe to say,' said Honor, doing a little *b-boom tish* with her palms on the table, 'There will be champagne corks over Bodlowe.'

Claire b-boom tished too. 'Fantastic.' When the news came, Honor would be in a great mood. 'That's something to look forward to. Just like the whole holiday is.'

Chris went to the bar. Ben entertained Honor with an anecdote about unravelling 'Carlos's capers' as his team had named the messes his boss had made before going off sick. Honor screamed with laughter and laid a hand on his thigh.

Claire was drunk in a heavy-headed way. To avoid Honor pressing a new bottle of wine on her she sat on the grass and played with Ottie, Pearl and Charlie and a box of mayonnaise and brown sauce sachets. For some reason the genteel guests gave this enterprise approving looks. Claire began to relax.

Later, rubbing his eyes, Charlie clambered onto Ben's lap. Ollie slouched into Claire's empty chair, and Honor, laughing loudly at something Ben had said, handed the boy her phone.

The pale sun slid down and a cool dampness drew in.

Ben called her name. Charlie was asleep with his head on the table.

'Maybe it's time to call it a night,' said Chris.

They walked back across the beach, Ben piggybacking Charlie. Chris raced Ben and and the kids up the steps. Claire climbed up behind them next to Honor.

'So look, Claire.' Honor stopped and turned towards her. She blinked, one eye shutting before the other. 'I've been thinking about you going freelance, and I've godda say, it's not just about talent, you need to be *on it*, and have *drive* to be self-employed.' She shook her fists to demonstrate that having drive required ferocity. 'But the great thing about you ...' She slapped a hand on Claire's shoulder and looked her in the eye and Claire found herself leaning forward to drink in what un-a-fucking-ssailable Honor had to say, '...is that I'm absolutely positive,' shoulder squeeze, 'that if it goes tits up,' shoulder squeeze, 'and they have room,' shoulder squeeze, 'your school would have you back in a heartbeat.'

'Oh,' said Claire. 'Yeah, thanks. Maybe.' She pulled her face into a smile and turned to the sea, which was beautiful and extremely useful as something to pretend to look at happily.

Back at the cottage, kids asleep, Claire plonked the chain onto the door.

She lay in bed knowing Ben was nodding off over his book, waiting for him to snore so she could get him to switch the lamp off. The moon shone through the curtains and her eyelids. Today had felt three days long and there were thirteen more. When they'd got back just now, Honor had said 'see you in the morning'. What time would that be? Because if Claire could have, say, ten hours a day Honor-free, then maybe she could manage thirteen days of fourteen-hour Honor shifts. No point in getting herself worked up about that now though, not in her free time, her lovely, peaceful fre—

'Hey.' Gelled fingernails tapped on the door frame.

'Jesus,' said Ben. Claire yelped and not just because he'd dropped his book on her head.

'Only me.' Honor was wrapped in a towel, her smooth toffee shoulders glowing in the moonlight. 'Our bloody shower's a gnat's dribble, going to use yours, 'kay? *Mi casa, su casa* and all that.'

'How did you? I put the chain on.' Claire scurried her feet out of the way as Honor planted her bottom on the bed.

'The door behind the little bookcase, well that's what it is on my side, you've got a chair. I didn't want to knock and wake the kids.'

She raised herself back up, swaying a little. Her towel slipped, showing the shape of her back. 'Call the owner about the shower first thing yeah, Ding?' She clicked her fingers at Claire and clucked, then swept out to the bathroom.

Ben turned to Claire and laughed.

'It's not funny,' she hissed.

'I know,' he said. 'I don't know why I'm laughing.'

Curtain rings clattered and the shower started. Claire leaned back against her pillow, outraged. 'Our *casa* is not her *casa*. Say something to Chris, Ben. Just say *oh, while I think of it, do you mind if we don't use that connecting door?* And then hopefully he'll say something.'

'It'll sort itself out.'

'It's important. You know, boundaries.'

'Yeah.' Ben yawned. 'Sorry, I'm shattered. Let's play it by ear for now.'

Honor was humming, off-key.

'Could you turn your light off please,' said Claire.

'I don't know, it's not very friendly when there's someone here.'

Claire curled her toes. Ben sighed and turned the light off and they lay there listening to gushing water.

'That's quite a shower,' said Ben.

Eventually it stopped and Honor called out from the stairs in a loud whisper. ''Night guys. Beach tomorrow. Sleep well.'

The connecting door banged shut and they sighed in unison and then laughed, breaking the tension.

Claire woke early. Replaying Honor's appearance in the room sent the chance of more sleep away. She crept downstairs and tilted the chair under the knob of the connecting door and set to sorting stuff out, moving buoyancy aids and water bottles and suncream and beach towels, fitfully disagreeing with herself about where they should go. She must look like a lab rat faring badly in an experiment. She took the chain off the door and slipped outside.

Sitting on the damp dawn AstroTurf in pants and T-shirt, Claire hugged her knees, bathed by the moon. The sea glittered and a ship's lights, a mile out, maybe more, moved almost imperceptibly.

Honor was confident of popping champagne corks. She had a full fridge and no self-doubt. But when it came to Claire, Honor *did* have doubt. She thought Claire should prepare for things to go tits up. And that made Claire nervous.

Chapter 25

'Drive? I'll show you drive, Honor Wellbeloved.' She pumped her fists like Honor had, then yawned and pushed the plunger on a second coffee. The window reflected a wild, bed-haired woman in a T-shirt with *Dreamzzzz* on it. She poured the coffee and opened the fridge for milk. She'd split the freezer bags of macaroni cheese between a roasting tin and an oven dish. She nodded at it.

'You will fulfil your destiny, macaroni cheese. Oh yes. You *shall* be eaten.'

She would prove she had drive. Fake laughs and smiles weren't going to cut it. There'd be no more feeling like a patsy with a drinks tray. Charlie must get his talent for acting from somewhere, maybe it was her. She would *act* the part of someone decisive and un-a-fucking-ssailable.

She picked up her coffee and an A3 sketch pad and pens from the art stuff she'd brought to Bodlowe. Propped on the sofa, she marked out the fortnight over two sheets of paper. They'd plan it together. Claire would do what Asif couldn't, and work with Honor. Into the square for the second Saturday Claire wrote **HOME**. She cried and hugged the sketch pad. It was all edges so she laid it on the floor and hugged a cushion instead.

She crept up the groaning stairs to shower, quietly humming the tune Honor had mullered the night before as sweetly as she could. Was that... no, it couldn't be kids' feet on the landing. Not this early.

Ben slept on while Claire looked in the wardbrobe. What outfit best said *Claire has drive and her shit together?* She wrestled into a sports bra and sleeveless running top and added leggings, trainers and a swishy ponytail.

Downstairs, Ollie was on the sofa with saucer-eyed Charlie and yawning Pearl. The connecting door was open. Claire prised apart her clenched jaws.

'You're up early, guys. My two, did you go next door?'

'Nope,' said Pearl.

Charlie pointed miserably at Ollie. The fricking Houdini. He had slipped round her chair trick. Chip off the old block, no boundaries.

She made up bags for the beach. Forgot what was in the bags. Made lists of what was in the bags. Had more coffee. Changed what was in the bags and wrote the lists again. At 8.30, she dropped some things off in the barn and knocked at the Fancy House. Honor opened the door with one eye closed, a cockscomb of hair standing up at the side of her head.

'Morning, Honor.'

'Kind of early, isn't it?'

'Oh no. Sorry, I didn't mean to wake you. I thought you might all be early birds. Ollie's been at ours a while.'

Honor looked Claire up and down. 'You look sleek and strapping.'

'Thanks. Combat classes.' She kick-boxed a leg to the side, surprising herself as much as Honor. 'I thought you and I could have coffee in the barn and, you know, chat through plans and stuff?'

Honor frowned. 'Are you sure you need coffee, Claire? You're acting like you've had a *lot* of coffee.'

'Ha, yeah. You might be right there.'

'Fine. I'll see you there in half an hour.'

'Great. I might as well have a run then.' Claire jogged away, pulling a face, her chirpy doofus words repeating in her head. She set back her shoulders: Honor might be watching.

She turned onto the coast road and relaxed her show-pony gait and ran onto a path along the edge of the cornfield, picking her way over dips and divots. Honor wouldn't want to give an inch, she wasn't lovely Fran who shared ideas. Claire would have to keep nudging. She'd need ... what was that word? Leverage. What did Honor want? Her shower fixed. And what was the thing *she* wanted most today?

'Easy!' she called into the air, 'I want her to eat my macaroni.'

It turned out cornfields were kind of samey, which meant Claire got kind of panicky, and kind of lost, and the run took a bit longer than expected. She hurtled back, slowing as she reached the cottages. As she wobbled to stretch a quad, Chris appeared at the top of the beach steps in cargo shorts and walking sandals. He waved as he crossed the AstroTurf.

'Morning, Chris.'

'Hey. It's going to be good weather-wise. Where did you go for your run?'

'Down the edge of the cornfield into some other corn-fields that looked exactly the same.'

He chuckled. 'Lucky to get you back, are we?'

'It was touch and go for a while.'

They laughed and nodded. Neither of them said anything. The atmosphere teetered towards awkward, she was so susceptible to his shyness. She loosened her shoulders. 'You're looking really well, Chris.'

'Thanks. I feel it.' He scratched his head, knocking off

sunglasses which he caught against his side. 'Honor's been holed up in town and Geneva with this big work situation for weeks, and I've been hanging out with the kids. If I'd known how much fun it would be not running a company I'd have sold it ages ago.' He rubbed the lenses on the bottom of his T-shirt.

'The three of us have made friends in the estate next door. We were biking through a while back and there was a table sale for a local charity so we got chatting to people.' He put the glasses back on his head. 'We've been getting to know the neighbours.'

Claire smiled. 'Sounds really nice, Chris.'

'It is. A nice community. Bit like you've got in Headleigh. And I've got this plan for this community thing, it's a—' Gritty footsteps. Honor was crossing to the the barn. 'Do you need to go?'

'Probably should. Me and Honor are doing some planning.'

'Sure. I'll tell you about it another time. Oh, before you go, how do you feel about that connecting door?'

Claire turned round. 'Um, in what way?'

'I think we should make it no entry.'

Claire exhaled. 'Great, me too.'

'I'll let everyone know.'

Lucky Ben. The only thing on his smoothing-out-the-holiday agenda had sorted itself already.

Honor was on the sofa with a bowl of yoghurt, fruit and seeds. She wore a bikini under a cream halter top and shorts, her long legs crossed at the ankle in tan sandals. Claire perched on the sofa, curling her ponytail round her finger. She gestured at the two sheets of paper she'd Blu-tacked to the barn wall. 'So, yeah. I wondered if we could make a loose plan for the fortnight. There's a week on each page and Post-its. I've got a little whiteboard I'll stick next to the planner so anyone can add ideas, and sketch pads and pens and paints so the kids can review places and do pictures.'

'Adorable. You're a loss to the classroom, Ding.'

Claire laughed nervously. There was a smear of yoghurt on Honor's lip gloss, a caramel shade that was too light for her.

'Have you told the owner about my shower?'

'Not yet.'

Honor tilted her head and doused Claire in disappointment.

'I will, when we're finished here.' The list in her hand was shaking. She laid it on the sofa between them, folding it towards her.

'I don't know how you and Katrina did things, so obviously tell me, but otherwise I thought we could pool ideas, pop any other traditions onto the planner. Are there outings you've got in mind? Boat trips, days out to St Ives, theme parks? We could use yellow Post-its for good weather stuff and pink for all-weather activities.' Honor was staring at her. She had the feeling she'd been talking very fast.

'God Claire, was there speed in that coffee? This is like being back at work.'

'Sorry. I don't want it to be un-fun, I just thought it would be good to be on the same page.'

Honor held out her hands for the pen and Post-its and rose from the sofa. 'Here's an all-weather activity.'

She wrote on a Post-it, filling the rectangle of pink paper with capital letters. She slapped it over the line between week one and two then plonked back on the sofa.

'"Chill", said Claire. 'Yeah, fair point. We could chill on

the planning for now, good idea.' She breathed out slow and jumpy as her eyes flicked to her list and she fought the urge to mute and power down.

Planning
Snacks
Bedtimes
MACARONI CHEESE!!

'So about snacks,' she said. 'That's maybe something to be on the same page about.'

Honor spooned breakfast into her mouth. 'Is this the *same* same page, or a new one?' A wink gave Claire the cue to laugh.

'Ha ha ha, yeah, see what you mean, I'll stop saying that, but anyway—' She cleared her throat. What was a driven and un-a-fucking-ssailable way of saying *when I'm helping my kids choose a single ice cream flavour, don't say 'pick two'*? 'Just thinking, as we go along could we have, like, mini pow-wows to decide about ice creams and stuff?' Her voice had wibbled high and pleading.

'Hmm,' said Honor. There was a yoghurty film on her gloss. 'Can't see mini pow-wows working for me. We'll just go with the flow.'

Claire folded the paper. She wouldn't mention bedtimes for now. It was time to go in for the kill. 'Can we talk about today's food?'

'Cool. Well, Chris wants to take us to the Pheasant tonight. They've got suckling pig so he's drooling already. The weather looks blowy but sunny, so we'll do a picnic and the local beach because the man will be round to get the shower sorted out, won't he, Ding?'

Don't get sidetracked into Brian. 'Macaroni cheese for lunch then?'

'Oh.' Honor's brows shot up. 'Not very lunchy.'

'People have it for lunch. We can have it.'

'But, won't it be a bit tired, Ding?'

'It defrosted and went straight in the fridge, it'll be fine.'

Honor sighed. 'Look, here's what we'll do. We'll bin the macaroni, and I'll knock up a picnic.'

'So, have the macaroni for dinner then?'

'Dinner is the Pheasant. I think you need to let it go.'

The dark nail of Honor's middle finger touched Claire's Lycra'd thigh. 'It's not personal. It just doesn't fit our plans.'

Claire pointed gun fingers at her phone. 'Macaroni for lunch or the owner doesn't get it.'

'Don't understand.'

'He doesn't get the phone call. About your shower.'

Honor closed her eyes, then seemed to struggle to open them, as though Claire's idiocy was gumming them together. 'If I don't agree to macaroni for lunch you won't phone the owner?'

Claire's heart thumped. 'Just joking. It's a joke.'

Honor sighed. 'Ding, You're being weird. No one will want to traipse back from the beach for lunch.'

Damn it. Good point. 'I'll heat it up and bring it down.'

'Won't that be a bit sort of hot, and mad?'

'It'll be fine.'

'You really want us to have that macaroni, don't you?'

Claire nodded, suddenly a three-year-old with a tray of mud pies.

'Fine. Be my guest. Macaroni cheese for lunch on the beach.'

Chapter 26

While Ben and the kids ate breakfast, Claire packed for all beach eventualities. She and Ben had a stand-off about how much they were taking, so Claire gave the kids KitKats to carry things, and Ben muttered about bribery.

They followed the Wellbeloveds down the steps to the beach. Claire cursed under her breath as Honor weaved around sandcastles and families, rejecting spot after spot, Pearl and Charlie bitching at Claire like it was *her* fault they were walking so far, which in a way it was because it was obviously to make her macaroni lunch run more difficult.

'Perfect,' said Honor, stopping in a space no different to twenty or so they'd passed.

Claire's secret practice puttings-up of the beach tent had taught her you had to start with the poles laid out in height order.

'I'll leave you to it,' said Ben, backing away, hands raised. And she got it. Old Claire would have goofed around with him and got the tent wrong and they would have laughed, but she would also have been laughed *at*. Threading poles decisively through loops, she glanced sideways and caught Honor *noticing*.

Yes Honor, we have a good quality beach tent, and I know how to put it together.

'Great tent.' said Chris.

'Thanks.'

Honor shook out towels looking for Ollie's goggles, while he fiddled in his trunks. 'Hands where I can see them, sunshine. Have a snack now, then if you eat all the lunch Claire's making, I'll get you an ice cream later.' She passed him the goggles then opened a food container.

'I don't want anything,' said Ollie.

'You're a growing boy. Growing boys are hungry all the time. Have a Scotch egg.'

'I'm not hungry.'

'Yes you are. Come on, eat it.'

Ollie threw a spade and it cut into the sand. Honor confiscated it and passed him the food.

Claire pretended to settle, reclining in one of the pair of lightly sun-faded camping loungers she'd snapped up at a discount, then spent the next couple of hours defending the Swift camp, its tent, enormous picnic blanket and hefty windbreak from invasion by sand, wet, disorder and, on the basis of Honor's covetous glances at her superior chairs, takeover. Eventually it was time to go and sort out the lunch.

'Already?'

'Yes, Ben. Already. I've worked out the timings.'

When Ben and Claire took the kids to Glasgow to stay with Margo, or visited Ben's parents in Lincoln, their packing would spew out of its bags and free-range around their room and they'd search for stuff as needed. But Bodlowe was all about tidying and auditing, so while the dishes of macaroni heated up, Claire busied herself round the house. She checked the bags in the hallway and the lists she'd attached with pegs.

Snorkels x 2 and spare swim stuff. Microfibre towel and spare clothes.

When the cheese reached peak brown, she took the food

out. While the dishes bubbled on tablemats she squirted perfume in the car and de-littered it, then put the foil-covered oven dish in the beach bag on top of melamine plates and cutlery.

Claire set out over the AstroTurf with the roasting tray, hip thrown out so the oven dish burned her side a little less. *I'm strong and single minded. This is not the obsession of a mad woman. When Honor tries it, I will become better in her eyes. Yes, it's a humble macaroni cheese – I know my place, but it's good, and it's worth it.*

On reflection Honor was right. Taking food from an oven to a beach *was* hot and mad. She'd thought that carrying the roasting tray with oven gloves would call too much attention to the hot madness, so she'd folded a tea towel in each hand. By the time she reached the steps, the heat in her palms was making lights flash in her peripheral vision, but she bounced down them, trying to make it look like she was having a great time and this was a super fun idea.

Honor was below, a hand to her forehead like a visor. 'Careful,' she called. Beach people turned and looked up. Claire missed a step with one foot and landed on her backside Cossack-dancer style, honking like a seagull as pain seared through her buttock.

A kid yelled, 'The lady sat down Mummy.'

Claire swallowed winded gasps. She blew hair from her sweating face, put the roasting tray to one side and clambered to her feet like it was nothing.

'You all right?' called Honor.

'Fine!'

'I've been watching Pearl swim,' said Honor as Claire reached the bottom of the steps, and began to follow her back to their camp. 'She's very able.'

Claire felt a moment's pride push through her pain.

'Has she got a coach? Ollie's come on terrifically since we started his coaching.'

'No. I mean they had lessons last term, but not a coach.'

'She should have a coach. You should take her, early mornings.'

'Yes, maybe,' said Claire.

'Having someone push you on is transformational. And if you're me, that means looking at Linton's Lycra bulgy bits with every crunch, so that's a bonus.'

Claire's body flared with heat and pain. She felt for rocks with her toes before putting down a foot. She had not gone through all this to trip and drop the food.

'The most important thing a parent can do,' said Honor, 'is provide opportunities for a child to excel in their interests. Well that's my opinion anyway.' She touched a hand to her chest. Why did Honor have a free hand to touch to her chest? Why wasn't she carrying something? Claire was suddenly desperate to scratch her nose. If only she felt she could ask Honor to do that for her.

'I mean Ottie's got this thing about cheerleading out of the blue.' Honor slid her fingers into the pockets of her shorts. 'And in my head I was *God no, tacky nonsense*, but of course, I didn't show that.'

The itch felt like a spider dancing on Claire's nose. She stumbled. The bag swung forward, the tray jerked. She broke into a sweat. Tears that had been welling rolled out of her eyes. Oh sweet hope! Claire tipped her head as she walked, hoping to divert a tear through the itch to soothe it.

'So I did my research and went to see the best club in the league and I was gobsmacked. These kids are athletes.'

Tears fell either side of the spider itch. Fuck. If she put the load down, she'd never want to pick it up again. Still, only a few more spots to pass that Honor could have picked.

'She'll need to manage her expectations mind you, because let's face it, Ott's never going to be top of the pyramid.'

Oh God Honor, shut up, stop talking. A kid ran across Claire, chasing a ball. She twisted out of the way. Twenty more steps, twenty should do it.

One, two, three…

'And even if they will take her as she is, I'm determined to shave six pounds off her before September, for her sake. It's important she doesn't feel too different.'

Nine, ten, wait. Did she say shave six pounds off Ottie?

'But back to Pearl and the swimming. If you and Ben needed help with the money—'

'It's fine. No thank you,' said Claire. 'We're all fine as we are.' *Including your daughter.*

Claire reached the camp and dropped to her knees. She placed the roasting dish on a wrinkled blanket, her bag swinging off her shoulder onto the sand. She rubbed a sore palm round and round on her nose. Was there a German word for pleasure in your *own* pain? Because this was it.

Claire peeled the foil from the roasting tray. The macaroni cheese looked glorious. Pearl and Ottie came and knelt by the food as Claire unpacked the plates. Honor was looking down the beach, swigging from a bottle of water.

'Smells amazing,' said Ottie.

'What is it?' asked Pearl, suspiciously.

'Macaroni cheese.'

Ottie clapped her hands and looked at Pearl, delighted. Claire's hands and bum pulsed with pain as she served up. She hated the overthinking that accompanied her portion for Ottie. *Don't skimp. Give her plenty, but don't overdo it.* She added an extra bit of crispy topping and handed it to her.

Pearl nodded at Claire, and Claire understood, she wanted hers like Ottie's.

'This is fantastic,' said Chris.

Ben gestured at his plate with his fork and nodded.

'Honor.' Claire stretched out to Honor with a modest portion. *Here you go. A cheese sauce that has not gone catastrophically wrong, that not even you can say 'this is a mess' or 'bless you for trying' or thud into your recycling caddy.*

Honor smiled and shook her head. 'I'm good thanks.'

'Don't you want some lunch?'

'I had some cashews and an apple.'

The plate went heavy in Claire's hand. 'Not even a bit?'

'I'm sure it's very nice. Nothing personal, just not my kind of lunch.'

Honor sat with her chest out and her legs bent to the side, looking out to sea while Claire ate, tilted onto her good butt cheek. Chewy, savoury, comforting, it was very good. And Honor not eating it was totally personal.

Charlie jumped up, wiping his hands down his little thighs and running off. 'Yummy, thank you, Mum.'

'You're welcome.'

Honor's stomach rumbled and she put an arm across her lap but the serene smile didn't flicker. Not even a mouthful to taste it. What annoying self-control.

Charlie ran back, sand kicking onto the blanket. 'Come in the water with me in a bit, yeah?'

'Yeah, I will,' said Claire. 'I'll come now.' She pulled herself into the wetsuit, strafing her hands as she wriggled it on, slowly slowly over her aching arse, reaching round for the tag to pull up the zip.

Honor laughed. 'Could you *be* any more insulated?'

The remark pinged off the thick neoprene. 'Fantastic, isn't it.'

213

Claire walked to the sea with Charlie. The food hadn't gone to waste, she'd stood her ground, she'd got it to the beach, and everyone else had enjoyed it. That would have to do. She stepped into the water. It was freezing on her feet but she kept going because her shins, then her thighs and torso didn't feel it. When icy water snaked in at her lower back, she thought she'd have to wade out again, but it soon warmed and the water cooled her bum and she swam and played with the kids and obeyed Charlie's requests to watch his endless twists and splashes.

She forgot about lunch, so later when she looked at the beach to check how far along she and Charlie had meandered, what she saw was sweet. Honor was sitting on her own, spooning macaroni into her mouth from the roasting tin.

'Yes. I rule,' she said to her son's pale soles as his feet smacked below the surface, showering her with water.

Pearl and Ottie came over with Ben, bats and a ball. Claire played with them for a while and then went back to base.

Clearing a space on the blanket outside the tent she saw the macaroni dishes, both empty, had been placed inside the beach bag. Honor must have liked it. This could be the moment things changed, that Honor grew a little faith in her. 'Lunch all got eaten,' she muttered, 'that's good.'

Honor glanced up from her Kindle. A smear of cheese sauce curled on her chin like a comma.

'Did it? Oh, well done.' Claire felt a moment of pity for Honor, eating in secret.

Honor stood up and stretched her arms behind her. 'I'm going in the water. Wetsuit seems to be working out for you, Ding. You could barely go in last time.'

'Yeah, I'm not good with the cold.' She looked up at

Honor and touched a finger to her chin. 'Honor, you've got a bit of...' she paused.

Honor wiped her chin and looked at her fingers. Claire picked up a crumpled towel and folded it. *Just admit you managed to force some down. Just give me that, you don't have to say you enjoyed it.*

'Claire, I've had such a fun idea. A cook-off on our last night. Mummo a mummo. You v me. Won't that be fun?'

'Oh gosh, um...' Clare turned to face her friend, the sea. Her hair whipped in the breeze and her heart sped up and beat *mummo a mummo a mummo a mummo a mummo...*

'Put it on your planner, yeah.' Honor threw back her shoulders and strode to the water.

It had not occurred to Claire that the macaroni might flick Honor's competitive switch. She'd overachieved. What a dumb move.

'And let's get that shower fixed,' called Honor, her hand thrown in the air. 'Phone the owner.'

Claire threaded her way round beach cricket to get a phone signal. She leaned on a rock at the back of the beach and cupped her hand over the screen to find Brian's number. Was there a bright side to ringing him? Yes! If he came to the cottages he could give her the key for the connecting door.

'Decided to talk to me have you?'

Claire winced. 'Hello Brian. The cottages are so, so lovely.'

'And what does Mrs La-di-da think? Up to scratch for her?'

'She's very happy, except for the shower. The one in the Fancy House doesn't work all that well.'

Brian guffawed. 'Ooh, she wouldn't like yours being better, would she.'

'Would it be OK to send someone to look at it?'

'Allowed round now am I?'

'Of course. Gosh. I'm sorry about the text. It's just I hadn't slept and my husband still thinks I was on a course when I was here so I panicked about having such a big secret with a stranger.'

'A stranger? Is that who I am?'

Claire imagined his huge eyebrows drooping. 'No. No no. Sorry. Course you're not a stranger.'

'I shared things with you I en't told no one. I thought we had a bond.'

Claire swallowed. 'You're right. We do.' She wished they didn't, but they did.

'This shower then. I'll be over at half four.'

'Great, Brian. Thank you.'

Chapter 27

'A cook-off?' yelled Katie, buzzing Claire's phone speaker. 'What a bag of cack.'

'It'll be "fun" apparently.' Claire put the phone between her cheek and shoulder and pulled out a trolley. She'd escaped in the car, telling Ben this would be a good time to go to the supermarket, asking him to let Honor know the owner would visit later. 'How are things in Norfolk?'

'Utter shite. Torrential washout since yesterday. Ed's put me in a café so I don't murder anyone. If this tea looks at me funny I will punch its stupid lights out.'

'Oh babe, I'm sorry,' said Claire. 'Weather's great here. Wish I could have your rain for you.'

'What a smugly pointless thing to say,' said Katie before gasping, 'Claire! I love you, sorry, I'm in a savage mood. Nice there is it? On the beach are you? Aaggh. I can't even ask polite questions without sounding aggressive.'

'It's understandable. Drink some tea. I'm at the supermarket.'

'But you've got sunshine you berk, why aren't you on the beach?'

'Because Honor's got a full fridge and we've got jack all.'

Katie sighed and slurped. 'So what are you getting?'

'Bit of everything.'

'When in doubt, overkill,' said Katie.

'Exactly. Guess what Katie, she loved my macaroni cheese.'

'What a bitch. Hold on. That's good, right?'

'Yes. But no. Because it gave her the idea we should have the last night cook-off.'

'Oh, I get it. The queen of the castle has seen the village idiot shinning up her ramparts, no offence. Woah. Stakes are raised. You could do steak. Or just kick her in the slats and say get to fuck.'

'Katie. Have you not slept?'

'No.' There was a rustling noise and Katie let out a sob. 'Sorry. You're so much better at no sleep, I could weep. I *am* weeping. Everything is wet. The dryer queues are ten deep. Remind me never to come camping again.'

'It sounds horrendous.'

'Thank you. I'm so jealous of your holiday.'

Claire pulled her trolley into an alcove by the toilets and texted a screen shot of the improving Norfolk forecast.

To my favourite savage. This too shall pass x

She pushed her trolley up and down, chucking things in at random. Everything she picked up felt wrong. When would they eat a chicken pie? Who even liked beef jerky? Her left ear was on full whoosh. A cook-off might be 'just a bit of fun' to Honor but it made her nerves jangle. Maybe she could untrigger her with a reset to full Ding mode. Offer up cheap baps with cheese slices and crap ham. Leave stuff at the cottage so she had to borrow. Pretend to be puffed out on walks. Klutz up everything until Honor thought *aw, bless, it's not worth it. I don't want a cooking contest with Claire, she's unworthy.*

She dropped her chin onto the muesli box in her hands.

Claire, if you stop trying, you'll feel worse, and what will be the point of everything you've done the last six months?

Her text alert sounded from her back pocket.

Hedding over to the cottages now.

Oh, you are kidding. He mustn't get there before she was back. She lurched away abandoning her trolley. But got to have food. And Honor would most likely stay on the beach as the sun was out. Claire hurried back to the trolley and rushed to the busy checkouts, chucking things in as she went.

She picked a cashier. Madge. Madge was a good choice. Through it all went. Beep. Beep. Beep. Into the bags, fast as you like. Here's the points card. Here's the debit card. Here's the receipt.

Madge's crooked finger pulled open the last bag.

'I've always wondered,' she said, savouring each syllable like it was an individual lump of fudge worth taking your time over, 'what beef jerky was like.'

'I'll come back and let you know,' said Claire, unhooking the bag, bunging it in the trolley with the others and legging it.

She drove back horribly, mangling every other gear change. She turned off the coast road onto the track and there was Brian's faded red Land Rover, and Brian hoiking up his trousers, and Honor sashaying towards him over the Astro-Turf, saying something. Claire braked late and hard. The car skidded on gravel and Brian and Honor scattered to either side. Claire opened the door and jumped out.

'Hey there.'

'Woah, Claire. Where's the fire?' said Honor.

Right here. And I'm the bucket of water.

'Afternoon,' said Brian, ignoring Honor's outstretched

hand and turning towards Claire with a weird stiff bow. 'Brian Baxter. Nice to meet you for the first time.'

See? Fire. Claire gulped. 'Claire. Nice to meet you too.' She shook his hand briskly, trying to transmit the message that if he thought he'd started well, he should … reflect on that.

'Honor Wellbeloved.' Honor pumped Brian's hand then gestured at the Fancy House. 'Shall we? I don't expect Niagara, but I can't accept a piddle.'

Brian's massive eyebrows undulated. 'Thing is Mrs Welby—'

'*Wellbeloved*, you're missing the "loved".'

'Thing is,' Brian folded his arms. 'That's just how it is, ain't one of them power showers.'

'I realise that. But mine's a dribble compared to my friend's here.'

Brian raised his bristly chin. 'Well sometimes it's other people gets the better stuff. Might be you just have to put up—'

'Please, Mr Baxter,' said Claire. 'If the shower could work better that would be great.'

'I'll do what I can.'

Brian went upstairs and stepped into the Fancy House bath, his cargo trousers clanking with tools, and took the front off the shower unit.

'You were right,' he whispered. 'That one thinks she's chocolate. I mean she's stunning and that but she's *awful*. "Can't accept a piddle".'

He examined Claire's face, the thickets above his eyes furrowing. 'You don't look too good.'

'I know,' said Claire, leaning against the closed door, an ear out for Honor. 'I haven't been sleeping well.'

'Is it that there stress?'

'Yes, I think so.'

'Bad business that stress. So, you like 'em? The cottages?'

'So much. They're absolutely lovely. The floors, the sofas, you've done a wonderful job.'

Brian beamed. 'I'm glad, Claire. I wouldn't want to let you down.' He rubbed his spiky chin noisily. 'Tell you what though, I'll just turn her pressure up a tiny bit. I don't want to make her happy, I just want her off your back.'

'No, Brian, please make her happy. Make it better than mine if you can. And be nice. She's used to people treating her like she's special.'

Brian agreed. When he'd finished, Claire called Honor up to check. She held a tanned hand in the water. 'That's acceptable.' She dried her hand and placed it on Brian's arm. 'Well done,' she said, like she was saying *See, not that hard was it?*

'My pleasure,' said Brian, dipping his head. 'If I could, I would give you the Niagara what you deserve, but I'm just a simple man giving of my best.'

'Fantastic. That's all done then,' said Claire. She gently hustled Brian from the bathroom, nosing him out of the Fancy House and penning him into his Land Rover like a cheery sheepdog. She waved him off down the track.

The key.

'Oh no. I forgot to ask about, um, departure time.' Claire told Honor and sprinted after him, waving. 'Brian. Mr Baxter.'

'Missing me already?'

'The door that connects the cottages,' Claire said, catching her breath. 'Do you know where the key is?'

Brian scratched his head. 'Nope, sorry. Never seen one.' He put his big chalky hand on hers. 'I could pop back and fit a bolt.'

Claire looked back down the track at the cottages. Honor's shower was sorted. The thought of Brian there again with Ben or Pearl around made her queasy and Chris had said he'd tell his lot not to use the door.

'Thanks Brian. Don't worry, it's fine as it is.'

Chapter 28

Claire turned over on the pillow and opened an eye. Beyond the flimsy curtain was the suggestion of sun and also greyness and rain. They'd had this keep-you-on-your-toes weather for a few days. Sometimes sun would turn to rain, others rain to sun. It was packing-for-all-eventualities weather. Claire stretched and shuddered, remembering the meeting with Honor on the first morning. Her holiday planner was still stuck on the barn wall. An empty grid with a Post-it slapped on it saying CHILL.

Claire's drive to succeed had choked and died when the macaroni cheese had landed her in a cooking contest. There had been no sharing or pooling of ideas since then. Honor announced what they were doing and when they were doing it.

'We thought the beach', 'a scoot round the galleries and St Ives', 'the beach and then the lifeboat station if it rains,' Honor would say. So that's what they'd do. And Claire tried not to feel wrong, or show it, or do the wrong thing. Ben and Chris went along with all the plans, their focus more on chat and challenges.

'How many roly-polies will it take Ben to get to that wall?'

'First person to name a bird that starts with S gets Chris's last piece of gum.'

'If we lay the knives and forks end to end, will they stretch two lengths of the tables?'

Claire pushed her pillow down to look at Ben. He was asleep on his side, an arm flung round his head. She smiled at the thought of his friendship with Chris. They brought out the best in each other, and the kids, and provided everyone with good humour. But when she and Ben were alone it had been tense. She couldn't chill, because she was always wondering what would be next. And because she couldn't be sure that Ben would get the nuances of meeting the intangible standards that came with Honor that so compelled her, it was easier to hope he'd just go along with things and not want to talk about any of it. So she packed and unpacked bags, made lists, shook sand and made sandwiches that might or might not get eaten according to Honor's whim. All the thinking was an effort too. And the effort it took to make it look easy, was more effort still. She was 'on' so hard, that when their exhausted children crawled into bed, so did she.

Her fingers walked across the pillow. She could touch him now. He'd wake up and they could have sex. Ben's breath caught and he made a clacking noise with his mouth.

Maybe not *right* now.

She pushed back the duvet and stepped out of bed. She moved the edge of the curtain, laying her temple to the glass. There it was. That glorious glimpse of the sea lit through the grey beyond what she now thought of as Macaroni Steps. The sea with its bright white foam that crashed onto the sand and shingle beach, that she would sketch as soon as she didn't feel Honor was watching.

She smiled. She'd come a fair way since she'd been here pregnant and miserable with Ben and Pearl. Being in the sea with the kids was a delight. It was an all-you-can-eat buffet of fun, and the wetsuit was her bowl. To be warm in the sea.

To zip her cold-sensitive body into top to toe warmth was joy. It gave her all the time she wanted, bobbing, skimming, towing bodyboards. She was appreciated and then unnoticed while pirates plotted their next capture of treasure as she waited for their instructions, zoning into their bubble as they clambered onto rocks and stuck hands out to be steadied for jumps, their small bodies given over completely to play.

It was bliss so deep it seemed to flow into arid gaps in her childhood and water them. Now *that* was quintessential chill. As long as she had that, she was free.

She peeked in on the kids sleeping, Dog in Charlie's fist. They'd wanted to share a bedroom. They tussled and bickered but romping in and out of the barn as a pack, Ottie's kindness gelled them together. Charlie buckled to Ollie though, dancing to order, bestowing his toys – but never Dog, Dog was sacred.

Claire went down to make tea. Katie had sent a selfie. A starburst of rays on the lens of her sunglasses, tent in the background. **Having a MUCH better time.** Claire replied *Whoop!!* with a line of alternating clapping hands and thumbs-ups.

While the kettle boiled, she packed stuff in the big patterned beach bag. She'd been carrying the enormous thing everywhere. 'You're so well-equipped Claire,' Honor had said, and sap that Claire was, she'd lit up like one of the arcade machines that they'd fed with the bag of coins she'd produced the day before.

Honor was carrying less. And Claire had become de facto sherpa-cum-donkey, and woe betide her if she came up short. Like when Honor wanted to go crabbing out of the blue, and was disappointed Claire had no raw bacon. Claire was in charge of *things*, trailing along with her enormous everything bag and an aching shoulder while Honor was in charge of *decisions*, heading them up at the front with a backpack so tiny it was basically jewellery.

Claire popped teabags into two mugs and poured on just-boiled water. She didn't mind the sherpa thing so much. What she did mind was when Honor sat on one of *her* chairs in front of *her* beach tent; now *that* was annoying.

She put the teabags in the recycling bag and saw the part-cooked sticky chicken she'd had to ditch last night when her joint barbecue with Honor had gone wrong. Ben and Chris had made a lovely carbonara the night before. She'd hoped their collaboration might go well too. Honor had lit the Wellbeloved and the Swift portable barbecues, which seemed thoughtful. Then she put a load of award-winning best-in-the-whole-world sausages on hers and just as Claire went to place her maple syrup and sauce-coated chicken on *her* barbecue, Honor laid out a batch of kebabs.

When they were done, she said, 'all yours,' and Claire had turned and turned her chicken over the ebbing heat. Then Honor called that it was dinner and scrunched her nose and said, 'Not happening is it, Ding.'

And that was Honor doing a barbecue *with* Claire.

What would a cook-off be like, 'Mummo a Mummo'?

She shuddered and grabbed a bag of chew sweets from the table, stuffing several in her mouth.

Ben was awake. He smiled and took the mug of tea from her hand. 'Thanks. How's your bum today?'

'What? Oh, the bruise.' She realised she had sat on the bed side-saddle. 'Guess it must be getting better if I had to think what you meant.' She held out the bag of sweets. Ben took one as though they were a fine dining delicacy.

'Ben, have you noticed our kids straight up ask Honor now when they want snacks and things?'

'One less thing for us to do.'

'Makes me feel like Maggie Simpson next to Marge. A pretend steering wheel in my hand and a dummy in my mouth.'

Ben laughed and gestured for the sweets again.

'You know she wants to do a her-against-me cook-off.'

Ben's face reflected back her feelings, and Claire laughed. 'When?'

'Our last night.'

'Didn't she put that Post-it in the barn?' said Ben. 'Doesn't she want everyone to chill?'

'I guess for her, competing with people *is* chilling.'

'You don't have to do it. Tell her you don't want to.'

Claire cracked the shell of a sweet between her back teeth. She'd be denying Honor her chance to shine. If she wussed out, the teasing and little jibes would keep coming. 'Oh, I'll do it,' she said.

'I'll help.'

'Pretty sure help won't be allowed.'

'Well let's see. But can we make a deal? Don't think about it till at least Wednesday of next week. If it pops into your head, think of something else.'

'Sure.' *Hey Taj Mahal. Guess I'll be seeing more of you.*

Ben was looking at the outline of her breast through her T-shirt. He picked a sweet out of the bag and licked it.

'My bruise has a lump in the middle,' said Claire. 'Want to see it?'

Ben tossed the sweet into his mouth and rubbed his hands. Claire grinned and put their tea on the bedside table. She whipped off her pants and climbed onto the bed on her front, giggling as he edged up her T-shirt.

'Woah. That is stunning. It looks like a purple Australia and you've got north and south New Zealand too.'

He lightly traced a finger over the non-bruised area of

her buttock. 'You'd love this colour palette. Shall I take a photo?'

'No. Don't stop. Stroke the other cheek.'

'But there aren't any countries on that one.'

'*You're* a country.'

She rolled onto her good side and pulled her body towards him. She kissed him and felt how hard he was and they let their tea go cold.

*

She was on a lounger with Hilary Mantel. The plastic cover of *Wolf Hall* warm beneath her hands. Today the sun had won. And she'd had amazing sex, and she was reading on the beach like someone on holiday.

Her eyes found her place on the page. She read most of a line, then looked around her again. Glittering sea, sky dotted with cauliflower-floret clouds, Ottie and Pearl patting sand in a bucket. Chris on duty on a blanket between loungers watching Charlie and Ollie. Honor having her swim. Ben back at the cottages for something, maybe a poo.

It was so fantastic to have a chance to read on the beach. *So read, Claire. Gobble it up. Yes, you should have paid more attention from the beginning, but just try and work out which Thomas she's talking about as you go.* She read eight words and looked up. *I'm reading on the beach. This is so delicious, I don't even mind which Thomas it is.*

Chris answered his phone.

'Hey Nick. Good thanks. You? Yes, back a week Saturday. Sure, do it while we're away. Yes, you can get access from the front entrance.'

Claire pulled her book closer. Read. You want to read. Don't think about what Nick's doing while they're away.

'Treated wood, yeah,' said Chris. 'On the bit of the fence that links to your road. So you'll maybe take out,' his head moved from side to side as he thought, 'just the one panel, yeah, I think so. Just a nice easy catch the kids can open. Great, Nick. Maybe the supplies place can ring me with the cost. Have you told Madison? Did she?' He laughed. 'I'm keeping it as a surprise for my two. OK, better go.'

Chris put away his phone. Honor walked up from the sea in her black bandeau swimsuit. She picked up a towel and rubbed it over an expanse of thigh then leaned over and pecked Chris on the lips.

'Nice swim?' he said.

'Extremely. Who were you talking to?'

'Er, the opticians. Need to make an appointment soon.'

Claire's eyes widened. She stared at the gap between two words. Pearl ran up. Before she got to Claire, Honor dropped straight-backed in front of her.

'Mummy's having some book time, baby cakes.' Honor's hands were on Pearl's skinny hips.

Pearl shrugged a smile and skipped off. Being Honor-generated, the notion of Mummy having book time was acceptable.

Charlie bowled over. 'Play wiv me Mum. I could bury you. Just your legs. Please.' His fists were under his chin. Claire put down her book.

'Claire,' said Honor. 'You're reading, remember? Clarity, consistency, boundaries.' She put on her sunglasses.

'Yeah,' said Claire. 'Look, I'm reading at the moment, Charlie.'

Charlie's eyes flitted up to Honor and back to Claire. 'How long?'

'Just for a bit.'

'Too vague, Claire. Show him how many pages.'

Claire flipped to the end of the not-sure-which-Thomas-this-is chapter. 'To here, OK Charlie?'

Charlie spun on his heel and pounded away.

'Eh, voila,' said Honor. 'Now Mummy must read.'

Claire picked up her book, humiliated. 'Thanks Honor.'

Honor made an 'it's hardly rocket science' gesture with her hands. She lay on the other lounger behind where Chris was sitting, knees up, ankles level with his shoulder.

'Gorgeous isn't it?' said Chris.

'Gorgeous,' said Honor.

'You know, I love the cottage here,' he said, angling himself towards her. 'We use all the space, don't we? Very ergonomically satisfying. Plus, if you yell to someone, they *hear* you. I always feel like I'm walking in our house. Walking to get close enough to yell to people.'

'Yes, Claire's cottages are cute.'

'We should live somewhere not much bigger Honor, seriously.'

'What charming nonsense.'

'We could build somewhere on our land and sell the house.'

Honor made a noise like someone shooing a cat off a worktop and flapped a hand at him. 'Stop that.'

Claire swallowed, appalled but amused. If that wedding had stayed cancelled, this wouldn't be happening. If they'd rented Perriwinton Manor Chris wouldn't be saying *let's have a bizarre looking erotic mosaic and some turrets and a nineteen fifties bar.*

'Anyway,' said Honor. Claire quickly looked at her book. This was her book time. She was supposed to be reading. 'Back in the real world. Did I mention the landscaping and pool design women I've been talking to?'

'Ha,' said Chris. 'No.'

Claire's body filmed with sweat at the friction filled silence. With unusually good timing Charlie and Pearl started bickering. She swung her legs over the side of the lounger. 'I think I'll just go and—'

'Uh-uh Claire, no,' said Honor. 'You're always sorting the kids out. Just relax with your book.'

Claire lay back on her lounger.

'Their schemes are phenomenal, Chris. Streams winding through trees into lagoons, you'd think they'd occurred naturally. It will be stunning and sound-insulating and *private*.' She put her arms behind her head. 'We'll use super mature trees, tall ones. Generics at the boundary, nice and densely planted, then exotics and flowering trees as you get closer to us and round the lagoon.'

'Honor, I have no interest in building a lagoon and some kind of magical forest,' said Chris amiably. He'd basically said no to Honor. Was that even an option? Claire gripped *Wolf Hall*, waiting to hear the next instalment.

'What? Of course you do, we talked about it months ago, you were really keen. Wait. Claire was there! Claire, sorry to interrupt your reading.'

'Honor, don't drag Claire in.'

Honor clonked her sunglasses onto her head better to capture Claire in her gaze. 'Claire. Remember when you came for lunch in the winter?'

A drop of tanning oil slid between Honor's breasts into her swimsuit. 'We were in one of the guest rooms. I was showing you how shockingly overlooked we are and I mentioned the plan to plant trees and have a pool and Chris agreed with it, didn't he?'

Claire raised herself onto her elbows. The sun was a blinding halo behind Honor's head.

'You remember don't you?'

'Why on earth would she remember that?' Chris held his hands towards Claire in a placatory manner. 'No offence Claire. I mean why would anyone.'

'None taken.' Of course Claire remembered. She remembered thinking, *Oh, Honor didn't ask Chris what his plan was.*

'Well anyway,' said Honor. 'Sounds like somebody needs some persuading.' She lay back and raised a leg and ran her beautiful foot over Chris's shoulder.

'Ow,' bellowed Pearl in a blood-curdling way that would lead to revenge.

'Better go,' said Claire, awkward, embarrassed for Chris. 'Nearly finished the chapter, so, you know … it's OK.'

Chapter 29

'Please tell Chef the lemon sauce was perfect.'

The gawky waiter, arms full of plates, gave Honor a slow nodding smile. It was sorrel, not lemon. Honor had offered Claire a taste on a spoon, the flavour had taken her back to the time she'd been to the restaurant on her own.

Claire hadn't known they were coming to the Pheasant again. When they'd been packing up on the beach, Chris had suggested wandering into town, which was what she'd dressed for. She'd come out of the cottage in jeans and old Birkenstocks to find Ben and Chris in short-sleeved patterned shirts posing for Honor in front of the fake roses. She was wearing wooden-heeled sandals and a silky sleeveless dress with a high neck and no bra. Claire turned to go back inside to change.

'Claire.' Honor held out her phone. 'Do pics of me and the boys for the Manchester alumni group.'

'Sure.'

Honor swayed over and wiggled silkily between Ben and Chris, an arm round each, pushing their cheeks towards her as she pouted, leg bent. There was no sign that Chris and Honor's conversation on the beach had left an atmosphere between them. Claire took a few photos, then handed back the phone. 'Won't be a sec.'

She ran up to the bedroom and looked dumbly into the wardrobe. She didn't actually want to change. She should have sent Charlie to the Fancy House earlier to scope out what Honor was wearing. He'd enjoyed doing that the other night.

'OK Claire,' called Honor from outside. 'We're off.'

Claire's eyes lit on her embroidered hessian bag. That hadn't had an outing yet. She transferred lip balm, water, games, a few bits of art stuff, keys and wallet inside its yellowed lining.

Outside, Honor was checking Chris had keys and money. She popped her lip gloss – the caramel one that was too light a shade on her damson lips – into his back pocket and squeezed his bum. Honor had no bag at all. She had completed her journey from go-to-Mum to woman responsible-only-for-herself.

On the way into Bodlowe, Claire had moved the embroidered bag behind her back and held it by its curved wooden handles, suddenly self-conscious of its home-craftedness.

Then Honor said, 'I'm on a campaign to win Chris round about the pool, Claire. I've booked at the Pheasant.'

Chris had enjoyed his starter, and the pork belly Honor had encouraged him to have.

'Mummy,' said Pearl, her elbows sliding a little on the white linen napkin she was leaning on, 'did you bring any games?'

'I did.' Claire lifted the bag onto her lap. Her daughter had been convinced no one would play these games, that Ollie and Ottie just went on Chris and Honor's phones, yet they asked for Uno, Bananagrams or colouring stuff every night.

'May I see?' Honor smiled and held out a hand. Claire handed her the bag and her pulse sped up as Honor ran her fingers over the felt and embroidery palm tree and the sunset edged in thick gold braid.

'I bring it on holidays,' said Claire. 'It's a bit fragile. It's the first time I've brought it away since the kids.'

'You made it?'

Claire nodded.

'Look at this. Claire, you're incredible!'

Claire felt like a small animal who'd walked some shaky steps on its back legs.

'Is there anything on the—' Honor turned the bag over, then gasped at the stitched-on poppies and cornflowers. 'Look Ottie.' Honor held the bag up and turned it.

'Its very stunning, Claire,' said Ottie.

Claire turned to Ottie, next to her at the end of the table, while Honor opened the handles and handed the drawstring bag of games to Pearl. 'Thanks Ottie. I sewed it when I was supposed to be revising for my A-levels. The hessian was just as faded then. I don't know how old the bag is.'

'Nineteen fifties,' said Honor. 'It's broken through to the lining in places.' Honor traced a dark nail over the brittle fibres, and the twisted gold braid.

'Chris, pass my lip gloss, will you.'

Chris put down the Uno cards he was dealing and handed her the tube.

'Look.' Honor tilted its gold twisted knob towards them. 'It's like your braid, Claire.'

'Oh yeah.'

'Is that your favourite lip gloss, Honor?' asked Pearl.

'It is,' Honor smiled at her. 'How perceptive of you.'

Pearl beamed, head on one side. A curl fell across her nose and she blew it away.

'How much was it?'

'Pearl,' Claire warned.

'Crazy lots,' said Honor, happily. 'It's discontinued.' She made it sound important. 'It means they've stopped making it.'

Pearl put a dismayed hand to her face.

'I tracked down as many as I could, Pearl. I searched every website and visited every big shop in London.'

Pearl looked at Honor with maximum respect. 'How many have you got?'

'I found three. This is the last one.' She stroked the tube. 'It's my most precious thing.'

Ottie looked down and moved her Bananagram tiles around.

'Honor,' said Pearl, one shoulder raised, 'if I'm careful, can I open it?'

Honor inhaled sharply, 'no' writ across her face, then her cheeks cranked into a smile 'Yes. All right then.'

Pearl wiped her hands on her napkin like she was about to handle the Koh-i-Noor diamond, undid the knob and slowly pulled. The applicator crackled from the tube. Pearl gazed at Honor and then sadly, because it meant the fun was over, pushed it back in again.

Claire went to the loo. By some miracle neither of her children had joined her. She sat and luxuriated in aloneness, mildly fatigued by everything to do with Honor's lip gloss and Pearl's fascination with it.

When she returned to the table, Honor was handing a stack of dessert menus back to the waiter.

'I ordered you a sticky toffee pudding, Ding. I know you love it. You had an enormous serving when I made it once.' Honor leaned over, newly caramel lips almost touching Claire's ear, breath hot. 'Split it with Ottie, Claire. But you have the lion's share. Just let her have a couple of bites.' She leaned back and mouthed, 'Cal-or-ies.'

Sticky toffee pudding? Delicious. I will need an entire portion and so will my small friend. Say that, Claire. Say it.

Her face moved around and no words came out.

The waiter arrived and Ben and Chris moved their card game to make space while Honor told them that it wasn't the same doing personal training sessions over video calls. There was dessert wine for her, cheese for Chris and a dessert to themselves for Ben, Pearl, Ollie and Charlie.

Claire wanted no part in this hustle of sharing and disappearing Ottie's food. It was way worse than Margo's haphazard provision of it. Her mother had been benignly self-absorbed, but Honor's control of Ottie was malignant.

The waiter put the bowl in front of Ottie and Ottie pushed it towards Claire.

'Mummy,' said Ollie. 'What do you call a man with leaves on his head?'

'I'm talking, Ollie.' It was important Honor wasn't interrupted from bitching about Linton's other clients whom she stalked on Instagram.

Claire stuck the bowl of her spoon against her chin and let it dangle, crossing her eyes. Ottie laughed. She was waiting for Claire to have first go on the pudding. Claire picked up a fork, put its tip into the gooey sponge then dabbed it in the ice cream. Waiting until Honor was drinking from her wine and distracted, Ottie loaded up and quickly put a spoonful in her mouth then shut her eyes and melted into a smile.

'Do you love it?' said Claire.

Ottie nodded waving the spoon dreamily. 'It's my favourite.'

The kid had given Claire, Pearl and Charlie tips on cartwheels and swum and run for hours. Policing her food like this was pathological.

'Your mum tells me you're trying out for cheerleading squad.'

'You don't have to try out.' Ottie looked puzzled. 'Anyone can join.'

'Oh. Cool,' said Claire.

'It's round the corner from my house. I'm going with my friend Madison. She's been teaching me the routines.' She glanced at Honor. 'Mummy doesn't know her yet.'

Claire nodded. Unlike Chris's resistance to forests and lagoons, it did at least sound like Ottie's and Honor's plans were *similar*.

Honor raised a slender arm to sip her wine. Ottie's wrists weren't slight like her mother's, they were wider like Chris's. Ollie shared Honor's bone structure, and that didn't work for Honor. She wanted to fatten him up and skinny down her daughter.

'All for you,' Claire mouthed at Ottie.

Ottie ate the sticky toffee pudding, darting the spoon to the bowl, chewing behind her hand. As cover, Claire leaned in to the conversation at the table. Honor glanced over. Claire spun back and picked up some ice cream on her fork.

'Claire,' said Honor. 'They've got a rack of leaflets at the back. Shall we take a look?'

Honor towered over Claire by the jumbled rack. Her nipples – *way* too far into Claire's peripheral vision – were like raspberries against the flimsy fabric of her dress. Claire turned and straightened a leaflet, hands sweating.

'You gave Ottie the whole bowl. Why? I asked you to have the lion's share.'

Claire curled her toes away from the heft and sharpness of Honor's sandals. 'I just, I didn't fancy it. Sorry.'

'Not like you to not eat something. Look Claire, we've

got ten days to get maybe five pounds off her. Wing woman, yeah?' She held her fist out for Claire to bump.

Claire clenched her fist at her side. She'd let Honor block her kids from her on the beach. Was that Honor being *her* 'wing woman'? Headwoman more like.

'Sorry but no.'

Honor jerked her head questioningly.

'I, I,' Claire swallowed. 'You said you didn't want her to feel different.' Her voice was thin and quavering. Honor looked confused. 'From the other girls at cheerleading. But she must be feeling different here all the time, the other kids aren't sharing food.'

'You've undermined me in front of my child and now you're questioning my parenting?'

'Sorry.' A sense of doom twisted under Claire's ribs. 'I... I think I might be getting my period?'

Honor withered at her. Fair enough. Her period wasn't even due until after they got home. *Be strong, Claire. Own this.* 'But even if I am. Please don't ask me to do that again. I don't think Ottie needs to lose any weight at all.'

'Well,' said Honor.

Claire glanced up. Honor's lips were trembling.

'No need to be sorry, Claire. This is actually amazing. This kind of real, strong, deep shit only gets said between friends who are *truly* close. So thank you.' She tugged Claire's hand. 'Thank you for letting me know how much you care.'

Chapter 30

Ben gestured to Claire through the Pheasant's window. He was outside with Chris and the kids.

'Look Charlie. Daddy's got Dog, I can see him.' Charlie crawled out from under the table and rushed through the door Chris held open for him.

Honor clattered back from the loo. Claire's shoulders shot up to her ears.

'Would you look after my lip gloss please, Claire?'

'Sure. Absolutely, yes, of course.' She'd overdone it, rushing to be agreeable, but it was a relief Honor had asked for something so easy to agree to. The hooped hands of the bag were on Claire's shoulder. Honor opened it.

'You don't mind do you?'

'No, I'd be happy to.' *I feel I owe you, although I know that's ridiculous.*

'Thanks.'

They walked home along the coast road. Claire, Ben and Chris mucking around with the kids, Honor pausing to wait for them.

Back at Murdon Farm, Ben joined Chris and the kids in the barn.

'Can I get my gloss, Claire?'

'Sure.'

Honor held out her hand as Claire opened her bag and riffled back and forth through the games, tissues and wipes.

She put the bag down on the porch and checked again. Not there. It must be there. Honor followed her into the cottage. Claire poured the bag out onto the sofa and raked, desperately. She turned the bag upside down and shook. She pulled it inside out and frisked it.

'Oh dear, look.'

Honor reached out. 'There's stitching missing in the lining, Ding, and some of the outside is broken.' Honor clasped an elbow with her hand. 'It's fallen out, hasn't it? It's gone.'

Her favourite thing, Claire. Her favourite thing.

'Oh God. I'm sorry. I'm so, so sorry.'

'We're just going to look for my lip gloss,' Honor announced to the barn. 'Claire was looking after it but it fell through a hole in her bag.'

'Mummy!' Pearl looked Claire up and down.

'Bad luck,' said Chris. 'You've got lots of others though, haven't you, sweetheart?'

Honor shook her head sadly. 'It's my discontinued Faron Odashi Absolute Nude.'

'Nude?!' Ollie hit himself in the forehead.

'Discontinued?!' said Charlie and did the same.

'Even so, it's not the end of the world if you don't find it.'

'Chris is right, Ding.' Honor clutched Claire's arm. 'But let's try. It's insanely hydrating, and literally irreplaceable.'

'You should try and find it Mummy,' said Pearl, an edge in her voice.

'Let's go while there's still some light,' said Honor.

'Oh no Honor, stay,' said Claire, a bit too fast. 'You shouldn't have to come. Ben, you'll come won't you?'

'I'll come Mum.'

'Thanks Charlie. And Ben, please?'

241

Claire and Ben shone their phones on the road. Claire hadn't known she had a hole in her bag. Why couldn't a tiny toy, or something of hers have fallen out? Why was it Honor's favourite lip gloss?

'I'll take Charlie back,' said Ben after they'd been on the coast road for a while. Charlie's hands were behind his back, his head switching from side to side playing boy searching for something.

'Have you found it?' he said.

'Not yet, Charlie. Go back with Dad.'

'What does it look like, Mum?'

Now he was asking? She kissed the top of his head 'It looks like the end of the sodding world, love.'

'It's only a lipstick,' said Ben. 'Why don't you leave it?'

'*Gloss*, it's a lip *gloss*. And it's irreplaceable.'

Claire searched in the tufty grass to the side of the slope where she'd run around with the kids, then walked on. She should have done things differently tonight, because everything else aside, an evening in which Honor remarked in a scary way on the depth of their 'truly close' friendship was one that had got away from her. She had gone beyond her remit. Honor was in charge of *decisions,* Claire was in charge of *things.* She'd shared an opinion about Ottie's weight, and she'd lost a thing. An eye for an eye. A gloss for a 'how dare you not agree to be my food-denying wingwoman.' It was karma. Maybe Claire should just have eaten the lion's share of the pudding. But sod that. It was shit of Honor to put her in that position, and damaging to limit Ottie, and Honor had needed to know.

Maybe Chris hadn't noticed what was happening. Honor was so quick. One second she and Ottie were sharing a waffle, the next it had gone.

Claire gasped and ran towards the twirled knob of the tube. It was a scrunch of gold sweet wrapper. She couldn't deny it, Honor had ambition for her children. She'd picked the cheerleading squad that was the best because she wanted them to be the best they could be. A parent should probably have ambition. Maybe in a *way*, Honor was right. Maybe it was Claire's pandery lack of drive that made her feel like cheerleading round the corner with Madison was right for Ottie. It wasn't surprising Pearl hadn't progressed on the piano with Edna. How well might she have done with a qualified teacher who could properly hear her? Luton Luvvies wasn't the best by a long stretch. Claire had literally chosen it because it was on Sunday, *to avoid Honor*. How un-child-centred and all-about-her was that? She was a terrible mother. She'd let her children, already weakened by her pandering, have their talent (particle of) luvvied into cheesiness. This anger inside her probably wasn't with Honor at all. She was trying to *project* it onto Honor but she was angry with herself, especially as, since she'd started gnashing this over, she'd been striding along *forgetting to look for the fucking lip gloss.*

Claire stopped dead and howled in frustration. She retraced her steps a little, then searched her way into town. At the door of the Pheasant she shone her phone torch through the dark window. She couldn't see a thing. She'd pop in tomorrow to see if by some brilliant chance, the gloss had fallen out before they'd left the restaurant.

She walked back head over shoulder to enjoy the lights of Bodlowe. When she turned onto the track, light was shining through gaps in the barn wall. Claire stopped at the corner. The door was open.

'I still think you need a solid plan B,' said Chris.

'No plan B required, Chris. *Asif*, the clue is in the name.

The job's mine. God, everyone thinks they know better than me tonight.'

Claire's lower lip crept under her teeth. She tucked her hair behind her ear.

'Here hon,' said Honor. 'Have a look at the pool company's website. Please.'

There was quiet for a while.

'Yes, they look completely natural. I can see why the designs win awards but it's not going to happen, sweetheart.'

'What do you mean?'

'I've got a plan for that space. Something that will benefit the community.'

'We're not part of the community.'

'We are.'

'*I'm* not,' said Honor sounding almost disgusted. Laughter kicked Claire's stomach. 'I have no interest in being part of the community.'

'Well the rest of us *do*. And while you've been in London and Hong Kong and Geneva, me and the kids have very much become part of it, and I'm having a gate put in this week.'

'A gate? Where?'

'On the boundary fence where you want your fairytale forest, so we can have quicker access to the neighbours. Nick's doing it next week.'

'Who the hell is Nick?

'Madison's Dad.'

'Madison?'

'Jesus, Honor, ask your daughter. Actually don't, it'll make her sad. She's a friend of Ottie's. Look. I'm not anti pool, there's a spot the other side of the garage block that would work. I'm also not anti the odd tree, but I'm anti waste and I'm anti being a decadent tosser.'

Movement. Wooden sandals.

'I'm going to see if Ben and Claire have any wine.'

'Don't,' said Chris. 'Their lights are out.'

'All right!' Honor sighed.

'So my project, if you're interested, which you clearly aren't, is to provide our hardworking neighbours, who mostly struggle to afford the houses you see as an eyesore, with something that will benefit them.'

'Yes. A fucking gate. Let the hordes in for picnics. Er, don't think so.'

'The gate's a gate. I haven't told you the plan yet.'

'Well, you're right. I'm not interested. I'm hurt you don't want what I want, and I think you called me a tosser just now, so g'night.'

'You're not going to knock on their—'

'No, I'm not Chris,' Honor yelled. 'Because actually, I think we've got another bottle.'

Claire shrank down the side of the barn. Honor exited, an angry flash of silk. Her steps receded and Claire heard the Fancy House door shut. She waited for Chris to leave the barn too and when he didn't, Claire tiptoed back up the track towards the coast road and returned, walking like Gunnar in her Footgloves, to rearrive and not surprise him.

''Night then Chris,' she called.

He turned and smiled. 'Oh, 'night Claire. Any luck?'

'Nope. I'll have another look tomorrow.'

'Great. She seems really attached to that lip gloss.' He rubbed his eyes. He looked worn out.

Claire let herself into the cottage. Honor *was* a decadant tosser. And she drank way too much. And why had she still not asked Chris what his plan was? So rude. Something that would benefit the community sounded great.

It was after midnight but Claire opened her laptop.

Honor was wrong, there were loads of Faron Odashi Absolute Nudes. She put one in a basket and clicked. No stock. Ah. It happened on website after website. Claire searched for Faron Odashi Absolute Nude dupes. There were none. It was irreplaceable and also inimitable.

Claire went up to the bedroom. She could hear voices from next door. Mostly Honor's, expansive and righteous. Ben was asleep. She felt around for her make-up bag and found her own lip gloss and put it in the embroidered bag and shook it. She tilted the bag and shook over and over.

'Claire. What are you doing?'

Claire startled. Moonlight glinted in Ben's eyes.

'Sorry. I thought I was being quiet. Why am I such a dick Ben? Why did I agree to look after something of Honor's with a hole in my bag?'

She put the gloss through the gap in the lining near the bottom of the bag and poked it up and out through a hole in the hessian. It could happen. It had happened. She looked up at Ben but his eyes had closed.

Chapter 31

She'd woken keen to run, and jogged to Bodlowe scanning the tarmac for the lip gloss. Why had she bothered last night? Searching in daylight was way more efficient. She cupped her hands to the window of the Pheasant. All she could see was a till receipt on the floor and fresh white cloths on the tables. Claire pulled her leg behind her to stretch her quads.

OK, that's done. You might be the one who lost it, but jeez, you've looked for that gloss, so let it go and carry on with your run. After all, Honor's on holiday too. It's not like she doesn't have time to look for it.

She hurtled up through Bodlowe, ponytail swinging as she exchanged a couple of hearty good mornings. Her steady energy surprised her. Some days it was like this and running was absolute life. She'd been so resistant at the start, shuffling round the park, grumbling at Katie. If it wasn't for running, she might be lying in bed right now, nauseously replaying Honor's truly close friendship spiel, but she was out here doing this instead. Mucho better.

She ran along the coast road and in down the edge of the cornfield. A gate pole with a twist of shredded orange plastic on it moved closer. And now the pole was beside her and now it was behind her. Running was perspective. Running showed you that you moved forward.

★

Claire bent over panting at the open barn door. Ottie, Charlie and Pearl encircled an iPad like it was a campfire.

'Morning kiddles.'

'Hey Mummy.'

'Hey Claire. Nice run?'

'Smashing run, thanks Ottie.' She stretched out her calves.

'We did our breakfast,' said Charlie, proudly.

Claire smiled, 'So I see.' She picked up the pack of cornflakes and the two still brimming bowls. One day, although maybe not till they were buying their own, they'd work out how much milk was enough. 'Ollie around?'

'He's on the beach with my dad,' said Ottie.

'Cool. Catch you later.'

She went into the cottage and put two slices of granary in the toaster. She texted Katie.

Top run just now. You? Xx

A text popped up. **OK OK!! I'm going now!!**

Ben was in the shower. She wouldn't fill the kettle just yet. It would shut off the hot.

She felt unexpectedly great.

Do it Claire. You know you have to.

It could kill this good mood.

You won't know till you try.

It was time to look at what she'd posted on the Headleigh Forum, in shock, having resigned in a wetsuit. That post was her calling card to the world. She had to see what she'd put out there.

CLAIRE SWIFT ILLUSTRATION
Dear Headleigh Forum folk.
Thank you so much for the kind things you've said about my work.

**Just to let you know, my new business is up and
running. Bring me your projects big and small. I'm
happy to quote for anything. Spread the word!**

Bit excitable. Definitely keen. But not completely mortifying.

She smoothed butter then Marmite onto toast and bit in.
A knock at the door. Claire swallowed the wrong way and
started coughing. She opened the door onto a waft of musky
perfume and coughed harder, circling a finger at herself to
say *give me a minute*.

Honor was leaning against the porch in a jarring patterned top and trousers. 'Someone's had a good run.'

'Yes, it was great, thanks.' Claire cleared her throat but the
cough wasn't finished. She let herself be turned so Honor
could clap her on the back. 'OK, thanks, I'm good now.'

Honor's eyes were puffy and lined with kohl. 'Do you
think you and Ben could have my two for the day?' Her
hungover skin was perked with shimmery blush, her lips
slicked in a pink that suited her loads better than the discontinued pain in the arse.

'Sure. Of course.'

'Thanks. I'm taking Chris out. Obviously we'll return
the favour. FYI, Ollie got out of bed the wrong side, so lay
down the law, Ding. He's basically a dog, so he needs to
know you're the boss. I'm not criticising your parenting, I'm
just saying what works best.'

Ten minutes later, Ollie was in the barn and Chris and
Honor were whizzing down the track in the Space Ship.
Trepidation at a day with Ollie swirled around elation at a
day without Honor.

The kids played in the barn. Claire had a shower while

Ben cleared breakfast, then she sat on the bench outside the cottage and looked up how to make dogs like you, how to play with dogs, and how to make dogs believe you're in charge.

Ben came and sat next to her and shuddered with a yawn.

'Are you tired because Honor and Chris were arguing?' she said. 'They were having quite a humdinger.'

'No. I'm tired because you woke me up about that lipstick.'

Claire turned away and mouthed 'lip gloss' and loathed herself. 'So what about today, Ben? Do we need a game plan?'

He pulled a face and Claire laughed.

'Honor said to treat Ollie like a dog,' she said.

'Charlie's not a dog is he?' said Ben. 'He's more like ...' he looked up, thinking, 'a middle-aged rabbit.'

Claire laughed again. 'Grant gives Ollie-ish boys lots of praise and exercise.'

'Pretty much what Chris does.'

She nodded. 'So shall we be more Chris, less Honor?'

'Yeah,' said Ben. 'Let's be two Chrises and if things go pear-shaped, you can be Honor.'

'I don't want to be Honor.' The words came out in a rush. She felt Ben glance at her.

'Hopefully no one will have to be Honor.' It was one of the most negative things she'd heard Ben say about anyone. 'We should mix it up,' he said. 'Do stuff we haven't done yet and keep things moving.'

'Sure. Sounds like a plan.' Claire smiled and felt herself relax. She'd forgotten he could be in charge.

When they were ready, they took the steps to the beach, the kids haring down them and somehow landing intact. They went to the slot machines and Bodlowe's little town museum, which Ollie blazed through in forty seconds until Ben pointed out some flaps and levers he could bang.

Lunch from Greggs was an exotic novelty for the junior Wellbeloveds. She wondered if they should have gone somewhere else. *Claire, stop caring what Honor thinks.* They took their food to picnic tables at the harbour via the Pheasant, which was closed due to staff illness. She'd try again later.

Ben was beach lifeguard while Claire sketched. She'd been too inhibited to draw on the beach in case Honor thought she was showing off. She sketched two women lying on towels. One of them was pregnant and kept tugging her tankini top up over her football of a bump. She sketched a woman and her teenage sons, all of them reading paperbacks, pages flapping in the warm breeze rolling in from the water. She sketched a big family group with four generations of humans and four generations of deckchairs, the eightieth birthday people from the hotel bar.

It felt so good to be her unfettered self.

Ollie annexed a den the kids had all made – chip off the old block – hitting anyone who tried to enter.

'Divide and rule?' said Ben.

'Yep.' Claire set down her sketch pad and scrambled into her trusty wetsuit. 'Ollie, let's you and me play together.' She thought he'd refuse, but he rushed to her beach bag and ferreted out a frisbee. They played in the sea. He liked it when Claire threw the frisbee so he had to swim for it and brought it back in his mouth.

'Good dog,' said Claire and ruffled his hair. He barked for her to throw it again, and again.

The problem with Honor treating Ollie like a dog, was that it didn't include the playing.

Eventually, he flopped out onto the beach. 'Will my mum and dad come back?'

Bless his heart. 'Of *course* they will.' She smiled her sureness into his hard-to-read face. 'Are you worried about them arguing?'

He shrugged and rubbed his eyes and then nodded.

'Everyone argues. I'm sure it's nothing.'

They went back to the others. Charlie attached himself to her like a limpet.

'Can we send a photo of us to my mum and dad?' asked Ottie.

They used Ben's phone, better camera, and huddled up for a photo.

'Hold on.' Claire arranged herself. In the event that this was gifted back to her as a massive englargement, she wanted to feel all right in it. The photos were fun. The kids' faces full of wild holiday energy. Ben texted one to Chris and Honor. He thought they should move things on again. As they walked off the beach, Claire found his hand and squeezed it. He'd caught the sun on his nose. Conversation starters popped into her head.

Have you noticed how Honor…

I wish Honor would…

I'm obsessed with Honor and I used that as an excuse to lie and do something you don't know about…

Better to just enjoy holding hands.

The kids got stuck in at the play park. It was perched on a high point and the view of Bodlowe was stunning. Different shades and textures of greenery interwoven with rooftops, patchworking down to the harbour.

Ben went to the kiosk for coffee and Claire sat on a bench by the play area. They'd sit here and gorge on the view and cement this nice feeling. She'd just check her phone. Nestled between a promo for the Luton Luvvies' summer scheme and one from a time management site she'd subscribed to, was an email from someone called Gemma Dillon with the subject *Illustration*.

Hello Claire

My neighbour Fran Achibe mentioned you to me, then I spotted your post on the Headleigh Forum. Clients of mine need an illustrator for a wide-reaching project and your work has just the kind of fun, quirky warmth they're after.

If you have availability in the coming weeks and would like to know more, please let me know.

Best wishes,
Gemma

Excuse me, *what* was that? Claire's chest thumped. This was incredible. This was the most incredible email ever sent. Wait. Was it meant for her? Fran. Headleigh Forum. It *was* meant for her. Lovely Fran! She read the email again. No one had ever told her they had *clients* looking for illustrators. But maybe the clients were Gemma's friends who wanted posters for pottery classes or something. She looked at the bottom of the email. Gemma Dillon was Director of Creative Development at Aldous O'Hare.

Ben whistled for her attention and handed her a coffee. 'You all right?'

'Yeah, yeah, good.' She put her phone under her thigh. She couldn't share the email straight off, it was too breathtaking, she needed time to take it in.

Ben was chatty. He was in such a good mood and Gemma had said her work had fun quirky warmth.

'Doesn't it?'

'What? Sorry, Ben.'

'The coffee. Smells great. Wasn't sure it it would.'

She sniffed at her cup. 'Yeah it does, thanks.'

'It's a gamble isn't it. You want to support the little places but it's *coffee*, so you're "Dudes, I don't know you. Can I trust you with something this important?"'

'Yeah, I know what you mean.' She smiled. *Ben's so lovely. What would he say about the email? It feels too good to be true. It probably won't come to anything. What's a wide-reaching project anyway?*

'Don't they, Claire?'

'Sorry Ben, sorry. I just had an email. Can I show you?'

He took her phone and she watched his eyes widen and crinkle as he read. He turned to her with his tongue out, gobsmacked. She laughed.

'See?' he said. 'Knew that course would kick things off for you.'

Claire nodded in a hazy way, felt sick, and threw scalding coffee into her mouth.

Chapter 32

'Claire,' Ottie had come over to the bench. She tweaked unselfconsciously at the crotch of her shorts. 'Do you think one day, you could give me a drawing lesson?'

'I'd love to. How about now?'

Ottie hopped and clapped her hands above her head.

Claire smiled. 'I'll take that as a yes.' She stood from the bench with the coffee and hooked the beach bag under her arm. She went to the grass near the play area, scoped it for dog mess then kneeled down and pulled out all the materials she'd brought.

'Art class is open.'

Charlie beetled over and kneeled next to her.

'Give Mummy some space, Charlie.' Pearl sat some way to the other side, demonstrating her superior understanding of Claire's need for space. Ottie kneeled in the gap. Pearl tossed her hair back, discombobulated, then to her credit, gave Ottie a big smile.

'Are you joining us Ollie?' Claire asked.

He flung his head from side to side.

'Me, Ollie and a ball I think,' said Ben.

'Won't be too long,' Claire mouthed.

'Take as long as you like,' he smiled affectionately and followed Ollie to the hedged-in area at the bottom of the slope.

'Can you show us how to make people look like people?' Ottie asked.

Claire sorted them out with paper and something to lean on and drew them each a vertical line and six horizontals, then showed them how to lay in a body with a head in the top section, feet in the bottom, hips in the middle.

While they were adding faces and clothes, she quickly googled Aldous O'Hare. It was a design and branding consultancy. There was a photo of Gemma. She had huge clear-framed glasses and a pierced eyebrow. Would Aldous O'Hare's Director of Creative Development write to her about posters for classes at the Halls? No. They would not. Claire must write back and not sound mad. Or amazed. Or overly grateful.

Hi Gemma
Thanks so much for getting in touch.
Yes, I'd love

Not 'love', it's too much …

like

Not 'like', it's too bland …

be interested to know more.

Claire put away her phone, nervously excited.

Ottie passed over her piece of paper. 'I've drawn you but it doesn't look like you.'

'Oh, it's fab, Ottie. I love the pattern on my top and you've given me the best eyelashes.'

'I've drawn Pearl,' said Charlie. His drawing was mostly orange curls.

'I've drawn me too!' said Pearl. 'Aw, well done Charlie that's really good.'

Charlie beamed and Claire chuckled. 'These are great.'

'Shall we take photos and send them to Honor?' said Pearl.

Honor's daughter's drawing of *another woman?* Hell no. 'Maybe later, Pearl. Let's do some more.'

Charlie pointed beyond the gated play area at a muscle-bound bald guy in a tight white T-shirt throwing a stick for a tiny long-haired dog. 'I'm drawing them now,' he said.

'Oh, me too,' said Claire tearing out a piece of the thick paper. She sketched an exaggerated version of them. Made the dog look like a mop head, gave the owner the proportions of Mr Incredible.

They were a funny pair. The man was throwing the stick for the dog, but doing most of the running. He'd chuck it. The dog would bound a few tiny steps towards it then look to the man and he'd scarper over. The man was running for the stick. Ha ha, the dog was in charge. She flipped her paper over and redrew them reflecting their power dynamic, making the little dog huge and the man teeny and eager to please.

The kids wanted to look. They thought it was hilarious. Charlie rolled around on his back, laughing. 'You should show the man, Mum.'

'Ha ha, hmmm, better not.'

'It's really funny, Claire.'

'Thank you.'

'Ottie's right, Mummy.'

What lovely kids. Claire smiled down at Bodlowe, enjoying the sun on her skin and the warmth within. *Claire, what's going on? You're not turning over what they said and looking for a weak spot to prove it's rubbish.*

No. I'm not. Because it's an exhausting waste of time. And anyway, I'm having what they said.

Why?

Because I believe them.

'I've learned so much today, Claire.'

'Me too Ottie.' Claire smiled and breathed out slowly. 'Hey, how about you paint this beautiful view.'

They talked about how the harbour wall snaked round and down into the sea. How the ribbon of sea behind swooped round to the wall. That the sweep of buildings were a long line with a shorter line behind. She talked about how drawing was looking. That you had to think about the big shapes before the details.

The kids pencilled in the big shapes then added their details in pencils and paint from a tin of watercolours.

'I'm doing the flowers at the edge of the park.'

'I'm doing boats.'

'Here are some clouds.'

With her favourite pen, Claire sketched Charlie and the girls as they painted, then wrote *fun, quirky warmth* in a fun, quirky way.

'I might give this to my grandma,' said Ottie, surveying her finished painting. 'Or Mummy and Daddy.'

'My granny Gogo is a painter,' said Pearl. 'Mummy, wouldn't Gogo love to see our pictures?'

In theory ... yes. 'Sure. 'Course she would.'

'Can I have your phone then?'

'Oh. You mean, right now?'

Claire's hand hovered over her back pocket. It was a recipe for a damp squib. 'I don't know, Pearl. You have to ring her neighbour and he goes and gets her.' Quite likely, David the neighbour would be grumpy, and who could blame him? And Margo hated being disturbed.

Ben and Ollie were laughing. They both had hold of the ball. Ben suddenly groaned and bent over. Ah shit, Ollie had whacked him in the nuts. Claire jumped up.

'Phone pwease, Mummy.' Pearl had her hands out.

Ben was still bent over.

'OK Pearl.' She handed over her phone. 'It's *Mum neighbour David* in contacts.'

She jogged down the slope, picking up more speed than she intended. 'Ben, you OK?' She laid a hand on his back.

'I hope it was a mistake,' he winced.

Ollie was thrashing his arms at the hedge. Either guilty or sulking, it was hard to tell. Claire beckoned him over.

'Sorry Ben.'

'OK. Play nicely bud, yeah?'

Claire joined the game, booting the ball inexpertly to Ollie. She glanced up the slope to see Pearl nattering at her phone and then turning it onto her harbour painting which Ottie was holding up, while Charlie elbowed in, determined to be on screen.

Well, Pearl had got hold of *someone*.

'You be in goal,' said Ollie.

'Er, OK.' She got into position by the hedge, crouching protectively. Ollie put the ball down and stepped backwards for a run up.

'Save yourself, not the ball,' called Ben.

She laughed. 'Good tip.'

The ball bounced off Claire's forearms. OK, she could handle this. Ben and then Ollie took turns to send the ball towards her. Some she saved, some she missed. Some she saved herself from.

'Mum.' Charlie had bum-shuffled part way down the

slope. 'Gogo said she wanted to see *your* drawrins, so she's looking at them now, yeah.'

'Um. OK, yeah.'

Wow. That hadn't happened in a *loooong* time.

They were meeting Chris and Honor in the square in Bodlowe at six. As she and Ben and the kids walked there, Claire asked Charlie what Gogo had said about everyone's pictures.

'She liked everyfing. She said they were all good.'

'Can you remember anything else she said about...' she wanted to say 'mine', but said, 'any of them?'

'Just they were all good.' he made a massive circle with his hands.

Honor was in a sleeveless denim jumpsuit. Chris gamely tried to pick Ottie and Ollie up, one in each hand, groaning like a strong man as they giggled.

'Jumpsuit looks incredible on you,' said Claire.

Honor stroked a hand down her hip. 'Got it in St Ives. That dress really does suit you, Claire.'

'Thanks.' She looked down at her belted below-the-knee button-through. Honor mostly meant 'you've already worn that dress', but it bloody did suit her, and after a good rest from Honor, and an email from Gemma Dillon, the comment was amusing rather than hurtful.

They wandered towards the Pheasant so Honor and Claire could ask about the lip gloss. Nothing had been handed in. Claire kneeled on the floor to check under the table while Honor went to the loo.

'I feel so bad about this,' said Claire, as they left without it.

'I know you do,' said Honor, bestowing a look of great sympathy. 'Come on. Let's forget about it, bestie.' She draped an arm round Claire's shoulder and as they strolled through town past people, blackboard menus and hanging baskets stuffed to bursting with geraniums and lobelia, Claire smiled, to offset the feeling she was basically in a headlock.

'We had a stupendous day, Claire. Couples massage, very sexy. Then some action movie I knew Chris would like with *un peu de* back row snoggage, bit of lunch and on the way back, a walk at that arboretum. I say walk,' Honor checked no one was looking then mouthed 'up against a tree' into Claire's face before mercifully releasing her from the headlock. Claire had been with Honor maybe ten minutes and her energy, steady all day, was suddenly draining.

'And I asked Chris for nothing, Claire,' Honor added, bumping her arm against Claire conspiratorially. 'Didn't even mention my lagoon. You see, if you get the subliminal messaging right, the U-turn will happen. The idea will dawn that he'll have to choose carefully if he ever wants sex again.'

*

They walked to the Clifftop Hotel garden. Honor and Ben went to get drinks and the bar menu for food. Chris wandered down to the lowest tier of the bushy garden to take photos of the kids. Claire checked her phone. Gemma had replied.

Hi Claire

Really good to hear back from you. At this stage I can tell you the client is part of a financial corporation with an excellent ethical reputation. We've been working with them for a few months and they're great.

I'll get a non-disclosure agreement ready for signing, then let's talk rates and if all's good, we can have a video call to say hi and tell you about the project and hopefully move you onto pitch stage.

All the best and thanks
Gemma

'You all right Claire?' asked Chris, sitting the kids at their own table.

'Um, yeah. Yeah, I'm good.' She was staring at her phone, wide-eyed. Non-disclosure, video call, pitch ... This was not chutney stuff. Financial corporation with excellent ethical reputation. Honor's world. So unlikely to be Honor's bank though. Surely.

Ben arrived with drinks. He took the kids' ones over with instructions to be careful. Honor put down beer and a bottle of red and glasses. Ollie rushed to Claire's side. She reached for her beach bag. 'Do you want some cars Ollie? The Jenga?' He threw stiff arms round her.

'A hug?' Honor was aghast. 'Ollie doesn't do hugs.' Ollie ran back to the others. 'What was that about?'

'I don't know!' Claire felt very hot and pulled a face like it was puzzling and hugs weren't even nice.

Honor glugged wine into the oversized glasses. Ottie appeared. 'Claire, can I show mummy what we painted?'

Claire reached into the bag for the watercolour pad. Ottie took it round to Honor.

'Claire taught me to look at the big picture before the details.'

Honor bristled. 'Well yes, that's definitely how to do it. Oh, look at this though. That's good enough to frame, Ottie.'

Ottie beamed. 'I loved it today, thanks, Claire.' She handed back the sketch pad.

'You're welcome.'

'Claire had an email about a job,' said Ben.

'Fantastic,' said Honor. 'Show me.' She opened and shut her fingers like a beak. Claire allowed herself to be mugged for her phone and Honor scrolled to the start of the exchange.

'I heard from them again,' Claire told Ben. 'While you were at the bar.'

'Hey, cool.'

'Oh.' Honor's mouth fell completely open. 'How extra-ordinary. It's First United.'

'Really? Are you sure?' Claire sank inside. 'How do you know?'

'"Excellent ethical reputation". That's First United. It's like saying the Scottish play instead of *Macbeth*. Wow wow wow. Guys, Claire's going to pitch for some illustration work with my bank. Isn't that just incredible?

'It's fantastic, Claire,' said Chris.

'First United?' said Ben. 'Woah.'

They all clinked glasses with Claire.

Honor glugged at her wine. 'I'm so delighted about this. Hey, why don't we all work for FU! Ha ha!'

Claire laughed nervously. Honor grabbed her knee. 'You must jump on this while we're here and I can help you. Isn't it perfect timing.'

'God yes, it's perfect. Thanks. Thank you.'

Claire went to the ladies' in the Clifftop to process what had happened. The soap dispenser waited till she'd moved her hands away, then dispensed soap. She wiped it up and washed.

Did she want Honor's help? Honor was scary, and a bit

mean, but she was basically good. True, she was manipulating her husband into building some kind of fairytale forest, but things only went wrong for Katrina because she stood up to Honor, and it's not like Claire was going to make that mistake again.

The dryer didn't work. Claire shook her hands over the sink. Given she'd lost Honor's favourite lip gloss, it was nice that she wanted to help. So the feeling she had, that she was being hustled onto a white-knuckle ride that hadn't been safety-checked, with someone who might push her off, was just... excitement? Yeah. It was excitement, with a tiny pinch of fear.

Bottom line though. If Honor decided she was helping her, she probably didn't have much of say in it.

*

'Get a wiggle on, you lot.' Claire placed a hand on her hip. The kids were trailing behind, larking along the hotel garden railings, stuffed with club sandwiches and chips that she herself had had little appetite for, and Honor had barely picked at. They'd be ages getting them back to the cottages at this rate.

She startled. Ploughing along behind the kids, overtaking now, the fabric of her nylon slacks and top pulling in all directions, was the B&B lady.

Claire twisted to hide herself. Static shocked her forearm.

'You shouldn't have sent that umbrella.'

Claire flooded scarlet. 'Sorry? I don't know what you ... sorry. I think you've got the wrong—'

'It's far too good. And so *heavy*.'

'O*kaaay*.' Claire shrugged and smiled and flashed a gurn at Honor, Ben and Chris before turning back to the woman who threw her hand in the air like the umbrella was the least of her problems.

'Well, anyway. It's the thought that counts.' She trudged on past them all.

'What was that?' said Honor, fascinated.

'Most random thing ever,' Claire spluttered, sick with herself. 'No *idea* who she was.'

'You OK?' said Ben. 'You look rattled.'

'I'm fine. She was mixing me up with someone else, I guess.'

'She seemed so sure,' said Ben. 'I suppose that's part of the deal with confusion.'

Claire couldn't breathe.

'Or maybe,' said Chris. 'You've got a doppelganger round here.'

Guilt churned like cement. 'Ha ha, maybe I do.' The secret she'd pushed to the back of a cupboard had thudded into her hands.

They meandered back through Bodlowe. She was trembling, the smell of her deceit in her nose. *You thought you had it sorted. Prinking along in your ponytail thinking you've solved life with running. Feeling OK about your forum post. Smugging it up over the kids' compliments.*

The secret had thudded out. And she was not sure she could bear its weight.

Chapter 33

Claire woke the next morning in brace position, head splitting. The celebration of her job news had continued when they got back to the cottages. Unsettled by the umbrella incident, she'd drunk Too. Much. Wine.

There were six sleeps to go. It was a lot. She felt next to her. Ben was already up, so she thunked into a starfish, peeking behind her through the slit in the curtain at the Tupperware sky. She crawled from the bed to the bathroom. She needed to put things into her body to stop it feeling this bad.

How could there be no headache pills in the medical kit? She tipped her head back and poured Calpol from a tiny bottle into her mouth.

The kids were in pyjamas in front of the TV. Dog was splayed on Charlie's head like a hat, his embroidered smile momentarily cheering. Ben was playing on his phone in the kitchen, feet crossed on a chair. He looked up at her and nodded. 'Hey.'

'Yeah,' she managed. 'Headache pills?'

'In the bathroom.'

'Nope.'

She frisked bags and coats and surfaces. Where had they gone? Calpol wouldn't cut it. This was an *adult* headache. She'd moved things around several times to stay on top of feeling organised but she'd always known where they were.

'Honor called round,' said Ben. 'They've gone into Bodlowe for breakfast. They lent us some milk, we'd run out.'

'I thought we had loads of milk.' Claire switched on the kettle and her phone and leaned her forehead on a cupboard. She had a missed a call from Honor.

'Honor, hi.'

'Hold on a sec, Ding.'

Claire heard gulls and a chugging boat that fell into rhythm with the pounding in her head and then out again.

'We're at the harbour. Ottie mentioned the boat trip we always do. It's a four-hour thing, you get a good couple of hours on a nice beach.'

'OK yeah. When shall we meet you?'

'It leaves at ten thirty, so at the ticket booth at ten fifteen latest.'

Claire put down her phone and looked at her watch.

'Oh shit.' She thrashed out of the kitchen. 'OK, TV off. Ready to leave in ten minutes, please.'

'I was watching that.'

'Sorry but chop-chop. We've got to get to the harbour. Dressed and out in five.'

'You said ten.'

'Don't argue. Teeth.'

'I can't, my toothbrush is lost.'

'Look for it. Ben, can you make some sandwiches please?'

'I'm having a shower.'

'Pearl. Get dressed.

You're not dressed.'

'It doesn't matter. I'm the mum.'

'But you're being a bad role model.'

'Get dressed anyway.'

Fifteen minutes later, the sound of the slammed door ringing in her ears, they set off.

Would she regret not bringing the beach tent? Should she have looked harder for Charlie's jumper? Where could the headache pills be? Things were in such a mess in the cottage. Pearl could only find one flip-flop. Towels Claire had thought were on the airer were crumpled on the floor, still damp. The factor 50 that didn't make her eyes sting was God knows where.

They steamed across the AstroTurf. Thank goodness the tide was out so they could take the beach route. They might be there by twenty past. Each one of Macaroni Steps was an extra thud in the head.

'Ben, I want you to take more responsibility for us being ready please.'

'Oh really?'

'Yes really.'

'Claire, you've been like a whirlwind for months. If I tried to put a hand in, it got blown clean off. So don't wake up with a hangover and think you can click your fingers and change everything.'

'I hate being in this family.' Pearl glared at Claire and put her arm through Ben's.

As they crossed along the beach, Charlie tried to carry the big bag of dishevelled beach paraphernalia.

'It's all right bunny,' said Ben. 'Let Daddy carry it, it's heavy, Mum's brought lots of stuff again.'

Bunch of sods. This was vile. So vile she was almost looking forward to being with Honor so everyone would behave.

'The boat,' wailed Pearl. 'Look. The boat's going.'

Claire looked at her watch. 'It can't be.' Honor and Ottie were waving sadly from the deck of a blue and white boat with Puffin Tours printed on the side.

'I can't believe it, Mummy. You got us here late.'

'But I didn't. Well only a bit.'

'I wanted to go on a boat with Ottie.' Pearl burst into tears, joined by Charlie.

'It's only twenty past,' said Claire, indignation rising. 'Honor said the boat left at ten thirty and to meet for tickets at ten fifteen.' She pulled out her ringing phone. 'Hey Honor.'

'Oh no, Ding, what happened?'

'You said it left at ten thirty.'

'No no. I said ten fifteen. Ottie's so disappointed. She was saying, "Claire will make it, they'll be here." The guy said they saw loads of puffins yesterday. We'll catch up this afternoon, I guess.'

Claire picked up the bag, walked off the jetty and dropped onto a bench under the cliff.

'We weren't late. Honor said it left at half past.'

'Why aren't you saying sorry?' said Pearl. 'Honor doesn't get things wrong, Mummy, and now I don't get to see puffins with Ottie.'

Claire rubbed her forehead. 'I'm sorry you're upset.'

'You don't like those sorts of sorries, Mum.'

'Look Charlie,' said Ben. 'Mum's not feeling great. She got the time wrong. Let's move on.'

Claire made a noise of frustration. A seagull flapped then sauntered away. 'I didn't get the time wrong.' Another gull strutted near her feet. She roared and smacked her hands and it changed direction, glancing back like it thought she was nuts. Claire breathed down, anger curling into sadness. She opened her eyes. A family with a teenage boy and girl strolled past. All four of them smiled and nodded. Claire looked at her own family, scattered and mutinous. Pearl, arms folded, Charlie standing directly in front of the cliff face like he'd been sent there to think about what he'd done, Ben rubbing his cheeks, herself collapsed on a bench, their badly packed belongings spilling round her feet.

'So what shall we do till they get back?' said Ben.

It wasn't fun weather, mild but grey and moody, like Bodlowe was hungover too.

Pearl stamped a foot. 'Whatever it is, it will be *rubbish*.'

'Fine.' Claire heaved herself off the bench. 'So let's go to the beach and have a rubbish time.'

She'd tempted fate. Charlie's goggles snapped as he put them on. Hysterics ensued. Pearl trod on Ben's calf as he suncreamed her. He yelled, she took aggressive umbrage. Claire had consumed nowhere *near* enough water or coffee for this shit. She took her wetsuit out of the bag and inched herself into it. The sea might be the answer. She couldn't feel any worse. She reached over her shoulder for the zip rope and pulled upwards but the zip didn't move.

'Ben, could you do me up.' She kneeled down. Ben tugged the zip, stood up and tried again. 'It's stuck. Maybe got some sand in it or something.'

Claire peeled the wetsuit back off again. She fiddled and pulled at the zip, her head throbbing. The zip was completely jammed. She bundled the wetsuit into her lap and hugged it. Her trusty second skin.

'Try without it,' shrugged Pearl, like it was simple.

She managed to go in to mid-calf.

'I know the water's not freezing for you, and I wish it wasn't too cold for me, but it is. Ben, I'm going to have to find some headache pills. Will you guys come, in a bit, or—'

'We'll stay here.'

Claire pulled on her jeans. A kid cantered past, a tie from some beach equipment as a bridle round their waist, a sibling geeing them on.

Honor had let the pony out when she was a kid. That was the gist of what she'd told Claire and Katie in Headleigh before her flight. Honor's parents bought a pony when Abbie came to live with them, and Honor had felt pushed out and replaced and hadn't wanted to share.

Claire shuddered, remembering how she'd spoken her mind about Ottie and the pudding. That Ollie had hugged her, and now Honor's bank had shown interest in working with her.

Claire put the wetsuit in a bag. Six nights to go. A cook-off to endure, a job to find out more about, and all while holding secrets inside a cupboard as rammed as Pope's Hill infants', pre-sort-out. There was a dry cleaner's in Bodlowe. Hopefully they had a tailor who could replace the zip. She needed all the protection and second skin she could get.

Chapter 34

The kitchen window rattled. Monday was definitely going to be a windbreak day. Claire made coffee and picked up her phone again. She'd messaged Fran to thank her for putting Gemma in touch.

Fran had replied:

Wicked, you'll love each other. Grant is missing you already.

She tapped the photo of Fran and Grant on the South Bank and beamed at their dopey, loved-up faces.

'Gorgeous.'

The kids were playing in the Fancy House. Ben was in the bathroom removing a splinter from his toe. Claire reached for the cereal. Wait. Was she running today? No. She'd gone yesterday afternoon. It had finally seen off her hangover.

She sat on the sofa in her jogging bottoms with her cereal. Her phone pinged again. An email from Gemma with the Non-disclosure Agreement.

Shit's getting real, Claire.

The NDA was long and baffling. Basically she wasn't allowed to talk about the First United project, or share materials attached to it. She auditioned her nails, writing her signature on her phone screen with the winner. Her name looked like it had been scrawled by a kid, but she didn't know how to redo it so she sent it.

★

Gemma emailed back a few minutes later.

Hi Claire
Thanks for the signed NDA. Crazy short notice but
are you available to Skype today at 11.30?
Warm regards
Gemma

Claire emailed back that she was available. She told Ben the news through the bathroom door.

'Fantastic,' he said. 'Are you going to tell Honor?'

'Of course.' She didn't know why she'd sounded so adamant. Perhaps she wanted to be seen as someone who didn't keep things from people.

She knocked at the Fancy House. Honor squealed in a most un-Honor way and threw her arms round Claire, squeezing the air from her.

'Why did you tell her?' said Katie, when Claire phoned her from near the scrubby bushes where the AstroTurf met the real turf, buffeted by a light wind. 'First United are global, Claire. You could have worked for them for years and she'd have never known.'

'She'd have known.'

'How did the job come up?'

'Through Fran's neighbour, Gemma. She sounds really nice.'

'What did Honor say?'

Claire glanced towards the Fancy House. 'That she's delighted.'

'I expect she'll be the best at being delighted about it *globally*.'

Claire sat on a boulder losing the view of the little

triangle of sand below. 'She wants to get me ready. She wants to "style and brief" me for the video call. How do I get out of it?'

Katie breathed in and hummed out.

'You don't. You *let* her. Cossetting you is a power play. It helps her see you as less.'

'Like she's a stallion and I'm her My Little Pony.'

'That's it.' Katie laughed. 'She wants to put ribbons in your mane with her great big clattery hooves.'

'Ouch.'

'Keep your frenemies closer. Anyway, it's Honor, so resistance is futile, and you don't want to be fighting her off all morning; you need to conserve your inner strength. Hand yourself over. Let her prettify your velvet glove while you focus on your iron fist.'

'She's not touching my velvet glove.'

'Ach, sorry, let's stick with My Little Pony.'

Claire laughed. 'Let's. And how are you?'

'Oh it's working out great, Claire. We should have bought a second tent sooner. We've basically put a restraining order on the boys. They have to stay ten feet apart unless we're eating or there'll be consequences.'

'What consequences?'

'I don't know.' Katie laughed. 'Ed sounded so terrifying when he told them, we haven't had to work that out.'

Honor packed everyone off to the beach and took Claire to her bedroom.

Claire sat on the bed like she was told to. Honor put an ambient tune through a speaker that sounded a bit like the First United hold music. She told Claire to relax and hotbrushed and wanded her while Claire watched trees and shrubs through the window leaning in the breeze. Her hair would blow straight as soon as she stepped outside, but she was in My Little Pony mode and not about to stick her neck out about anything.

Honor showed her tubes of sunscreen and primer. Claire 'oohed' dutifully. Honor dabbed them on her face. Close up, Honor smelled of mint. Her own make-up was immaculate. She wore a light coat of caramel gloss which presumably she had less love for than the Faron Odashi. Beneath the artful cosmetics, her complexion was … weary. Her under-eye was dark. Her bones cut her cheeks. As Honor applied make-up to Claire's eyes, her hand vibrated. Her overly controlled eating and uncontrolled drinking were written in her body.

Honor stepped back and scrutinised. 'All done, but stay there.' She rolled up her make-up bag and presented Claire with a Stella McCartney top and some silver earrings. 'Just try them. See how they look.'

Claire turned her back and slipped on the top. She put in the earrings by touch and Honor steered her to the full-length mirror on the wall.

She had planned to say 'oh wow amazing thank you so much I love it' even if Honor had turned her into Widow Twanky. But it *was* oh wow amazing and she *did* love it. Her hair tumbled around her shoulders in artfully imprecise waves. And rather than drawing some other Claire onto her, it was her, at her best, with glowing skin and bright eyes.

She thanked Honor and agreed with her suggestion to go to the beach for a while. They set off towards the steps with Honor belting out 'Isn't She Lovely', clicking her fingers and sidestepping along beside her.

'Yowch,' Honor leaned on Claire's shoulder. 'I forgot these had given me a blister.' She was wearing the wooden sandals. 'I'm going to pop back and change them. See you down there.'

★

Claire joined in with the game of beach cricket, fielding in a place from which she was unlikely to have to run, holding up her hands to protect her hair.

'You look gorgeous,' said Ben.

'Thank you.'

He kissed her gingerly so as not to disturb the tinted balm on her lips. 'I know it's not a done deal but it's great to get this far.'

'Is it a chat or an interview?' asked Chris.

'Chat. Just to say hi and tell me about the project. At least, that's what they said in the email.'

Honor had arrived in trainers. She took the bat from Chris. 'Don't look so worried, Claire. Chris, you've made her nervous. It's a chat and she'll smash it because she's talented and delightful.'

Claire smiled at Honor and looked at her watch. 'Think I'll head back,' she said. Fifteen minutes gave her plenty of time. Ben and the kids gave her a hug.

'Good luck Mum.'

'Just say the right things, Mummy.'

Honor walked back along the beach with her.

'Now, Claire. Finance people are straight, so facts before funny. Give one firm answer and decide what you're going to say, *before* you say it. Firm not flabby.'

It wasn't bad advice. 'Facts before funny. Firm not flabby, yup, got it.'

'It can't be a business-to-business initiative, so it won't go through corporate. It's probably a project with a domestic feel.'

'Yeah,' said Claire, feeling a bit iron-fisty.

'Do you remember coming down here with your macaroni, Ding? You looked hilarious. Who'd have thought you'd be going up these steps for an interview with my bank.'

Chat. It would definitely be a chat not an interview … wouldn't it?

Honor tossed back her hair. 'How hilarious if you went home from Bodlowe with a job at First United as well as me.' She sighed. 'Well. Off you trot then.' She clapped and Claire leapt to the steps with a shriek, thinking Honor was going to chase her.

'Hey, Claire.'

She turned round. Honor was rubbing her palms together.

'When this is all out of the way, it'll be time to plan our cook-off.'

Claire nodded like that was fun. Her anxiety switched up a notch. *Don't think about the cook-off. The cook-off is Friday, it's Monday now.* Ben was right: think about it three days before. Claire blew out a long breath as she climbed the steps. Fast and focused. Facts before funny. Firm not flabby.

She pounded over the AstroTurf, the breeze picking up her hair.

Password.

What was her Skype password? Funky Town. Definitely Funky Town, then exclamation mark, then door number. Cool, right. Got it. Wait, no. *Not* door number. It hadn't felt right that she'd told it to Honor, so she'd changed it … to what though? Nerves fogged her brain. Hold on, yep. It was one of the kids' birthdays. Pearl's. No. Not Pearl's, Char— Katie's! Katie's birthday! She entered the cottage and grabbed the laptop. God, she'd let Honor make her life complicated. She should have left her sodding passwords alone. She'd never had any problems with Claire1234.

No wi-fi. How no wi-fi? The wi-fi had been faultless all holiday. Claire flew to the router on the dresser. There were no unplugged cables. A light was blinking. Did it usually

277

blink? She hadn't given it a thought since she'd typed in the password when they'd arrived. She switched the router off and on again. Her entire tech troubleshooting repertoire had now been deployed. Lights flashed fast. Time ticked by. Her heart hammered. The slow useless blink returned.

Claire. Don't just stand here like the spinning wheel of doom. What happened to fast and fucking focused? There's no wi-fi. You need your phone!

The barn was where the signal was best. She hurried there, opening Skype, seeing the hopeful waving smiley Gemma had already sent.

Here, just here. Four bars on her phone. Claire dropped onto the dusty floor, pen and open notepad in front of her and crossed her legs. Late. She was late for her first-ever proper freelance meeting. It was crushing.

She liked Gemma immediately. And Gary from First United. He had a flop of sweaty fringe which he couldn't leave alone and the longest, boniest fingers Claire had ever seen.

She apologised for being late. And on a phone. Wi-fi trouble. Gemma apologised because they were on day three of a London heatwave of sauna-like proportions and Aldous O'Hare's eco policy was anti air-con. 'So we might have gone slightly mad, Claire.' They all laughed and then Gemma asked about the Post-it behind Claire. Aw hell. 'CHILL' on the empty planner. Turning a deeper fuschia Claire explained she was on holiday, and it had been a directive from one of her companions. 'Great advice,' said Gemma, flapping her black and white Peanuts T-shirt.

The call swung along, with Gary explaining in a funny and not unflabby way that the illustrations were for a campaign about customers' local pursuits, to create the sense that the bank still had a branch on every high street. Gemma said they planned to commission 'a dozen or more' over several months from the same illustrator. 'So we'll need someone we like working with who has good availability.'

There was an almighty crash. Gary had been passing a fruit bowl to Gemma and they'd dropped it, cherries had rolled all over the floor. Once they'd picked them up, Claire having taken some calming breaths, Gemma said they were getting pitches in over the next week or so and Claire said that was great and Gemma said it had been really great to talk to her and she'd send through the brief, and Claire said she felt like eating cherries now.

The call had been funny, flabby and not all that fast, although, at several points, it had been fairly focused.

Claire's hair bounced as she skipped back across the Astro-Turf. Fair play to Honor's wand, the curls had stayed in. This was probably a bit how it felt to be Pearl.

Chris and the kids were out in the dinghy.

Ben took off his headphones. 'How was it?'

Claire set next to him on the sand. 'Nearly a disaster. I couldn't get wi-fi. I had to ditch the laptop and use my phone in the barn.'

'Oh God, stressy. *Then* how was it?'

She was about to say fantastic, but Honor was walking along towards them so she restrained herself. 'It went well,' she said, including Honor. 'Focused, firm, lots of facts.'

'Cool,' said Honor. 'Terrific. Said you'd smash it.'

Fruity, thought Claire. It had been more fruity than she'd expected too.

When the kids could no longer be staved off with snacks, they headed back to the cottages for lunch. Chris's weather app suggested a beach where the waves would be great for bodyboarding. So that was their afternoon plan.

In the cottage, the router was steady again. Claire eyed the connecting door. The chair in front was sitting forward a few inches. One of her family *might* have nudged it, or maybe that was as far back as it could be pulled *before a gelled finger had to retreat the other side.*

Oh, but come on. No.

It was *windy* today. Wind could have affected the router. Honor wouldn't have spent all that time getting her ready if she hadn't wanted the call to go well. She'd been to change her *shoes* after she'd serenaded Claire across the AstroTurf, not fiddle around with the router in their cottage.

But it wasn't like Honor *hadn't* used the connecting door. And it was odd they'd been out of milk the other morning, and that Claire hadn't been able to find any headache pills.

It did seem, to be on the safe side, that a little less *mi casa su casa* was called for.

Claire strolled up the track and called Brian. 'I'm probably just being paranoid, but could you please put a bolt on the door like you said?'

'What's been going on, Claire?'

'I don't have any proof, but the router wasn't working and we've lost a few things. Flip-flop, toothbrush, headache pills and suncream. I'll probably find things are still getting lost, but if there's a bolt, at least I'll know it's on me.'

'Bet it's her. Mean vibes she gives off.'

'Look, it's just a hunch. I can't prove anything. We could come back from being out, and be like, "Oh, he must have just got round to that"'.

'Wilco, Claire. I'll pop over in a couple of hours and sort something out for you.'

Chapter 35

The beach was several miles away. Chris's app had been spot on, the waves were perfect. Claire watched the roiling water spit the bodyboarders onto the sand. High on the buzz of it, Chris suggested he and Ben take the kids for a day at an adventure park before the end of the week, maybe Thursday.

Claire had no chance of going in the water without insulation. It seemed even icier here. She and Charlie built giant strawberry sand sculptures, with stones for seeds, and seaweed for stems. The possibility of the job with Gemma and Gary made the kids seem adorable and the beach more beautiful. Claire breathed deeper, felt lighter.

Honor kept asking whether Gemma had sent through the brief. Claire told her, 'Not yet,' but the email had arrived mid-afternoon. She planned to throw Honor off the scent when they got back. Maybe she'd go for a nap to read it in peace.

'Oh Pearl, your arms.' They'd parked up at Murdon Farm. Pearl was attempting a handstand. She had sunburn. The top of her arms, her forehead and nose were scarlet. One missed dose of suncream. She and Ben had slathered it on every other time. You'd think you might get a free pass.

Chris had sparked the kids' interest in ping-pong after a couple of days of no one bothering. Claire left them in the barn getting into teams and went for aloe vera.

'Claire,' called Honor. 'Pearl needs aloe vera.'

'I'm just getting some.' She pulled a face. Did Honor think she didn't have eyes? Chris passed with a tray of glasses and a jug of lemonade. Claire went into the cottage, blushing. A chunky iron bolt, fully deployed, had been screwed onto the connecting door. Oh yes. That would do it. She pulled her phone out as she went upstairs.

'Brian, it's Claire.' She entered the bathroom and reached her free hand into the medical bag, finding the tube of aloe vera straight away. 'Thanks so much, the bolt is great.'

'You're welcome, Claire. That should sort your troubles out.'

She trotted down the stairs. 'It's probably nothing to do with her.'

'Just one thing to let you know, though Claire.'

'What's that?'

'I got a bit angry.'

Claire stopped at the bottom of the stairs. 'Angry? What about?'

'Madam waltzing into yours and messing things up. So seeing I had the door open, I messed with her back.' He sounded almost proud of himself.

'What kind of messed with her back?' She dropped onto a stair, painfully waking her bum bruise. 'Brian, what did you do?'

'I went in her wardrobe.'

Claire flashed with an image of Honor's clothes in revenge ribbons.

'I knocked a frock off its hanger. I know it was wrong. Silky it was, it'll be all creases.'

Claire honked a laugh and shook her head. 'Is that all? Dresses fall off hangers, it's not a problem.'

'That's a relief. I thought you might be upset with me.'

'No, it's fine.'

'That's good. Oh, and then I remembered you said

summink about her being a good cook, so I switched off her fridge freezer.'

'Oh God,' Claire whispered. 'Did you ... did you do anything else?'

'Er, yeah. I chucked some tablets what I found on her bed table in the kitchen bin. So I reckon you and her are quits.'

Her head simmered like a ham in not enough water. There was no time to discuss the rights and wrongs. She just had to get off the phone and sort it out. 'Thanks so much for fixing the bolt. I'm going to have to go now. Bye.'

Think. What to do? She rang Ben, palms filmed in sweat. While the call connected, she yanked the bolt and it shot back like a gun going off.

'Ben, whatever you do, don't let anyone out of the barn for a couple of minutes.'

'Why, what's going on?'

'Could you just do it.'

'I want to know why.'

'Um, because ... because the owner's been round and I'm, er ... I'm tidying some mess he made, that I don't want to bother Honor with.'

'Why didn't you just say that then.'

Claire opened the connecting door. She would like very much to get away with this. She really didn't want to be caught *undoing* sabotage. She scurried to the kitchen. She looked for a plug on the wall by the fridge and couldn't see one. She felt around in the warm fuzz behind, found a plug, switched on and the fridge shook and hummed. She opened the bin, pulled the blister pack of tablets from the bin and hurried out to the stairs. *Don't look at the tablets, they're private. Don't look.*

Up in the bedroom, she glanced from one bed table to the other. Hand cream and eye mask or John Grisham? She stepped round and placed the tablets by the eye mask.

Honor's voice boomed out. She was calling something into the barn and heading to the cottages.

Shiiiiiit.

Claire rushed to the stairs, drummed down them and through the connecting door.

The aloe vera! She'd left it in Honor's kitchen. She darted back into the Fancy House. Honor had her back to the window, checking her phone. Claire flew across to the kitchen. Safe to go back the way she came? Nope. Honor was on the move. She unlocked the kitchen door. If she could just get out and round the back of the cottage—

'Claire. What are you doing?'

Honor was justifiably suspicious. Claire swallowed. She had one shiny, distracting thing she could throw at this. 'Looking for you,' she said, trotting up with a smile. 'She's sent it. I've got the brief. I can start on the pitch.'

'Ha,' said Honor. 'Perfect timing. Come.' She beckoned with her index finger. 'Something to show you.' She clasped Claire's shoulders and steered her to the front of the cottage, and past the table tennis table, sandpit and toys that had all been set out on the AstroTurf.

'Ben. For Pearl, catch.' Honor took the aloe vera from Claire and bowled it to Ben.

She marched Claire to the barn. 'I've created a space for you.'

In the middle of the floor was an old writing desk and a wooden chair.

'I found them at the back of the barn. It's a safe space for you to work in, Claire.' Her breath was warm on the top of Claire's head. 'You can draw your pitch and no one's allowed in except me, to help you.'

'Great.' A deep unease rippled through her. 'Thanks, Honor.'

Chapter 36

Uncomfortably hot in running shoes, Claire repositioned her feet under the desk. The 'safe space' had felt more like a threat than an opportunity and she'd managed to swerve it the day before, but when she'd come back from her morning run just now Honor had intervened.

She'd been in warrior pose outside the cottages in harem pants and a tank top that was mostly arm hole with a bandeau underneath. She steered Claire into the cottage for her laptop and art stuff.

'I've got a week or so,' Claire protested.

'Yes, but who gets the worm?'

'The early bird,' she muttered.

'Exactly. Do you want to be the first person who submits, or the eighth? Who knows, they might have Skyped twenty illustrators.'

Twenty?! That hadn't even crossed Claire's mind. She'd planned to think about the pitch in Bodlowe then bear down on it at home at the weekend. But Honor's early bird idea might be a good one.

She laid her laptop on her sketch pad with her paints and pencils and let Honor hustle her into the barn. Honor brought her a tray. Coffee, a pint of water and a delicious not-big-enough bowl of granola with yoghurt and some pear and raspberry compote that Claire saw off in three spoonfuls.

Honor perched on the barn sofa to read *World of Interiors*, like Claire was taking an exam and she was the invigilator. Claire read the design brief again and studied the series of reference photos. A community choir and leader in mid-song accompanied by two people with African drums.

She jiggled a pencil between her thumb and finger, watching its two ends become four.

It's just people Claire. You know what to do. Just pretend it's for a poster at the Halls.

She soaked up the faces and began to swell with fellow feeling.

A glossy page swiped over and Claire jumped. 'Honor, would it be OK if… I'm usually on my own.'

'Not a problem.' Honor closed the magazine and stood up as though a request for solitude was Claire whimsy. 'I'll leave you to it, and I'll make sure you're not disturbed.' She pulled the barn door shut and sun shone in through the gaps like light through bars.

Claire looked at the photos again. They were the starting point of something that didn't exist yet, that she was going to have to create. She opened the other attachment. Information about the campaign and a slogan: *Like you are, we're global and local*.

She scrolled to the design brief.

Using the photos as a starting point, create a choir with nine members to include a leader and two drummers. Think:
Community
Sameness/difference
Personality
Underdogs/overachievers

Transformative power of music
Hearts on sleeves
Endeavour for a common goal

She opened a pad and picked up her pencil as the first moments of flow entered her bloodstream like a sip from a strong cocktail.

I can do this. Yeah. Let's go.

'Uh-uh, no!'

She jumped at the stentorian tones from outside and her pencil skittered to the floor.

'Claire is *working*. No going in the barn. Do *not* disturb her.'

★

'Let's see what you've been up to.'

Honor was standing over her. After around an hour and a half of working, Claire had popped out to the loo and been followed back into the barn. She stretched her arms over her sketch pad.

'Come on. Show me,' said Honor, laughing and nudging Claire's shoulder.

'I don't know, Honor; I signed a non-disclosure thing.'

Honor laughed again. 'Claire. I *am* First United.'

'It's just practice stuff. No one looks right. You have to do lots to work out what you're doing.'

'Like priming the pumps,' Honor said, taking the sketch pad and opening it. 'You've got to flush out all the crap first.'

Claire rubbed at her thumbnail, feeling slightly sick as Honor leafed through the pages with detached amusement. She continued to leaf like she was welcome to look at anything, which she was not, and Claire sat clenching every muscle while this talent (particle of) she supposedly had was silently assessed.

Honor placed the closed pad on the desk, the tips of her fingers tented on its cover.

'Ding, I'm a colossal fan of your work, but you need to manage your expectations. The likelihood of you cutting through at First United is small. Your work is darlingly oddball but FU is a straight-line place. I'm not going to sugarcoat it, these people you've drawn this morning are a bit wobbly and weird, whereas here,' she flipped through the pages, 'this sketch you've done of Ottie is good, you've drawn her well. It's not too cartoony, she looks normal. It's almost as good as a photo.'

'That's life drawing though, Honor. It's a different discipline. I make people up. People with flaws, who have jealousies and worries.' She felt sudden affection for the characters she'd thumbnailed that morning. 'People who are trying and failing.'

Honor crinkled her nose. 'If you want this Claire, you'll have to change up your style. Be neater, make the people look more successful at life.'

'But my Skype call...'

'I know your call went well, but I've looked up Gary, your contact, and he hasn't been in post long.' She gestured, palms flat, shoulders raised. 'Cut me and I bleed First United, Claire. There is no better person to steer you on this.'

Claire's mind whirred. Gemma and Gary were running the project and they'd picked her out because of her style.

'If it's not on-brand, corporate will push back.'

'I thought it wouldn't go through corporate? Not that I know what that means.'

Honor smiled, tight-jawed, like there shouldn't be a need

288

to explain. 'Take my advice Claire. Don't be like the people you draw. Don't try and fail.'

Honor was convincing, and perhaps she genuinely wanted and *could* help Claire land this. Claire had no proof she'd fiddled with the wi-fi. Maybe she *had* misremembered the boat time? Maybe Claire *should* make the people less fallible. Make them winners like Honor, because whatever Honor's faults, she would never go on about how hot she was on a conference call or drop cherries everywhere. Honor was un-a-fucking-ssailable.

'OK. I'll do it.'

About an hour later the door opened and Claire lifted her head from the desk. Ben eyed her from across the barn.

'I can't do it, Ben.'

'You so *can* do it.'

He came over and dropped down beside her. She grunted with frustration and shook her head. 'Honor's been giving me advice, and I've got the design brief but I don't know how to approach it. Should I go with what feels natural and obvious, or is that wrong, or lazy?'

'How could it be lazy?'

'So you think it could be wrong?'

He winced. She'd dug her fingers into his arm. 'Sorry.'

'That's OK. I realise I didn't specifically *say* it couldn't be wrong, but—'

'First United is very straight-linesy, Ben. It might be a mistake to just be me. At the least I need to be a better me. You know, like me, but in a well-cut suit and maybe a bit taller. But then, what would that look like literally on paper?'

Ben picked up one of her hands. 'I wish I knew what to say.' He looked thoughtful. 'You need advice.' He brightened. 'Talk to someone from Andrea's course.'

A veil of guilt dropped over her.

'Tell them about the call, show them the brief. They'll know how to play it. What about Tanya? You said she was nice.'

Claire swallowed noisily. She had made up a Tanya. Who Ben had remembered. Acid curled through her stomach.

'I bet it's nothing like as bad as you think,' he said. 'Hey.' He propped her chin up with his fingers. 'Do you want to have a break and get cake?'

She fell on him and squeezed her arms around his back. 'So much.'

*

Claire stripped off the running gear and stepped under the shower. Ben was waiting to take her for cake, and he was lovely and she wished she wasn't holding this shitty secret. She should have told him. But when? After she'd checked in at the B&B? Or from this bathroom when she was newly Sandy and about to take on Brian's decluttering? Or perhaps from the crazy golf. *Don't worry Ben, that's not Ivan. It's some old bloke I'm playing crazy golf with in Bodlowe. I bricked it and didn't go on the course because I felt like I was a joke.*

She rubbed shampoo in her hair and groaned. Maybe it was funny enough not to be awful. Except it wasn't funny. And Ben would think it was even less funny because he would know what had driven it. Because along with the breach of trust it told him how she felt about herself, deep down, *still.*

She'd be letting him know she had romped off hand in hand with the part of herself who stopped her from hearing his encouragement. Turning away from Didcot was a shame-ful hook-up with that other Claire. Proof that despite all his efforts since they'd met to persuade her to believe in herself, what drove her still was her insecurity, not her ambition.

She sighed and let water rain on her scalp. The moment she'd first seen Ben in the art shop swam into her head. How he'd strolled across the worn parquet in his navy Crombie and she'd thought, '*You're* here,' her tower of erasers tumbling around her. To find out he was already thinking about her, had come in just to *speak* to her, had blown her mind. Her gorgeous Ben, who'd spent years trying to coax her from her self-doubt. He didn't know that despite her small skill in catching humanity on paper, she couldn't extend the forgiveness and acceptance she had for others to herself. That she felt at her core like an error in human form. An embarrassing mistake slipped out into the world.

Which was why she had to tell him, she decided, switching off the water and stepping out to towel her hair. Tell him how Honor made her feel and how she'd allowed it to become an excuse to run away. She would tell him so she could start all over again, journey right back and search out her self-belief. If she could tell him, it was a start in the right direction. It was the *only* start.

Claire put on sandals and a short wrap dress and walked into Bodlowe with Ben.

The tea shop was the first café they came to on the pedestrianised lane that sloped off the coast road. They went inside and sat on clattery metal chairs at a tiny circular table and gave their order to an unsmiling white-haired woman. They talked about how compared to Charlie's trunks, Ben's were really quick-drying even though the fabric looked the same. How in photos of both the girls, the bluey-pale tones of Pearl made Ottie's caramel skin look almost orange. They pondered whether you'd stop noticing the sound of seagulls if you lived in Bodlowe. Claire paddled the tiny, safe, conversational tributaries off the white-water topic roaring in her head.

A tray arrived with tea things and cake. She would eat a bit and then tell Ben she hadn't done the course, that she'd come here on a recce. And she'd tell him why.

Ben folded chocolate cake into his mouth with evident satisfaction. The topping of Claire's carrot cake was almost fizzily sweet and the cake was stuffed with walnuts that went dry and bitter in her mouth. She put down her fork. Ben picked up a napkin and wiped his mouth. He scrunched it on the plate. 'Dee-lish. You OK?'

'Ben, I— I've got something to tell you.' The table scraped and wobbled. Claire startled. Someone had caught a metal leg as they passed.

'Pardon me.' Claire's body flashed with sweat. Brian's eyes flickered nervously. 'Oh, hello there.'

'Hello.' Ben was waiting an introduction. 'Er ... Ben, this is Brian Baxter, he owns the cottages. Brian, this is Ben, my husband.'

'Hello.' Ben stood up and shook Brian's hand. 'You joining us? We'll find another chair.'

Claire jumped up, her chair scraping noisily. 'We should go actually, Ben. I need to get back to the barn.' She took out her debit card and waved it at the woman.

Ben shot her a frown. 'Oh, OK. I'll just go to the gents.'

Brian watched Ben head to the rear of the tea shop. 'Looks like a lovely fella,' he said, showing approval like he was her favourite uncle.

'Thanks, he is.' Claire's eyes bored into the back of the woman.

'Taking your cake with you?' asked Brian.

'You can have it, if you like.' She turned and quickly smiled at him.

Brian nodded, giving the offer consideration. 'I'm just back from the hospital, Claire. Brian Junior's broken his shoulder.'

'Oh no. Sorry to hear that. Um, excuse me, hello.' The woman turned and gave her a look that said *yes, I know, be patient.*

'Worst of it is, we might not be able to play at the Harbour Fun Night on Friday now. Be the first time in seven years we haven't. We're a big draw. Here, your bloke play the bass?'

'No! No no, he doesn't.' Claire waved the card wildly. 'Sorry.'

Ben came back and the woman came over with the payment machine and clumped Brian on the back.

'All right Brian.'

'All right Jill.'

'Playing at the Harbour, Friday?'

Brian shrugged his shoulders and exhaled. 'Depends. Is that niece of yours around?'

Claire stretched over and beeped her card on the machine. 'Thanks. It was great. Bye then.' She moved to the door and pulled it open, gesturing with as much charm as she could muster for Ben to go out ahead of her.

''Cause if I can't find a bass player we'll have to pull out.'

'Erm,' Ben was almost, almost, at the door. He stopped and part-raised his hand. 'I play bass.'

Jill looked daggers at Ben and turned, blocking him out of Brian's eyeline. 'Demelza would *love* to help you out, Brian. There's nothing she likes more than playing live.'

Nice one Jill.

293

They emerged from the café and Claire hurried up the lane.

'What was that about? Why are you in such a hurry?'

'He rambles on and on, Ben.' She slowed to let him catch up.

'I wouldn't have minded.'

'I saved you, trust me.'

He frowned disapprovingly. 'What was it you were going to tell me?'

'Erm … Oh, right.' *Abort! Abort!* She shrugged, laughed and shook her head 'Can't think what it was now.'

She had nothing she wanted to tell Ben. *Nothing.* It had been confirmed by seeing Brian, who knew things Ben didn't and *just no*. Her journey to find her self-belief would have to start from somewhere else.

Chapter 37

Claire had gone straight back into the barn. Having made out to Ben she was in a hurry to, she didn't have a choice, and Honor would have shooed her in there anyway.

She pushed back her cuticles with the end of her pencil. She could no more act on Honor's 'strong lines' steer now than earlier. It wasn't just the horror of the near miss with Brian that was putting her off her stroke. It was the fact that Gary and Gemma were her potential clients. *They* were the ones who'd sent the brief. If you cut Honor and she bled First United, that was sad, but not a reason for Claire to consciously change the way she drew.

She wanted Honor off her back. So that meant producing something. But it didn't have to be something she intended to send.

Claire fell towards the desk chuckling at how easy it actually was.

She looked at the reference photos and then without a thought for composition, sketched some people standing close together. She gave them no common focus, no energy. She went over the pencil with neat, continuous pen lines, making peoples' postures better than they were in the photos. She broadened shoulders, reduced double chins and trimmed stomachs. She erased her pencil marks, added watercolour then stood back to take in the big picture. Nine blank-faced people in neat strong lines. In the arena of reflecting human nature, there was nothing going on whatsoever.

Let judge only those who know. If Honor can't see this is wrong, that it's bland and nothingy, then I'm one hundred per cent going with my instinct from now on.

When it was dry, she took the pad outside. Ben and Chris were playing table tennis. Honor was on the bench in front of the cottage watching them. She'd thrown on a jumper and looked like she was posing for a knitwear catalogue.

Claire approached, sketch pad under one arm. 'Done.'

Honor held out her hands. 'Show me.'

Claire teased open the pad and presented the illustration. Honor's gaze roamed it happily. The objective failings were most likely lost on her, but she would see that what was on the paper was *not Claire,* that she'd nudged Claire out of the picture, and thereby out of the running for the work.

'Aw, poppet. That's so much better. Well done.'

Claire plonked down on the bench and crossed her legs at the ankle. She felt almost elated. 'Thanks.'

'And you've emailed it, yeah?'

Honor loomed at her. She couldn't read a composition but she could read a face and Claire's had not reacted correctly. 'We'll do it now then. Hold up the sketch pad. We'll email my photo straight to your contact.'

Honor swiped for her camera. Claire's chest thumped.

'Claire. Come on.' Honor, sunk a hand onto the flesh above her knee. 'You just need to have faith in yourself.'

'I do have have faith in myself.' She swallowed. The words had simply been there. A bespoke order dispensed from some kind of self-esteem vending machine. She pulled the sheet of paper from the sketch pad, folded it, crumpled it. Her hand, like her voice, knew what to do.

'Gemma gave me a week.' She grabbed a breath. 'So I'll do it in my own way, in my own time.'

'D'you fancy mixed doubles?' called Chris.

'Sure.' To Claire's surprise, she was on her feet, her hand out for a bat.

She and Ben darted round the AstroTurf. They were being *pulverised*, but ha! What did Claire care about winning table tennis? She'd just properly won a battle with Honor. She crouched, waiting for Honor's serve, still buzzing.

Honor tapped the ball on her bat as though it was an egg she was cracking. Oh jeez ... Egg. A fan of anxiety waved through Claire's chest. The cook-off. To Honor, the cook-off would be everything. It would decide the war.

Honor's serve sliced past her. As Claire lurched off to collect the ball, a throaty rumble reached her. A faded red Land Rover rolled down the track and the colour disappeared from her. It pulled up outside the cottages.

'Afternoon,' Brian called as he walked round the car, tugging the waist of his cargo trousers upwards. In the back, squashed next to an amplifier, sat a heavier-set younger Brian with tame eyebrows. He waved through the window with his non-strapped-up arm.

'Sorry to disturb your game.' Brian's eyes left the ground to dart uneasily between Claire and Ben. 'Just been round Jill's niece's. Turns out there *is* something she likes more than playing live, and she's over his house Friday 'cause his parents are coming down the harbour.'

Claire's ear whooshed.

'What do you reckon?' Brian was addressing Ben but glancing at Claire as if to communicate that he was sorry, but his need was greater than hers.

'What's going on here?' Honor was playful, but with an edge of *why am I not up to speed on this?*

'So you ...' Ben circled a finger between himself and Brian. 'Want me to play with your band?'

'This sounds good,' said Chris.

'He's our only hope,' said Brian. 'We've got a rehearsal room booked now as it happens.'

★

Ben still hadn't texted back.

It had been hours.

They were called *Brian's Band*. 'Does what it says on the tin,' Brian had shrugged, apologetic. Their set list for Friday was 'easy listening, with a surprise'. He probably meant Hullfire but it was other surprises that worried Claire.

Ben had gone into the cottage to get his stuff. Claire had followed, her mind churning with how to stop him from going. He reached for his wallet on the kitchen table and her hand flew out.

'Ow.' Her nails had scraped him. 'What the fuck?'

'Sorry!' She was as appalled as he was.

'That really hurt.' He flexed his fingers.

'So sorry. I didn't mean to ... Ben, please don't go, with Brian.'

He looked at her, confused. 'Why not?'

'I— we don't know him.'

He tucked the wallet into his jeans, baffled. 'We're renting his cottages. The tea shop woman was happy for her niece to play with him.'

Claire wiped her lip with the back of her hand. 'I'd prefer it if you didn't.'

He laughed in disbelief. 'Are you kidding? You're being

a bit weird. After all the encouragement I've given you the last few days ... It's kind of a one-way street.'

'You're right. Sorry.' She pushed a hangnail back and forth on a quivering finger. 'Hey, how about I come with you?'

'Back seat looks pretty full.'

'I could follow in our car,' said Claire. 'Like your groupie.'

Ben pulled a hand across his brow and shook his head, clearly confused as to why she was pushing this agenda. 'Could I just go on my own? I'd like to go on my own.' He went over to the stairs. 'And now I'm going for a pre-rehearsal dump because I'm nervous. You can come to that if you like.'

Claire went outside. Brian was leaning on his car, arms folded, watching a game of mixed triples. When he saw her, he held out his hands appeasingly.

'God rest my ma's dear soul, I won't mention you come here.'

She pretended to watch the table tennis. Ben emerged and waved at the kids. Brian opened the passenger door for Ben, then jumped in the driver's seat. 'Right then.' The engine coughed into life. Brian nodded at Claire. 'Bye Sandy.'

Their eyes locked. His face reddened. He crunched into gear mouthing, 'Sorry.'

Claire watched the vehicle swing round and hurtle up the track. Brian was a loose cannon. His Fancy House antics had been born of loyalty to her, but when loose cannons misfired, they injured people on their own side too.

It would be so much worse coming from him. Song titles went through Claire's head.

Bad Karma Chameleon. When A Man Loves A Lying Woman. Signed Sealed Delivered I'm Fucked.

★

It was after ten in the evening. How long was this rehearsal? She'd texted Ben for the address so she could collect him but he hadn't replied. She decimated another fingernail. Heat rose through her and she pushed back the duvet. She was still in the wrap dress, ready to jump in the car. Brian would *surely* have been more careful after his ridiculous slip. With a gig on Friday and a guest bassist, the rehearsal would be focused on the music, not chat or confessions. As long as Ben got back to her with the address and didn't get a lift back with Brian, it might be OK.

Her phone lit up. At last. She threw off the duvet and put her feet in her sandals.

Ben: Drinking with the band. Going to be a late one. Don't wait up x

Chapter 38

Dawn light silvered the wooden stairs. Claire felt her way down for water to the aroma of fermented apples. She thought she hadn't slept at all and that Ben hadn't returned but he was sprawled on the sofa, a beach towel for a blanket, a foot on the floor, shoe unlaced but not removed.

She shuddered as she poured a glass of water, relieved he was there but dreading what would come next. He stirred as she came out of the kitchen, then lurched upright, his shoe almost tripping him over as he pelted up to the bathroom to be sick.

Claire climbed into bed. The bathroom door opened and he crawled in beside her, a new minty top note added to the smell of him. 'Close the curtains,' he said.

'They're closed.'

He groaned. 'Close them properly.'

She gestured her annoyance at his back. They were closed as properly as they could be. She posted a towel over the curtain rail which fell on his head.

'Sorry,' she said quickly.

He tutted and flung it on the floor.

Sleepless adrenaline drove her into running gear. She jogged up the track. Taking in a huge breath, she stumbled on a stone. She bent over, winded, then gave up, walked back and paced around on the AstroTurf, glancing up at the cottage.

Honor came out of the Fancy House. 'I've been watching you Claire. You look incredibly stressed.' She announced it like a compliment.

Claire told Honor that Ben was hungover. Honor said Claire should pack the kids' 'day bags' and send them round once they were up.

She did. If Ben knew. If Brian had told him, it was better no one was around when he recovered enough to pull the pin from the grenade.

In the kitchen, she and Ben bumped up against each other, reaching for a cupboard, the kettle, at the same time. Claire knocked over her coffee. By the time she'd wiped it up, he was putting his toast plate in the sink. 'I'm going to practise for Friday in the barn.'

He lumbered out. The door banged behind him.

She started a text to Brian.

Did you say anythi

It made her feel gross. She deleted it.

Tiredness fell on Claire like a skipful of laundry and she hauled herself into bed. For ages she nearly slept, sinking to micro-bonkers dream stage before startling awake hearing the bass rumble from the barn.

A vehicle drove up. Someone thudded at the Fancy House. Claire moved the curtain. A van with curlicued lettering on the side.

FORDHAM'S
Purveyors Of The Finest Comestibles.
Butcher, Baker, Cheesemonger, Greengrocer.

She went out and took delivery of a vast crate of groceries, evicting things from her fridge to house a wooden box with *Refrigerate Immediately* stamped on it in ink.

The cook-off. *Fuuuuck.*

The cook-off still stupid mattered. At the level of not screwing up, at not being a laughing stock, however much she wished it didn't, the cook-off really did matter.

★

Claire switched on her phone and watched a video Katie had sent.

'Hello friend.' Katie's lightly sunburned face and voice were dreamy. 'Look. Peace has broken out.' She turned the phone round and Claire saw the back of the dark-haired twins stepping their way across the grass of the campsite, arms round each others' shoulders. 'My kids have gone to buy bread together.' Katie sighed luxuriantly and flipped the camera back onto herself. 'Just wanted to show you. OK, hope things are good with you. Peace out.'

'Oh that's gorgeous.' Tears blurred Claire's vision as she replied with a dozen heart emojis.

She drank some orange juice and sat at the table to draw. An Honor-free day was the perfect time to do the pitch but her hand was like a separate entity she had no connection to, and the marks on the page were all wrong.

Claire put her drawing things away and climbed back into bed with Hilary Mantel. She turned back to the beginning of *Wolf Hall* and read up to the bit where she'd confused the Thomases.

When hunger propelled her to the kitchen in the middle of the afternoon, her phone had clocked up several texts and photos from Honor. The first was from the stables they'd been to that morning. A close-up of Charlie with a daft expression and Dog spreadeagled on his head. Honor's caption said, **Bad news ... We lost Dog.**

'No!' Claire gasped, a speck of cheese and cucumber sandwich flying onto the screen. She scrolled up. The next photo was of Charlie grinning teethily, clutching an overstuffed knitted toy whose eyes were too far apart.

Wait. Claire scrolled back and then forward. Photo of Charlie, pulling a face with infinitely wise-eyed Dog on his head. **Bad news ... We lost Dog.**

Next photo, Charlie clutching a knitted toy. **Good news ... Meet Noah! Isn't he gorgeous? Charlie wuvs him.**

Claire toggled between the two photos as her heart twisted and a piece came off.

We lost Dog.

Meet Noah!

'What, and that's it, sorted?' Claire gestured angrily at her phone. Honor had responded to a chasm of awful by making it a shopportunity. She'd taken Charlie to Yummy Snowflakes, or whatever that fancy toy shop in Bodlowe was called, and bought him a mindless-looking stuffed toy like it fixed things.

When Claire lost things, it was classic Ding and called for her to do a town-wide search. Had anybody even looked for Dog? Claire jabbed the call icon above the photos.

Where did you lose him? What have you done to find him? Don't you feel so wretched to lose something so important you'll search and search and search for it like I did?

The call went to voicemail, and Claire hung up. More photos pinged through. Charlie and Noah. Pearl and Charlie and Noah. Ottie and Pearl and Charlie and Noah in a group hug with Ollie in the background.

She rang Ben. He was less than a couple of hundred feet away in the barn, but this was urgent, plus using the phone seemed to sidestep round both her betrayal and his cider fug. His phone rang out. She felt sure it was beside him, but instead of speaking to her, he was choosing to concentrate on the far more straightforward and reliable bassline to 'What a Difference a Day Makes'.

She looked at Honor's photos again. Maybe Charlie did 'wuv' Noah. Maybe he saw something in the gormless knitted lump that she couldn't.

'Ha ha ha!' yelled Charlie, clambering out of the Space Ship, shoving the toy in Claire's face.

Honor demanded her Fordham's order. Claire reassured her it had been refrigerated immediately.

Ben came out of the barn with an arid pallor, but put on a show. 'Who wants to play beach cricket?'

They went down Macaroni Steps to the beach, Claire's buttock spasming post-traumatically. Grey clouds lurked low. Charlie had left Noah on the dresser in the kitchen. No one mentioned Dog. He was the elephant not in the room.

Honor was wearing sunglasses the size of reentry shades and more caramel-coloured ligloss. Obviously it wasn't the Faron Odashi because Claire had lost that, but it was a really similar shade, to her untrained eye anyway. Everyone played except Honor, who lay tapping her phone. Claire pretended to be in as good a mood as Chris, who whipped the game up so well it attracted some other kids too. Later, Claire watched Charlie play hotels with the girls but they got pissed off with him being an angry guest who trashed all the rooms.

'Testosterone,' declared Honor.

Testosterone at five? Really? 'You did... look for him? Dog?' She was blushing. Why was it so hard to ask?

'To be honest Claire, we didn't know *where* to look. We

had such a fun-packed day, it could have happened any time, and it wasn't like Charlie asked for Dog at any point.'

Claire jostled a hangnail. She'd looked for hours for Honor's irreplaceable lip gloss. Her kid's irreplaceable toy? Not so much of the looking.

'He had him when you went riding. You sent a picture. He had Dog on his head with a horse in the background.'

'But then we walked into Bodders for lunch and Chris came and got the car and we drove to the chocolate sculpting place and then along to the beach where we did bodyboarding. It was only once we got back to Bodlowe that he noticed. And then we whizzed to the toy shop and I saw Noah. Well obviously we didn't know that was his name yet, and I thought, perfect.'

Oh my God. Charlie hadn't even chosen Noah. Honor had thrust Noah upon him. Claire set about a different hangnail. She'd grown a crop in the last couple of days.

'Right Claire, listen up. I've been working on the rules for our cook-off. No help with prep or cooking. All hot food must be cooked entirely on the barbecue, served hot and on time. We'll keep it simple, a main, plus a hot side dish, and a salad or vegetable accompaniment. We serve at six thirty p.m. Friday. I'll provide a mark scheme for presentation, taste etcetera on the night, and you and I can vote on each other.'

'OK,' said Claire. She stood up and ripped off her hoodie and jeans. To the sound of Honor's patronisingly amazed whoops and applause, she waded in her sleeveless T-shirt and underwear into the excruciating water where she stood chest deep until until she lost control of her teeth. Her wetsuit would be ready to collect tomorrow. And although that was good, she felt her protection needs had, in a number of ways, outgrown what it could offer.

*

When they got back to the cottages, Charlie rushed off to play with Noah in the barn. He hadn't mentioned Dog. Claire quietly followed him in, and sat on the sofa with Hilary Mantel as a decoy, observing him as he pushed the witless toy through the sandpit in what had been Dog's limo. Claire had thought Dog would be in their lives forever. Dog had been family. She tipped back her head, tears tracking her cheekbones. She felt like all the stuffing had been knocked out of her. Why was she so miserable when Charlie seemed fine? Maybe the attachment was hers. Maybe it was all linked and Charlie calling her from the school medical room was because *she* needed the reassurance?

Charlie put Noah under his arm and marched round the barn shrugging his shoulders up and down. Claire quickly rubbed her fingers over her face and smiled at him. He stared through her. He was being odd and annoying, but he was fine. If he wasn't, he'd be clingy, a whining human apron, arms clamped round her hips. Mind you, bedtime would be the real test.

Pearl arrived and reached inside the unzipped case of Brian Junior's bass, which Ben had left against the wall. She tweaked a string, then skipped over and perched on the sofa arm. Claire laid a hand on her knee.

'How do you think he is, Pearl?'

They looked over at Charlie.

'I thought he'd be sad,' said Pearl.

'Me too. But he seems all right.'

'Noah cost forty-eight pounds ninety-five, Mummy.'

'I know.' The handwritten tag tied to Noah's leg with silk ribbon proclaimed as much.

'It's too much, isn't it?' said Pearl. 'If something's too expensive, you shouldn't buy it.' She gently pinched the skin on the back of Claire's hand. 'Like trees. If a tree is a hundred and seventeen pounds that's a lot.'

'Yeah, it's a lot.'

'And buying thirty's nuts, isn't it?'

'I agree.' Claire held out her arms. They exchanged a smile and Pearl pushed back into Claire's lap. Claire squeezed then let go, expecting Pearl to wriggle away as usual, but Pearl stayed, her nose nestled into Claire's neck. Claire inhaled the sherbety sawdust of her daughter's hair and held her until her heart overflowed. When Pearl eventually skipped away to find Ottie, she felt drunk. She didn't know whether she had Ben. Charlie had Noah and not Dog, but Claire definitely had Pearl.

Chapter 39

In the end, in an anxious blurt, she just asked him.

'So, what did you talk about with Brian at your rehearsal?'

They were washing up breakfast things before Ben and Chris took the kids to the high ropes place. He still looked like someone with a hangover, but had stopped alternating between looking like he might die and then rallying and suggesting cricket, and seemed resigned to life.

'No one got much of a word in once Bucket got started,' he said, drying a plate.

'Bucket?'

'Brian's guitarist, Gut Bucket. Good job he's got long arms.' He mimed someone playing a guitar a long way from their body. 'He's one of those story blokes. Doesn't do being interested in people or conversation, just stories.'

Claire laughed nervously. 'Bit like your uncle—'

'Uncle Peter, yeah.' Ben reached for another plate. 'He got kind of intense about his ex-wife once he was pissed. Brian I mean.' Ben made his brow heavy. '"It's secrets that break a marriage." That kind of thing.'

A soapy mug slid from Claire's hand and smashed on the flagstones. Ben tried to help clear up the pieces. She waved him away.

'We'll get a replacement,' he said, laying out the local paper for the bits.

'Yeah,' said Claire, knowing where to get one because she'd bought it with Brian, in secret.

Ben went upstairs to brush his teeth. Claire took out the dustpan and brush.

'Who will buy this wonderful morning!' sang Charlie, arriving in bare feet, stopping at Claire's gesture to stay back because of the broken shards. 'It is wonderful, isn't it Mum?'

'Yes. It is.' She squashed the newspaper in the bin and kissed his whirl of hair. He made a messy bowl of cornflakes and sat at the table, little legs dangling. He was pale. Maybe he was coming down with something. Although he usually told her in detail when anything was even mildly awry with his health. He hadn't come into their room in the night. He'd said he'd felt fine at bedtime, scrunching his eyes closed. He hadn't wanted Noah in bed. Didn't want him to 'get dirty'.

Ollie, Ottie and Pearl were in the Silver Bullet. It was warm and they were lively. Chris's enthusiasm for this trip he'd suggested while buzzing from bodyboarding seemed to have waned a little now it was here.

Charlie clung to Ben, laughing, persisting in the idea he could remain papoosed around him while Ben drove.

Honor came out to see them off. She stood next to Claire in her huge sunglasses, a wide-brimmed hat and sleeveless maxi. As she waved, the muscles in her arm rippled under tanned skin. Once the Silver Bullet had disappeared onto the coast road, the two of them sprang apart.

'All right if I borrow a lounger?'

'Yes,' said Claire. 'Sure. They're in the barn.'

Claire showered and dressed in low tops, jeans shorts and a soft orange T-shirt. She tied a hoodie round her waist, checked that the ticket for the dry cleaner's was in her phone case with her debit card and popped it into the empty beach bag with her keys. She walked into Bodlowe, a baseball hat pulled low over her eyes.

She passed the fancy toyshop and looked away from its saw-you-coming window. Weakened by thoughts of Noah and Dog, she could no longer cope with the stone in her shoe and leaned against the pillar of a holiday letting company to shake it free. In the window was a photo of Perriwinton Manor with a Post-it underneath. *Available this week!* It looked like the on-again off-again wedding party had ended up off.

'Glue?'

As the man in the dry cleaners nodded, his eyebags were magnified and then not magnified in the glasses at the end of his nose. 'Yes. Glue.'

'You're sure? Glue in the zip. You're completely positive?'

He nodded again, growing weary now. Claire extracted the wetsuit from its plastic cover.

'I didn't have to replace it. Just soaked it in acetone.'

The zip worked perfectly.

'Sorry, just a minute.' Claire was light-headed. She leaned on the counter and inhaled a few restorative breaths of dry cleaning chemicals. Here was proof. Everything was clearer now. The things that had gone missing. The boat she thought she was on time for. The excellent wi-fi that had malfunctioned at a crucial time. It was more than likely Honor had been glueing it all up.

Claire cantered back to the cottages and straight down to the beach with the wetsuit in the beach bag.

Honor was lying on Claire's lounger with her arms above her head, her body glistening with oil in the sun. She'd set up not far from the steps. Of course she was near the steps. After all, it wasn't like she needed to inconvenience anyone bringing her a hot meal.

Claire put down the beach bag, punchy with adrenaline. She took out the wetsuit and opened the zip from top to bottom. Honor had closed her eyes. Was she blushing? Her golden cheeks had definitely turned rose. Claire rushed with fearlessness and fear as she wobbled around yanking the material up her legs.

'It's mended,' said Honor. 'That's good.'

'They put acetone on it. It breaks down glue.' Her voice wobbled too, but it was good and loud. She'd planned to death-stare Honor when she said 'glue' but in reality she couldn't look at her. That was OK though. Her work here was done.

'Think I'll have a stroll.'

Claire sauntered away along the beach, creamy water simmering onto the shingle.

Take that, Honor Wellbeloved. She snorted a laugh and sighed. Oddly, she didn't fancy going in the sea. The thought had popped into her head that trouncing Honor the day before their cook-off wasn't great timing. Now that she'd paraded the wetsuit, new things would be occurring to Honor about how to undermine and show her up, and with so much else going on Claire hadn't even thought about what she was cooking. She must go to the supermarket.

Claire trotted along the back of the beach. She didn't want Honor to ask where she was going or really ever talk to her again, so she left her bag where it was and sprinted up the steps. She didn't have her keys, phone or debit card, but she could work around that. Everything seemed brighter now she had her second skin again.

'Yes.' The downstairs window had escaped Brian's

renovations. Claire nudged it open then slotted a leg through and scissored herself into the cottage. Upstairs, hot, but not wet from the sea, she found herself re-enacting the panicky escapologist routine from the charity shop changing room. As she was off to a Cornish supermarket, not a job interview with Gunnar, it mattered less to stay in the wetsuit, so she threw a T-shirt over it and slid her feet into her well-worn Birkenstocks.

She stepped off the Park and Ride shuttle. Despite a building sensation that evoked approaching Christmas with no plans made or presents bought, while still at the cottage she had managed to find recipes – nothing inspired, hopefully doable – for what she would cook, and wrote out a list.

A tall stack of disposable barbecues lined the supermarket entrance. Claire put two in her trolley. It would be just like Honor to annexe her actual barbecue again. She walked the aisles, filling the trolley with stuff for the cook-off. She'd forgotten a pen, the only thing in her bum bag was the joint account card, so she folded her list as she found each item. Her aim wasn't to win. She just wanted to meet the criteria and give Honor no justification for legimate laughter. She wished her ambition was greater than that. She would love to do something amazing.

She pushed towards the checkouts, searching for Madge, the cashier, to let her know her that beef jerky was like leather in salt, but Madge wasn't around. She joined a queue behind a man with a toddler in a trolley, a bedraggled toy cat in its lap. The child held a wooden block and a plastic teacup in her sticky hands. As she stretched towards the conveyor belt to poke the food with the block, the cat slid to the floor unnoticed.

Claire picked it up and handed it to the man. His gratitude

was immense, as though the toy were oxygen. Claire opened her mouth to reassure him there'd be a time when the cat didn't matter so much, but she couldn't, because a feeling like one of those standing-still-but-moving-at-the-same-time film moments rolled through her, because that time had *not yet come for Charlie*.

Singing 'Who Will Buy?', his face pale ... Dog was still oxygen and Charlie was *acting*.

We have to bloody look for Dog.

The dad popped the cat beside the toddler. She squawked and clanged her block in her cup and held it out to him.

'Hmm, my favourite,' he said, taking the cup and pretending to eat the block. The kid shrieked, delighted.

Claire's mouth dropped open.

Because that was her cook-off inspo right there.

Because at the end of the day, nothing mattered more than letting your people know that you knew, and loved them.

Claire reversed out of the queue.

She returned every item from her soy and sesame pork, spiced apple slaw and hot flatbread menu to its shelf. When the trolley was empty, she started her shopping again. Honor was calling it *mummo a mummo*, and Claire couldn't lose.

The cook-off would settle things once and for all.

*

Claire missed the Park and Ride shuttle by moments, and with a sudden rush of blood to the head decided to walk the two or so miles back to Bodlowe. She strode away from the supermarket, bicep-curling the shopping bags and sweating into the wetsuit with an exhilarating sense of balance and perspective. The panicked Christmas feeling from earlier had dissolved into a yearning to hold Ben, and the kids, and wrap them all in love.

She was quite a long way down a B road before she realised she hadn't seen any signs to Bodlowe for a while. She retraced her steps, asked for directions at a roadside burger van, paid a visit to some cows at a gate.

When she eventually arrived back at Murdon Farm, the Silver Bullet had returned from the high ropes, but the Space Ship was absent. She weighed up whether to see if anyone was in the Fancy House with her things or leave that until later and head into the cottage.

'Claire.'

'Chris, you made me jump.'

'Where have you been?'

He was shaking. 'What's wrong?'

'Here.'

She dropped the shopping and took her phone from him.

'You'd better call Ben.'

'What's happened? Has there been an accident? Where are the kids?'

'Just call Ben, now.'

Chapter 40

People had gathered to watch the lifeboat be winched up the ramp. A couple hurried their kids away. Claire wondered if they found it harrowing that there was no rescuee in the boat with the crew and silently sent a message. 'Don't worry. It was sent for me and I'm fine.' She shuddered at the waste of time and money, then spotting Ben sitting on the sand with his knees up, rushed towards him.

Their phone call had been short. He'd spluttered, 'God. You're there. Right.' He'd sighed hugely and told her to come to the lifeboat station. 'I'll tell them you're OK.'

'Ben.'

He glowered at her. She sat on the sand a few feet away. Her body feeling the lack of the hug she'd expected.

'Why did Honor call a lifeboat?'

'Fuck, Claire. Seriously? You were gone hours.'

'I was at the supermarket.'

'Oh. The supermarket? That's nice.' He grinned and nodded manically. 'You left your stuff on the beach.'

'I told Honor I was going for a walk.'

'You left your phone, your keys, your clothes.'

'I told her, Ben. I didn't say I was going swimming.'

'You left your *shoes*. You disappeared in a wetsuit, what was she supposed to think?'

Claire shrank back from his gesturing. Ben was not on her side and the weight of the thousand micro-aggresssions she'd borne from Honor since she'd met her hit her all at once.

'Ben, why are you being like this, is it shock? You thought I'd drowned and I'm right here.'

He glanced at her and picked up a razor shell, scraping it through the sand. 'Are you? Doesn't feel like you. Often hasn't felt like you for months. "Dear Claire, I'm on holiday in Cornwall, wish you were here.".'

Her breath caught. 'Don't say that.'

He looked at her, one eye closed against the sun. 'I've never been more scared in my life. And maybe, now I know you'd jaunted off to the supermarket, maybe I'd be able to process it, except Brian rang me earlier.'

Claire's insides lurched like jelly tossed out of a mould. 'What did he say?'

'That he'd promised you he wouldn't say anything. That he found you breaking into the cottages one Saturday.'

She squashed the fingers of one hand with the other till they hurt, seagulls jeering above them.

'You said you were on Andrea's course, Claire.'

'I'm sorry Ben, I'm sorry.'

'I thought she'd got through to you when I couldn't. You told me what the ice-breaker exercise was.'

'I Googled them.'

'Is Tanya made up?'

She nodded.

'So the woman a few days ago who thought she knew you: you *had* sent her an umbrella. She's your *real* friend from that weekend, right?'

'I stayed at her bed and breakfast.'

'You missed the Halls open weekend, Claire.' He wiped his cheek with the back of his hand.

Claire burst into tears. 'I know! I didn't plan to come

here, Ben. It was right at the last minute. I literally turned the other way as I got to Didcot.'

'Oh, I see. One of those impulsive moves that always work out so well for you. Jesus.' Ben exhaled and pushed his hands through his hair.

'I wanted to do the course. It petrified me, but I wanted to, and I so nearly got there but the cottages... they looked *off*, and Honor had rushed me into booking them.'

'Are you blaming Honor?'

'You should have seen them, Ben. Did Brian say? Threshing stuff all over the garden, full of junk inside.' Claire dropped her head. Through the lens Ben was seeing her, this was bleating to teacher that Honor had pushed her while she had a lighter in her pocket, when it was she who'd set the school on fire.

'He says you pretended to be his dad's cleaner.'

'That makes me sound like ... Villanelle. I mean it's true, but he assumed it. I just went along with it.'

'A man I just met knows more about my wife than I do.'

'I should have told you what was going on in my head.'

'But instead you went off your own merry way.'

'How do I get back?' she asked quietly.

He raised his palms and shoulders. 'I dunno. Ask Tanya?'

'Ben,' she pleaded.

He clambered to his feet. 'To be honest, I don't know if you can.'

'Ben. Please. Don't go.'

Ben stormed to the harbour. Claire followed him, sobs welling as she tried to wrap him in the wave of love she'd felt when she left the supermarket, hoping he'd turn round. A mob of seagulls circled, shrieking like they were saying *Fight! Fight!*

Ben didn't stop. She remembered the wetsuit and plucked at her arm. 'Ben,' she called. 'Did you see? I'm wearing the wetsuit. The zip was glued. The dry cleaner fixed it.'

A woman opening a buggy looked at Claire like she hadn't expected entertainment.

'The zip, Ben,' Claire shouted. 'Honor a hundred per cent put glue in it, the man said.'

At the top of the slope Ben was swallowed in a sea of happy holidaymakers.

Claire dropped onto the hard sand, waking the lump of bruise. Through tears she watched two seagulls scrap over crab guts spilled on the sand.

I've fucked up. And I can't ring Katie because she's having a lovely time with the family she hasn't fucked up.

The disdain on Ben's face pierced her, and she cried until she felt picked as dry as the crab.

She needed someone to lean on, to listen, to tell her it would all be OK. She needed her mum. And because her mum was Margo, she'd have to go through someone she'd never met to get her.

'David here.'

'Hi. Sorry to bother you, it's Margo's daughter Claire. I need to speak to her, if that's possible. It's important.'

'Sure,' he said laconically. There were some murmurings.

'Claire.'

'Mum. I need you.'

'Let me call you back.'

Claire stared open-mouthed at her phone. Margo had slipped through her fingers yet again. Her mother was an outrage. If there was a retrospective after she died, Claire would make them call it: *Margo Macklin – It's Not a Good Time Right Now.*

Her phone rang.

'I just had to check the oven,' said Margo with a degree of pride. 'I'm roasting a chicken. It's quite a nice idea. Makes a meal an occasion. I'll do one for you some time. It was idiotic of me to say don't visit, by the way. I'm quite bereft knowing you aren't all coming as usual.'

'It was your idea we didn't come.'

'I know,' Margo sighed. 'I was an ass. Anyway, you've got something important to say.'

'Yes. I'm in a mess, Mum. I need to talk it through so please just listen. I'll try and make it simple. It's not, but try to wait and ask questions after.'

'All right darling. Just a sec though.' Margot covered the phone and said something about potatoes. She was apparently eating with the neighbour.

'Right. I'm here. You've got all my attention. Take as long as you need.'

Claire breathed in deeply. Where to begin? What thread would pull from this tangle?

A banana boat ripped across the sea where the lifeboat had been earlier. Claire suddenly swelled with an urge to enact a rite of passage. She was thirty-six years old, and for the first time in her life she felt she had enough attention from her mother to make a decent show of hanging up on her. So she did.

She expected to fill with rage, or regret, or sadness.

She felt fantastic.

Wow, Claire. Well done. Not for hanging up, because that shouldn't really be encouraged, but for demanding to be heard! That was awesome!

Hey, positive self-talk voice, thanks. And thanks for showing up.

I was here all along, Grasshopper.

Brilliant. In that case you probably know what I'm going to do next.

320

Of course. You trust yourself. So you're going to do what's in your heart.

And she *was*. And although it wasn't the point, if it showed Ben she was journeying back to what was important, having been off on her own merry way, that would be really great.

Chapter 41

'Hi Chris. I'm just ringing to find out where you all are.'

'We're at the crazy golf. Ben's just arrived.' Chris's jolly tone conveyed he didn't know what was going on, but he knew it was bad.

Claire ran sweatily through Bodlowe. This could easily be the longest anyone had ever worn this much winter-weight neoprene and not got it wet *at all*. She felt weak but ran as fast as she could, ducking and darting round wandering tourists as though sprinting might stop her life from falling apart.

She saw Pearl first, on a patch of manicured grass near the walking-the-plank hole by the railings, a line of townhouse bed and breakfasts behind her. She was stepping over her golf club then trying to swing it over her head like a skipping rope.

'Mummy!' Pearl slammed into Claire and pasted herself along her body and Claire spread her fingers to make contact with as much of her daughter as possible.

'I knew you'd be all right,' said Pearl, showing no sign of letting go. 'Because it's not very wavy in the sea today, and you don't like to go deep.'

'You're right. I don't.' Claire kissed the top of her head.

'Thank God you're OK Claire,' said Honor, her hand on top of her plastic golf club like it was a walking cane. 'Chris and I have made a full donation to the lifeboat, so don't feel bad about that.'

Right. She was clearly supposed to feel bad about that.

Standing there in the wetsuit Honor had glued up, Claire felt suddenly raw. She scanned Chris and the kids. They looked raw too, like prawns with recently peeled-off shells. 'Where's Charlie?'

Honor gazed round disinterestedly. Charlie was by a tiny hillock on Treasure Island, crying. Quiet gulping sobs. Claire's heart cracked. She rushed over and crouched beside him.

'Chris's club caught him on the shin,' said Ben, arriving the other side of Charlie and rubbing the boy's cheek gently with his thumb. 'It was just a tap really though, wasn't it, bunny?'

Charlie held a bunched up T-shirt under his chin and Claire knew her heart had been right. She touched the scrunched fabric gently. 'Not the same, is it?'

'No.'

'Oh Claire,' said Honor. 'Really. He's moved on.'

'I'm fine though,' Charlie swallowed a crunchy sob. 'I don't mind about Dog.'

'I'm sorry I haven't paid more attention,' said Claire. 'Are you *pretending* to be fine?'

Charlie banged his knees together. He looked straight at Claire, desperation in his blue eyes. There was a swish of technical fabric and Claire assumed Honor was crossing her arms.

Yes Honor, I'm pandering. I'm a panderer.

'Come on Charlie,' said Honor in her best child-friendly voice, proffering her flimsy club. 'Don't you want to play?'

Charlie's eyes widened, his gaze dawdled for a brief moment towards Honor, and back to Claire.

'When he bangs his knees together, it means he's got something to say. I'm listening Charlie. Tell me anything.'

'I'll give you five shots at the treasure chest,' said Honor.

'I've tried to be brave!' he yelled, pudgy fists clasped to his chest.

'Oh baby, no one said you had to be brave,' said Claire.

He hunched over and uncurled a finger so only Claire could see. Someone *had* said he had to be brave. Claire boiled. Honor had thought she could replace a thing her child loved and make him pretend to be fine.

'What about Noah, Charlie, hmm?' said Honor. 'Don't you love Noah now?'

Charlie tucked his chin into his neck and shook his head. Claire angled round.

'You can probably get a refund on Noah. He's sitting on a shelf with his price tag still on. Charlie,' he looked up at her. 'We're going to look for Dog.' He tipped into her arms. 'And we'll try really hard to find him.' Her voice gargled, his shoulder pressing her windpipe.

He let go and kissed her precisely on the tip of her nose. 'And that's a promise,' he said.

Before Claire left with Charlie to draw up a Lost Dog poster, Ottie gathered Charlie, Pearl and Ollie together for a group hug. 'A grug' they called it. Honor wasn't watching; she was attempting one of the holes that had been man-splained to Claire by the man in head-to-toe taupe on her Bodlowe research trip.

'What do you think?' Claire asked Ben. 'Worth trying, isn't it?'

He passed her a tenner and looked at his feet and nodded. 'Yeah,' he said. 'Nice one.'

Charlie's choice of café had bits of driftwood and dusty teapots strewn randomly in the window. Claire laid her phone on the table in front of him. 'While I'm getting our drinks, find the best photo of Dog.'

'All photos of Dog are the best.'

She queued up with the sticky menu. She'd allowed Honor's hobbled heart to dictate that Dog didn't mean much, should stay lost. She should have taken action sooner, and that was on her. But to tell a child not to feel their feelings was...Was it unconscionable? She'd never knowingly thought that word. Yes. It was un-fucking-conscionable.

Charlie pushed the melting island of cream against the side of the tall glass with a teaspoon. Claire squidged her mint teabag on the side of her cup and dried her hands on her T-shirt and wished she'd had a hot chocolate too.

'The thing is,' she said, reviewing the photos Charlie showed her, a bubble of air rippling down the back of her wetsuited thigh, 'you can't really see Dog. He's always a bit sort of squished on you.'

'You'll have to draw him from rememory, Mum.'

Claire smiled. 'OK.' She opened the sketch pad and pen they'd bought at the pound shop. 'Ears out or tucked in?'

'One in, one out.'

She'd drawn Dog too big. There wasn't room for all the essential wording: *LOST TOY! REWARD! PLEASE BAIL ME THE FUCK OUT I'VE PROMISED TO FIND IT!*

While she started another drawing, Charlie folded the first, and slid it under his chin.

'We'll need lots of posters, Mum.'

'I'll get copies of this one.'

'OK. Get seven.' He sucked cream and sighed. 'Someone will know where he is because you promised.'

Claire smiled at him and her lips trembled. What had she done? She needed serious sugar on board to push forward with this. She glanced at the counter. Maybe a rock cake.

And a giant cookie.

And better order fast because one of the last rock cakes had just been dropped into a bag with a pair of tongs.

Dropped in a bag. With tongs.

Tongs.

Dog on the end of tongs. The disgusted look on Honor's face back in her kitchen in January when she dropped him in a bag and zipped it up like he was ready for incineration.

'Oh my God,' said Claire, as she took an overdue breath. 'Charlie.' Claire rushed back to the table and put the lid back on her pen. 'I think that if Honor thinks really hard, she might know a bit more about where Dog is.'

Chapter 42

Charlie tugged Claire through Bodlowe by her fingertips.

'Sorry', she warbled to everyone he squeezed through and she bashed into.

The others had finished crazy golf. The kids were playing on the pirate ship while Ben, Honor and Chris looked on. 'Hey, um, Honor,' Claire called from a short distance away. Honor looked round.

Trust yourself Claire. Remember the tongs and the bag.

She swallowed minty saliva.

'So I was drawing a poster just now when I wondered if you knew anything else about what happened to Dog?'

Honor looked at her pityingly. 'He got lost, Ding, I've told you what I know.'

The kids and Ben and Chris watched anxiously. Sweat rolled down Claire's back.

If I push this and she doesn't crumble, I'll look insane. Ben might leave me. Our family will break. And if she crumbles ... how will we be punished? This is too risky.

Charlie squeezed her hand. Hope and love rushed into her, and she felt like she could lift the pirate ship clean over her head. 'I think you know more than you're saying. And we would like Dog back.'

'Er, why is this happening?' Honor held out her golf club and looked around, as though one of the people who were watching – and there were several, because crazy women were more interesting than crazy golf – might tell her.

'Claire,' Ben warned.

Keep going, Claire. 'Maybe Dog fell in a bin?'

'This is absurd.' Honor bulldozed towards her. 'We'll talk privately.'

Claire swerved, combat class reflexes kicking in. 'No.' She pushed her hand in front of her in a way she'd never done with unruly Strawberry table at school. 'I'm staying here. And *I'm* telling *you* what's happening. You're going, right now, to get my kid his dog.'

*

Claire paced over the AstroTurf. Chris and Ben were in the Fancy House making pasta and the kids were in the barn. Beyond the trees, inky clouds clustered and orange sunlight, fake and electric-looking, cast a glow over the rooftops. Claire peeled a hangnail with her teeth.

It was almost unbelievable. She'd told Honor to go and get Dog, and Honor had held her hands out to the side of her and walked off like she was saying 'Right, so … I'm just going to pretend to do what this *insane* person says,' and Claire had felt like Wonder Woman.

They'd been back at the cottages for over an hour. Claire had wrestled off the wetsuit and showered, nerves making her clumsy, dropping the shampoo and getting it in her eyes.

Her head was buzzing. Did Honor even know where Dog was? And if she did, was she finding him? Or getting drunk and asking around for a hitman?

Claire crossed to the open back door of the Fancy House. 'Hey, hi. Have you heard from her?'

Ben carried on slicing pepper with his back to her, and

Claire dropped her head to avoid looking at Chris because she'd accused his wife of doing something horrible.

'She's not picking up. She was at the Clifftop Hotel for ages and now she's here.' Chris handed Claire his phone. 'It's a road near the stables. She's been near there about fifteen minutes.'

Claire added running shoes to her shorts and T-shirt.

It was interesting that Honor, who'd said she had no idea where Dog had got lost, had zeroed in on this one location. She glanced in the barn as she jogged past. The kids were lying on the floor drawing, like children with functional parents.

It didn't take long to run there. As she approached the junction, she slowed to get her breath back. She was pass-ing Perriwinton Manor. The house sat back from the road behind a yew hedge, bathed in the stagey orange light. The sandstone turret, crenellated walls and leaded windows had a gaudy friendliness. Rather than defend itself fortress-like, it looked like it would roll over and let its tummy be tickled if you went towards it. At the edge of the grounds she turned onto the verge of a road lined with brambled hedgerow. A wooden sign to Bodlowe Stables hung from a tree. And there was Honor, the zip of her silky silver running jacket catching the light as she poked the hedgerow with a big stick, a hand in the pocket of her tapered joggers which looked like Katie's Primark ones but were probably Dries Van Noten.

Claire approached and Honor's body swooped around. 'Ah!' she said expansively, revealing she'd had wine, maybe two large glasses, at the Clifftop. 'Reinforcements.'

'Hey.' Claire's mouth was dry. She wondered why she'd let Chris's phone draw her to Dog's likely location when it was *Honor's* location.

'Nice of you to join me, Ding.'

Resentment shuddered through her. Honor really deserved a nickname of her own.

Honor pushed her arms out behind her and her face and tits to the sky. 'I'll take a little break, seeing as you're here.'

Claire parted low branches in feeble fury. Where was the warrior who'd dispatched Honor to bring Dog home?

'You went too far earlier, Claire.' Honor stretched an arm over her shoulder and reached the other up her back, interlocking her fingers. 'You basically accused me of knowing where the dog was. Way out of line.'

'But,' Claire gestured weakly at the hedgerow. 'We're here. Doing this. So—'

'God only knows if it's here. The important thing is that I've worked out how you can make amends. Whether or not we find it, when we go back you can apologise to me in front of everyone, and say you now realise I knew nothing. I'll accept the apology and I'm prepared to leave it at that, as long as you promise to get help once you're home, OK?'

'Sorry, *what*?' Claire examined Honor's face.

'I mean, come on. What were you *like* at the crazy golf? I thought you'd spontaneously combust, Ding.'

'Don't *call* me that.'

A bird flapped out of a nearby tree. Honor crouched back. 'Woah, Claire,' she said, gleefully. 'Keep it calm over there. Look,' she prodded the hedgerow with the stick. 'You've got a problem. I tried to help you when we got to Bodlowe. That's why I said chill. I could see you were trying to keep up with me, I just had no idea you were so obsessed. And now, because you can't deal with your own inadequacies, you've developed this persecution complex. I get it, you've lost your grip on reality, but it's not cool to try and bring me down with you.'

'My grip on reality is just fine.' Claire blinked hard, blocking out the look on Ben's face when he found out Tanya was imaginary.

'What you said about your wetsuit being glued. We know it's not true, don't we?'

'It is true. The man in the dry cleaner's said so.'

Honor raised an eyebrow and pulled a mock sad-face. 'Dry cleaners are notorious, Caire. They invent stains and say they've fixed them to get extra money. Do you really think I'd bother glueing a zip to thwart you? Sorry to disappoint, but I just don't think about you that often.'

She sighed. 'There might be some narcissim mixed in with your persecution thing.'

Honor's phone was ringing. She pulled it from her jacket, looked at the screen and tossed the stick. 'Need to take this. It's work. You carry on.' She swirled an arm in the general direction of the hedgerow and strutted down the verge, phone to her ear, elbow high.

Dry cleaners notorious? Claire didn't know that. *Had* he looked shifty? Was she persecuting Honor? No, wait, stop. He'd charged her way less than what he'd quoted for a new zip. All of this was bullshit.

Honor warbled with obsequious laughter. Claire stuck her hands in the hedge and searched through ivy and hawthorn and swathes of mean, unripe blackberries that didn't look like they'd come to much. She was *not* a narcissist. She did *not* have a persecution complex either. A tiny brown mouse shot past her feet and disappeared under a wodge of mud and leaves. She removed a Greggs bag from a slapdash nest and stood back to slot it in her pocket.

Honor was thirty metres away, side on to Claire, back straight. 'Uh-huh,' she said to her caller. 'Uh-huh, uh-huh.'

Claire reached back into the hedgerow. Her eyes fell on

a dirty cream and beige bundle rammed into the brambles. Pain at the bundle's taunting nearly Dogness whelped into joy. Dog it was Dog it was Dog. Claire grabbed Honor's stick from the verge. She poked it into the sharp jumble and hooked Dog out; his arms flopped one side of the stick, legs the other. The stitched line of his mouth smiled widely. This was good. This was wonderful. He smelled of moss. Claire inhaled him.

Honor strutted back, hands in the jogger pockets. She reached Claire and stared into the middle distance. Claire waved Dog in front of her. Honor slammed a hand into her chest and paced, gasping, her face and her damson lips suddenly bloodless. Her knees buckled and she dropped onto all fours in the road.

'I think I'm having a heart attack. I don't want to die here, Claire,' she gulped. 'Help me.'

A car swooshed round the corner. Claire tucked Dog tightly into her waistband, pulled Honor up and and helped her along the verge.

They reached a wooden gate and Claire bundled Honor under an arch of greenery into Perriwinton's grounds. The driveway was empty. No one answered the clanging doorbell in the enormous oak door.

'Hello! Hello, is anybody here?'

Claire led Honor to the rear of the building. The door of a pool housed in a smeary glass extension was open a couple of inches. It rolled grittily along its track.

'Can anyone help us please?' She led Honor across smooth sand-coloured ceramic tiles to one of half a dozen sumptuous poolside loungers. 'Lie down, I'll call an ambulance.'

'No.' Honor swiped Claire's phone and tossed it down. She rose to her feet, filled with rabid energy. She paced round the pool, chest rising and falling, clawing at her arms and chest. This wasn't a heart attack. And she wasn't an invalid, she was a wild animal.

'Here.' Claire bundled a thick lounger mattress in half and placed it against the wall as Honor completed a circuit. 'Hit this.'

'Fuck off, Claire.' She tore the mattress from Claire's hands and lobbed it overhead into the opaque pool. Water curled out and Claire cringed back, arms in front of her face.

'I'm just trying to help.'

'I don't need your help.'

Claire peered out from beneath her arms. Honor couldn't decide which way to pace.

'Did you ... Did you get some news on the phone?'

'What? No. And anyway, mind your own fucking business. Jesus Claire, look at you cowering, you're such a wimp. I remember the night I met you. You told me you'd failed your degree before we'd even ordered drinks. You'd had three sips of your mojito when you blurted out that you'd never met your father, and your mum had barely known him.'

'OK, and?' Claire's body rumbled with hot shame. She wouldn't deny it. She used to tell people all the time that the only thing her mother could tell her about her father was that he'd been 'an excellent life model with Michelangelo thighs', and that she'd been conceived immediately after the life drawing class had ended, in the room where it had taken place.

'What's that got to do with anything?'

Honor laughed and shook her head slowly. 'You marked yourself out. Broken through and through and so keen to share it.'

Claire's shame was flipping into anger.

'Poor fractured Claire. It's always fascinated me that you

gave the information away like that. That you didn't have the self-respect to keep something so mortifying to yourself.'

She wants you to lose it with her. Don't lose it with her.

'Have you ever thought, Claire, that if someone had popped back to the art room for their student card, you might never have existed? You only *just* made it. From that one grubby fuck. Funny isn't it?'

Rage tornadoed through Claire. She yearned to shoulder Honor into the unfiltered swirls of the water. But then Honor would tell Ben and Chris she'd been attacked, and what an own goal that would be. She straightjacketed her arms around herself. 'Do you really think that's funny, Honor? It's such a nasty thing to say.'

Honor shrugged carelessly. 'Bet you were a good little girl, weren't you? Obedient. Craving approval. Doing your little pictures in the shadow of your mother's genius. Actually, nothing's really changed, has it?'

She is my negative self-talk voice incarnate. Don't react. Rise above it, distract her.

'I know you're trying to make me lose it, but I won't.' Claire kneeled at the pool's edge to reach for the sodden mattress. She dragged it onto the tiles like a drowned body and leaned it up against the mosaic freize. The act of restoring order was calming.

'You know, this might have been our holiday home,' she said, examining the mosaic wall frieze. It depicted carousing naked people with grapes and jugs and goblets. She lifted one of several pieces of paper someone had duct-taped onto it. Beneath was a pair of rosy buttocks and a cock made up of different shades of tiny tiles.

'Well that would have been fucking weird,' said Honor.

'I know you glued my wetsuit, Honor.' Claire lowered the paper and turned to face her. 'And I think you took

334

things, messed with stuff in our cottage, before I had the lock put on.'

Honor threw back her head. Her wailing groan clattered off the tiles. 'None of this matters Claire. It's nothing. I didn't get my fucking job. *That* matters. Asif got my job, that's what the phone call was about.' She wiped a hand across her eyes. 'Oh fuck it, hey, why not?'

She flung out her arms. 'Let's all kick Honor when she's down. Yes, I messed with you. You were trying so hard, with your little ponytail bobbing away, doing so well. *Jogging* and going in the *sea,* and your macaroni cheese was actually edible. And yes, probably Ottie should have had her own sticky toffee pudding. There, happy now?'

Honor sloped off round the pool and grabbed up a bottle that had been left in a corner. Liquid circled in the bottle. Jagermeister. She opened it and sniffed, lips parted.

'Honor,' said Claire. 'Please don't drink that.'

Honor stared at her and took three long gulps.

'I'm having a swim.' She screwed the lid back on the bottle and tore off her jacket. Something fell from the pocket, clattered off the tiles and plopped into the water where a jet sent it to the middle of the pool. It bobbed on the surface. A tube with a braided golden knob.

'That's your Faron Odashi Absolute Nude.'

'Dur. I know.' Honor flung her joggers to her ankles and stepped out of them. 'I told you I'd found it.'

This woman was the living fucking end. 'No you didn't! Wait a minute. Did I ever actually lose that lip gloss?'

Honor groaned like a busted teen. 'Fine! I never put it in your bag, OK. Happy now?'

She stripped to a plum lace bra and thong and climbed down the steps into the water. Claire eyed the bottle of Jagermeister then dropped heavily onto a lounger. No. She would not drink any. And no, she would not lob it at Honor. Even though Honor was a batshit crazy cow bag. Asif would need to watch out. Honor could easily arrange for him to lose millions of pounds with his name on.

Honor put the gloss on the side, swam a few fast lengths then climbed out and sat hunched on the edge, dripping.

'Look, Honor, about your bank. About everything. You don't *have* to punish people you think have knocked you off your pedestal. Leave First United. Move on. Stop repeating what happened with Abbie.'

Honor pulled her heels onto the edge of the pool and hugged her shins.

'Because,' Claire spoke more gently now, 'the pedestal's not real. And are you even happy up there?'

Honor tilted her head towards Claire. Her expression said, *I'm not. And now that you know, what do I do?*

Claire, stood up, aching all over. 'Let's go. I want to get Dog back to Charlie.'

They walked back along the coast road in falling light and silence, Honor raking her fingers pensively through her hair, until the corn hissed towards them on the breeze.

'Would you like us to leave?' asked Honor. 'We can be gone first thing in the morning.'

'No,' said Claire, wondering for a moment why she'd rejected the offer, then realising why. 'It wouldn't be fair on the kids.'

They turned onto the track. Claire's heart swelled to be reuniting her boy with his skanky first love. As they got close to the barn and laughter from a game of Twister, Honor slowed to a stop. She looked wretched. Smaller, with spidery splodges of mascara down her face.

'Claire. I'd rather the kids didn't see me like this. When

you've given Dog to Charlie, would you please ask Ben and Chris to come out here?'

Claire tilted her head. 'You do know you haven't offered me an apology, right?'

'Sorry.' Honor dropped her head, then raised it and with difficulty, found Claire's eyes. 'I'm sorry. I am.'

Charlie's mouth fell open and he shook his arms into a blur. He looked at Claire like he owed her his life, because yes, oxygen, and then he grabbed Dog and pressed him onto his head and span round and clonked his ankle on the corner of the sandpit. He fell down, drew breath to wail but when the breath came out he looked at Dog and the cry was two-thirds laugh. Claire joined in, bending down to hug him.

She told Ben and Chris Honor wanted to talk to them and waited by the barn door, intrigued. Not long after they'd gone, she heard them coming back down the track, then Honor trotted past, her arms across her body, hands cupping her elbows. She disappeared round the corner and the Fancy House door shut behind her.

Chris walked into the barn. He passed Claire and shook his head and blew out and Claire returned the look because yes, they really had all been through it.

The kids strung up bunting they'd made to welcome Dog home. Charlie was hyper. The other three indulged him. Ben had gone to sit on the bench outside the cottage. He stood up as Claire walked over and they sat back down together. The sky was streaks of orange. Claire breathed in and smelled the sea.

'She said she'd behaved horribly,' said Ben. 'She said she knew you hadn't gone in the sea, and we should believe anything you tell us because it will be true.'

'Wow.' Claire clapped her hands onto her knees. She

hadn't lost her mind. Honor had been hiding it from her. And so much – not Ben yet, but so much else – was restored to its right place, even the freaking Faron Odashi lip gloss.

'I'm sorry, Claire.'

She looked at him in surprise.

'I didn't realise what a psycho she was being.'

Claire smiled and felt hopeful.

The families drifted to their cottages for the rest of the evening. Ben found *Chitty Chitty Bang Bang* on TV and he and Claire and Pearl and Charlie squashed onto the sofa in front of it.

'It's nice being just us,' said Pearl, through a mouthful of chocolate digestive. 'Cosy.'

'Yeah,' said Charlie, Dog held to his neck, hovering a biscuit by his open mouth, transfixed by Truly Scrumptious on her music box.

Silent tears rolled down Claire's face. She'd trusted herself, gone out on a limb about Dog, and been right. She looked at her family, side by side eating biscuits and watching telly, and she shut her eyes, because this was bliss.

Chris texted Ben later offering to listen out for Pearl and Charlie if Claire and Ben wanted to go out.

Ben opened the connecting door so Chris could babysit from home.

Claire was waiting for him outside. They walked down Macaroni Steps to wander on the beach as the tide went out and the moon reached through the dissipating cloud to sparkle the sea. They sat on the stones. And Claire told Ben that Honor hadn't actually put the lip gloss in her bag and that she was to blame for much more. She told him that Honor's safe space hadn't been safe, and her encouragement hadn't been encouragement, and it didn't go down like tittle tattle from the school arsonist. It solved the equation Y + Claire = Bonkers Claire. Because Ben understood now. Honor was Y.

Claire turned a perfect chalk-white shell in her hands. 'Ben, did you know Chris for long before he met her?'

'Four, five weeks? Seemed longer because the first term's so intense and he was in the room opposite.'

'What was he like, before?'

Ben smiled, his eyes crinkling. 'Same lovely bloke. Messier haired, heavier, not so well-dressed. They met at some innovation seminar and within a month, she'd shagged about a stone off him, found him an amazing biotech internship, and replaced his entire wardrobe. If they hadn't been under his pillow he'd have lost his pyjamas. He'd wear them for days when she was away, which seemed significant but mostly gross.'

'Did he really like her?'

'Smitten. Couldn't believe his luck. It was like, you know how a Tesla is a fifty-grand computer inside a forty-grand car? Honor was the car he needed to get him moving. She roared up, pulled him in and she's been driving him ever since.'

'Did you like her?'

'She didn't really hang out with us,' said Ben, after a pause. 'She was in a flat in the centre with other rich kids; he'd go and see her there. I'd never spent much time with her till you came along, all friendly and lovely, and she wanted a piece of you.'

'You haven't answered my question, Ben.'

'I didn't actively like her,' he said, clambering over each word.

Claire nodded at his decoy 'actively'. 'But you didn't say anything to Chris?'

He wrinkled his nose. 'It's difficult isn't it? Cuts deep. How do you say, "I don't like your girlfriend" to your best friend?'

'If you felt that way, why haven't you been looking out for me? "Dear Ben I'm in Cornwall with a toxic bitch, why haven't you been here?"'

'You're the one who wanted to come to Bodlowe with them.'

'What?' She jolted to face him. 'Are you on drugs, Ben? I dreaded this holiday for five months. It was you that wanted to come.'

Ben groaned. 'I thought you wanted it. I know you weren't comfortable about them paying at first, but you'd said she was one of your best friends.'

'I would *never* have said that.'

'You did. When we drove back from lunch at theirs in the winter.'

Claire shook her head hard and the horizon bent at either side.

'We were in the car with the kids, Claire. You said she was incredible and generous with advice or something.'

Claire raised an eyebrow. 'I must have meant *thinks she knows everything and makes me feel useless*. Wasn't Pearl going on about how we all had a Wellbeloved special friend? I probably just didn't want to be the bad guy.'

Claire laid the shell on Ben's knee. He picked it up and ran a thumb over it.

'We were a good team,' he said. 'We were Luton Town, and then you decided to be Man United on your own so nothing Luton Town did was going to be right. It's been really lonely.'

'I'm sorry.' Claire pulled Ben gently towards her. The friendly kindness was back in his face. 'I want to be Luton

Town with you, only with being more honest if something or someone makes us feel bad.'

'Sounds good. I'm sorry you didn't feel you had a choice. So what now?'

'I'll tell you what now,' said Claire. 'The best revenge I can think of is to start enjoying this bloody holiday.'

Ben held up his palm for a high five. Claire missed, smacking her hand on his thigh. They laughed, and kissed, and the wave of love she'd felt as she'd come out of the supermarket was finally delivered.

Chapter 43

Pearl stood in the dinghy, swaying from side to side. 'Me and Ottie's go should be longer because we blowed it up.'

'But that wasn't the deal you all made, was it?' said Claire.

'Nope,' said Charlie, his arms wrapped round the dinghy oar.

'So what do think is fair?' Claire leaned behind her to toss a towel into the tent from the lounger. Honor had been looking pained while she'd arbitrated this squabble but Claire had not been cowed into passing sentence. The kids ran off in the end, deciding not to bother with the bloody dinghy.

'Honor. I don't like it when you look at me like that. It's not pandering. The kids need to be heard.'

Honor lay back and shook her head slowly. 'I wasn't judging you, Claire,' she said quietly. 'It was the opposite. I was thinking about the feedback I had from work. They said I dictate rather than motivate, that I don't listen.'

'I see.' Claire examined Honor's newly vulnerable features with cautious interest, the snarling banshee from Perriwinton still fresh in her memory. 'Honor,' she began carefully, 'what was it that made you put Dog in the hedgerow?'

Honor breathed in slowly and out again. 'We were walking into Bodlowe from the stables,' she said, eventually. 'Ollie had been a tit, literally scaring the horses. Ottie was moody. And Charlie and Pearl had been adorable. The stables woman kept going on about Charlie's lovely posture.' Honor turned and smiled at Claire bravely.

'Oh, nice,' said Claire. *Please don't tell me he's a natural horseman.*

'We were walking along and I took Charlie's backpack because he was being a pony, and Pearl was being charming to Ottie, and Chris was stopping Ollie from running in the road, and I thought, what if Claire gets the illustration thing, and Asif gets my job? What if all I've got is puberty, and waywardness, and a garden full of neighbours, and no trees or lagoon and no department to head up. I don't even know if I've got Linton, Claire. Some lingerie entrepreneur woman offered him double for my slot. And it was like the ground came up and swallowed me. I had Charlie's backpack in my hands, and this dirty biscuit smell wafted out and it was too much. I slung him out and kept walking.'

Honor ran her hands along her thighs and pulled her bent knees towards her. Claire was surprised and oddly touched that she had referred to Dog as 'him'.

'My kids love you, Claire.'

Claire spluttered. 'Your kids love you, Honor.'

Honor scrunched up her face. 'I bet they wish I was more fun and kind and patient. I bet they wish I was more like you. I'm going to be more like you.'

Later in the afternoon, Claire phoned Katie from the top of Macaroni Steps. Peace still reigned in Norfolk.

'It's amazing. The twins have never got on better. The weather's fantastic, today's been brilliant. It's like the last few months never happened.'

'That's so good.'

'How about you?'

'Fine. Great actually. In fact, the weather's fantastic, today's been brilliant. It's like the last few months never happened.'

'Huh? How? Spill.'

Claire caught Katie up on Bodlowe goings-on.

'And Honor wants to be more like me. Hey, why don't I make her a sort of Be Better Before the End of Bodlowe list? It could be *Miss Congeniality* again but her as Sandra, and me as Michael Caine. I could go flat out to transform her for the sake of her family, neighbours and future employers,'

'OK, this is fun, but have you sent in your First United work?'

'No. But I will, soon.'

'Claire …'

'I will. I really will. Katie, I will.'

*

Honor went on a cliff walk with Chris to ask about his plan for the community. They came back hand in hand. She let the kids choose what was for lunch and the families ate pizza, delivered by push bike, on the AstroTurf in the sun. She let Ottie and Ollie eat as much as they wanted and drank water, having announced she was drastically cutting down on alcohol. Ottie had drawn a community heat exchange.

'So how it works,' said Honor, wiping her mouth on some kitchen roll as Pearl and Charlie looked at the diagram, 'is that everyone who is part of it has their rubbish burned in a big oven, deep underground, and then the heat that's made is sent through pipes back to their houses for their radiators and hot water.'

'That's brilliant,' said Pearl.

'Isn't it.'

'And you're doing it instead of all the big expensive trees and the pool, Honor?'

'Yes, yes we are.' Honor smiled at Chris.

Claire licked garlicky tomato from her fingers and shut her pizza box. It was as though Honor been waiting for someone to tell her to 'stop', and she was the one who had done it. Her. Claire. She had.

Brian came to collect Ben for their sound check at the harbour. He gestured sheepishly to Claire. She joined him in the shadow of the barn.

'I know I swore on my ma's grave I'd say nothing, Claire. But I realised she wouldn't rest in peace if she knew I had a secret between a man and his missus.'

'It's all right, Brian. It's worked out OK.'

Brian clumped her arm. 'Lovely jubbly.' He walked into the sun and clapped his huge hands together. 'Beautiful weather all weekend,' he said. 'You'd be welcome to stay till Sunday.'

'What do you think, Ben?' She realised she wanted him to say yes, which he did. Ben raised an eyebrow and gestured a subtle thumb at Chris and Honor. Claire nodded.

'What about you two?' asked Ben. 'Fancy staying an extra night?' Honor and Chris exchanged a questioning glance.

'Stay,' said Claire, like it was obvious.

Honor touched her chest and mouthed, 'Thank you.'

Claire turned to the sea and laughed to herself that she'd chosen to spend a fifteenth night on the holiday she'd been counting down to leave.

The cook-off became a cook-out. Claire took out the shopping she'd shoved in the freezer before she'd run off to the lifeboat station.

'Is it something fancy?' asked Ben worriedly, arriving back from the sound check as Claire lit their barbecue.

'Not fancy. Special though.'

He laughed when Claire brought the tray to the table later. 'This is a Swift family favourite. What is it we call it?'

He joined in with Charlie, Pearl and Claire. 'Burgers à la bap de potato smile.'

'With an accompaniment of cucumber au slice and carrot au stick,' Claire added.

There was enough for everyone, which was good as Honor had agreed with Claire that the pigeon she'd planned to barbecue smelled a bit … Funky Town.

Once they'd eaten they went to Bodlowe Harbour for the Fun Day. There was a magic show, and a set from a sea cadet band. Brian's band were good. Ben looked gorgeous on the bass. They played a Hullfire track as an encore. Brian's metal voice was a vast terrifying growl. People surged away from the stage as though torrential rain had started. Charlie rode to the back to the cottages on Ben's shoulders and Ben announced he was definitely joining a band when they got home to Headleigh.

When they arrived back, everyone else went in the barn and Claire set up on the weathered kitchen table and fell on her work. She flicked back and forth through the reference photos, taking in intention in faces and body language. She thumbnailed thoughts, working out characters and their relationships. She marked them onto paper, all tilting towards their kookily empassioned choir leader, mid-note. She blocked a wash of colour on a jumper here, some earrings there. Then she rose from the flow of it, taking a breath.

She rubbed her eyes and pushed back the chair and stood to take a look.

Nice one Claire. She'd made a choir. A bunch of flawed and funny people who looked like they met each week to sing.

Claire slipped into the barn to ask Ben to pop back to the cottage with her. They sat on the sofa and she showed him what had poured from her. He looked at it for ages, chuckling gently.

'I'll hit up Ikea for new frames when we get home.'

'Thanks. But hold on. See if you think I've met the requirements.'

She opened the laptop to the briefing that she'd under-lined, and highlighted, and enlarged words of, until it was an all-singing all-dancing yell of importance.

Ben read it carefully, checking back with the artwork: 'Community, hearts on sleeves, endeavour for a common goal ... You've definitely met the requirements, babe. It's lovely, really.'

Claire smiled. 'I don't suppose doubt ever goes away completely. But next time it won't budge and I think I might do something stupid like tell a massive lie, or rip up months of work, or buy a car, I'll find you and tell you.'

'Definitely do that. And I won't think it's nuts, I promise. And I'll do what I can to help.' He moved some of Claire's hair behind her shoulder.

'Good. Thank you. And I'm not going to put up with anyone who messes with me or makes me doubt myself ever again.'

'Excellent.' He stroked the back of her neck meaningfully.

'Great. Thanks Ben. Now go back to the barn, because I

want to send this to Gemma. No offence, and I'm sure we can make some magic later, if you like.'

He stood up. She pressed compose and typed Gemma into the recipient box.

'I am going,' said Ben, 'but first, I need to tell you something.' He dropped his head, brow heavy.

'What, Ben? What is it?' Her heart hammered.

'I haven't been straight with you, Claire. Silver Bullet Two, I like it, I like it a lot.'

When she went to the barn a little later, Ottie was teaching a routine from Madison's cheerleading club. Honor had said she could start there in September and Madison would be invited for tea when they got home. Honor was crap at the footwork and looking lovingly to her daughter for tips on how to improve.

Claire noticed kids' writing on Post-its saying 'SMILE', 'FART', and 'OLLIE IS KING' had been added to 'CHILL' on the planner. Yeah, in the very end, they did chill.

When they would have been travelling home on Saturday, they were on the beach.

'I'll make lunch,' said Honor. 'Shall I bring it down or do we want to go back for it?'

Claire glanced at the kids. Charlie and the girls were immersed in another hotel game.

Ollie had planted a big stick in the ground and was running round it, playing up the dizziness when he let go.

'Do it later.' Claire swung her legs off the lounger and stood with a smile. 'You've got more important fish to fry. Stay there.'

Claire plucked Ollie's stick from the sand. She feinted left and right as the delighted boy tried to catch it, then stopped and held it out.

'I'm tired, Ollie. Ask your mum to play.'

Ollie glanced at Honor and looked doubtfully at Claire. 'Seriously. Go and ask her.'

Claire held her breath as the boy approached his mother.

'Please Honor,' Claire muttered to herself. 'Please get this right.'

Ollie was by the lounger, talking. Honor didn't stir.

'Oh shite,' Claire said softly.

Then Honor's hands flew out. She sat up and her 'Boo' floated over on the breeze. Claire watched, laughing, as Honor chased Ollie, catching and tickling him. Ollie yelped with laughter then Honor took off, but not fast, giving him the chance to catch and hug her.

Claire raised damp eyes to the sky.

In the evening, before leaving for dinner in a pub, she overheard Honor on the phone.

'Is that Abbie?' Her voice was soft and hopeful. 'Yes, it's Honor. Is this a good time?' And it must have been, because clutching her phone to her ear Honor walked slowly away across the AstroTurf towards the steps, talking to her sister.

On a whim, Claire pulled out her phone and rang David's number. Her mother was there.

'Claire. How extraordinary. I've just come to tell David I've had my mobile fixed. Next stop was to text you.'

'Sorry I hung up on you.'

'That's all right,' said Margo cheerily.

'Mum. Is David your boyfriend?'

'What? Oh gosh darling. Hold on.' A door closed and Margo came back on the line. 'It's a bit confusing. Maybe.'

Claire laughed silently. It sounded like her mother, at

sixty-seven, was caving in to her first relationship. 'Can I ask you something, Mum?'

'Yes, absolutely.'

'Do you ever wonder if your paintings are any good?'

'What do you mean?'

'Like, whether you're good enough.' Claire moved a few steps up the track. *Oh God, I've offended her.* 'Hello? Are you there?'

'Yes, I'm here. Do I ever tumble down the old vortex of doom, you mean? Of course I do.'

'And what do you do about it?'

'Well, usually, I give it about fifteen seconds to have its way with me, and then I kick it out the door. It's just a feeling, always passes.'

'You just push on and value yourself anyway.'

'"Value yourself anyway". I like that. Staying productive helps.' She sighed. 'Claire, I'm missing you. All of you.' She spoke with a hunger. 'It doesn't feel like August without you. Let's text about getting together. And oh my goodness, Claire.'

'Yes, what?

'The little ones showed me your drawings. What joy. And what a voice. Your work's so true and touching. I bow to your wisdom.'

A Mexican-wave of pleasure rolled from Claire's knees right up over her head. 'Thank you. Thanks Mum. I'm really glad to hear you say that.'

'Mummy and Daddy,' Pearl ran up to Claire and Ben where the low tide lapped the sand. 'Can we dig a heat exchange thingy on Bevvy Road?'

It was Sunday morning and the kids had lobbied for one last beach visit. Claire reached for Pearl's nose, gently slotting it between two fingers. 'No. But you could go and look at Chris and Honor's one, when it's built.'

Pearl mulled Claire's answer as though the final say on who built heat exchanges was hers.

'All right then.' She ran into the water. 'Come in and play with me and Charlie.'

Ben took Claire's hand. 'What do you think? Can you handle it?'

Claire looked down at her swimsuit. 'Let's do this.' She ran into the shallows with Ben and Pearl and Charlie, the four of them in a line, holding hands.

And then she ran straight out again. Because it was fricking freezing.

She pulled on her wetsuit. Better. Perfect.

They became a family of dolphins. Pearl insisted they communicate only in clicks and then was the absolute worst at breaking her own rule. In a cave that they reached by escaping evil mermaids, they saved Ben from a sea monster before returning to the beach.

'Woah,' said Ben. 'That was amazing. I feel almost drugged.'

Claire smiled at him. 'Endolphins.'

He laughed. His gorgeous tanned face creasing.

She towelled herself and checked her phone. Gemma had emailed. Hands trembling, she showed it to Ben.

'Decided to drop you a line,' he read, 'as I'm in the office prepping a launch. You were top of our list in any case and you've totally nailed it.'

She had the First United job. Ben congratulated her hand and kissed her then wiped her tears from his lips. He nodded towards Honor, playing cricket up the beach.

She scrunched her face. 'I don't mind her knowing at some point. But not now.'

Claire took her euphoria back in the water. She floated

on her back, the sea rolling under her and spritzing her face. The air tasted freshly made. The clouds were meringues. A boat chugged. Laughter, yells and the sounds of gulls and kids lapped around her.

★

Claire sat Charlie on a suitcase so she could zip it up.

Her phone rang.

'Hey Katie.'

'Hey. Where are you? I thought you were coming home yesterday.'

'Just packing up in Bodlowe.'

'Jeez, you *must* be having a good time. I knocked for you this morning. You and me were going to whup a double circuit.'

'Did you do it on your own?'

'No. I want to do it with you.'

'Tomorrow we whup.'

The Wellbeloveds were ready to leave first. Pearl and Charlie were in the car, but Claire and Ben were still loading.

'Here's a thought,' said Honor, laying her arm along the passenger window frame, reentry shades atop her head. 'Same time, same place, next year. What do you say?'

Claire's breath departed her. Ben seemed similarly stunned.

Chris jammed in his seat belt and fired the engine. 'Well,' he said, 'safe home. Thanks guys, love you lots.' He launched the Space Ship up the track like a rescue vehicle rushing to a shout, although he'd saved them already. Claire and Ben waved them out of sight then burst out laughing.

'Mummy, what are you and Daddy laughing at?'

'Something Honor said.'

Pearl eyed them askance. 'Can't have been *that* funny.'

Claire's eyes met Ben's and she knew he was thinking the

352

same thing. That if Honor meant it, it was hilarious. And if she was joking, it was hilarious too.

Claire drove up the track and onto the coast road. The corn rustled, a gull cawed. The summer holiday was over. She set the wipers to clean the windscreen.

'Ben, our shed's got power sockets, hasn't it?'

Eight Weeks Later

Claire popped a couple of pens back in their tin and rolled herself away from her drawing board. She'd come back to this theatre poster fresh in the morning.

When she'd asked Ben what he thought about her using the summer house as a studio, he replied that he'd suggested it himself a couple of years ago.

'I don't remember that,' she'd said.

'Maybe you weren't ready to hear it.'

They'd boot-saled unneeded shed stuff and anything they wouldn't use again from the holiday, and it was amazing how quickly the summer house had felt like her space. Her safe space. Her works in progress, reference materials and pictures Pearl and Charlie had made her were stuck on the edge of the shelves that she and Ben had put in. They'd painted the wooden panelled walls a milky yellow. She'd found a junk-shop chest of drawers that fitted perfectly and Katie had lent her a plug-in radiator from work.

'It's from when the heating broke down. If anyone notices, I'll have to grab it back again.' Claire had used it for the first time today, reaching over in her wrist warmers to plug it in; she was warm in minutes.

She'd written to Andrea telling her what had really happened when she reached the A34, but also what had happened since. That she was doing a campaign for a bank and that her contact had introduced her to a cookie company who were using her drawings of robins on their packs of Christmas biscuits. Andrea had written back offering to mentor Claire, and linking to the course marketing specialist's channel on YouTube.

Claire smiled through the window at the lean-to Ed had helped them build for their bikes and garden stuff. 'Nice guy,' Ben had said when he'd gone.

'Shall we all go camping with him and Katie next summer?'

'No.'

Claire cackled. He could not have said it faster.

Margo had booked rail tickets to come for Pearl's birthday.

'Mum,' Claire had said, 'when you come, come and see *us*. Come *to* see us.' A silence dangled. She hoped Margo's cogs were turning.

'Yes,' said Margo, returning Claire's fervour. 'Absolutely, I will.'

It sounded like she'd got it.

'And there are exhibitions at Saatchi and Tate Modern I'd love to get to.'

Oh. Maybe she hadn't.

'Sure,' Claire said. 'The Turbine Hall is great for running around, so that would be fun.'

'Of course.' The fervour again. With a side order of penny dropping. 'And the South Bank will be fun for the little ones, won't it? Where else is good for running around?'

'The adventure park where Pearl's having her birthday party. Bring Valium.'

So they'd had a visit, not from Margo Macklin, but from Claire's mum, who was Pearl and Charlie's granny, and Ben's mother-in-law. She'd looked after the kids while Claire worked on the First United campaign and travelled into

London for a couple of meetings. Charlie had popped out of the living room when she got home, exhausted, and nestled his chin on her stomach.

'We're all so tired Mummy, but we've had a lovely day.'

The kids gave the exhibition at the Tate fair shrift, and Ben arranged to meet Claire and Margo in the Turbine Hall. Claire was standing next to Margo, looking at the last piece, when Margo's hand crept into hers.

'Are you done, darling? I want to look at my grand-children now.'

Ben and the kids were playing a game, taking turns to peer around the edge of a sculpture, with an unexpected expression on their face. Claire and Margo leaned against a wall, unnoticed, to watch them.

'What a lovely man you chose, Claire. I'm sorry I couldn't do that for you. I must seem bloody careless.'

'It's OK.'

'If I have ever let you doubt, for one minute, that I wanted and loved you, then that is the biggest regret of my life.'

'Oh Mum!' Claire enveloped Margo in a hug.

'I admire you so much, Claire. I want to deserve you. All of you.' Claire's tears sank into Margo's smoky, perfumed scarf.

'Thank you. That's a lovely thing to say.'

'Grug!' Charlie's voice bounced off the huge walls and his feet slapped across the concrete towards them, followed by Pearl's.

'Come on Daddy. Grug.'

Ben ambled up and let Margo pull him in. And it was *lovely*.

Claire locked the summerhouse, stepped over to the back door and went inside.

'Good day at the office?' asked Ben.

'Great. Commute was an arseache though.' She kissed him and hung the key on the hook attached to the wall screwed into a wooden block that said STUDIO.

Ben had been coming home happy from work. He had been tipped off that Carlos's contract wasn't being renewed, and that it was hoped he'd go for promotion. He didn't feel un-a-fucking-ssailable but Claire was pretty sure there would be champagne corks over Headleigh.

Tonight there was excitement in the house. Ms Achibe and Mr Reader were coming for dinner with the grown-ups. Charlie had made Dog a book from a tiny piece of paper and Pearl had arranged all her teddies on her bed. Claire had made them promise that Grant and Fran would be allowed to have a glass of wine in their hands before they were swept upstairs for introductions.

Claire cleared the remnants of the kids' tea from the table and wiped it down. Ben held out chilli on a wooden spoon for her to taste. 'Is it hot enough? I pepped it up once I'd fed the kids.'

'Just right,' she said.

He smiled then gestured the spoon at their corkboard. 'I pinned your rail tickets up there, if you're wondering. They were kind of floating around.'

'Thanks.'

Claire was travelling to Glasgow the following Thursday for Margo's exhibition opening.

'While you're with your mum,' Ben reached up for wine

glasses, 'now we know how good she is with the kids, see if she'll come and look after them for a couple of nights in November.'

'Ooh. I like where this is going.'

'I know,' he said. 'Good idea, huh. I thought we could fly somewhere for your birthday.'

'Awesome. How about Gdansk?' Her arms circled his waist.

'Why Gdansk?' His crinkled eyes danced.

A laugh fizzed from her. 'I had the letters when we played Scrabble the other night.'

'Then it was meant to be.'

They kissed, then they pottered, chatting about their trip, getting ready for their guests.

Poland in November would be cold. The straggly blue coat wouldn't cut it. She would invest in a winter coat. Something cossetting and feathery. And maybe warm boots. Other than that, she was fully equipped.

Acknowledgements

Thank you to Kate Shaw, my agent. You contacted me while I was on my own summer holiday to ask for the rest of my manuscript and turned an already great family holiday into the best ever. Your commitment, energy, support and our straight-to-the-heart-of-it phone calls are so appreciated.

To Clare Hey, who along with Kate leaned towards me smiling when I found myself pitching this book, a special moment I'll always remember. To Victoria Oundjian for suggesting the major cut that made it deeper and better. To Charlotte Mursell and the whole team at Orion, I'm so excited to be working with you on this book and what's next.

To Jean Kitson, my script agent, for reading an early draft and saying things that helped and sustained me through many more.

Three people read this book and gave feedback. From single word to big picture observations, everything that Emma Carver, Jane Clegg and Jenny Landreth said was full of insight and deeply helpful. I'm so grateful for your encouragement and the time and thought you gave.

To Tanya Cornish for generous help with the illustration sections. To Hannah Law whose coaching helped set goals and inspire confidence that resulted in less time thinking I couldn't write a novel and more time writing it.

To Ellen Brock and to Emma Darwin for the brilliant

free online writing resources, and to all the 'strangers on the internet' for the tons of writing advice I've hoovered up over the years.

I value laughter so highly and the following people generate heaps which keep me going through the hours of sighing and snacking and typing. To Candida Goulden, thank you for more than thirty years of treasured friendship. And to Sophie Wellings who goes back even further.

To the Material Girls – Rosy Fordham, Alison Joseph, Gerry McNulty, Georgia Pritchett, RK Saroff, Sue Teddern, and the Girls no longer with us, for years of everything and crisps and clothes swapping.

To Helly Charman, for fast walks where things fall into place. Thank you for the understanding, the hope and the joy.

To Philippa Johnson and Lewis Marks and to the Carvers and the Flacks for family holidays I would never want to get out of.

To Andrew Brenner, Sam Dransfield and Davey Moore, my scriptwriting friends for all the text banter and the bands. Days would be lonelier without you.

To three special South London parks (you know who you are). Walking in you always helps untangle a story or any other problem. And to Sainsbury's Three Bean and Tomato Soup, avocados and crackers: without you, I'd have to think what to have for lunch.

The first people I shared my writing with were my parents. Mum and Dad you'll always be with me. You never sugar-coated your feedback, so it really meant something that you made me feel I had worthwhile things to say. Further thanks go to Jane for the fun and the top notch sistering (and the ram jam and backflips).

To Mark, thank you for proof reading the manuscript and for sharing your life, your good humour and your talents with me, and to Jess Jones thanks for being awesome and for having him to stay that time. To Amy and Mel, thank you for your wisdom and for seeking my opinion (see what I did there?). You bring so much interest, love, excitement and great hair to our lives. And finally, thanks to Simon for nine years of feline excellence. Never stop sitting at the table like you're a person.

Credits

Jo Clegg and Orion Fiction would like to thank everyone at Orion who worked on the publication of *The Summer Holiday* in the UK.

Editorial
Charlotte Mursell
Olivia Barber

Copy editor
Sally Partington

Proof reader
John Garth

Contracts
Anne Goddard
Paul Bulos
Jake Alderson

Design
Rabab Adams
Joanna Ridley
Nick May

Production
Ruth Sharvell

Finance
Jasdip Nandra
Afeera Ahmed
Elizabeth Beaumont
Sue Baker

Editorial Management
Charlie Panayiotou
Jane Hughes

Audio
Paul Stark
Amber Bates

Marketing
Tanjiah Islam

Publicity
Ellen Turner

Operations
Jo Jacobs
Sharon Willis
Lisa Pryde
Lucy Brem

Sales
Jen Wilson
Esther Waters
Victoria Laws
Rachael Hum
Ellie Kyrke-Smith
Frances Doyle
Georgina Cutler